JULIET IN VERONA

JULIET IN VERONA

ALESSIA SAINT

Maria DeKoning

Alessia Saint

Juliet in Verona

ALESSIA SAINT

ISBN-13: 979-8-9855067-1-6

Cover design by: Alessia Saint
Edited by: Maria DeKoning

Printed in the United States of America

To my family...vi voglio bene

Juliet in Verona

Ciò che il cuore conosce oggi, la testa comprenderà domani.

What the heart knows today, the head will understand tomorrow.

-Seneca

Prologue

I looked over to the middle of my room. It'd been sitting there for about two days now, unpacked and holding all of my time abroad. It was time to admit that whatever we had was over and that I was back home, back to my regular life. I reached over to grab the heavy luggage. It was frayed all around the sides and the zipper looked as if it were going to burst from the amount of clothes and souvenirs I packed into it. I debated whether I could actually do it; unzip the bag and reveal everything from my trip. Tears were already forming around my eyes as I began to pull on the zipper. The contents spilled out as if they were finally taking a deep breath after being hidden for so long. I was afraid to see it, afraid of what emotions were going to well up inside of me. As I turned back around to face the suitcase, there it was.

I

Uno

Un'Avventura (nf) = An Adventure

Okay. 60 minutes to Milano train station. 73 minutes to Verona. Get there before 4pm. I looked around desperately for a clock since my phone was buried somewhere in my bag under my passport, snacks, and three lists my mom made for the trip. I was not typically a numbers person at all, which is why I decided to major in languages and teaching, but making sure I got to the director's office on time made me count the seconds.

I spotted a clock on a wall directly across from me. It's only 1:45. A bead of sweat trickled down my neck. Why was I sweating in the middle of February? I took in the frenetic scene of the Milan airport, not at all familiar with it since I usually landed in Rome when I visited my nonni in Calabria. I twirled my hair, looking at the tips of it and noticing the new caramel highlights I just added brightened up my brown strands. I looked out to the luggage carousel, praying that my polka-dotted luggage would come out next.

"Relax, Juliet," Matt said sitting right next to me. "You look like you are about to take one of Professor Rossi's Dante exams."

I looked over at him as he adjusted the dark green hoodie he always wore under his jean jacket. His face had his usual expression, one that never showed an ounce of worry. Here we were, about to start an adventure in a completely new place where our lives could be changed forever, and he seemed immune to any of the impetuous emotions that I was currently experiencing.

I took a second to imagine myself older, retelling the stories of the semester I spent abroad in Italy to my grandkids, filled with all of the crazy adventures I had. I got jolted back into reality though when I realized that none of these adventures would take place if my polka-dotted luggage didn't show up within the next ten minutes. I would have to start a frantic search of missing underwear, bras, and clothes and find a way to replace them.

"No, Matt. This is worse than any Dante exam. Giorgia told us we need to get there by 4pm, or *16:00* like she wrote in the email." I mindlessly twirled my hair between my pointer and middle fingers, anxiously watching the minutes as they ticked by.

I loved how the Italians insisted on military time for anything scheduled, the trick was to subtract twelve in order to figure out what they meant in regular time. This time I had memorized the exact time we needed to be there since I've had this trip planned since my freshman year.

Matt reached out and pulled my hand down from my hair. "Juliet, we will make it. She can't send us back home just because we show up late to her office. Plus, there's nothing we can do about this. Let your hair be. Whenever you are worried, you twirl it at record speed."

I took in a deep breath and relaxed my hand. I always envied how

Matt was able to be so calm during stressful moments. He's been exactly the same since I first met him freshman year. I remember him walking into our Italian class on the first day of classes and how every girl subtly shifted their focus to him, secretly hoping that he would sit next to them. He took a seat next to me though and I silently jumped up and down inside, trying to maintain a cool composure while I just nodded my head slightly to him. My secret crush was short-lived when I found out he had a girlfriend, but we oddly ended up becoming really good friends anyway.

"Listen, let's think of something else to do while we wait for your bag to come. That couple over there," Matt said, pointing to an older couple waiting across the airport for their bags at another carousel. "They're from England, in their mid 50's, they are both accountants traveling to Italy for an adventure. While they're here, he is going to surprise her with a hand-gliding excursion."

I looked at him and let out a snort, trying to suppress my giggle as I imagined the fear across their faces as they tried hand-gliding. We had always played this game back at Binghamton University, where we would try and guess the backstory of other students and professors we would come across as we walked between classes.

"Your turn Juliet. Girl in the red dress next to the boy who can't stop staring at her. Go."

"So," I said, taking a big inhale, "both of them are around our age or a year or two older, they are students staying in Italy for a week and then traveling to France after. He is secretly in love with her, but she has no idea. That's why she is not nervous at all while talking to him. He is dying to tell her that he is in love with her and will do just that in front of the Eiffel Tower. *Très romantique.*"

Matt's eyebrows raised as I told him that story, he shook his head and started laughing.

"So, you speak French now?" He asked suspiciously with eyebrows raised and a goofy smile across his face.

"*Oui,* but it stops there because that's all I know." I smiled back at him. He shook his head, dirty blond hair momentarily covering his eyes before he pushed it back and let out a chuckle. I took another strand of hair between my fingers when I noticed the carousel stopped moving completely.

"Juliet, let's go and report your luggage as missing. You should've brought just one bag like I did. You girls and your twenty shoes and thirty hair products." I rolled my eyes and shoved him. He wrapped an arm around my shoulder and we walked over to find the lost and found counter. I was grateful to have him with me here right now.

When he found out I applied to the study abroad program in Verona, he argued he had to come too since he didn't want to break the tradition of us always being in the same Italian classes. We especially did not want to break the tradition now since we were graduating in June.

We reached the lost and found and approached an agent who was seated behind a computer screen.

"*Mi scusi. Ho perso una valigia.*" I explained to her how my luggage was missing. She looked up at me and cocked her head, her short black hair swishing to the other side before she spoke.

"*Sei del sud?*" She asked, wanting to know if I was from the southern part of Italy. "But I also sense an English accent too. Do you speak English?"

I was a little stunned that she detected that my accent was both Southern Italian and English so quickly. I tried really hard to perfect my Italian back at school because I wanted to fit right in when I got here.

"Yes, I do." I knew my mom would yell at me for resorting so easily to English because this was the perfect opportunity to put my Italian to use. I was too upset to even care at this point, I would learn German if it meant I got my luggage faster.

"Okay, so what is your surname and first name?" The agent said, adding an "a" at the end of every word.

"Um...surname?" I asked.

"Oh! You are American, right? I sometimes forget that Americans say *last name* and the British say *surname*." She seemed content with the brief language lesson, but I was growing more anxious as the minutes ticked by.

"It's Fiore. F-I-O-R-E and my first name is Juliet, J-U-L-I-E-T." I spelled out both since there are typically many ways to spell each.

"Ah *Fiore*, very pretty. You know that means flower, right?" I could see her smile pull wide as if she had been the first person to ever let me know that. My nonni told me first when I was very young, and every year, my Italian teachers and professors would remind me.

"Yes, thanks, I know. Do you know where my luggage is?" The smirk on her face disappeared and she went back to her computer, typing the information in.

The typing stopped and I saw the agent look up towards a taller man dressed in a suit making his way across the room to us. She called out to him and he gave her a sultry smile back. I felt the pit in my stomach fill with nerves like boiling water. This man was definitely going to be a distraction.

After five minutes of hearing *sei davvero carina*, you are really cute, and *ristorante...stasera*, restaurant and tonight, I grew even more impatient. "Um, *signora*? My luggage, can you tell me where it is?" I interrupted them as the woman was now playing with his tie.

"Yes, one moment." The woman said shortly. She then turned back to the man and batted her eyes a few more times before saying *ciao*.

"Ah, okay good news. Your luggage is here, in the Malpensa Airport, but we are going to have to take some information from you while you wait for it. Please give me your phone number and the address of where you are staying while you are here."

"I don't know where I'm staying yet. I'll find out today." I felt another bead of sweat trickle down from my forehead and my stomach flip-flop, threatening to bring up the gnocchi I had on the plane. "Can I give you the address of our director's office?"

She scrunched up her nose and looked down at me as if she wanted to tell me *to pull it together.* Instead, she just nodded her head.

After she typed all of the information I gave her, she lifted her head and looked back at me. "Okay, the man that will bring you your luggage is on break. He will be back in five minutes. Wait there and I will call you when it is here." She dismissed me pointing to a set of chairs and turned her attention back to the man who never left after she said *ciao.* I looked over and found Matt sitting down and scrolling through his phone. I walked over and slumped into the chair next to him.

"Hey Juliet, don't worry, we can still make the train. We'll just have to run." Matt smiled, placing a hand on my arm. I looked up at him, nodded, and realized that I was probably going to give myself a heart attack if I didn't calm down.

"Let's look up stuff to do in Verona while we wait." Matt flicked through his phone, pulled up a map, and scooched closer to me. I could smell the usual citrus and light woodsy-scented cologne he wore. It always gave me a feeling of warmth and comfort. He was the only one at Binghamton that lived within fifteen minutes of me back home and we were able to see each other during breaks. Lately, we have been hanging out more and more since he and his ex-girlfriend broke up just over a year ago. I was used to seeing his ex-girlfriend as a background picture on his phone, but now it was just a big picture of the Red Bull soccer stadium.

"There are a million *gelaterie.* We would need to visit at least three a day in order to try all of them." Matt said, referring to the little Italian ice cream shops that sold gelato.

I felt my shoulders loosen and I chuckled. "We also need to make sure that we try all of the flavors before we leave. Promise me?" I said, waiting for him to hook his pinky into mine to secure the deal.

"Promise." We both laughed but then I felt his gaze stay on mine slightly longer than it should, his light blue eyes hovering on mine as if he was debating whether to ask me something else. He looked down instead and reached into his bag to grab his Italian phrase book.

"Listen to this, *Vorrei ordinare il risotto con le gambe.*"

"Matt, you just ordered risotto with legs. You meant to say *gamberi*, shrimp, right?"

We both laughed together and then I looked down at my phone to check the time. "Fifteen minutes have already passed! I'm going back up."

I marched to the counter and interrupted the agent who was now whispering something in her admirer's ear with her back to me.

"*Mi scusi*," I said firmly, "is the man back from break to give us our luggage?"

"*Signorina*," the agent said as she whipped around to look at me. "He is on break. Americans think things happen quickly around here. Here in Italy, you have to learn patience. When he is back, he will bring you your luggage."

I skittered back after her response, my mouth slightly opened as if I were trying to answer her, but I closed it when I saw a short, bald man pushing a cart full of bags out of the corner of my eye.

Right on top was my polka-dotted one that had a pink ribbon tied to it that my mom made me attach at the last minute. *So you can spot it better at the airport*, she said. What good did that do if it didn't even show up when it needed to? But, nothing mattered anymore as I got excited that we might still make the train.

After confirming with the agent that the polka-dotted bag was actually mine, Matt and I ran across the floor of baggage claim and out of the doors of the airport. We found our bus that would bring us to the train station and boarded it quickly.

I watched the battery drain on my phone as I kept the screen bright, watching the minutes tick by on our way to the train station. An agonizing hour later, we had finally arrived, only to find out we had just missed the train we were supposed to take by a few minutes.

"*Mi dispiace, signorina.*" The ticket agent apologized to us then told us that we would have to wait for the next train to arrive which would take an hour longer because it was a local train meaning it made more stops.

I wiped my forehead with the back of my hand and felt that the tiny hairs along my crown were frizzy from sweating all day. It made the situation even more upsetting. Matt turned to me, put his arm around my shoulder, and pulled me into a side hug. I felt defeated, wondering if this was a precursor to how my trip would be, running around everywhere just in time to miss everything.

"Juliet, don't worry so much. We're both tired from the plane, and the jet lag is making everything seem worse than it is. You have all of your luggage, right? You are in Italy, right? So what if we missed a train! The director isn't going to tell us to go back home, we'll just have to make the best of it."

"You're right." I said, giving him a small smile. "I guess I'm nervous because I've never really travelled anywhere on my own before." I've visited my nonni in Southern Italy with my parents during the summers, but never really had my own independent adventure. I remember my friends begging me to go on Spring Break with them to Acapulco or Cancun but after watching videos of all of the crazy things they did while they were there, I was always too nervous to go.

My phone started buzzing and I looked down to see my mom's face popping up. I was hesitant to click accept on FaceTime and hovered over the icon a few seconds before finally pressing it.

"Sweetie, is that you? *Studenti—guardate. Questa è mia figlia!*" It was too late to hang up, I noticed she was in front of one of her classes. I thought about pretending that the phone didn't have good reception and saying only half of every word, but I didn't have the energy to even feign that.

"Mom? Everything is okay, but it's a little crazy now. I'll call you later." After introducing me to the class as her daughter, she was now parading the phone around her classroom, eager students were saying *ciao* to me, as I continuously tried to pat down my hair from the Medusa spikes that were forming.

"Wait, *aspetta! Studenti, come si dice "train station" in italiano?*"

I squeezed my eyes shut and felt the blood coursing through my body and settling in my cheeks. I couldn't believe she was using me as an example to her Italian students right now. She had been excited for me for this trip, explaining how this would be the perfect experience for me to really perfect my Italian before I started teaching and how it would help me stop speaking the dialect that I would sometimes resort to.

My nonni spoke the dialect to me whenever I would visit them at their house in Calabria for the summer, and I would naturally start to pick it up. Each region was known for its own dialect, with words and pronunciation being different even within a thirty-minute drive of the next town, but at school, they all learned the same Italian. As soon as I got home, my mom would turn on her teacher-button and make sure I could conjugate all of the verbs correctly. If there was anything I hated, it was definitely conjugating verbs.

"Mom, I have to go. I love you, bye." I said in one breath and hung up the phone. I was afraid she was going to start quizzing me in Italian in front of her students, and I was already stressed enough as it was.

The next train came shortly after I hung up. We boarded it, and were finally headed towards Verona. The train was crowded, and older looking than I would have imagined. We took the first two adjacent seats we could find. Matt helped me put my luggage in the overhead bin and we both plopped down simultaneously and stared out the window.

The landscape outside was beautiful. There were small hills and olive trees scattered around. It was definitely different from the scenes I was used to seeing back home, which were streets lined with oak trees and houses on perfect sharp rectangular-shaped properties with white plastic fencing around. Here the houses were minimal and the fields blended into soft greens, browns, and yellows. Wheat fields and tilled dirt seemed to show a sense of pride in taking care of the land. I wanted to keep staring out the window but exhaustion was taking over so I sat back and closed my eyes. My nerves were finally melting away, enough to make me sleep.

"Juliet." Matt lightly tapped my leg.

I quickly shot up and I noticed the train slowing down. I rubbed my eyes, looked out the window, and with a wave of relief I saw the sign for Verona and realized I had been asleep for over an hour.

"We're here!" I said as I pulled up the directions the director sent us.

"I think it would be easier if we just get a taxi," said Matt. "We really don't know our way around the city yet." I nodded, trying to shake the jet lag that was trying to pull me back into sleep. I forced myself to fight it, grabbed my bags, and trailed behind Matt as we got off the train.

"Wow, look at this building. It's got to be at least 400 years old." Matt said, staring up at the building the taxi pulled up to. "Can you believe how old these buildings are around us? Back home, it's rare to see buildings built earlier than the 1970s!"

I laughed at him, realizing he was right. We walked through the big, heavy doors that welcomed us inside.

"*Benvenuti a Verona!* Giorgia, your director, will be with you shortly." A woman seated at the front desk greeted us and ushered us to follow her. "You must be Juliet Fiore and Matthew Connell. Your friends from the program already arrived and are now in their rooms, but you came just in time, Giorgia was just about to leave for the night."

I looked over at Matt and he turned his head toward me with a look of relief on his face. We just made it.

She reached her desk and picked up the phone, dialing a number and speaking in Italian too quickly for me to understand. "Giorgia will see you both now. Come this way, please." She led us through a narrow corridor into the director's room.

Giorgia was sitting behind a large, dark desk with papers piled all over. She had short-cropped reddish hair with bright red-rimmed glasses. She was very petite and dressed like she was ready for a Milan runway, with tight, black pants, and a tweed blazer paired with a perfectly-matched patterned silk scarf. Her eyes came up from the paperwork she was looking at and she stared at us over her glasses, smiling smugly.

"There you two are. The last two on my list to check in." she said. "You are both very lucky. I was just about to leave for the night. I had given you precise directions to come here, no?"

We both quickly explained what happened but she interrupted us as if she didn't care enough to hear.

"Yes, well, I have these two rooms left and I have already assigned them. Matt, you will be in this building here, number 43, apartment 10. The rest of the people in the program are also in that building. Juliet, I'm sorry but you will be in another building, here,

41, apartment 28." She said as she pointed to a map. "There was no more room in building 43. The Italian students stay in building 41, but you will just have to join them. It will be good practice for your Italian anyway.

"Okay, here is some more paperwork and information about the program as well as your keys. If you have any questions, you can reach me at this number, sounds good?" Giorgia seemed in a hurry as she handed us all of the paperwork and information. "My secretary will call another taxi so you can go quickly to your apartment. Oh, and here is a map. Explore the city when you have free time. By the way, Juliet," she turned to look at me directly. "You must have picked this city because of your name, right?"

I figured she was talking about the fact that Romeo and Juliet took place in Verona and that Juliet's original house was here. I had seen pictures of it online when I was researching Verona and made a note that I would have to visit it. I gave her a timid nod yes, clutched all of the papers and keys, and turned to leave.

Giorgia's secretary got us a taxi as promised and we went to check out our new apartments. The taxi driver drove faster and crazier than a New York one, which I thought was impossible, and ten minutes later pulled in front of our apartment buildings.

Matt reached over and grabbed my hand that was mindlessly twirling my hair again. "We will be fine Juliet. I promise." Matt said in a soft voice as he leaned closer to me.

"No, I'm fine. It's just, you know..."

Matt chuckled as he leaned over to reach the handle to open my door. I breathed in a deep sigh as I pushed the door the rest of the way open.

The taxi driver dragged out our luggage and placed them in front of us. Matt squeezed my arm gently before picking up his bag.

"I'll stop by your apartment tomorrow morning. We can go exploring and find a good place to grab a *cornetto* or something else for breakfast." Matt said as he took a few steps backwards towards his apartment.

He turned around and headed off giving me one last wave and I was looking at the building that I would call home over the next four months.

It was already dark so I couldn't see much but, all of the buildings surrounding mine seemed to all be very similar. They all were about five stories tall and seemed fairly modern compared to the other historic buildings I had seen so far. Each apartment had a balcony facing the street. I saw a few that had clothes blowing in the wind, on Matt's building and noticed that many of the windows were lit with shadowed movements behind the curtains that were drawn. The balconies on my building looked bare and I only saw a faint light on in one of the apartments.

Even though it was February, I didn't notice the cold. Somehow, the frigid air would settle itself into your bones back home, no matter how many layers of clothes you wore. Here the air felt different. There was no ocean 15 minutes away. Here we were surrounded by hills, valleys, and mountains that stood off in the distance. Somehow, the air made me notice just how far I was from home.

I entered my building and started to search for apartment 28. I found it on the second floor, all the way to the right of the building. Even though it was my room, I felt odd opening the door and entering myself. I knocked several times hoping that the sweet Italian girl I envisioned as my roommate would answer it and give me a hug. After waiting a few moments, I concluded that no one was going to answer so I used my key to unlock the door.

I blindly searched for the light switch with my fingers, pressed it on, and dragged my bags to the center of the room. Seafoam green cabinets lined the side of the wall adjacent to the door and in front of them was a table with four chairs tucked in neatly. I looked for a place to set my jacket and found a coat rack sitting right next to me. On the opposite side where I was standing were french doors that opened up in front of the table and led to what I guessed was the balcony.

"*Permesso?*" I asked, walking through the room towards a hallway, wondering if anyone was there.

It was only seven in the evening, so I figured they wouldn't be asleep. There were two doors in the hallway, one slightly opened, showing a stark white sink and dark blue tiles on the floor. I opened it further and chuckled quietly to myself when I spotted the bidet, a bowl that delicately sprayed water and washed your more *intimate* areas. My parents had insisted on having one in our house and my friends would always ask why we had a second toilet in the bathroom. I would then explain what it was and quietly laugh at their disgusted faces.

I knocked carefully on the other door, since it was fully closed, wondering if my roommate was in there sleeping. I decided to open it a few inches after not hearing any response. I quickly found the light switch next to the door and scanned the room to see which would be my bed. I noticed one was already done up nicely, with a dusty-rose colored bedspread and matching pillows. There were pictures scattered all over the walls around it. The nightstand had a small nightlight with more pictures in picture frames surrounding it. Next to the nightstand, there was a desk covered with books neatly stacked in a pile.

I looked to the other side of the room and saw the same setup, only this one was completely bare. There were not even bed sheets covering the bed yet. I unzipped the luggage, took out my sheets, and made my bed. I decided to unpack all of my things so that I wouldn't have to worry about it tomorrow. When I was done I checked my phone and saw that it was already past ten o'clock.

I wanted to go to bed soon so I could be on Italian time and not fall into the trap of jet lag. I felt a nervous flutter in my stomach and tears started to sting my eyes. Maybe it was from all of the running around, or maybe it was that I was completely by myself, in a dark building, with no one around.

I wished I was in the other building with the other students that were studying abroad. I could have someone to talk to or laugh with at this point. I took out my phone and found my favorite Italian playlist, put my earbuds in, and tried to fall asleep, as a few tears slid down my cheek and onto my pillow.

All of my doubts and worries hit me all at once. I couldn't help asking myself if this was all a big mistake and I worried that I would ever fit in. What if my Italian doesn't get better and I'm not a better teacher? A shudder went through me as I replayed the time I shadowed my mom in her classroom and tried to teach a lesson. I could see the pity and shock in her students' faces as they realized I was not a natural teacher like my mom. I barely got through the lesson, stammering between a mix of English and Italian, and almost gave up on the dream of becoming a teacher afterward. My mom insisted all I needed to do was study abroad and then when I came back, I would get my Master's in Education, and be ready to teach alongside her. I still didn't feel confident that I would be good enough to do that. I buried my face in the pillow, breathed in the familiar fabric softener my mom used, and got lost in Laura Pausini's melodramatic songs that I was praying would help me go to sleep.

2

Due

Gli Amici (nm)= Friends

I woke up to someone knocking on the door. Was it 9am already? I looked at the time on my phone but was confused by what it said because the room was still pitch black. I walked over to the window, my mind still fuzzy and not fully awake, and pushed the shutters open. Sunlight spilled into the room and I squinted my eyes trying to adjust to the sudden brightness. A chuckle escaped as I remembered that most houses back home have shutters for decorative purposes, but here I would actually have to use them.

I heard knocking again and wondered who it could be this early. I assessed myself quickly in the mirror, brushing back my hair so it wouldn't look like I just woke up, and splashed some water on my face. Thankfully my face was only slightly puffy. I found my purple fluffy slippers that matched my flannel pajamas and rushed over to open the door.

There was Matt, looking me up and down. He had an amused smile on his face.

"*Buongiorno*! I see that someone has just woken up."

I blushed a little, looking down again at what I was wearing and making sure that it was not as embarrassing as I thought. "Yeah, I guess I was tired after our journey yesterday."

"No one is in this building, huh?" He said. "If I had known last night, I would have told you to come over to mine. Everyone was up until at least eleven and I met a whole bunch of new people. A lot of them are from different countries like Spain, England, Germany, and even France. It's convenient too because they all speak English better than Italian. I want to introduce you to everyone today."

A pang of jealousy hit me because Matt was already making friends with everyone while I was stuck in a seemingly deserted building all by myself.

"Wow Matt, that's great." I was happy for him but still wondered why no one was here.

"Well, today is everyone's first day of the second semester, so they'll have to be back soon." A female voice behind Matt said.

Matt moved to the side so I could see Valentina, a petite girl that was born in Ecuador, but moved to NY with her family when she was young. Her dark brown hair was pretty much always pulled back into a ponytail and she always wore dark-rimmed glasses that seemed to overpower her small dark brown eyes.

"You see," she continued as she fiddled with her shirt and patted down her jeans, "Italians usually go home for the weekends and on breaks. They typically live relatively close to the colleges they attend so they can go home to spend time with their families, boyfriends, or girlfriends. They should be back today. I'm not sure if they'll be coming straight to their apartments or going to their classes first. It's the first day of everyone's classes except for ours. We'll get our schedule today and start tomorrow instead."

Matt had rolled his eyes during Valentina's long explanation and looked over at me as if to say *here we go again.* Valentina's family spoke Spanish fluently, which made learning Italian a cinch for her.

Valentina seemed satisfied with the lengthy explanation she gave us. In our classes back home she always had to make sure she knew the answer to every question and gave more information than was needed. Professoressa Rossi loved her and always complimented her on her knowledge of Italian history and culture.

"I found the rest of the study abroad gang in the lobby as I was walking out, and they wanted to come along with me to wake you up." He motioned next to him to show John and Jess standing a little bit further down the hall, they were the other two students from our program on this trip.

John, "the rich kid from Westchester" as Matt referred to him as, had unruly, curly hair and an outgoing, fun personality. He was slightly shorter than Matt, and not as fit. He always bragged about his *perfect year-long tan* thanks to his Dominican dad and Sicilian mom.

Back at school, John was part of a fraternity that would host parties every Friday night at their house. He would always make an announcement at the end of class that his frat was hosting a party and that we were all invited. All John had to do was make his perfect smile, showing off his gleaming white teeth, and then half of the class would show up.

Matt has asked me in the past if I wanted to go to one but I always told him I wasn't interested in frat parties. The one time I went, freshman year, I had beer spilled all over me and someone threw up right in front of me, splashing vomit back onto my clothes. It was not fun for me like it was for others.

Matt always laughs whenever I tell him that story and says that I shouldn't shun all parties just because I got traumatized at one. I never ended up going to another one though and just hung out with my friends in our dorm rooms.

"Hey, Juliet, nice pajamas," John said, snorting a little while laughing and looking around. "So, where's your hot Italian roommate? When are you going to introduce us to her?"

"Already, John? You're insufferable." Jess said as she pushed him aside to give me a hug hello. She was a lot shorter than everyone and usually wore clothes that hid her figure. She's always very closed in when she sits at her desk at school. Her toes and elbows tucked into her sides as she quietly took notes. I always thought she was sweet, with her short, curly blonde hair and light green eyes that sparkled any time someone talked about something she loved.

"So, are you excited to go on the college tour today?" Jess asked, her voice softer than the others and her hands clasped together in front of her.

"College tour?" I asked, looking at Matt puzzled.

"Yeah, Giorgia forgot to tell us. We are supposed to go on a college tour in an hour. I wanted to make sure you'd be ready in twenty minutes to catch the bus to Giorgia's office again." Matt said.

"Okay, I'll be out in a bit, I just need to change." I closed the door and ran to the bathroom to take a quick shower. I tried hastily to turn the hot water on and got dressed in whatever looked the least wrinkled before making my way out the door.

When we arrived at Giorgia's office for the tour, I started getting excited again as she explained what classes we would take. Matt found out that his engineering classes would be in one building, while my Italian classes would be in another. A language professor called us individually in his office to quickly assess what level we are individually at in the language.

When it was my turn, I spoke the best I could, trying to use all of the grammar tenses correctly. I saw the professor biting the edge of his pencil and knitting his eyebrows together before he said anything as a response.

"Do you have family from the South?" He asked in English, which surprised me.

"Well, my dad was born in Calabria and my mom's parents were born in Naples."

"I see. You are good enough to be in the advanced program, but I hear some words of dialect mixed in. I'll put you in the intermediate class for now. It will help with your accent."

I was a little surprised that I was not ready for the advanced level yet and could already see the look of disappointment on my mom's face when I told her. I thanked the professor and left the office. I felt better when I found out that Jess and Matt were placed in the same level as I was. We would have one language class together Mondays, Wednesdays, and Fridays, while Valentina was placed in the advanced level and John was placed in the beginners. I decided it was probably better this way so at least I could stick with Matt. After the tour, Valentina convinced us to try a place she found for lunch and was sure we would like it.

"What is a *Piadineria*?" John asked, trying his best to pronounce the sign hanging above the door where we stopped.

"So, it's basically an Italian sandwich shop, except the bread is flat and homemade. They usually put prosciutto, soft cheese, and other toppings on it and then they fold it over!" Valentina explained, excited that no one else knew what it was.

"Wait, so like a quesadilla?" John asked, his face scrunched.

"Ugh, forget it John. Let's just go in." Valentina quipped, pulling John's arm inside.

We all ordered a different piadina, wanting to try all of their toppings to see which one came out the best. John and Matt each got a lot of toppings on theirs, brie, mozzarella, onions, spinach, and a few more that I couldn't see under the fold of the bread. Jess, Valentina, and I opted for a lighter version that had only one topping each.

"I love pronouncing this cheese— *Squac-que-ro-ne*! But it's even better to eat it!" I said after taking a bite of my piadina with this new soft cheese that I loved.

"Okay, and after this, I know exactly where we need to go. They are supposedly the best gelateria in the city!" Valentina said, pointing to a place on her map.

We all shrugged our shoulders in agreement, still biting into our *piadine* and enjoying every last bite.

After we were done, Valentina led us to the ice cream shop, where we quickly became overwhelmed with all of the possible choices we could get.

"I might need to order at least five scoops!" Matt said, his eyes widening as he kept looking at all of the different flavors.

"I know you are joking Matt, but I really might need to get five with all of these amazing flavors!" I said, my eyes absorbing all of the flavors, and my mouth watering. Matt and I decided that I would order two flavors and he would order three so we could both taste a variety and see which was better.

"Oh my God, that *tiramisù* flavor is the best!" I exclaimed after trying a spoonful of Matt's.

"Your *nocciola* one is so good too though," Matt said, after taking a spoonful from my hazelnut scoop.

We decided to walk around the city center, gelatos in our hands, and absorb the view around us. It was all very peaceful and charming until all of a sudden Valentina started talking.

"Do you know they say that *Piazza Brà* is one of the biggest piazzas in all of Italy?" She asked. When none of us responded, she took it as an invitation to keep going. "Here is the statue of Victor Emanuel II, the first King of Italy when it was unified. Also if you look over there at that arena," she continued, pointing across the piazza. "They are typically the hosts of many concerts and operas, we should definitely try to go to one." Valentina was about to go on, when John interrupted her.

"Wait, what is this piazza called again?" John asked. Matt, Jess and I knew exactly where this was going.

Valentina seemed thrilled that someone was paying attention to her, she repeated *"Piazza Brà*, John, where..." she stopped as soon as she realized why John was asking and saw him laughing hysterically.

"Piazza Bra? Now that is my kind of piazza!" John exclaimed as Valentina made a face back at him.

We all laughed and continued to walk a little more. The sun was sinking lower into the horizon, and I took out my phone to see it was already 5 o'clock. I felt excitement starting to build up inside of me as I figured that most Italians must have already finished classes and my roommate might be in the apartment.

"Should we start heading back?" I asked the others, hoping they would agree. Matt nodded yes emphatically and the others agreed as well. As annoying as Valentina could be, she was handy with directing us through the city and back to our bus.

3

Tre

Il Compagno di stanza= roommate

A huge smile spread across my face, ready to greet my roommate the way I had been practicing in my head all of this time. I raised my hand up to the door ready to knock. My mind swirled with all of the possibilities that she could be like. I took one deep breath and allowed my fist to make contact with the door. It sharply swung open to reveal a dark-haired girl in jeans and a white sweater, wearing a puzzled expression on her face.

"*Ciao, chi sei?*" She said, asking me who I was.

"*Sono* Juliet, *la tua compagna di stanza.*" I answered back, explaining that I was her roommate, but in a less enthusiastic way than I had imagined.

"Oh, *l'americana.* Giorgia told me today you were my roommate. Well, you know your name Juliet is perfect here for Verona?" I was surprised that she spoke English so well, but even more surprised that she wasn't as excited as I was to finally meet.

"Yes, I know." I said, feeling a little defeated that she had decided to speak in English.

"Well, I see you know where our room is, since all of your things are here." She said with a little smirk on her face as she turned around. She was about my height, but with long, straight, jet-black hair. She was slightly thinner than me and walked slowly to the room. She turned around, and said, "by the way, my name is Elisa. I was just about to have dinner—would you like to have it together?"

A smile immediately spread across my face. Maybe she was the perfect roommate I had envisioned after all and I was just judging her too quickly.

"*Bene!*" I said, hoping that she would start speaking in Italian to me instead of in English. "*Cosa mangiamo?*" I asked, curious about what we were eating.

Elisa lifted her eyebrows and said, "Well, we are eating a soup that I brought from home that my mum makes. It's with turkey, chicken, carrots, some celery, and tomatoes. It's actually popular here in Verona, but no one makes it better than my mum."

She paused for a second, looking at me like she was trying to figure me out. "Are you from Southern Italy? Your Italian sounds like a mix between Southern Italian and English."

Was it that obvious? No one from back at home would point out that my Italian was Southern. When I visited my nonni in Calabria, everyone sounded like me, or so I thought. It made me wonder if it was a bad thing to sound more Southern Italian. I never questioned it before, but after hearing it three times in the past two days, it started bothering me. I quickly shoved the thought to the back of my brain and decided not to overthink it.

As we were eating, we talked about how Elisa was a language major. She spoke in English the entire time, even when I tried to respond in Italian. When I did, she would look at me funny and then continue to carry on in English. Midway through the conversation, I decided it was easier to just stick with one language instead of flip-flopping between the two of them.

"I'm fluent in French, German, and Spanish, and I just started taking Greek after visiting Santorini last summer." She said this in between sips of water. "I don't really have a plan with what I'm doing with all of these languages, but I'm having fun learning them."

She continued talking as she fished a carrot out of her bowl of soup. I noticed that something about her exuded confidence when she spoke and I admired the air of coolness in her words. I felt a little bit self-conscious when she spoke about her plans and the multiple languages she speaks because I wasn't even sure if I was fluent enough in Italian yet to teach it after I graduated.

"Let me see your class schedule," she said, putting down her spoon and holding out her hand. "I want to see what building you are in and if I know any of your professors."

I was a little taken aback by the direct command she gave me, but nonetheless, I went to my room and retrieved my printed-out schedule.

She took it from my hand, surveying it for a couple of minutes. "The classes you are in will be difficult." She said before turning back to her soup and handing the paper back to me. "But you will be in the same building as me, and a few of my friends have taken classes with some of your professors. It will not be easy though."

She said this with a small smirk on her face, which made me wonder if she found it funny that I might struggle through my classes. "Tonight I will introduce you to my friends that live in the building. After dinner, I can show you all my pictures of them."

When we finished eating, we walked to the bedroom and I was reminded of all of the photos Elisa had above her bed. Last night I hadn't taken the chance to look at them too closely.

"This is Luca," Elisa said pointing to a boy with dark brown hair in one of the pictures. "He is studying computer science and is very funny." She started laughing at a memory she must have remembered.

"This is Pietro, he studies engineering and lives with Luca as well." She said, showing me a picture of another boy with longer, light brown hair.

As she was saying this I felt my eyes drift towards another picture where a group of people was having a barbecue, holding bottles of wine. Everyone in the picture looked like they were having a really great time and smiling.

"This is Giacomo." She said while her finger moved to point him out.

In the picture, Giacomo was leaning against a wall with his legs and arms crossed in front of him. He had beautiful, big eyes that looked a cross between brown and green, and hair that was the same shade as oak, tousled perfectly away from his face. He was smiling with his eyes crinkled slightly around the edges while he looked straight at the camera. I couldn't stop staring at him. He was gorgeous. Something about his smile seemed so genuine. I immediately knew I had to find out more about him.

"So, Elisa, what does Giacomo study?" I asked casually.

Elisa raised her eyebrows signifying that she caught on to why I was asking about Giacomo. Her mouth turned up slightly on one side as she turned back to look at Giacomo in the picture.

"Oh, he studies engineering, with Pietro." She turned back to me and narrowed her eyes so they became tiny slits. "We are very good friends, me and Giacomo. In fact, we are practically, how do you say it in English, boyfriend and girlfriend?"

Of course. How could a good-looking guy like that not be taken? Elisa was gorgeous herself so it made sense that they would be the perfect couple. The inner part of my mind started thinking selfishly.

Maybe he's arrogant or has a really bland personality. At least then I wouldn't feel so bad that he was taken.

After looking at his picture again, I couldn't imagine someone with that smile, and those eyes being anything besides perfect.

"He looks like a nice guy!" I tried my hardest to sound sincere, "It's great that you two are together."

Elisa looked at me a little bit odd as she sensed that it was difficult for me to say that. "*Grazie.*" She said, smiling contentedly and moving on to explain the rest of the pictures. "And this is Marcello."

I looked at them too and then noticed that Elisa only had guy friends.

"Wait, you've only shown me pictures of your friends that are guys. Are you friends with any girls?"

Elisa started to laugh and said, "Of course, but these pictures are of my university friends. Many of the students in this building are studying engineering or computer science and the majority of them are boys. So, naturally, I became friends with a lot of males here." She sounded amused that I asked that question. "But, here on my, uhm, how do you say *comodino* in English?" She continued as she walked towards the side of her bed.

Elisa's brows pulled in and I could see from her expression she was searching for the word.

"Nightstand." I blurted out when I became sure that she wouldn't think of the word herself. A smile formed across my face because I was finally able to show some language skill.

"Yes, I remember, *nightstand*. Anyway," she continued, brushing off that I helped her, "on my nightstand are pictures of my family and friends from home."

My mind began to wander as she was telling me about her family and friends from home. I tried to sneak a glance back at the picture of Giacomo but didn't want to make it too obvious. I finally fixed my eyes on his again and had a feeling that he was looking right back at me, enticing me.

Elisa looked at her watch and then looked at me and her eyes widened. "They are all home now." There was a tinge of excitement in her voice, "We should go see them!"

Elisa went to the bathroom, fixed her hair, and put on some lip gloss. I also took a quick glimpse of myself, and added my favorite frosted, pastel pink lip gloss, hoping to make a *bella figura*, or a good impression.

"You see," Elisa said, while closing the door behind us and walking towards the stairs, "some apartments have two people, like ours, and some apartments have four people, like theirs. Giacomo and Luca share a room while Marcello and Pietro share the other."

We walked down the stairs together and knocked on the door. I caught Elisa fixing her hair again. "*Ciao!*" She exclaimed when a boy slightly taller than us with short dark-blond hair opened the door. A quick flash of excitement crossed his face as his eyes jumped between the both of us.

"Marcello, *questa è* Juliet." Elisa said, introducing me to him. I froze as he reached over and kissed me hello on both cheeks.

"*Piacere.*" I managed to say, praying I was not blushing. I felt like I was already failing the first part of knowing how to act like an Italian by being surprised by a kiss hello.

"Don't worry, Juliet. Marcello is very friendly." She said, smirking at him.

"Juliet *è americana. Studia lingue come me.*" I had understood exactly what Elisa was saying, explaining how I studied languages like her. I was excited to finally be able to speak in Italian, so I continued to talk to Marcello.

Elisa made her way past Marcello and into the room before turning around to ask him if Giacomo was home yet. Marcello shook his head no, and then turned back and continued talking to me while moving to the side of the doorframe, leaving room for me to walk into the apartment. Their setup was similar to ours, they had a kitchen and a living space as soon as you walked in, also lined with the same colored cabinets. There was a soccer ball that caught my eye in the middle of the room and over in the sink there were a bunch of dishes piled up. The counters were also filled with a few empty pasta boxes and bottles of wine. I saw Elisa looking around the room before she sat down in a seat with her phone in her hand, typing a message.

Marcello seemed nice and attentive as I explained to him my story of travelling here, and how I missed the train and almost lost my luggage. He felt bad about that happening to me and was quick to share a travelling mishap of his own that he once had when landing in the same airport.

I was beginning to like him because he was a quick laugh. He loved my imitation of Giorgia I did by pretending to adjust a fake pair of glasses and looking down at him. I even received a compliment on my Italian saying that I should have been put in the advanced Italian course even if I did speak a few words in dialect. The conversation then shifted to me explaining how I wanted to be a teacher and how I, in order to do that, needed to receive a Master's degree back home.

For the first time on the trip, I felt myself relax as I was talking to Marcello. He even grabbed his side as he laughed when I told him I wasn't used to actually opening and closing shutters in the morning and at night. This sparked a conversation about the differences I've noticed between where I live and Verona so far.

In the middle of our conversation, the door opened again. I turned around quickly, wondering who I was going to meet. This time, it looked like Luca, but I wasn't sure yet.

"Ehi, ciao ragazzi!" the boy exclaimed as he walked in. He was a lot

taller than Marcello, but slender like him. He was wearing square-rimmed glasses which showed off his dark brown eyes perfectly.

"*Ciao, sono* Luca." Luca smiled widely as he said hello to me. Unlike Marcello, he just extended his hand in the form of a greeting.

"*Ciao, sono* Juliet." I explained who I was and that I was Elisa's roommate. Instead of sitting down next to Marcello, Luca walked over to Elisa and talked to her.

I looked over at them and Luca had his hand on the back of Elisa's chair as he spoke to her. I could tell that they were close even if I couldn't make out what they were saying. Elisa asked *dov'è Giacomo*, probably wondering where he was.

I was still talking to Marcello, but this time about football and how we all watch the Superbowl. He excused himself to go to his room to grab a football jersey that his cousin sent him when he visited New York.

When he returned, the door opened again. This time I was sure it was Giacomo who walked in. He was even better looking in person, and I was shocked at how that was even possible. There was a smile already on his face as he walked in, and we instantly locked eyes with one another. My stomach did a front flip, and it suddenly became a little bit more difficult to breathe. It was insane to me how the presence of a singular person could completely change the entire dynamic in the room and make my body feel like this.

His eyes were even more inviting than the picture. I could see the array of green taking over the subtle hints of brown. His hair was brushed back, slightly wavy. It all complimented his face perfectly. His smile caused a slight indentation in his right cheek. I never realized how adorable it was to have only one dimple. His body was toned and very well-dressed in jeans that looked freshly pressed and an overcoat that had the collar popped up. He did a quick survey of the room, before deciding to walk right towards me to introduce himself by holding out his hand.

"*Sono* Giacomo. *Ciao.*" He said, still staring into my eyes.

My body betrayed me and I felt a wave of heat rush my cheeks as I took his hand. "Uhm..*sono...sono*...Juliet." I stammered, looking down and trying to break the tension I felt building up between us. I sounded like an idiot who could barely remember their own name.

"Giacomo." Called a voice from the other side of the room, breaking me out of my dream haze. I turned around to see Elisa giving me a glaring look. "Giacomo," she repeated before saying something in Italian fast enough that I couldn't understand it.

Giacomo turned back to me, giving me an apologetic look, and turned to Elisa. From her quick cadence of speech, I noticed that she seemed flustered.

Luca, Giacomo, and her then went into the room adjacent to where they were sitting and closed the door behind them. I looked over to Marcello but he just shrugged his shoulders and went on talking about sports and all things American while I politely listened, stifling yawns. Tiredness was starting to hit me after a long day. I explained to Marcello that I needed to get back to the apartment to get some sleep for the next day. I gave him a wave goodbye in hopes that we wouldn't kiss each other hello and goodbye every time we saw each other.

Thoughts were swirling in my head as I climbed the stairs to reach my apartment. I was replaying all of the conversations that I had and my stomach started to tense. It hit me that I was 3,000 miles away from home and that even though these people were nice, I did not know them. I reached into my bag, took out my key that looked like it came from a medieval novel because of its comical size and fancy design.

As I was doing this, I made the immediate decision that I did not want to be sad in Verona. I was going to make the best of this. I was going to make friends with as many people as I could, and just enjoy every minute that I had in Italy.

I entered the room and noticed a sink full of dishes and let out a quick sigh before starting to wash them. I started to think again of each person I met. And then I thought about Giacomo.

Even though Elisa was with him, I could not seem to shake him out of my head. I tried to tell myself that it wasn't right to continue thinking about Giacomo like this, but I couldn't help it. There was something about him and the way he looked at me that struck straight into my soul. I broke out of my trance when I noticed the sound of water trickling on the floor and soaking through my socks as the sink began to overflow. I shut the water and mopped up the mess.

As I was cleaning, I was amazed to find out that it was only 8pm, according to the clock above the stove. I walked into the little seating area we have and flicked on the TV. There was a man and a woman speaking rapidly to each other in Italian and my brain was too tired to pick any of it up. I was about to retire all my thoughts and resign to my comfortable bed when I heard a dreaded knock on the door.

Dragging my feet and heading over, I assumed that it must be Elisa and she had forgotten to bring her key to the guys' apartment. I leaned my ear against the door and said, "*Chi c'è?*" A familiar man's voice responded, trying to speak in Italian.

"Matt!" I said smiling as I opened the door.

"*Ciao bella!*" He said with a smile on his face. I opened the door wide to let him inside and we both sat at the table both giving occasional glances at the Italian show.

"Can you understand what they're saying?" I asked him.

"Um, what do I need to understand? I mean look, the girls are barely wearing anything. I think that's the entire message and goal of this show right there." Matt said, chuckling and gesturing toward the girls wearing skimpy outfits.

I laughed at that because it was very true. "I think all Italian shows are like this," I told him. "I remember when I would visit my nonni I would have to turn away half the time because the girls were wearing practically nothing. I would always feel embarrassed and look at my nonna wondering what she thought but she would just smile at me since she knew that it was not something I saw every day. I honestly think she got a kick out of it."

I suddenly was not in the mood to watch the half-naked ladies anymore so I turned the television off and rested my head on my hands letting out a big sigh.

"Hey, what's the matter?" Matt put his hand on my shoulder and scooted closer to me, trying to study my face.

"Nothing, why?" I said, but my voice cracked a little.

"C'mon Juliet, you're thinking about something," he paused for a second before his eyes widened. "Or maybe it's someone! Wait! Juliet, did you meet a cute Italian boy and not tell me about it! Come on, what's his name, do I need to go beat him up?" He said, teasingly nudging his elbow into my arm.

I nudged him right back, and he grabbed onto my hand, not letting go. I laughed, trying to pull it away, and jokingly yelled *basta* at him, so he would stop. He dropped my hand down with his onto my lap before looking up at me.

I stared into his eyes taking notice of the color and shape. They were the nicest shade of aquamarine, the type that you could just picture diving deep into and getting lost inside of. We looked at each other longer than we were used to and I felt my heart skip one of its regular syncopations. What if the natural connection I had with Matt was natural for a reason?

My thought was interrupted when I suddenly heard a set of keys, turning in the lock on the front door. The door quickly swung open to reveal Elisa in the threshold.

"Oh, *mi dispiace*, sorry." Elisa said loudly, taking in the scene that she just walked in on. A huge smile began to form on her face as I pulled my hand away from Matt's, and sat back in my chair.

"I'm Elisa." She said approaching us, reaching her hand out to him. "Juliet didn't say she had a boyfriend!" She was smiling at me in an almost sinister type of way. I furrowed my eyebrows and squinted at her trying to understand what she was thinking about us.

"No, he is not my boyfriend." I replied sternly. I saw Matt in the corner of my eye deflate a little bit, but decided not to think anything of it.

"I'm going to go." He said getting up abruptly. "*Piacere* Elisa." He gave her a terse smile as he got up and shot me a confusing look before he opened the door.

"Good luck tomorrow on your first day. I'll text you tomorrow." He said as the door snapped shut behind him. I brought my hands to my face and noticed that my cheeks were still heated from the unexpected moment I just shared with Matt.

"So, what do you Americans say? Ah yes, are you *friends with benefits*?" Elisa asked as soon as he left.

"No, nonono! We definitely are not. Matt is just my really good friend."

"Oh, I understand." She said, but from the smug smile on her face, it didn't look like she believed me at all.

I didn't feel like pursuing this conversation any longer so I got up and went to the bathroom. What *was* that? Why did she have to embarrass me like that in front of Matt? I took my time applying a bunch of different creams on my face, trying to take up as much time in the bathroom as possible, hoping Elisa would be sleeping once I got out.

I opened the door slowly not wanting to wake her up, but once it was opened, it revealed a very annoyed-looking Elisa who had been waiting a long time for me to come out. She was propped up against her bed frame, legs crossed, and filing her nails slowly.

"So, why isn't Matt your boyfriend? Do you not like boys? I won't judge if that's what you're worried about. My brother has a boyfriend for three years now and my parents adore him."

I sat down on my bed and tried to embrace the fact that we were inevitably going to talk about this. "No, I like boys. It's just that we get along really well as friends and I don't think he looks at me in that way."

"Well, he is cute, Juliet."

I nodded my head, hoping that that was the end of the discussion, and reached for my earbuds and phone, searching for my playlist.

"Oh, by the way, Marcello said you're nice and he enjoyed talking to you. I think he likes you. He will be sad to know you have a boyfriend."

"He *isn't* my boyfriend! And yeah, I think Marcello's nice too, but I'm not looking for anything serious here. I don't think a long-distance relationship would work.

"Giacomo says you seem nice too." I noticed Elisa said this much quieter as if she hoped I wouldn't hear and her smile disappeared.

"Yeah?" I answered, "I liked him too. I bet you two are happy together."

Elisa mumbled something under her breath that I didn't catch and then said goodnight. I put my earbuds in and wondered why I felt so happy about Elisa's boyfriend thinking I was nice. I turned around, put one arm under my pillow, and tried to turn my mind off. After a while, the music began to drown out my thoughts and I went to sleep.

4

❧

Quattro

La Scuola (nf) = school

I hated to admit it but Elisa was right. The classes I was in were extremely hard. I had two poetry classes, one cinema class, and my language class three times a week. Matt made our language class enjoyable by stealing my pen and passing notes while the teacher had her back to us. I would give him a jokingly stern look and then would start to laugh too. I guessed that any awkwardness that might have happened between us last night was resolved and we were back to our usual ways of joking around.

Elisa seemed to warm up to me and we started having dinner together every evening. She would usually make the dinner and I would take on the role of washing the dishes. We always had polite conversations, in English, about university and her family at home. She mentioned to me how she lived about an hour from the university and she described what her villa was like. She showed me pictures of her property surrounding it, with vineyards organized in neat rows up and down the hill.

Her brother, who was two years older, marketed the wine they produced and was a sommelier to local restaurants while her parents oversaw the seasonal workers they hired to harvest the grapes and store them to make wine. I saw pictures of her whole family, and by the end of it felt like I knew them personally. Her mother looked exactly how I envisioned her. She was a striking woman, always dressed elegantly, and had the same long black hair and hard expression as Elisa. Her dad had a gentle look about him. He was shorter than the mother, with thin, white hair.

It was odd to me but, the way Elisa's hands looked, and from the pictures of her parents, it didn't look like any of them worked in the vineyards themselves. I remember my nonno's hands were hardened with callouses from working outside on the farm every day and his skin was always deeply tanned. I could tell that even though she didn't say anything about it, Elisa's family had money.

Throughout the first week, I began to fall into a routine. I started waking up earlier, and going for runs around the neighborhood, taking in all of the beautiful sites around me. The views were amazing early in the morning. I could see the beginning of the Alps on a clear day, and I breathed in the beautiful smell of chimneys burning wood in the crisp air.

Although classwork was tough, I managed to set aside time at night to read and practice some of the new Italian I learned. I also planned time to get an espresso with Jess and Valentina during our breaks between classes. We would joke and try to mimic the native Italians by leaning against the counter and slowly turning our espressos with the tiniest spoons. We ordered a *brioche* or other delicious Italian pastries and ate every bite of it.

"*Ciao Gianni! Per me, un macchiato, per favore.*" We practiced saying to the bartender. We quickly were on a first-name basis with him and he gave us small espresso cups filled with a touch of milk and a smile when he found us amusing, his dark eyes crinkling at the sides. He was probably around my dad's age, with dark hair combed over to the side, almost giving him a classic look that reminded me of an older movie actor. Gianni had warned us that if we really wanted to look Italian, we should never order a cappuccino after 11am because that's what the tourists did. We made sure to listen since he told it to us in a serious voice while he was drying some glasses.

Elisa made a routine out of visiting the boys' apartment during the week and I usually followed along.

"*Questo è* Pietro," Marcello said, introducing the only roommate I hadn't met. I gave him the usual *piacere*, pleased to meet you, and shook his hand.

"*Cosa ascolti?*" I asked, curious about what he was listening to after noticing his earbuds. I knew a few names of some Italian singers that were popular now, but I mostly listened to whatever my parents played in the house, usually something from the early or late 90s.

"Ah, *questa è l'ultima canzone di Fedez*. Here, listen." Pietro responded, explaining how it was Fedez's latest song. He switched the audio to his phone and played it out loud. I instantly fell in love with the catchy beat and was happy to be able to add more modern Italian songs to my playlist.

"*Bella!*" I replied, trying to stop myself from moving my hips so I wouldn't embarrass myself in front of my new Italian friends. Pietro smiled and then our attention all shifted to Elisa after she let out a huff.

"*Dov'è Giacomo?*" Elisa asked where Giacomo was, disappointment clearly showing on her face.

Marcello quickly explained that he was still on campus, working on his research project. He then turned his attention back to the rest of us, continuing his accurate imitation of his engineering professor and eventually making us practically roll on the floor with laughter.

I turned my head towards the door when I heard a key fumble in the lock and Giacomo walked in. He had a sad and tired look on his face. I locked eyes with him but looked away to notice that his shoulders were slumped. He dropped his bag on a chair and walked across the room towards us.

"*Va bene*, Giacomo, *su, prendi un caffè*." Luca patted him on his back, trying to bring up his morale with a cup of coffee.

"*No, vado a letto. Divertitevi.*" Giacomo answered, telling us to have fun, while he walked straight to his room to sleep without looking back.

I hadn't seen him in a week since I initially met him. I couldn't help the selfish thoughts I had been fighting back all night, hoping that I would get a chance to talk to him again. I paused for a second though, when I realized that neither of them acknowledged each other. Maybe that's why she assumed me and Matt were "friends with benefits" because that's what her relationship was like with Giacomo.

"*Buona notte, gnocco!*" Marcello jokingly yelled good night after Giacomo, calling him *hot* in Italian. Marcello then continued another hour entertaining us, bringing back the fun mood from before.

***

The next day after our Italian class, Matt decided he would skip the class he had after and ride the bus home with me. He invited me to his apartment a few times during the week, but after Elisa had asked if he was my boyfriend, I kept coming up with excuses not to, feeling like I should give him space, and also worrying what Elisa would think if I went over there a lot. He began texting saying we saw more of each other back at Binghamton than we did here.

"Okay, listen up," he said, turning towards me in his seat. "I'm having a party on Friday and my roommate is making the best paella ever. And no excuses, you need to come."

"I don't know, I mean, I have a poetry assignment I have to do."

"I swear, Juliet, if you do not say yes right now, I will come to your room on Friday night and drag you there!" Matt said, imitating in air how he would pull me away from my books.

"Well," I thought about it. It would be fun to meet the people in Matt's building. "I suppose I could work on it tonight or Saturday. Are Jess and Valentina going to be there?"

"Yes! I slid an invite under every door in the building." Matt said, chuckling.

He said that his roommate loved having people over and at times it made it difficult to study, but it was nice meeting new people. I needed to make more friends, and this party was probably the best way to meet more people and fill the lonely weekends.

"So, what time should I be there?" I said, pulling my lips into a smile. I noticed that his eyes lit up at my response.

"Awesome!" he said, hugging me. "I honestly have no clue because Europeans are weird with time. One time Javier, my roommate, told me that everyone would come around 9, but they all showed up at 10 and were still hungry for dinner." He pulled out his phone and began typing out a message. "I'm going to ask Javier tonight but I'll text you tomorrow and let you know for sure."

The rest of the bus ride home, I told him how I met Pietro for the first time and how we've been hanging out in the guys' apartment some weeknights. He told me about his roommate's friends and all of the amazing Spanish food he's been eating.

By the time Friday came, I found myself very excited for the party. I was fidgeting with nervous energy all through my classes, imagining what the party would be like. I had very little party experience and hoped that it wouldn't mimic the frat party I went to freshman year. I wondered if there would be a language barrier between all of us or if we would all try to speak either English or Italian.

I got back to my apartment a little bit earlier that night, so I could get ready. I used my curling wand to create some soft curls and then shadowed my eyes with a shimmery, brown eyeshadow and a soft black liquid liner, being sure to apply it all neatly and concisely.

I began to hear my old roommate in my head tell me, *enough to enhance but not overpower.* She would always brag about how she saved me from overusing bronzer and blush before going out, and looking like a clown. We began a tradition that anytime I put on makeup, I would take a picture and send it to her. I took a look at myself in the mirror and my usual doubt crept up inside me. I sent her a picture for a confidence booster and immediately received a reply back.

DANIELLE: **Make those gorgeous big brown eyes pop more!**

DANIELLE: **Are you having fun? Any Italian hotties?**

DANIELLE: **Bring one home for me too!**

I smiled as I read her rapid-fire texts and then went back to the mirror to enhance my eyes like she said.

JULIET: **Any more mascara and I will look like a raccoon.**

JULIET: **Also, I'm going to a party tonight so I will keep an eye out for you!**

DANIELLE: ♡

I only saw Danielle at school since she lived close to Binghamton, but over breaks, we would meet up in the city to go shopping.

At 7:30 I began heading out of the front door of the building when I saw him. He was carrying a duffel bag and was headed towards the parking lot. He turned around for a second and instantly noticed me. He squinted his eyes to make sure and he waved in my direction.

5

Cinque

Divertirsi= to have fun

"Ciao, Juliet— *vero?"* Giacomo said surprised, confirming that he remembered my name correctly. I saw him start to make his way towards me and I instantly felt a rush of heat enter my cheeks.

"Yes, umm.... *Sì....* What are you still doing here?" I said in a mixture of nervous Italian and English. "I thought you would already be home by now?"

"I'm sorry, but I am not good at speaking English. I left my bag in the apartment and had to turn around to grab it."

I smiled as he took his time saying each word correctly. I found it funny how every European I met so far didn't think they spoke English well, but compared to many of my friends learning a second language, they were practically fluent.

He smiled back at me and walked a little closer. He was about five or six inches taller than me and his hair was perfectly in place with gel giving it that "purposely messy" look. He had amazing, big hazel eyes that I found myself getting lost in once again.

"Juliet, *ti piace Verona?*" Giacomo asked if I liked Verona.

I told him, in the best Italian I could, that the city is absolutely beautiful and the views were amazing. He seemed proud of my answer and explained how he only lives about an hour from the city center, in a small town up on a hill.

"Your Italian is *incredibile!*" he told me and I blushed even deeper. "Maybe you can now teach me English."

I immediately broke our eye contact and looked down as I started thinking about Elisa.

"But Giacomo, Elisa speaks English well too, maybe you should learn from her."

"Yes, that's true. But Marcello told me you want to be a teacher, and I can be your first student!" he said.

I promised him I would only teach him if he promised to help me with my Italian too. He agreed and his smile grew even wider as he nodded his head. I wondered if Elisa would be okay with what I just agreed to and if I should let her know.

"*Allora, ciao.* My friends are waiting for me back home." He said hesitantly, as he looked down at his watch then back at me, eyes softening. I watched as he headed back towards the parking lot, forgetting that I also had somewhere to be.

I was instantly shaken into reality as I realized I probably looked like a doofus standing in front of my building with a smile on my face and watching him go. I tried to stop smiling but I couldn't. I looked at my reflection as I passed a window and noticed that my hair was still in place and there were no mascara smudges under my eyes. I skipped a little on the way inside Matt's building and instantly felt even more excited about the night.

I felt my nerves surface themselves again as I stood in front of

Matt's door, hesitant to knock. I could feel my heart, beating like a bass drum, thumping to the beat of the music on the other side of the door.

Go, Juliet. I thought to myself and let out a huff before grasping the cold, metal doorknob and entering the scene.

The apartment was packed, people gathered in small groups talking to each other with red cups in their hands. I could smell roasted chicken and shrimp and guessed that it was the paella as soon as I took a step in the door. The music was so loud that the vibrations from it traveled through my body, replacing any other thought I had. I could make out some Spanish words from what sounded like a classic pop song from back home. I looked around, hoping to see a familiar face, and finally spotted Jess and Valentina, and quickly felt a sort of comfort as I walked towards them.

"*Ciao!*" I yelled over the music. Valentina was standing extremely tense, looking around the room while holding a plastic cup in her hand. My body oddly relaxed after seeing that Valentina was definitely more nervous than I was. I hoped that I did not look up-tight. Jess, on the other hand, had a red face and a vibrant smile and was holding onto a glass of sangria.

"Oh, *ciao*, Juliet!" Valentina said, her shoulders dropping in relief as she kissed me hello on both cheeks. Of course, Valentina had to show off that she even knew how to greet a friend at a party, just like an Italian.

"Hey! The paella is amazing- you need to try it!" Jess said, hugging me. "You look so gorgeous tonight, how many of those Italian boys are chasing after you?" She said while taking a sip of sangria.

"Thanks, Jess!" I said. I got a little upset that I felt like such an outsider here. "I am actually jealous you all live in the same building. You must have made your friends right away!"

"It's not all that great," Jess answered, laughing. "Yeah, they do have great parties and fun every night, but I know Valentina is actually a little bit jealous of you living with the Italians." She said, her thumb pointing over to an annoyed-looking Valentina who nodded in agreement.

"Did you see John? He's already kissing a girl that he met tonight. He's unbelievable!" Valentina quipped, pointing over at John.

John was leaning over to talk in a girl's ear and then putting his hand on her waist. She was giggling with him and seemed to love it when he got closer to her face.

"Do you know her?" I asked, curious to find out.

"I think she's one of my roommate's friends," Valentina answered. "She's from England. So...I'm sure John won't be needing to learn Italian any time soon." She let out a little huff as she said that.

"Hey look at the *belle americane* over here!" Matt said while walking over to us and putting his arms around me and Jess.

"This is such a great party. You're so lucky to have Javier as your roommate." Jess said, taking another sip of sangria.

"I'm glad you like it. Jess, did you try the tapas?" Matt asked, noticing that Jess was almost finished with her plate while Valentina wasn't holding anything. "You and Valentina should try it and tell me what you think."

Valentina, still looking tense and uncomfortable, said that she was going to head back to her apartment and Jess went to look for her roommate so they could try the tapas together.

Matt and I hugged Valentina goodnight and we watched her wiggle her way through the crowd. He turned towards me with a look of excitement in his blue eyes.

"Alright, Juliet, you need to eat. I'm going to make you a plate of paella." Matt took me by my hand and led me over to the kitchen where he handed Javier an empty plate to fill.

"Ah, so this is Juliet," Javier said, smiling. "Matt told me so much about you. He is a good kid, but he needs to learn how to cook." He looked at Matt and playfully hit him in the stomach before handing me the filled plate.

"Yeah, yeah. I did watch you cook the paella, though." Matt said, dramatically rubbing his stomach. "I promise you I will be making dinner by the end of this trip." Matt laughed.

I took a fork-full of paella into my mouth and had to refrain myself from letting out an audible moan. An explosion of savory flavors instantly coated my mouth and made everything stop for a second.

"Oh my God Javier! This is delicious! Matt, please learn how to make this so we can have it back home too." I piled fork-full after fork-full into my already stuffed mouth.

Javier thanked me while Matt shook his head and chuckled. "Alright, Juliet, let's get you some sangria."

He filled up two red cups and we moved to the other side of the apartment, chatting with some friends he introduced to me. When they started talking about their engineering classes, I took it as an opportunity to scan the apartment. The setup was similar to ours. They had the same furniture and layout except it was in the opposite way. I was happy to realize that no one was obnoxiously loud or drunk and spilling beer. I instantly began to relax.

There was a couple sitting on two chairs facing each other, chatting and sipping sangria, and another few friends along the wall. I spotted John kissing the girl he had been flirting with earlier and laughed to myself because it oddly reminded me of back home. I continued sipping the sangria, letting the mix of wine and soda calm any remaining nerves I had. After a pause in the conversation, Matt's friends excused themselves to go get more drinks. Matt looked over at me, smiled when he saw me take a sip, and then peered into my cup as I took it away from my mouth.

"Finished already?" He said, his smile still holding mine. I felt slightly buzzed since I was not used to drinking at all.

"Do you want to go outside and get away from the noise?" Matt said, leaning into me. A small shiver went along my back as he whispered it into my ear.

"Sure," I said, probably not loud enough to hear over the music. Matt had understood anyway and grabbed my hand and led me outside of the apartment. The sangria had to be stronger than I thought because my hand felt tingly as Matt held it.

We walked outside and were instantly greeted with cold air. I was surprised that it wasn't the usual bone-deep Long Island cold I was used to. We walked further out and leaned against the railings that lined the balcony.

"What do you think of the trip so far?" Matt turned to me and asked, his hands in his pockets and his shoulders shrugged up from braving the cold air.

I said the first thing that came to mind. "Well, this view is beautiful, for one, but I'm still a little nervous about it. Some deep part of me says this will be an amazing adventure, but I'm worried that I put too much pressure on it." I felt some reprieve in the cold air after being inside the stuffy apartment, but a small breeze sent a shiver down my body as it hit my face.

"What about you?" I asked. "You must be having a blast with Javier as your roommate."

"Yeah, it's great." He paused for a second turning his body completely towards me and locking his eyes on mine. "Juliet," he put his arm around my shoulders, sending warmth down my arms, "What are we going to do?"

"What do you mean..." I started to say. His expression was unreadable, nothing like his usual playful self. I was trying to understand, but between being slightly tipsy and the cold breeze, I found it hard to think.

"Matt, *dónde estás?*" We both looked up to see Javier out on the balcony, looking down at us and calling out to Matt. "We need more Fanta for the sangria!"

"Ugh, I guess I gotta help out Javier. Come on, *bella*, let's go back to the party." Matt grabbed my hand again, leading us back. I noticed my stomach was now fluttering.

I took the time to meet the other students that were studying abroad. I met a girl from Southern Germany, Kristin, who spoke English really well and who happened to be in the same poetry class as me but on a different day, and her roommate Ana who was from Spain. She was studying to become an environmental engineer.

I instantly thought of Giacomo since he was also studying to be an engineer and wondered if Ana had some classes with him. Moments from our meeting recurred in my head. I subconsciously smiled thinking of him, but quickly brushed those thoughts away remembering he was Elisa's.

"I have a great idea!" Kristin said, beaming and breaking my thought bubble. "Let's go shopping tomorrow in Verona!"

"I'm in!" I said, smiling at both of them. We made plans to meet at the bus stop around 10 and have lunch together in the city center.

6

Sei

Fare spese = to go shopping

The noise of the people bustling and chattering with bags on their arms filled the main street of Verona, Via Mazzini. I admired all of the stores as we walked along the street. They were a mixture of high-end and affordable shops, complete with professionally decorated window displays that enticed me to want to buy everything inside.

"Follow me girls!" Kristin shouted, leading us into the Louis Vuitton store. We started giggling, like school girls about to enter a candy shop.

All of the clothing, accessories, and shoes were elegantly displayed. We pretended to act serious while we browsed in the store, but couldn't help feeling shocked at all of the masterful displays and exquisite clothing covered in bold patterns and sparkling jewels.

"*Mi dica, signorina.*" A shopkeeper asked if I needed help. From the look on his face, it was visible he was only asking me to be polite and to satisfy some type of protocol they had for greeting customers.

"*No, diamo solo un'occhiata.*" I responded, saying we were just going to look. Ana looked at me with her eyebrows raised and her thumbs up for the Italian I used.

I picked up a scarf and wrapped it around me before turning to Kristin who was trying on a backpack. We laughed when Ana walked up to us, wearing Louis Vuitton sunglasses and pouting her lips in an exaggerated way while taking a picture of the three of us on her phone.

After Louis Vuitton, we decided to shop more seriously and head to stores that were in our price range. These stores were all over Europe so Kristin and Ana were more familiar with them. They led me through a few and we picked out some outfits. I ended up buying a military green bomber jacket that I was sure people back home would know came from Italy. When we were done shopping, we had gelato twice, just to try as many flavors as we could, and we made sure to have a *caffè* with a *brioche* at a bar.

It was a little after five when we arrived back at our apartments and I noticed that I hadn't talked to my parents much since I'd been here. I did quick math of what time it would be at home and realized they would probably be eating lunch. My mom had answered on the second ring, excited to hear my voice.

"What are you eating?" She pressed right after greeting me, "Are you sure you are getting enough food? Are you taking enough pictures? You could use those in a portfolio when you become a teacher!"

"Yes, yes, Mom I know. I'm taking a lot of photos and eating really great food," I said.

My dad broke in after realizing I was responding to my mother in the monotone voice I used whenever she asked too many questions. "So, how's my little *italiana* doing?" My dad said, with his heavy Italian accent not pronouncing the "h" in how.

"Just fine, Dad. It's beautiful here. It's a little different from Nonna and Nonno's house since, well, there are no chickens or bunnies running around."

My dad let out a little chuckle. "Listen Juliet. Have fun there. Enjoy yourself and relax. Don't let your mom get you worried. Enjoy each day while you are there. Oh, and don't forget to call Nonna and Nonno. They can't wait to see you for Easter. Did you buy the tickets?"

"Not yet, but I looked into it. There are lots of flights that go to Calabria from Verona, so it will be easy." I continued explaining to my dad what airline companies flew there and I could almost hear him smiling through the phone. I know he felt guilty that he wasn't able to visit them this year with his work schedule, but he was happy that I could go.

We talked a little more and then hung up. I was about to put my cell phone down when it started lighting up and saw that Ana was calling.

"*Pronto?*" I said in a joking way, trying out my Italian.

"*Pronto!*" Ana said, letting out a little laugh after. "Juliet, you need to come over and have dinner with us tonight. A bunch of us are getting together and we're all making something to eat around nine, is that okay?"

I quickly thought of what I could make and asked if potato croquettes were okay. Ana seemed thrilled with it and admitted she had never tasted them before.

I got off the phone and looked at the clock. It was now almost six. I knew the Italian stores closed earlier than American stores so I prayed that I had all of the ingredients in the house. Even though I could've made something easier, I wanted to make a good impression and I could always trust my potato croquettes to come out delicious.

I learned the recipe from my nonna when I was little and we would make them together when I visited her. We'd put them in the freezer or give them to other relatives, and my nonna always bragged that I was the one who made them.

Luckily, I found the mozzarella, eggs, cheese, and potatoes I bought a few days before, with the intention of making them one night for Elisa. I searched through the cabinets to see if she had salt, bread crumbs, and oil to fry them in. I ended up finding exactly what I needed, and I took a mental note of what I was taking so I could replace everything on Monday when the stores opened again.

After two hours of boiling the potatoes, mashing them, mixing them with some grated cheese and bread crumbs, I rolled the potato dough around a piece of mozzarella, dipping them in egg and bread crumbs, and was ready to fry them. It was almost eight when I looked up from my frying and my stomach let out a deep rumble.

I remembered our Italian teacher telling us that Italians eat a little later than Americans do, and Spaniards even eat later than them. I wondered if this was a normal dinner time for Ana and if it was her decision to plan it.

After the last potato croquette was done, I took a quick shower, towel-dried my hair, and put it in a loose ponytail. I put the croquettes in a nice dish and kept about five extra in the refrigerator so Elisa could have them when she came back on Monday.

Kristin greeted me at the door with a big smile and Ana came running over to give me a hug.

"Wow, Juliet, that smells so good! I didn't know Americans could cook!" Ana said, teasing me.

"Well, you'll have to taste them first," I said, winking back and smiling too.

Ana and Kristin invited a few more friends, who also went to Javier's apartment last night. I met Kate, a girl from England, her roommate Sarah, and Marie, a girl from France.

I joked around with all of them and tried all of the different foods everyone made. I found out who was hooking up with who, who everyone had crushes on, and where a lot of other people in the building were from.

"Matt is cute." Kate had said in her British accent that made me smile. I saw that several of the other girls had nodded their heads as well.

I felt comfortable. My bundle of nerves had finally untangled and I felt myself truly relax. We spent the next few hours talking about our lives back home and comparing some of the differences.

"So when did you all start learning English?" I asked, impressed by how well everyone spoke.

"I actually started in first grade," Kristin said.

"First grade? We don't start learning a second language until 6th grade!" I answered, astonished.

"Wow! It must be hard learning a new language that late. Usually, we are already learning our second foreign language by then." Ana chimed in.

We continued the rest of the night eating and laughing. I couldn't wait for what the rest of the trip would bring if I continued to hang out with this group of people.

***

"*Stai ancora studiando?*" Gianni asked if I was still studying while he served a new customer that took a seat near my table.

"*Sì. È molto difficile.*" I said, expressing it was difficult. "*Un altro macchiato, per favore.*" I ordered another espresso hoping it would help me stay alert.

The weekend went by fast and it was already Monday, which meant back to classes. I had spent all day Sunday studying and catching up on reading. I noticed that I was able to mostly follow along in my class today, even though the professor spoke Italian at marathon speed.

"*Grazie,*" I said when he came back with an espresso cup and a little cookie on the side.

"*Per aiutarti con gli studi.*" Gianni said, motioning to the cookie he gave me, telling me it was to help me study.

I thanked him again and went back to pouring over all of the books, making sure to take little notes on the margins, and to refer to my phone for any quick translations.

When it got closer to four, I gathered my stuff, waved a quick bye to Gianni, and headed to my Italian class. As I walked up to the language building I noticed Matt standing outside, holding two books, and talking to Jess who had her arms folded in front of her.

"*Ciao, Matteo! Ciao,* Jess!" I yelled, calling Matt the way Prof. Rossi would call him.

"*Ciao, bella!*" Matt yelled back. Jess turned and waved timidly, only barely uncrossing her arm to do so.

"Hey, *siete pronti per la lezione d'italiano?*" I said, asking if they were ready for class. We walked in, grabbed our usual seats, and sat for the next two hours.

After class, the three of us headed back to the bus stop. It was a great feeling to not rely on a map or ask the locals where the bus stop was anymore. We were starting to make ourselves at home.

The bus was crowded. Jess grabbed a seat in the front while me and Matt found two seats in the back. Matt gave me a gesture to sit down first and then he took the seat beside me.

"*Grazie mille!*" I said to him as he let me sit down first.

"*Non c'è di che.*" He replied while smiling. We had just learned that phrase in class.

"Show off," I told him, nudging him in his ribs. His smile grew wider.

We didn't say much for the rest of the ride. I felt an awkward tension between us that was never there before, I didn't know what to say to him. It was finally our turn to get off and I realized that I recognized a lot more faces after meeting them at Matt's party on Friday night.

Jess waved us both goodbye and headed to her apartment. I walked next to Matt when he turned to me.

"So," he said, looking straight ahead with his hands in his pockets. "What's for dinner tonight?"

"I don't know. Elisa is probably home, so maybe we'll make some pasta together."

"We should have some pasta together one night."

I looked at him. He seemed more serious than normal. It was hard to tell whether he was just saying it to make conversation. I remembered how the girls from last night thought he was cute. I looked at him and smiled, understanding why they could think that.

"Yeah, sure. I'm curious to see how well you cook pasta." I said jokingly to him. He chuckled a little and then looked down.

"Alright, I mean it though." He finally made eye contact with me. "Okay, go and have fun with Elisa." He headed towards his apartment, turning around to wave at me once he reached the front door.

As I walked towards my building, my stomach tensed. I opened the main door, walked up the stairs, searched for the key in my bag to open the door, and walked into the sound of familiar voices.

"*Basta*, Luca!" Elisa yelled while laughing.

As soon as they saw me, Elisa shot up straight, her laughter dying down. Luca stood up from where he was sitting and took two steps back. Elisa gave me a quick glare without saying hello, and continued talking to Luca in Italian.

"Hi, Elisa. Hi, Luca." I said in a low voice, uncomfortable with the greeting she had given me.

"Hello, Juliet. So, you cooked this weekend, right? Let me guess, something with oil and bread crumbs, no?" Elisa said, with an exaggeration of sarcasm in her voice.

I felt the blood rush to my cheeks and I held in my breath. I forgot to replace the ingredients I used over the weekend.

"Oh, um. *Mi dispiace.* I'm so sorry. I...uh....I...I was making pota.."

"Don't worry." Elisa said, waving her hand for me to stop talking. "It's okay. I don't need it tonight for dinner."

Luca looked over at Elisa with a slight look of confusion, while Elisa got up and walked over to the fridge and opened it.

"So what do you call these?" She asked while nodding towards the potato croquettes.

"They're potato croquettes. Have you ever had them before?" I said, my voice cracking slightly. I didn't know why I always felt so belittled whenever I talked to her.

Elisa made a disgusted face like my offer offended her. "No. They look heavy. Right, Luca?"

My mouth dropped a little at her blunt response. I didn't know if she realized that her answer was rude or not.

"Well," I said, now a little bit angry. "You can try one if you want."

I almost wanted to throw away the whole dish so she couldn't have any but, I couldn't help but let her get away with what she said instead of speaking up for myself.

Luca looked like he was calculating what he should say. "We should try them, Elisa, Juliet obviously saved them for you." He said.

Elisa gave him a face and then shrugged her shoulders. She took them out of the refrigerator, setting them on the table.

The awkward situation was released by a knock on the door. Grateful to escape the tense situation, I walked over and opened it.

There he was. He had on a collared shirt with a sweater over it and dark jeans. He locked eyes with me and I looked down to see his mouth form a sweet smile. His full lips pressed together softly while going up slightly on one side. I looked back up to his eyes and couldn't think of what to say.

"*Ciao,* Juliet."

"Hi, Giacomo. Come on in. *Entra.*" I don't know why I became flustered with just the two words he said. My brain couldn't form a coherent thought in either language.

"Ahh, *cosa sono questi?*" He exclaimed, walking straight to the table, curious to know more about the potato croquettes sitting there.

"*Provane una.*" I told him, inviting him to try one.

"*Buonissima!*" Giacomo said, taking a bite of one.

I looked over at Elisa who had her arms crossed in front of her.

"Juliet, you made this?" Giacomo asked.

"*Sì.* Do you like them?"

"Yes. Can you teach me how to make them?"

"Sure," I replied, then glanced over quickly at Elisa whose face was turning redder by the minute.

Giacomo hadn't even acknowledged Elisa and she looked as if she were going to explode. After Giacomo reached for a second potato croquette, Elisa huffed, turned around, and headed towards her room.

"*Cosa ha?*" Giacomo said, looking up at Luca and asking him what was wrong with Elisa.

Luca responded too fast in Italian for me to understand, but I saw Giacomo shrug his shoulders as he took another bite. Luca then also proceeded to take a potato croquette off the plate with a smile on his face.

"Juliet, you are a very good cook," Giacomo said, smiling at me.

I smiled back at him but became worried at how Elisa was acting. Why was she so offended? Luca was tapping his foot and frequently glanced over towards the bedroom, but Giacomo seemed content to just eat the croquette.

Luca said something fast in Italian to Giacomo. He nodded to Luca, took the last bite of his potato croquette, and wiped his hands. I looked over to see Luca knock on the bedroom door, open it, and close it behind him.

At this point, I became confused as to why Luca was consoling Elisa. Shouldn't Giacomo talk to Elisa?

"So, when do we practice English?" Giacomo asked.

"Giacomo, you already speak English really well."

"You are kind. But no, I do not," he said before his eyes lit up. "Hey! Let's start now."

"Wait, hold on," I said, very confused at all that was taking place. "What is wrong with Elisa?"

Giacomo smiled again, rolled his eyes in a comical way, and said "No idea, she acts like that a lot."

"Do you think you should go talk to her?"

"No, it is okay, Luca's doing it."

The way Giacomo reacted so indifferently about Elisa's feelings made me wonder if he was a good boyfriend or not. The bedroom door swung open and Elisa and Luca stepped out.

Elisa's eyes were still narrow and she pulled her long black hair into a high ponytail. She approached the table, sat down next to Giacomo, and completely changed her mood. She said something fast in Italian while reaching over for a potato croquette and then chuckled at herself. Luca laughed too, while Giacomo had his head turned the other way.

"So, what were you guys talking about?" Elisa asked us, before taking another bite.

I didn't want to say we were talking about her. "Well... Giacomo was telling me about how he wanted to practice English." I answered, looking over at Giacomo for confirmation. He now turned to face me. His eyes were so intense I looked down.

"*Basta.*" Elisa said, finally using Italian to say enough. "*Guardiamo la* TV. Luca, *chiama* Pietro *e* Marcello." Luca grabbed his cell phone quickly and probably started texting the boys so we could watch TV together.

Giacomo shrugged his shoulders and whispered close to my ear so no one could hear. "We can practice another time."

I felt the hairs stand up on the back of my neck and instantly got goosebumps from his close proximity.

The rest of the guys showed up to the apartment and they watched a show they all seemed to love while I pretended to under-stand and laughed when they laughed.

The whole night, Elisa sat next to Luca and talked mostly to him. During the commercials, Giacomo talked to Pietro and Marcello about school and I tried to follow along with the conversation as much as I could. I started feeling left out since I wasn't able to talk about school with them and I didn't understand the show either.

Everybody decided to go back to their apartments to sleep after-ward. Elisa walked everyone to the door while I just stood back and waved to them goodnight. I went into the bedroom, put on my pajamas, and started getting ready for bed. Elisa walked in after and turned towards me.

"Well, goodnight. I must sleep since I have classes early." Elisa said, rather abruptly and each word pronounced very carefully.

"Elisa, wait. Are you okay?" I started. "Did I do something wrong? I felt like something was off tonight. If it's about the bread crumbs and oil, I'm so sorry. I really don't want us not to be friends for that."

Elisa's face softened a tiny bit and she went to sit on her bed with her legs crossed.

"No, I'm not mad. It's not that. It's something else." She said while looking down.

"Is it with Giacomo?" I said. I didn't even know why I said it, since it was probably none of my business anyway what was going on with them.

Elisa looked up at me. Her eyebrows furrowed slightly and there was a tiny crinkle in the side of her nose.

"Well, he told me he doesn't want a girlfriend," she said, letting her guard down. "So we are just good friends. Apparently, he wants to concentrate on studying first."

I was kind of upset that she told me they were dating when they weren't, but I continued listening because it seemed like she was finally telling me the truth.

"I like him though, and he likes me." she continued very calmly as if trying to convince herself that it was the truth. "So we can wait."

I nodded and pulled the covers over me. "Well, I'm sure things happen for a reason." I said, "It's probably good for both of you to concentrate on school for now."

She nodded and scootched down lower in her bed, turning away from me.

"*Buona notte* Elisa," I said, wishing her good night and hoping that my words were encouraging enough.

I laid in bed imagining how Giacomo told her. I wondered if it happened recently and if that was why Elisa was sad tonight.

Thoughts of Giacomo rattled around my head all night. I couldn't deny that something pulled me towards him. I wondered if he felt it too.

7

Sette

Un Desiderio (nm)= A wish

The next couple of days went fast since I spent most of the time attending classes and reading when I came home. Elisa acted a little nicer towards me and we had dinner together most nights.

One day after class, I met up with Kristin and Ana for coffee and they caught me up with what was going on in their apartment building. They mentioned how everyone was going to get together on Friday and go to a club in the city center. A memory flashed back from freshman year when I went to a local bar with my roommates. Even though I had a good experience at Matt's party, I still didn't have enough courage to go to a bar. I felt relieved when Kristin said she understood and whenever I felt ready to go, they would come with me.

Thursday night, I decided to visit Jess and Valentina to see how they were doing. I stopped by Jess's apartment and she had just finished a load of laundry and was about to hang everything to dry.

"I really miss dryers." She said, "I don't know how Italians do it. I mean, after I hang the clothes up, I have to iron them too! Who has time to iron socks?" Jess chuckled and continued taking the clothes out of the washer and shaking them before hanging them.

"Have you seen Valentina?" I said.

"I just texted her that you were here. She said she'll stop by."

Valentina greeted us with a yawn at the door and was already dressed in pajamas.

"Wow, Valentina, you were in bed?" I said, surprised since it was only eight.

"No, I was actually trying to read some of the books for my classes. I can't seem to catch up." She said while rubbing her eyes and yawning again.

"How many classes are you taking?" I've never seen her this stressed about a class. She was always somewhat anxious back at Binghamton, but never looked as overwhelmed as she did now.

"Well, including the Italian class, six. I think it's too much though. There are too many books for each class. And, well, I'm not really enjoying myself here. I seem to be reading all the time."

"You need to drop some classes," Jess said. I was shocked at how she was still standing. "Who knows when you'll get another opportunity like this! I bet you don't even need the credits. Come on, let's have some espresso and chat."

Jess made a pot of espresso and set out some cups. She took out some *cantucci*, which were a version of crunchy almond biscotti, and we all sat down around the table.

We talked about classes and their roommates. Valentina wasn't crazy about hers since she stayed out late and made noise when she came home, but Jess loved hers and had already invited her to visit her back in NY.

They mentioned that John was actually getting pretty serious with the girl he hooked up with at Matt's party, and how a lot of the girls in the apartment building thought Matt was cute.

"Yeah, I always saw him with his messy hair in Italian class, but he is cute when he's dressed nicely," I said.

Jess and Valentina exchanged glances and smiled when I said that. They grabbed their espresso cups in unison and took a sip.

"What? What was that?" I asked.

"What was what?" Jess said, putting down her cup and still smiling.

"You know what! That look you just gave each other. Do you guys know something?"

"So, anyway," Valentina said changing the subject. "Saturday we're going to see Juliet's house in the center of Verona. We can take pictures on the balcony and see where Juliet's statue is. There's also a wall where you write you and your lover's name in the hopes that you stay together forever."

I couldn't believe they just breezed past my questions. "Yes, and if you touch Juliet's statue, you will find love," Jess added.

"Yeah?" I said defeated, accepting that the moment had passed. "I never heard of that before."

"You know, my cousin went to Verona, touched the statue, and the next day met a man and now they're married!" Valentina said.

"Okay! I am down to go!" I said, excited to have the chance to see more of Verona. "We'll meet up early, take the bus, and have lunch there too."

***

The next night, Ana called to see if I changed my mind about going to the club, but I still didn't feel comfortable enough to go.

Instead, I decided to stay home by myself and relax while reading some more books for class.

I decided I read enough about the Neorealist movement in Italian cinema and the popular works by Federico Fellini to put on the TV to relax. It was getting boring staying home by myself so I turned to the same show I was watching with Elisa and the boys and tried to see if I understood it better than before.

Surprisingly I was able to. I straightened up the house, swept the floor, and took out the garbage. The Italians recycled vegetable and food scraps, something I never did back home, so I had to make sure to throw it out often before the fruit flies swarmed the pail.

It was still a little chilly outside, but I braved the cold without a jacket and ran to the garbage bins, dumping the trash in the right recycling compartments.

On the way back, I noticed a faint light in Giacomo's apartment. Hadn't everybody gone home for the weekend?

I let out a shiver as I stepped back into the warm apartment, and took out my phone, thinking it was probably a good time to call my parents.

"Hi, Juliet!"

"Hey, Mom!"

She answered right away and I saw that she was sitting on the couch in the living room. I could make out my dad's shoulders at the edge of the screen, leaning against my mom. I always hoped for a relationship like theirs.

Every Valentine's Day, my dad would read out the card he wrote to her, describing how he knew she was the one when he spotted her eating gelato in the piazza across from him. I would pretend-gag acting as if I couldn't stand their PDA, but I secretly enjoyed hearing the story.

She was visiting Italy one summer and was staying in the town where my dad lived. He always exaggerated how he felt a bolt of lightning hit him when he saw my mom.

Seeing them together made me wonder if there was a magical love lightning bolt that would hit me when I met "the one."

My love life was always disappointing. I had a few boyfriends in high school. One was thanks to a friend who told this one boy, Frankie, I thought he was cute, and one in college two years ago that lasted only a few months. I knew he was immature when he greeted all of his friends with "*bruh*" before each of his lacrosse games I went to.

"Hi, honey! I thought you had forgotten all about us since you haven't really called." My dad said.

"Sorry, it's been a little busy here. I've been doing some fun things, though."

"Hope there aren't any Italian boys involved, Juliet." My mom said, very on-brand for her.

"Oh my God, Mom, no." She had warned me before I left not to get involved with any Italian boys since she thought I would get my heart broken. I always thought it was a little hypocritical of her to say that, and typically shrugged off the advice. All I heard her say was how my Dad was different from other Italian men because he waited for her to finish her degree and never pushed her to give up her dreams for him. But it made me think of why she didn't have the confidence in me to find a guy like that. I couldn't help but feel a little offended.

"I've been hanging out with mostly Matt and two other girls who studied abroad and then I met two girls from Germany and Spain."

"How's Matt doing? Is he speaking any Italian there?"

"He's fine, Mom, and yes, he is speaking Italian, he's in the intermediate class with me." Even though it was kind of a lie since I honestly heard him only use maybe two sentences in Italian outside of our Italian classroom.

"Ciao, *principessa*." My dad said, positioning the phone to him. I was grateful I was going to avoid a further inquisition from my mom.

"Hey, Dad. Any new wines that you are taking on?"

"Well, there was one from Barcelona I wanted to check out. In fact, the owner wants me to visit the vineyard in a few weeks. Too bad it's far from you otherwise I would swing by for a day."

My dad started his own import and export business when he moved to New York with my mom. I could tell he was proud of himself and his company, especially since his family struggled with money growing up. In Italy, he tried to take on any odd job he could to help my nonni on their farm. He quit school at 15 to help work. My nonni did not approve, but he knew that they needed the extra money.

"Oh, that would've been nice. My roommate's family owns a vineyard." I thought, but then I almost wanted to take it back since I was afraid of how the rest of her family would act if they met Elisa.

We continued talking about my classes and life in Verona. I missed our talks. With the time difference, it was hard to get him alone on the phone. My father was always easy to talk to, and I usually turned to him with any drama or boy trouble going on in my life. He always listened, never judged, and I really appreciate that about him. His advice was usually the same, *give it some time, things always magically worked out for the best.* I felt comforted hearing those words.

***

I woke up early the next day, eager for my day in Verona with Jess and Valentina. Skipping down the steps, I spotted them at the bus stop waiting for me. I gave them a quick wave back and jogged to meet them, before stopping abruptly in front of Valentina's gruntled expression.

What happened?" I asked.

"Her roommate," Jess said, a mocking smile forming on her lips.

"You don't understand, Jess." She turned towards me searching my face for understanding. "She came home at 2am, reeking of cigarettes and slamming all of the cabinets. I swear she wore wooden shoes because her footsteps could have woken the whole building. I'm asking to switch rooms tomorrow. I can't deal with it anymore."

Jess's eyes twinkled and I could see she was trying everything not to laugh. I tried to do the same but a small chuckle managed to escape.

Valentina shot us both a glare that made us stop, but as soon as she looked the other way we both turned to each other and smiled.

When we reached the city, we followed Valentina since she knew her way around. Our first stop was Juliet's house. We entered through the gates and walked towards a small courtyard, surrounded by cream-stuccoed buildings on all sides. The walls in the small corridor leading to the courtyard were covered in writing of all languages. There were hand-drawn hearts everywhere. The space was filled with people taking pictures up on Juliet's balcony.

We decided to tour Juliet's house and ventured to the second floor so we could stand outside on the infamous balcony. A small woman who spoke French kindly offered to take a picture of all of us after seeing us struggle to get the right angle.

"That's right, we have to touch the statue for good luck in love!" I said.

"Um, no thanks. Did you see where you have to touch it? How embarrassing." Valentina said. Her cousin probably left out that detail in the story.

"Valentina, so you touch her chest. It's not that embarrassing." I said, trying to calm her down.

"Juliet, there are a lot of people here. I don't want to touch her boob in front of everyone." Valentina said, her voice low.

Jess's eyebrows were raised and she nodded her head in agreement too. "Sorry Juliet, I'm shy as it is. I'm not helping you out either."

"Fine, I'll go. Jess, can you at least take a picture of me?" I said. Jess took my phone in relief.

I approached the statue and hesitated a second. Her chest was worn out from all of the different hands that touched her over the years. I thought it was kind of interesting how metal could get worn out from the warmth of enough human hands. Her neck and her face were a dark brown bronze color, while her chest was shiny gold. I was conflicted with laughter and sympathy for the statue because of all the times it must have been violated.

I touched the statue, then started laughing while Jess took a picture. I rushed towards her to see how it came out.

"Oh wow. This is too funny. I wonder how many people believe in the power of the statue." I said.

"Well, now you never know Juliet, any cute boy you meet now on this trip might be your soulmate," Jess said, laughing at the same time.

We went to a pizzeria for lunch and each ordered a personal pizza. I ordered a *capricciosa*, which had ham, olives, artichokes, and mushrooms. Jess ordered a *quattro formaggi*, with four different types of cheese. Valentina just ordered the *margherita*, with tomato and mozzarella.

I bit into the pizza and was instantly reminded of how different the pizza tasted from back home. The fresh taste of mozzarella, thin crust, and the simple ingredients filled my taste buds and coated my mouth with the perfect mix of sweetness from the sauce, savory sourness from the mozzarella, and crunch of the crust. The pizza ended up being more than we could eat, so I decided to wrap up the rest to take home to enjoy during a late-night study session.

"No!" Valentina said as she saw me about to wrap it up. "Are you crazy? No one takes food home in Italy from restaurants. Especially from pizzerias!" She nearly shouted, which made both Jess and I flinch back.

"Ah! Okay, noted." I said, laughing a little and glancing towards Jess who looked like she was going to die of embarrassment from the scene Valentina just made. "You're right, Valentina. I will eat the rest." I added while bringing another slice to my mouth, slightly glad for the excuse to eat the whole thing.

When I had one slice left, not able to fit another bite in my stomach, and looked over at Jess who was struggling to finish hers as well. Valentina was wiping her mouth, her plate completely clean.

"I'm stuffed, but I'm not going to say no to gelato." I said to them both as we walked out of the pizzeria.

We ended up finding a gelateria around the corner and I made sure to continue on my quest of trying all of the flavors, this time choosing *bacio,* made after the famous Italian chocolate, and *caramello,* caramel, on a cone.

On the way back home, we couldn't stop talking about the day. We looked back at the pictures and laughed at the one where I touched Juliet's statue. I posted it onto my Instagram and laughed at the comment my old roommate Danielle wrote under it, teasing me that I was now a "changed woman". When the bus reached the apartments, we said goodbye and split off to walk towards our buildings.

I reached my room and texted Kristin and Ana to see what they were up to for the night. I felt bad not going to the club with them, so I decided to bake some lemon cookies and bring them over.

I got the recipe from my nonna. We would make lots of them to-gether. After I put the cookies in the oven, I changed into my comfy, ripped jeans, a beige t-shirt, and a burgundy colored cardigan that made me warm enough so I didn't need a jacket. I reapplied some lip gloss, put on my favorite white slip-on sneakers, and pulled my hair up in a quick ponytail.

The buzzer on the oven rang, and I took the cookies out. A delicious smell of warm cookies and lemon filled the room and instantly put me in a happy mood. I started putting them in a dish but stopped when I heard a knock on the door.

8

Otto

Capire (v) = to understand

"Ciao."

My heart stopped at the sight of Giacomo standing in my door-way. He was wearing a pair of jeans and a white buttoned-up shirt, with the sleeves folded up neatly.

"Ciao," I said slowly, my heart racing at this unexpected visit. "It's nice to see you, but I thought you were going home for the weekend."

"No, not this weekend. I needed to study. At home it is too, ah, what's the word.... noisy?"

"Yeah, noisy," I said, nodding that he found the right word.

"I was taking a break and going for a walk when I saw your light on." He said, his smile making my heart jump a little.

"Would you like to come in?" I was extremely nervous and he sensed it. He smiled, nodded, and walked in.

"Now, we can practice English together. Do you have time? If you are busy, don't worry, I don't want to bother you." He said it so quickly, I could sense that he was now nervous too, which oddly made me calmer.

"Yes. Actually, I just finished baking some cookies. We can have some if you want."

I started wondering whether I should mention that I was going to see Ana and Kristin, but then I thought that I could just see them tomorrow. They would surely understand.

Giacomo took a seat at the kitchen table and I placed some cookies on a plate and brought it over. His eyes lit up when he saw them.

"*Sei bravissima a cucinare!*" Giacomo exclaimed, saying how good of a cook I was after he put one in his mouth.

"*Grazie.*" I said softly, feeling the warmth rush to my cheeks.

We sat together and talked in English. I decided to start on the topic of families since it's usually an easy one to talk about.

"Juliet, please correct me if I make mistakes."

"Deal. Tell me about your family." I was actually curious to hear what his family life at home was like.

"I have two older brothers, they are both married to great women." He said with a smile on his face. I could tell that he enjoyed talking about his family. "Both of my parents are nurses at a hospital, but my mom hasn't worked in a little bit."

His smile instantly faded and I could feel the weight in his voice.

"She tells us she is okay, but I don't know."

"I'm sorry," I said involuntarily, reaching for his hand and squeezing it. "I'm sure everything is going to be okay, but I understand worrying about the people you love."

He looked up at me and gave me a faint smile, willing himself to believe it.

We changed topics to his town and his friends. He mentioned

how he's known Luca since they were two because they grew up on the same block. I only had to correct his English a few times, since he spoke so well. He seemed less nervous with me as the conversation went on and I also felt myself begin to relax. I realized I was leaning my head onto my hand, relaxed, as he was talking.

"Now, tell me about you, but let's speak Italian." Giacomo said, smiling with his lips closed as he crossed his arms in front of him.

I didn't even hesitate to start speaking because I felt at ease with him. I started with my family, how I was an only child, and how I lived on Long Island in New York. I mentioned how my mom was an Italian teacher and my dad owned an import and export company for wines.

We talked about my nonni's house in Southern Italy and how I helped them on their farm during the summers. I explained how I would help them gather and sell the peppers as soon as they were ripe and learned how to make different types of cheese and cured meat.

"You help your nonni on their farm?" Giacomo asked, with a surprised expression on his face.

"Yeah, they taught me everything I need to know. I know which types of grass to feed the animals, how to take care of them, and how to plant vegetables."

Giacomo's mouth had dropped as I continued telling him how every summer I would visit them and take care of the vineyards and drive their tractor.

"Are you sure you are American?" Giacomo asked, now laughing.

"Yes, why?" I asked, giggling too.

"Because not even my friends do this. You are incredible." I was flattered that he was impressed with me and knew that I was going to be repeating this conversation in my head over and over again tonight.

We continued talking when I heard a knock on the door. I got up to go answer it and saw that it was Matt.

"Hey! Come on in." I said, excited to see him and introduce him to Giacomo. "I just made some lemon cookies and I was talking to Giacomo."

I saw Matt look towards Giacomo and nod his head slightly in his direction. He looked down, his face becoming very serious, and he dug both hands in his jeans pockets.

"No, it's okay, I just wanted to see how you were." Matt said, stumbling over his words.

I was confused why he didn't want to come in if he walked all the way here.

"Matt, come in, just for a second."

Matt hesitated and walked in. I introduced him to Giacomo, explained how he lived on the first floor, and they shook hands.

"You look familiar," Giacomo said while trying to concentrate on how he knew him. "Yes, you are in my class, right?"

Matt furrowed his brows and thought for a bit before responding. "Yeah, you are in the class with Professor Biondi?"

"Yes!" Giacomo exclaimed, a lot happier than Matt. In fact, Matt's lips were pursed and he barely made eye contact with him.

Giacomo continued to chat to the both of us, but Matt didn't seem as interested in the conversation as we were. I tried to include him as much as I could, but he would just shrug or nod without adding anything.

About twenty minutes later, Matt said he had to go. I asked him if he wanted to stay longer, but he replied saying he was tired. He didn't seem like his usual self, so I walked him to the door as he was leaving.

"I'll see you tomorrow?" I asked, leaning against the door, looking out at him standing in the hall. I was hoping for at least some type of joke or comment back from him.

"Yeah, I guess." He shrugged his shoulders and turned around heading down the hall, toward the stairs.

I looked after him to see if he would turn back around or make a funny remark, but I just heard his footsteps getting further away.

"Matt seems nice but quiet," Giacomo said as I closed the door and came back to the table.

"He usually isn't quiet. I don't know what's going on with him tonight." He looked so uncomfortable as if he couldn't wait to get out of there.

"You know, let's go outside. It's not that cold and it's a nice clear night so we can see some stars."

I nodded my head and walked with him to the balcony and he held the door open for me.

There was a slight chill in the air, but the thick cardigan I had on was keeping me warm. The air smelled crisp, with a hint of the burning wood from the chimneys in the nearby buildings. The usual view of the hills that were scattered in the background was now covered in a dark backdrop.

We both leaned our elbows against the balcony and stared up at the night sky, not saying anything. I never saw these many stars back home. Tonight, the sky was so clear the bright light of the stars shone individually against the black background, twinkling. It reminded me of the field trips I used to take to the planetarium when I was younger. I almost expected to see meteors dashing through the sky.

I hadn't noticed how close I was standing to Giacomo all this time until I looked over and realized our hands were close enough to touch. My nerves started kicking in, and I was mad that I was feeling this way next to him. Why does my body have to betray me the second I am close to an attractive guy?

Besides his obvious good looks, there was something that was drawing me to him, he was so easy to talk to. My fingers started fidgeting and I realized that I was holding my breath. I exhaled allowing my shoulders to drop and relax, hoping he wouldn't notice how nervous I was.

"I have to ask you a question," Giacomo said, turning to me now, his face looking serious, with a slight hint of a smile forming.

"Go ahead."

"Is Matt your boyfriend?" He asked, with curiosity in his eyes. He was now leaning against the railing on one elbow, his body turned towards me.

I let out a nervous chuckle and shook my head no. He stood up straighter, crossing his arms in front of his chest, his expression now changing to confusion.

"Okay, Elisa told me he is your boyfriend, I don't know why she would do that."

"I told Elisa that he wasn't my boyfriend!" I was annoyed at how she seemed to do whatever she wanted. "We are just friends," I said.

"Wait." I continued after a moment, wanting to get everything straightened out once and for all. "Can I ask you something?"

"Of course." He said.

"Elisa told me that you aren't together right now because you have a lot of schoolwork. Is this true?" I wanted to hear from Giacomo what his side was because I'd been figuring out that I should take everything Elisa says with a grain of salt.

"*Cosa?*" Giacomo exclaimed, wondering what exactly I asked. So, I repeated what I said, in the best Italian that I could.

"Juliet, what did Elisa tell you?" He looked a little bit irritated over what I said, but not surprised. "We never were boyfriend and girlfriend."

"I don't know. I thought you were together, and she told me that you were, but just recently you decided to take a break so you could study for school." I explained.

"No. We were never together." Giacomo said, his tone serious.

and his words chosen carefully. "Yes, she likes me, and she's told me, but I do not like her." He said, then he continued saying some sentences in Italian that I couldn't make out, but from his expression, he was still upset.

Giacomo shook his head a few times, looked up at the sky, took a deep breath, and then let out a small chuckle.

"Well, maybe it is a compliment, no?" Giacomo said, his expression softening.

I looked at him, smiled, then looked up at the sky again. "It is a compliment. I can see why she likes you."

I couldn't believe I said that.

He looked at me for a few seconds before saying anything.

"*Grazie.*" He said, his words much softer and gentler than before.

I turned to look at him and he reached out his right hand to grab mine, holding on to my fingers lightly. I immediately felt a burst of electricity run through my veins and all throughout my body. My heart was pumping as if I was running a marathon. Giacomo looked at me, squeezed my hand, and then let go. He looked up at the stars again, and we both stood silently for the next few minutes.

I slowly regained my senses, and I forced myself to look forward and not at his profile standing next to me. When we started talking again, he asked me what I was doing tomorrow.

"I don't know, I was going to read a little for my class."

"Come with me. Let's go to the city and I will show you the Verona I know. Please say yes." His eyes begged me to come, but I didn't need any convincing. My heart was already screaming yes.

"Okay, sure." Trying to act cool. "What time do you want to go?" My hands were betraying me from how much they were shaking.

Giacomo's face lit up and we started to sort out all of the details. He would come by my apartment before lunch and we would visit some of his favorite places.

"I should probably get going if we are going to have a big day tomorrow." He said, looking at the watch on his wrist.

We went back inside and I walked him to the door.

"*Buona notte,* Juliet," Giacomo said. He hesitated for a second and then left, pulling the door softly closed behind him.

I turned the lock after he left and then leaned against the door. I was left with those overwhelming feelings as I replayed the whole night over in my head. I felt like I wanted to tell him everything about my life. I took a breath, looked at the clock. It was 9:45. I had to tell Kristin and Ana about what happened. I looked for my phone and dialed Ana's number. She answered after the third ring and was surprised to hear from me.

"*Ciao,* Ana!" I said, excited that she answered.

"Hey! I was going to call you. Are you home?" She said all in one breath. "Come over! Kristin and I were bored by ourselves."

9

Nove

La Confusione (nf)= Confusion

"So, do you like him?" Ana asked while taking a bite out of one of the lemon cookies I brought over. Kristin reached over and grabbed one too. I just finished catching them up about what happened.

"Well, I mean, he's really sweet and very good looking...so..." I said, my words trailing off as I recalled the way he touched my hand. I just wanted to shout out *YES*, but I didn't want to seem too eager.

"C'mon Juliet! It's obvious, of course you do!" Kristin exclaimed, jumping up with the cookie in her hand.

"Okay, yes. I mean, I guess so. But I don't even know him well enough. Plus, I don't know if it's worth it. I live on the other side of the ocean!"

A feeling of sadness overwhelmed me as I realized that it would be silly to start something. Maybe he knew it too and was just interested in being friends.

"Oh," I added, just remembering something else from the previous night, "Also, my roommate likes him too." I couldn't believe I forgot to tell them this. "And, she told me they were together but were taking a break."

"Wait, what?" Kristin said, astonished.

"Yeah, I know! When I asked Giacomo about it, he got angry and said that it wasn't true at all. She made everything up because she likes him." I said the last sentence in a higher pitch, on a roll spilling all of the gossip.

"Your roommate likes him? Oh no, this could be a disaster." Ana said, her smile getting wider while Kristin looked down and shook her head.

"Ugh, there's something about her that I don't like." Kristin said, still shaking her head. "Watch out for her. I feel like she's going to cause lots of problems for you."

"She is probably territorial and doesn't want some American girl coming in and taking him. Wait until she hears how you spent an evening together with *Giacomooo*." Ana said.

Kristin glanced over to Ana and gave her a look that made her shrug.

"Ana, you don't understand. I had a *friend*" she said, making air quotes with her fingers, "back in Germany that did something similar to me. There was a guy I liked, and I told her about him, and she ended up friending him. She told him lies about me to get him to like her instead and now they are dating. I ended up looking like the bad guy and, well, I kind of came here to escape from it all." Kristin's voice seemed to drop off towards the end. Ana wrapped her arm around her, noticing the seriousness of the situation, and gave her a squeeze.

"*Lo siento.*" Ana said, saying sorry in Spanish to Kristin.

"Don't worry." Kristin said. She became noticeably more relaxed, grabbing another cookie and wiping her eyes.

"Juliet, but what about Matt?" Kristin said, changing the topic.

"Matt?"

"You're not together, right?"

"No!" I said probably more sternly than I needed to. "Why does everyone keep asking me that?"

"Well, I think it's how he looks at you. It just doesn't seem like a platonic relationship."

"Actually Juliet," Ana chimed in. "Javier told my friend that he likes you. You had no idea?"

"What?" I said, my brain running a mile a minute trying to process. "He told Javier that he likes me?" I said.

"Yeah," Ana said as if the whole world knew besides me.

I stood there a minute taking in what they said. I thought back to our last interaction and how weird he was acting when he saw me with Giacomo and wondered if the dinner he asked me to was an attempted date.

"Juliet, are you okay? You look like your head is going to explode." Kristin said.

"I'm fine. It's just that, well, I had no idea he liked me." I said.

"Ooh! So, now you have to decide. Will it be Giacomo or Matt? This is like a real life Rom-com." Ana said with her eyes lit up.

"She doesn't have to decide," Kristin added, her tone more serious than Ana's. "She has to just go along with it and do what her heart tells her. Right, Juliet?"

"Yes, of course." I could do that. Go along with it, see what happens. "Let's talk about something else."

I was getting overwhelmed with all of the events from the whole night. I felt every emotion moving through me and I couldn't figure any of them out.

Ana switched conversations to what was happening in the apartment building. Kristin put on a pot of espresso and we kept munching on the cookies. As much as I tried to distract myself by listening to their recounts of who everyone was hanging out with, my mind kept going back to Giacomo and Matt.

Stop thinking about what-ifs. Nothing has even happened yet. Why am I worried about a choice that I may not have to make? The same scenes kept flashing in my head— one when I was on the balcony with Giacomo tonight and another when Matt held my hand at the party and I swore I felt something.

When I headed back to my apartment, it was nearly impossible to fall asleep. My stomach felt like it was being squeezed in a tight knot.

I remembered that I was supposed to meet Giacomo tomorrow.

I shut my eyes tight hoping that I would fall asleep. After an hour of tossing and turning, I gave up, scrolled through my phone, found some slow Laura Pausini songs that slowed my heartbeat and made my thoughts fall into darkness.

***

I counted the church bell nine times as I laid in bed the next morning, not quite ready to get up. Remembering the plans I made for the day, I shot up out of bed, more excited than nervous, and ran to the bathroom to get ready.

The long, biting hot shower was exactly what I needed. I focused on my makeup and hair and thought about what outfit would work. It had to be comfortable enough to go sightseeing in, but cute enough for a sort of date. I went over to the closet and as I was about to open the door, I saw a flash between the bedroom shutters and heard a large rumble. I ran to open the bedroom shutters.

As they both opened, my heart dropped. What should have been a bright morning sky was completely covered with black, threatening clouds. The lightning danced through them and the rumbles came shortly after; as if they were confirming that it was, in fact, a thunderstorm. I looked down to see the concrete covered in drops of rain painting the balcony dark grey.

"No!" I said out loud. I hoped that it was a passing storm, but looking outside, the clouds extended in all directions, and the rain picked up even more.

I closed the shutters. I wondered if he would decide to do something else. As I walked towards the kitchen, I stopped when I saw the doorknob move. Then I heard keys.

I couldn't even finish my thoughts until they were confirmed. To my horror, Elisa stepped through the door. She was home a day early.

"Ugh, it's raining a lot outside, look I'm wet," Elisa said, exasperated. From the looks of it, she had no umbrella with her.

"The weather forecast said it would be sunny. Can you believe this rain? I had to run from the bus stop to the apartment." Elisa said, taking off her rain-soaked coat and hanging it up on the coat rack.

She narrowed her eyes to look at me. "What's the matter, Juliet, no hello?" Elisa said, her voice happier than usual while taking off her boots and putting them on a rug to dry.

"Oh, um, hello. It's just that I'm surprised to see you home today. I thought you would be home tomorrow." I said, my face obviously showing how shocked I was that she was home.

"Well, I'm so sorry if I am home early," Elisa said dryly, with an exaggerated tone of sarcasm in her voice. "Did I ruin your plans?" She added, smirking.

"Why would you ruin my plans?" I said, confidently. Her sarcasm started to annoy me.

"Okay, well then, I am just going to make a cup of tea. Would you like one?" Elisa said complacently, rummaging through the counters looking for the teapot.

"I would love tea," I said between closed teeth, trying to seem as cheerful as I could while trying to figure her out.

Elisa put the water to boil and prepared two cups. She must have found out from Luca that Giacomo was here this weekend. I had recreated all of the scenes while Elisa brought the cups over to the table.

"I'll get the water," I said to Elisa as soon as I heard it boiling. I needed to move and do something. I couldn't believe that she actually came back a day earlier. I thought back to what Kristin said about how a similar situation recently happened to her.

"So what are you doing today?" Elisa asked conversationally while I poured the boiling water into the cup.

"I don't know. I wasn't expecting it to rain." I said, pouring the remaining hot water into my cup.

"Well, maybe we could do something. We can make lunch together, play cards. Whatever you want!"

"Oh, uh, okay. Yeah, sure. Why not." I said, not sure of how to respond since I didn't know what my plans with Giacomo were going to be.

Elisa sensed my insecurity and added, "If you don't want to stay with me, it's okay. I understand." She seemed sad, but I didn't know whether to trust her anymore.

"No, it's fine. It's not that. I did have plans, but I don't know if I'm going to be able to do them with this weather."

"But it's raining, come on. Let's play scopa. It's my favorite card game, I can teach you!" Elisa said, already looking for the playing cards.

"Okay, but don't worry, I know how to play," I said. Elisa turned her head to the side and gave me a surprised look. "I used to play with my nonno."

He taught me all of the rules and tricks to play. I loved it so much that I would beg him to play almost every night. I became so good at it that I began beating him. He would laugh and say how I should play with his friends. They would be surprised at how well a young, American girl can play cards.

Elisa and I started playing and I could tell she was shocked at how well I was doing. I was already beating her four to one when we heard a knock on the door.

Elisa got up faster than me and ran to the door.

"Cosa ci fai qui?" I heard Giacomo's surprised voice asking Elisa what she was doing back already. Elisa opened the door all the way and Giacomo made eye contact with me before entering the apartment.

"Ciao, Giacomo, you're just as surprised to see me as Juliet was. Maybe I should ask what *you're* doing here?"

Giacomo said some sentences in Italian to her that I wasn't able to understand. From what I got, Giacomo mentioned *studying* and *the weekend.*

"Hi, Giacomo." I said, my voice softer than normal. Elisa was looking back and forth between us.

"Ciao. I don't think Verona is great when there is bad weather." Giacomo said, with a smile on his face. "I am sorry, we will have to see Verona when it is beautiful." He added, being careful to say every word correctly in English.

"Ah, so these were your plans, Juliet. Well, then we can stay here and play cards together. What do you think, Giacomo?" Elisa said, her eyes had narrowed and a small smile formed on her face as she was saying those words.

"No, it's okay. I have a lot of studying to do anyway. *Divertitevi."* Giacomo said, adding in Italian to have fun. He looked at me one last time before turning and walking out.

My heart sank when I saw Giacomo go. Why didn't he stay or change the plans? I decided not to think into it too much, and concentrated on beating Elisa at scopa instead,

We continued playing the game for the next 15 minutes in silence. I could see from Elisa's expression that she wanted to ask me something, but every time she looked as if she was going to open her mouth, her expression would change and she would just continue playing cards.

"So why were you going to Verona with Giacomo?" She said, her words sounding very icy and precise.

"I don't know, he offered and I didn't want to be rude and say no." I said, trying to be relaxed about it.

"Well, I can show you Verona if you'd like. Then he doesn't have to." She studied my expression like I was her test subject and she was playing with my emotions.

"That's fine too, but I don't see why it's a problem if he wants to." I rebutted, trying to be confident. I was sick of Elisa walking all over me.

"No, it is not a problem. I didn't say that. It's just, well, I don't understand." Elisa said, but her words were trailing off. She didn't know that her jealousy was obvious on her face.

I didn't want her to be jealous that Giacomo made plans with me, but I also didn't want to tell him no to them. I liked spending time with him. Maybe he wasn't interested in me in that way, but I still wanted to spend more time with him.

"Want to see what we can make for lunch?" I asked, hoping to change the conversation and make Elisa stop thinking about Giacomo.

"Sure," she said, willing to let it go.

In the middle of rummaging through the cabinets, there was a soft knock on the door.

I wondered if it was Giacomo again. My stomach twisted in a knot as I went over to open the door.

Matt stood there beaming at me. I relaxed a little but then felt my stomach twist as I remembered what Kristin and Ana told me. *Matt likes you.*

"Hey." I said, grateful that Matt didn't have any mind-reading skills and couldn't see the craziness going on in my head.

"Oh, hello, Matt! Nice to see you!" Elisa called out, from the other side of the room.

Matt waved hi to her, and then turned to me. "Are you busy? I made lunch and it's way too much for just me and Javier."

"Well, me and Elisa were just going to make lunch. If you want, you can join us." I said. I had a bad feeling about hanging out with Matt alone.

"Juliet! Go have lunch with Matt." Elisa said, throwing a wrench in the plans again. "Don't worry about me. Actually, I will be mad if you *don't* go."

Matt raised an eyebrow as a slight smile spread across his face.

"Okay...I guess I have no choice." I grabbed my raincoat and headed outside with Matt.

We walked the whole way to his apartment in silence and I started feeling a little bit sweaty. I wished I didn't know.

"I tried to make something that Javier taught me. I thought you would like it. It's chicken, peppers, onions, and some other spices." Matt said while reaching for his keys.

"That sounds good," I said, following him in.

The kitchen was filled with the delicious smell of the spices he used and the whole apartment looked so immaculate that it was unbelievable he had a party last week.

"Wow, Matt, it smells *insane* in here!"

"I'll just set the table and we can eat." He said, his face showing excitement. He only put two plates on the table.

"Is Javier going to have lunch with us?"

"No, he is actually over his friend's, I'll save him leftovers. It's just you and me." He said, adding a nervous smile.

He took the food out of the oven and placed it on the plates. As we sat down I felt my heart begin to race again. It was so hard to know how Matt felt about me when I was so confused over my own emotions. I almost felt pressured to like him back, but I wasn't sure if I did. I instead tried to stay in the moment and looked down at the plate he placed in front of me. It was very colorful with tri-colored peppers and a piece of chicken that looked moist.

"This looks great Matt," I said, sawing into the chicken and stabbing a pepper. "What made you decide to cook this today?"

"Well," he said, chewing and swallowing his first bite, "I saw it was raining out and I really wanted to try making something by myself. I hope you like it because then I can make it for you again in the future."

"We will see. But I'll warn you that I'm going to be your toughest critic. Not because I want to be mean, just because I want you to succeed in your culinary journey." I took a bite of the chicken and chewed it for a while, gathering my thoughts.

"Hmmm," I said after swallowing. "Well, the chicken is cooked nicely, there is a good amount of seasonings and juices to make it tasty and not dried out." I looked up and saw him hanging on to my every word and laughed. "The peppers are good, not overcooked to the point of being soggy and still sustaining a nice crunch. I'd say it deserves a 95."

"Wow, a 95? Alright, I'll take it." He had a huge smile on his face. "That's better than I do on most Italian exams, so I'd say it's a win."

Soo..." Matt said, "who was at your apartment last night?" I could tell he'd been dying to ask me this whole time.

"Oh, just Giacomo, a friend of Elisa's."

"Right, Giacomo. He seems like a nice guy, right?" Matt kept his eyes focused on mine, trying to catch my immediate reaction. I looked down and felt my cheeks getting warm.

"Yeah, he's nice."

"Do you *like* him?" Matt asked like a little school girl.

"Well, I don't know if I *like* him, but... I don't know!"

Matt let out a small chuckle with my answer. Then he let out a sigh and poured me a glass of aranciata, a popular Italian orange soda.

"Oh my God, this is my absolute favorite!" I wondered if he knew.

"Mine too. I wonder if *Giacomo* likes it."

I let out a laugh, and so did he, and then I continued to eat quickly, trying to cover the silence with food.

"Thanks for lunch, it was really great." The air felt stagnant. I needed to get outside. "Do you want to get dessert?"

"You know me." Matt said, smiling at my suggestion.

I could see it was still raining, so I grabbed my raincoat and Matt grabbed his hoodie. We made our way out of his room and to the front of the building, stopping in the street and looking at each other. The rain was still coming down aggressively.

Matt looked at me in a very suspicious way before saying "Let's race, there's a bakery right down the road from here." He had a mischievous sparkle in his eye.

"Oh," I said, my heart rate already starting to quicken. "You're so on." I looked at him, lining up evenly next to him. "Ready- *go*!" I spat out quickly.

I took off sprinting, not looking back when I heard him yell, "Wait, what! You never said *set*!" He started running, but still yelled, "It's ready, *set*, go!"

I let out a chuckle but did not let it hinder me from running as fast as I could. It felt good to move my legs like this, like a little kid sprinting in the schoolyard away from the person that was "it" in tag.

Even while giving every ounce of effort I had, with the air squeezing my lungs, I could still hear his heavy footsteps gaining on me. I hated that men got an unfair advantage with their long legs.

I looked up and saw the bakery ahead of me, only about two stores away. Matt was right behind me, I could almost feel his rapid breaths blowing into my neck. I couldn't give up, not now. I pushed my legs faster, feeling the wetness of my shoes saturating my socks and drenching my toes.

Now side by side, we crossed the threshold of our made-up finish line, pretending we just finished the 100-meter dash in the Olympics and ran in the same heat as Usain Bolt.

I bent over my knees heaving oxygen into my lungs. I felt a hand on my back and saw another one in front of my face.

"Good race," Matt said winded. "Even if you cheated."

I reached to shake his hand and stood to my full height, "Whatever you say, slow poke." I comically rolled my eyes.

"C'mon let's go inside, I'm absolutely drenched." He had a nice smile on his face. It made me feel warm even though I couldn't feel my feet from numbness.

Inside, we both settled on a *bombolone* or doughnut, Matt getting a Nutella-filled one, and me an apricot jam. We sat down by the window to watch the rain with a warm cappuccino each to defrost our hands, not caring it was after 11. We deserved it after our sprint.

Matt invited me to his apartment to watch TV on the way back, but I declined thinking I should probably do some reading for my class. He gave me a hug goodbye, and I thanked him for the delicious lunch he made.

I stood outside my building for a little while because the rain was stopping and the sun started coming out, warming the street. Even though it was almost spring, I could see strong mountain peaks covered in snow in the distance.

I skipped up the last few steps to my apartment and pushed open the door, but halted when I saw Elisa smirking and standing near the front door.

"You just missed Giacomo." She said moving across the kitchen to grab a glass. "I told him you were out with Matt."

Why was this girl so involved in my personal life? I looked at her trying to figure out what point she was trying to make.

"He seemed a little sad." She continued, "You should be careful with who you are teasing, Juliet." She filled the glass with water and sat down by the TV putting her earbuds in and flicked through her phone.

I didn't even want to comment on what she said. It wasn't worth asking anything else, so I just headed to the bedroom and laid on my bed. I stared up at the ceiling, put my earbuds in, and thought a bit. I was listening to Laura Pausini, the Italian singer with the perfect vibrato who sang of broken hearts and confused feelings, when I saw a text come in. When I was younger, my mom always used to play her songs on high volume as she cleaned areas of the house. As I grew up listening to her sing, I associated her voice with being at home and hearing my Mom sing along.

KRISTIN: **I just passed Matt in the hallway. He had a big smile on his face. What happened?**

I caught her up with the events of the day and mentioned how Giacomo came to look for me.

KRISTIN: **I don't like this one bit. Come over, espresso pot is on, and we will talk!**

I was about to text her no but decided it was still early and I could use advice. I looked over at the pile of books on my desk that still needed to be read, and I promised myself that I would spend the next night studying and catching up as much as I could.

I checked the window on my way out of the bedroom to see if the rain really had stopped. I grabbed my jacket and keys, said a quick goodbye to Elisa, and headed out.

I skipped down the stairs, in a really good mood. I felt silly when I noticed Giacomo coming up the opposite side of the stairwell from me. He looked up at me, his eyes had a slight sadness to them.

"*Ciao*. I heard you stopped by the apartment before." I asked in a soft voice.

"Yeah, I did," He said. "I wanted to know if you still wanted to see Verona even if it was raining." He looked like he was holding something back. "I actually got a call from home and my mother is not doing well."

I walked up to him and put a hand on his arm for comfort. He was worried since none of the tests she went for came back conclusive.

"I'm sorry, if you need to talk, I am here," I said. I felt bad that he was going through such uncertain times.

"Thank you, I appreciate that," Giacomo said. This was one of the most comforting things I've heard in a long time. "They think it might be, um...how do you say, *cancro*?" I knew that word, and my body shivered thinking of what it would mean to him.

"I am so sorry."

"Do you have time to go for a walk?" He pleaded to me with his eyes.

"Sure," I said. "I have time."

We spoke in Italian since it was easier for him to explain what the doctors said about his mom. I didn't understand all of the medical terms in Italian, but still followed along well. I made a mental note to look up all of the new words when I got back home so I would be able to understand better the next time we talked. He mentioned how his dad had been worried and how his brothers weren't able to help out much since they were busy with work and taking care of their families.

"I might go back home this week just to be near her. I know she is worried and I want to help." Giacomo said while we walked down the road. We reached a piazza and decided to walk back before it got too late.

"Hey— *ti va una pizza*?" Giacomo said, suggesting after stopping in front of a pizzeria in the middle of the piazza. I looked down at my phone and noticed four unread text messages from Kristin.

"Oh my God! I completely got sidetracked. I was supposed to meet my friend." I said. "Would you be able to go again another time?" A big part of me regretted saying no but I knew I had to be a good friend and meet with them.

I texted Kristin that I would be there in 30 minutes and would explain everything. She responded with a thumbs up.

The conversation became less serious on the way back home. We discussed our favorite pizza toppings, mine varied from different vegetables but he swore that *speck*, a cured meat similar to prosciutto, gorgonzola, and walnuts was the best type of pizza to have. He asked if I had ever had pizza with horse meat toppings and I told him I had to draw the line somewhere with what went well on pizza.

Then he told me stories about Luca and him when they were younger about how they would often get into trouble with the old ladies in their town with all of the tricks they would do.

"Luca? But he is so serious! I can't picture him doing something like that!"

"He looks serious now, but trust me, he was not always." He said, wagging his finger and chuckling.

I was sad when we reached the apartment buildings so quickly and it was time to go.

"I think I am going to leave tonight to go home. Thank you. I needed this walk and someone to talk to." Giacomo said, turning towards me.

I hadn't realized he was close to me at this point. I held my breath as I saw him look at my lips and then back at my eyes. My whole body froze and now I was looking at his too. He put a hand on the side of my arm and leaned in to give me a kiss on both cheeks to say goodbye. He held onto my arm a bit longer as he looked into my eyes. There was a look on his face that told me he wanted to say something else, but instead, he just smiled and said, "*Ciao*, Juliet."

I tried to gather myself before I got to Kristin and Ana's. I turned around to see Giacomo entering our apartment building before I turned to enter theirs.

"*Wait*," Kristin said after I told her where I was. "So you mean to tell me Giacomo asked you to go get pizza and you said no because you had to come here?"

"No, no, *no!!*" Ana dramatically, pointing her finger at me. "We would have totally understood! We invited you over because we thought you were sad and needed to talk!" She shook her head, laughing about the choice I had made.

"I am sorry, but if a cute boy asks me to dinner, I am breaking the plans I have with you," Kristin added. I couldn't believe how adamant they were about this. "Tell us about your day from the start, filled with all of your boys and your dramatic roommate. Go."

I did while Kristin pulled out a bowl of chips to snack on like my life was a movie.

"You had more excitement in one day than I've had my whole time here!" Kristin exclaimed. I reached over and grabbed a handful of her chips.

Ana started telling us about a cute guy she bumped into on the way home from class the other day. She said they briefly made eye contact and he smiled at her.

"Oooh, Ana! Why didn't you tell me yet?" Kristin said with her eyes lighting up. "You definitely should ask him for his number next time!"

"I don't know Kristin. I mean, he's Italian and I'm already having a hard time even keeping in touch with my mom while I'm away. I don't know if I would want to get myself involved in a long-distance relationship. I feel like I could never make that type of commitment." Ana said.

"Well, who says it has to be serious?" Kristin winked. "Maybe you can just have some fun for now and then part ways when you have to go back."

"Well, I guess it would be fun to be with an Italian guy," she said, considering it. "But that's not really me. I almost always have a wedding planned with two cute babies in a pretty house with flowers all around whenever I start talking to a guy."

I understood what she meant, I never really did anything with a guy either unless I knew that there could be a future.

"Oh no, Ana, Juliet is thinking about something." Kristin laughed while nudging her as she sat down after putting the espresso pot on the stove.

"Maybe I'm overthinking everything. Here I am wondering all about Giacomo, but maybe he just wants to hook up and nothing more. And then you guys say that Matt likes me, but what if he just wants to hook up too because we are far away from home. Maybe he thinks it would be an adventure for him." I said, a little sad as the new reality stuck in.

"Juliet," Kristin started, her hand resting on my shoulder. "How about you stop thinking for just now and just enjoy your time here. Whatever is going to happen is going to happen, no need to stress about it."

I relaxed, she was right. "Okay okay. I guess my mind is making up more than what's actually there." My shoulders dropped and I heard the espresso machine bubbling, signaling it was ready.

Ana jumped up to turn off the gas and poured espresso into each of our cups. She served us and added a little piece of chocolate next to the cup on the saucer.

"Okay Gianni, I mean Ana, I see you trying to impress us with your fancy little espresso chocolate," I said, impressed. Ana beamed at the compliment.

We talked some more until we realized it was getting late and we had to wake up early for classes.

"*Buona notte.*" I said, wishing them a good night and hugging them goodbye. It felt good to have a set of friends I could vent to and get advice from at the same time.

I walked home and by habit, I looked over at Giacomo's apartment. No lights were on this time. I turned around to look at Matt's building to see where his apartment was. I saw Javier's paella pan leaning against the inside of one of the balconies and saw some shadows moving around behind the door. I looked down at my phone and contemplated texting him, but decided against it. I turned back to go straight to my room and tried to relax my thoughts as I went to sleep.

10

Dieci

Piacere (v)= to like

The next few days met Verona with a warm spell. People were out on their bikes riding around town, going for espressos, or on scooters weaving through traffic and honking their high-pitched horns to alert cyclists or other drivers near them.

I decided to walk around after class one day instead of taking the bus back. I walked up Via Mazzini, past the expensive boutiques and the Arena. I continued up towards Juliet's balcony and found a small shop selling souvenirs and little trinkets.

"Questo è il vetro di Murano." The shopkeeper pointed to the statue I was looking at, letting me know it was Murano glass. "Do you speak English?" He added, in a thick Italian accent quickly after.

I looked down to see what I was wearing if it was that easy to recognize I was a foreigner, but nothing really stood out that screamed *I'm an American.*

"No, signorina," The shopkeeper then continued, letting out a chuckle as if knowing exactly what I had been thinking, "I normally get tourists in my shop to look at these pieces. Your family is Italian, no? You have the look of an Italian."

"Yes, they are from Southern Italy though." He nodded his head and then moved the statue closer to me.

"This is a beautiful piece." I continued. "I remember learning about Murano glass at school, but I forget where it is made."

He went on to tell me how they make this glass on an island in Venice, where the gaffers would carefully create amazing statues and jewelry pieces for the public to buy. The one that I was looking at was a simple flower with a twisted stem. The flower was a clear glass with streaks of green and flecks of silver around the center. He pulled up a video on his phone to show me how they are made. The work of a glassblower always astonished me. It was mesmerizing how they used their hands and the weight of gravity to create such breathtaking pieces. Each time they heated up the glass they built on their current template and created something so detailed and ex-quisite. The flower was one of the more simple pieces to create, but I caught myself staring and imagining how the lime green streaks were created.

"Here, take this pamphlet. You should visit it." He said, hand-ing me a tri-fold paper, with pictures of the different statues and jewelry pieces scattered all over it.

I took the pamphlet, thanked him, and browsed the shop more. I found a set of Italian playing cards I'd never seen before and decided to buy them. When I was 10 years old, I started a collection with my dad with all of the different types of Italian playing cards that existed. Each time we went to Italy, we tried to complete our col-lection. I loved the different pictures depicted on the cards, noting how they were different from our classic American style. American playing cards have 52 cards in their deck, but most Italian ones were missing 8,9, and 10 and therefore only had 40 cards. We were able to collect most of the styles in Southern Italy, including the *Napoletane* which was my personal favorite. I grew up playing with the *Siciliane* and the *Romagnole* decks. My cousin who lived in that area gave it to us as a gift when he visited my grandparents one summer. At the airport one year, my dad and I high-fived each other when we came across a *Milanese* deck and the following year we found the *Piacentine* deck.

"*Quanto costa?*" I asked the shopkeeper, this time using my Italian to ask him how much the cards were.

"*Hai un bell'accento.*" He commented on my accent, saying it was nice. "*Cinque euro, per favore.*"

I handed him a 5 euro bill, in Italy the tax is already included in the price. He placed the cards in a small brown bag and handed them back to me with a nod and a "*buona giornata*" to wish me a good day. I walked out and got my phone out of my bag to send a picture of the deck of cards to my dad.

DAD: **Brava! You got the Trevisane cards? Wait til you see what they look like!**

I felt a little pang in my heart after I realized how much I missed him. We FaceTimed every couple of days, but it was difficult with the six-hour time difference.

We continued to text and I sent him a selfie of me standing next to some of the Carnevale masks hanging on display out a store window.

DAD: **You should visit Venice soon, you will love it. Ciao, principessa. Have fun!**

I loved how my dad called me princess since I was little. It always made me feel like I was important to him.

I hadn't thought about Venice much. It was one of the first places I promised myself I'd visit when I got here, but I got swept up in these imaginary romances and studying that I completely forgot.

That will change. I found an information point for tourists and collected all of the pamphlets they had on the city. I looked online for the train times and texted Jess and Valentina to get ready for our next adventure.

***

Elisa and I continued to have dinner together every night that week and visited Marcello and Luca only once. I went there hoping that Giacomo had come back early, but got disappointed when I opened the door and he wasn't. Elisa and Luca seemed a lot closer that night. Luca even chased her around the apartment at one point with a dead fly. She was screaming and laughing and at the same time running away from him who held the fly by its wing. This was the Luca that I pictured when Giacomo described how they acted when they were younger.

"Want to know something?" Marcello sat down next to me on the couch and talked in a hushed voice.

"Sure," I said.

"Luca is in love with Elisa, but *shhh*! You didn't hear it from me." He held a finger in front of his lips.

"I honestly was suspecting that. Why aren't they together?"

"Because Elisa likes Giacomo. It's really just one of those triangles of love." Marcello said, laughing at his own words. He went on to explain in Italian, that when they all met last year, Elisa right away told Marcello that she wanted to date Giacomo and he needed to help her. But when Marcello told him Giacomo came up with an excuse that he didn't want to date someone he didn't know well. Elisa got mad and thought that flirting with Luca would make Giacomo jealous. But instead, the only thing that happened was that Luca thought Elisa was hitting on him for real, and now really likes her.

"*Che casino.*" Marcello added, saying how messy it all was.

"*Hai ragione.*" I said, agreeing.

Things definitely became clearer now that I had a backstory to how everyone felt. I wondered why Elisa didn't give Luca a chance though. They seemed to get along much better than she and Giacomo did. I continued to watch them as Luca grabbed Elisa around her waist with one arm and dropped the insect creating a peace treaty.

"So tell me what you know about *Venezia*," I said, turning my attention back to Marcello.

Marcello took out his phone and showed me Venice and all of the places to visit. He would start writing them down on a piece of paper, but then quickly would remember another place and add it too.

"Make sure you wear your best walking shoes." He looked down to see the shoes I was wearing. I felt conscious of him judging my footwear and crinkled my toes in my white stained Vans hoping he wasn't looking at the dirt on them.

"I know you Americans don't walk a lot." He added, chuckling a little when he saw my expression. I rolled my eyes at him and told him to stop making me into a stereotype. Marcello's phone buzzed in his hand and his eyebrows drew down as he read the text.

"*Interessante.*" He said after looking up from the phone. "Giacomo is asking about you."

I blushed a little bit and hoped he didn't notice. He noticed my surprise though, so he flipped his phone around to show me the text.

GIACOMO: **Juliet è con voi? Di cosa parlate?**

I read the text three times, making sure my eyes weren't tricking me and that he actually was asking if I was with them and what we were talking about. I looked back at Marcello and shrugged my shoulders since I really didn't know what to say.

"Lo sapevo...lo sapevo..." Marcello repeated to himself, saying over and over how he knew it. *"Gli piaci..."*

I mentally translated what he was saying, confused with the verb "piacere". Does that mean I like him or he likes me? Or maybe he just likes something? Prof. Rossi would drill into our heads how the verb "to like" in Italian is nothing like the English verb at all. In Italian she would always say that it is like the verb "to be pleasing." I was trying to work my way through it when Marcello noticed my expression.

"Juliet, I think he likes you." He said, probably noticing the confused look on my face. "Why would he ask about you?" He threw his hands up in defeat. "Welp, there goes *my* chance with you." I laughed at how dramatically he said it. He even got up from the couch and acted like he needed to "walk it off." He sat back down and let out a sigh, but also threw a smile my way to let me know he wasn't actually serious.

"Sul serio," Marcello then went on in Italian, "If Giacomo is asking about you, it probably means he likes you.

"Ugh c'mon Marcello, I promised myself I wouldn't think too much into it. Why do you have to point it out?!" I told him laughing.

"I just call it as I see it. Nothing I can do about it." He shrugged his shoulders, displaying an innocent look on his face. "Why don't you want to think about it?"

I remembered what Kristin said the other night. "I don't want to get in a relationship while I am here. I am here only until June and I don't want to miss out on experiencing all of Italy because of a boy." I said, noticing Marcello's expression change.

"*Brava. Finalmente una ragazza con il buon senso.*" Marcello said, proud of what I said and emphatically patting me on my back.

Elisa walked over to us. "Are you ready to head back?" She asked.

"Yeah, I'm ready." I texted Valentina and Jess that I had big news to share with them so they should meet me at Gianni's bar after class.

***

"So, what is it? You had me worried all night!" Jess said, swirling her spoon in her espresso cup while we sat at a table instead of at the bar.

"Juliet, this better be good. I was supposed to meet this Italian girl and copy her notes for class. The Italians take amazing notes. Have you *seen* the pencil cases they carry around with all of the colored pencils and pens? My notes don't even compare!" Valentina said, showing a picture of a page of notes she got from the Italian girl previously. It was full of different colors outlining different aspects of a poem they read.

"Why is it on graph paper?" I asked.

"They can take more organized notes with the lines and fit more information on one sheet." Valentina said. She was so excited about this that I turned to Jess and gave her a sideways glance while she giggled and sipped her espresso.

"Okay, girls." I said, getting their attention. "I got all the info we need to visit Venice. We are taking the train really early Saturday morning straight there and then visiting *la Basilica di San Marco* first. Then, we will find a cheap hotel, stay the night and visit Murano the next day."

"Oh, I have always wanted to see Venice! Are we actually doing it? Do you know how to take the train there, Juliet?" Jess asked.

"I'll go," Valentina added, showing more confidence than Jess. "I assure you, we will not get lost. I was also planning on going soon, but I am glad you did it first, Juliet." I smiled a little at her realizing I would never get a real compliment and this is the closest I was going to get.

"Okay, if we are all on board. Let's talk logistics. We need to take the train from *Verona Porta Nuova* at 7:30 and arrive at *Venezia Santa Lucia* at 8:50. From there we can get breakfast and walk to Piazza San Marco following all of the signs on the buildings." I remembered Marcello mentioning that last night and thought it would be fun to wander through Venice.

"I love it! Did you text Matt yet? Or John?" Jess was practically squealing. "Ever since John hooked up with that English girl we haven't seen much of him."

I didn't even think about asking Matt or John. It would be more fun to have them around though. "Okay, I'll text both of them our plans. In the meantime, pack a small bag for Venice. Nothing crazy since we don't know how much we will be walking."

I took out my phone and texted them right away.

JULIET: **So...get ready for Venezia on Saturday!**

MATT: **Nice! Count me in!**

...

JOHN: **If I come, can I bring Kathryn?**

JULIET: **Sure! The more the merrier!**

John finally put a name to the "English girl" we kept referring to. We never saw John with the same girl around campus. Matt and I often joke around about who we would see him with next. This girl must be pretty special. I told them both to meet us at the bus station at 6:30.

11

Undici

Perdersi (v) = to get lost

When Saturday came, I didn't even need an alarm clock to wake up. I got out of bed at 5:30 with excitement rushing through me. I grabbed a bigger mug than usual to pour some espresso in and filled the rest with boiling water. Gianni from the bar explained to me how to make an "*americano*" cup of coffee. I added a touch of milk and started getting ready. I packed my bag last night, and put on the outfit I laid out. I chose the new jacket I had bought when I went shopping with Kristin and Ana and paired it with a cream-colored thin sweater. I picked my favorite pair of ripped jeans and slipped on my white Vans. I gathered my hair back in a low ponytail and applied just a touch of mascara and lip gloss.

Valentina was already at the bus stop nervously fidgeting and looking down at her phone while Jess was covering her mouth and stifling a yawn. I didn't notice before, but Jess looked different. Her jeans were slightly baggy and her brown, fuzzy coat looked a little big on her.

"*Buongiorno ragazze!*" I greeted them, giving them both a quick hug.

"Sorry," Jess said, still stifling another yawn that was coming, "I don't know why I'm so exhausted this morning."

"I know why." Valentina said, matter of factly. "You were up until midnight with your new English friend that you met." Jess laughed a little, not bothered at all by Valentina's reaction.

"That's great, Jess! What's her name? Oh, *wait*," I said, realizing something. "Is this a friend or a *friend?*" I prodded. Back in Binghamton she hung out with this one girl pretty often and she told us it was casual, but they definitely cared about each other as more than friends. She was upset when one day she found out that the girl was also hanging out with multiple other people in the same type of way, and never told her.

"Her name is Jane. She said everyone calls her plain Jane because of her looks. But I don't see it." Her eyes were bright with each word she said. "I'm not sure how I feel about her, but I do know that her hair is so shiny and you have to see her do yoga!" I laughed, happy that she was putting herself out there again.

"Maybe she can teach us some stuff. I always wanted to try it." One time I tried a YouTube guided yoga video and fell on my butt a few times before I gave up and turned it off.

"I want to start taking care of myself more," Jess added, this time looking more awake than before. "I've been walking around Verona in between classes and eating more fruits and vegetables. I still eat all of the delicious Italian food, just not *too* much of it."

I was about to say something when Matt jumped right behind us and yelled "*Buongiorno!*" scaring us awake. We jokingly hit him and then saw John and Kathryn right behind him holding hands. I caught Jess and Valentina looking at me from the corner of my eye and we all smiled at Kathryn and extended our hands to introduce ourselves.

"Oh come here! I've heard so much about you three already!" Kathryn exclaimed in her British accent, squeezing the three of us into a hug with her. I looked up from the embrace of her strong arms at John and saw he had the biggest smile on his face.

We chatted a while, asking what life in England was like, and she told us all about her house near Dorchester, and the farm her family lived on. We continued talking until we saw the bus climbing up the hill to our stop. When we climbed on we each greeted the driver in Italian, and punched our little bus ticket into the machine. The bus ride to the station was short. I looked out my window, taking in the early morning streets of Verona, watching everyone waking up and moving around for the first time. Once inside the train station, we checked the timetable to see if our train was running on time and looked to see what track it was on.

"Soo," I said looking over at Valentina. "Do you want to order our tickets for us? You're Italian is definitely the best out of all of us."

"Yeah, go ahead, Valentina," John added teasingly, "show us the best Italian you got and get the tickets."

Valentina pretended to be annoyed, but promptly marched up to the agent and asked in perfect Italian for six tickets to Venice. She handed one to each of us and we gave her the money while waiting for the train to come.

John and Kathryn were off to the side by themselves holding hands and whispering to each other. Every once in a while John would kiss her on her cheek or hug her tight to him. I looked over at Matt who was already looking at me and we both rolled our eyes at the scene.

A train pulled up on the opposite track and Valentina made sure to shout that it wasn't ours as if there was any confusion. The trains here were definitely different from those at home. I remember watching a documentary in 4th grade that warned us to never step on the tracks and only cross at pedestrian crossings. But here I saw some people walk across the tracks calmly and there was no 3rd rail in sight. I kept looking around on the tracks to see if it was hidden somewhere.

"The train gets the energy from the wires on top," Matt said, pointing up. "I saw you looking at the tracks all confused." He added, proud of knowing this fact. He continued to explain how the trains ran and then pointed out another train that was called *Frecciargento*, a bullet train that could go up to 155mph.

"Wow! When did you become a train expert?" I asked. "So what's that train over there?" I pointed to a train that was similar to the *Frecciargento* but instead was colored in Italy's flag- green, white, and red.

"Now that's the *Frecciarossa*. It goes up to 190mph, it's even faster than the *Frecciargento*." I looked at Matt, still in disbelief.

"Where have you been hiding this train information all this time?"

"You'd be surprised what else I know, Juliet." He said, his eyes crinkling as he let out a laugh.

I turned around to see the train pulling up exactly on time. It was a surprise because lately, I've noticed that nothing was really ever on time in Italy. We had to validate our tickets by putting them in the small yellow machine on the track that stamps the time and date on it. Marcello warned me that if you didn't do this the conductor would write you a ticket.

Matt explained that our train was called the *regionale veloce*, which was somewhat fast, but still a local train. He sat next to me, while Jess and Valentina sat in front of us, and John and Kathryn took two seats in the front.

We both looked out the window and I noticed that the rolling hills got smaller as the train neared Venice. We passed through

Vicenza and Padova and saw open fields with a few trees scattered here and there and houses and buildings that looked similar to the ones in Verona.

"We're almost there!" Valentina said, turning around and smiling at us. Valentina loved to take control of situations, and most of the time I let her. There was one time at school when another student wanted to put a play together in Italian for the local people in the town, and she took over by deciding what play to do and assigning roles to everyone. It got me angry at the time, but I could never find it in myself to tell her to stop. Matt and Jess would often do the same.

We got up when the train stopped and stepped off onto the platform. The air was definitely different in Venice. You could smell the saltiness of the sea water as the breeze blew.

"Okay, so we should head this way if we want to walk towards Piazza San Marco." Valentina said, after consulting the map on her phone and pointing directly in front of us. "Then if we..."

"Valentina," Jess said rather abruptly, "let's take it easy today. We are staying the night so there's no need to rush. Not everything needs to be planned. We always find ourselves in the end."

Jess's words hit me. I had written a few things down after I talked to Marcello the other night, but I decided to leave the paper in my pocket. We will always find ourselves in the end. I repeated those words in my mind.

Valentina opened her mouth to object, but then stopped. She looked down and I saw her shoulders relax. She took a deep breath and switched her bag from one shoulder to the other, nodding to Jess while we continued walking.

The cobblestone streets were lined with cart vendors selling souvenirs of masks and shirts. I went over, picked up a dark red t-shirt with a gold emblem of *Venezia* written on it and asked in Italian, *quanto costa*, how much.

As I was going for my wallet, I spotted Matt trying on a classic *gondoliere* hat, a woven hat made of straw with a black tie around the crown. "*Quanto costa?*" I asked the vendor again, this time pointing to the hat Matt was wearing, deciding to buy it for him too. The vendor made me try a white and blue-brimmed hat that was wider than Matt's and floppier, and then directed me to a mirror. I tipped the hat, moving my head side-to-side, and decided to buy it as well.

"*Grazie, signorina!*" The vendor said, obviously happy with the sale. I went right up behind Matt, tapped him on his shoulder to show him my new purchase.

"*Che bella!*" Matt exclaimed, admiring it. "What do you think of this one?" Matt asked, taking it off.

"Well," I said, walking around him. "Put it back on."

He put on the hat and posed.

"Yes, yes. That will do."

"C'mon Juliet. You think I should get it?"

I walked up next to him and pretended like I was whispering a secret in his ear. "I think we should steal it." I said.

"Juliet, what? No." The look of confusion on his face was priceless.

"Too late!" I said, grabbing the hat and starting running away with it.

"Juliet come back!" I heard him yell this after me, I could hardly contain my laughter as I ran away. I stopped a little bit down the road and waited for him to catch up.

"Wow!" He said, jogging up next to me. "The vendor didn't even care that you took that. Juliet, you don't steal, what's up with you?" He was looking at me differently, not sure if he was liking what he was seeing.

"Relax," I said, rolling my eyes and now cracking up. "I bought the hat for you when I got mine."

"*Whaat?*" He was in utter disbelief. "Juliet, did you just trick me?"

"Yeah, kinda." I said, still laughing so hard my stomach was starting to hurt.

I saw a big smile appear on his face, and he began to laugh too. "You really got me." He put the hat back on and playfully pulled my hat over my eyes so I couldn't see.

"HEY!" I said, still laughing. He pulled me into a hug and fixed my hat so I could see his face.

The hug caught me a little by surprise. When he pulled away he put his arm around my shoulder and said *"Andiamo, Juliet."*

We started walking back to the cart to find our friends. He left his arm around my shoulder, making my stomach flutter. Jess and Valentina were at another stand, admiring all of the different masks that were on display.

"This one creeps me out." Jess said, picking up one that resembled what the doctors wore during the black plague. It had a long beak, like a crow. "What do they do with these masks anyway?"

"It's for *Carnevale*." I said, "Remember? Prof. Rossi showed us a slideshow of what people dressed up in during the few weeks before Lent. It's like Halloween for the Italians, but it's usually in February or March instead. I'm pretty sure we just missed it."

"Yeah, Juliet is right." Valentina said, her voice definitely quieter than usual. "Venezia is the place to be for *Carnevale*. The streets are so packed you can't even move. The women and men dress up in elaborate costumes and wigs and they all wear masks. Wait, I'll show you." She pulled up an image of it on her phone and showed Jess. "See?"

"Wow, that's crazy! We need to come back next year to see this. How did we miss this?" She looked back at the mask she had in her hands.

We browsed a few minutes more and then continued walking. John and Kathryn were further back than us, holding hands and pointing to various landmarks. I looked up at the buildings and

noticed some of them had yellow or white signs with arrows pointing in different directions and the words *"Per Rialto S. Marco"* above
them. We decided to follow the signs, hoping they would lead us to
Piazza San Marco in the end. I had noticed that the general flow of
tourists looked as if they were following the arrows too.

My stomach started to grumble and I realized we hadn't stopped
for breakfast. "Is anyone else hungry?" I said, motioning towards a
little espresso bar to my left.

"Starving," Matt said, already making his way to the door.

"Actually guys, do you mind if Kathryn and I continue walking?
I have each of your numbers so we can always meet up later." John
asked, still holding onto Kathryn's hand.

"Sure, we will text you later to tell you where we are," I replied.
A small smile formed on my face after I saw John perk up and
squeeze Kathryn's hand before he gave her a kiss and they continued
walking.

"Okay, what's up with this new John? I actually kind of love
it." Jess said, a look of shock crossing her face. "Wasn't he always
hooking up with different girls at school? Now he's swooning over
the first girl he meets and hooks up with at Matt's party? What's
happening here?"

We all nodded in agreement and looked at the display case at the
counter with all of the pastries in it. I opted for a cappuccino and
a *cornetto,* an Italian pastry that looked like a croissant, filled with
marmellata or jelly, while the others picked a *cornetto* with *crema,*
pastry cream.

We took a seat at a table and the waiter brought our coffee
and pastries to us. I took a big bite of the warm croissant, making
sure not to drop any jelly onto my sweater, and closed my eyes as
I enjoyed the taste. I noticed everyone was quiet, just focused on
eating their pastries and drinking their cappuccinos. I took a sip of
mine too, letting the warmth of the espresso and milk fill my belly.

"Oh, Juliet," Matt said, wiping away a bit of frothy milk on my lip with his finger. I smiled at him, dipped my finger in my cappuccino to grab a little bit of froth, and wiped it right on his cheek. He tried to dart back in his chair to avoid me, but I still managed to get some on his ear.

"Oh my God, you two are like little kids!" Valentina said, staring at both of us. She then brought the cappuccino to her mouth to take a sip also revealing a frothy mustache. She smiled a little, knowing what happened, and continued saying, "I mean, I can't take you anywhere!" Now we were all laughing, Valentina included, as she wiped her lips.

We finished drinking, trying not to draw any more attention to ourselves since we got a few stares from the other people in the bar enjoying a quiet breakfast. I almost reached for my bag to leave a tip on the table out of habit but stopped when I remembered that it wasn't customary.

I stepped out of the bar and felt the sun beating down on us, warming the morning air. It was warm enough to take off my jacket. We continued walking along the same narrow road, lined with little shops and restaurants. It was nice not to have to worry about cars or bikes, just people walking slowly and absorbing the city around them.

The streets themselves were lined with stones and the buildings varied in colors from a warm, burnt orange, to a light pink and cream stucco. Some people walking already had gelatos in their hands, even though it was only 10am. I could picture Gianni from the bar saying *americani*, implying that an Italian would never have a gelato that early.

We stopped every so often at a shop, browsing all of the trinkets and buying souvenirs for our families back home. I picked out a mask for my mom that she could show her students. Matt got a Murano necklace for his that she would love.

JULIET: **Mom, look at this mask. Do you like it?**

I texted her a picture of it, not expecting a reply back since it was only 4am there.

I was placing my phone back in my bag when I noticed it started buzzing.

"Mom?" I answered, "What are you doing up so early?"

"Juliet!" Her voice was still a little groggy but full of enthusiasm. "You are in Venezia? Isn't it romantic?"

I laughed. "I don't know if it's romantic Mom. I think you're biased from when you and Dad were younger, but it is beautiful."

"Well, have fun and send me all of the pictures you take! I'm going to brag to my students that you went."

"Okay, love you." I hung up, happy that I was able to share this moment with her since, deep down, I wished she was here too.

"Not romantic, huh? I need to step up my game, Juliet." Matt said, his face beaming at me as he got down on a knee and pretended to propose to me in front of onlookers. My face must have turned purple as I shushed him, grabbed his arm to pull him up, and looked over at Jess and Valentina who were laughing uncontrollably.

"Matt! Don't embarrass me like that!" I yelled as I swiped his arm, my cheeks slowly returning to their normal color.

"Okay, okay. I promise I won't do it again. But, I can't promise you that I won't embarrass you in other ways." I rolled my eyes at him before we continued on walking.

We took pictures of the gondolas when we walked over a canal. I teased Matt that since he had the hat, all he needed was a striped black and white shirt and he could give us a ride. He started belting out *"O Sole Mio"* in the middle of the street and we all quickly ducked our heads in laughter, running away from him. He caught up to us, laughing as well. We went through the narrow streets and heard the bells chime from a church nearby.

"I don't know about you ladies, but now that John left me to be the only man in this group, I feel like I need to make a decision that we should find a place to eat." Matt said, trying to act all serious as Jess, Valentina, and I all stared back at him with a pinched expression of annoyance and a slight smile.

"Aww, *il bambino ha fame!*" I joked, saying the baby was hungry. "But you're right, I burned off that croissant a few hours ago!"

Valentina pulled out her phone and typed in *ristorante* and *Venezia*. We looked at the map view and found a small *trattoria* close to us with great reviews. *Trattorias* were known for their local food, casual ambiance, and more affordable prices compared to other restaurants.

Matt texted John to see if he wanted to meet up with us, but he responded back that he was on a gondola ride with Kathryn. I imagined them on the ride, holding on to each other. Maybe Venice was romantic after all.

The menu on the stand outside of the restaurant looked heavenly. Mouth watering, I led the group inside to find a table. I realized this was the first time I was eating a formal meal on my trip. Before this, I was either eating at home with Elisa or just going for a cup of espresso and a pastry at a bar.

"*Allora, cosa ordiniamo?*" Matt said, in his best Italian accent asking us what we want to order.

I scanned the menu and asked the waiter about the foods I'd never heard of. We decided on a *frittura mista di pesce* for all of us, which was various fried fish including calamari. Both Jess and Valentina ordered the *Orata*, a typical fish from the Mediterranean for the main course. I ordered *Spaghetti con vongole*, figuring that ordering clams near a sea would have to mean they were fresh and Matt ordered *Spaghetti al ragù di manzo*, a meat sauce.

I picked on the *grissini* that were in the middle of the table, unveiling all of the different types of crunchy breadsticks there were. The waiter came by and offered us *acqua frizzante*, sparkling water, filling our glasses to the brim. Our *frittura mista* came first and we all scrunched our noses when we saw the whole shrimp fried, antenna and head included.

"Okay, I like seafood, but that might be a stretch for me." Jess said, her fork touching an antenna and moving the head of the shrimp around.

"Don't be a baby, Jess," Matt said, and took it from his fork and deshelled it with ease. "I mean, this is what real food looks like!" He popped the shrimp straight into his mouth.

"Wow, this is good!" I said, my mouth still full of some of the fried mullet. It had a crunchy, salty taste to it.

The waiter brought out our main courses and we each took a bite of each other's. The *orata* that Jess and Valentina ordered was grilled perfectly and had a meaty flavor that reminded me of a red snapper. I tried Matt's spaghetti and was surprised to taste all of the different spices.

I closed my eyes as I was hit with buttery wine flavors from the clam sauce in my dish. The clams were as fresh as I had imagined and the spaghetti were cooked perfectly *al dente*. It had the right *bite,* or literal translation of *to the tooth*, between not crunchy and not soft.

We talked about our roommates while we ate, Matt was definitely the happiest with his, while Valentina the most bitter about hers. Jess's roommate seemed nice, even though she was out most of the time hanging with other friends. I talked about Elisa and some of the drama involved between her and Giacomo.

Matt had stopped eating and listened carefully to how I described the love triangle between Luca, Elisa and Giacomo, and how she had lied when I first met her telling me she was dating Giacomo.

"I don't trust Elisa one bit." Jess said. "She sounds like the type of girl that will create drama just to get what she wants."

"Yeah, but Juliet is not telling you two the whole truth. Go on Juliet, say how cute you think *Giacomo* is." Matt said, adding an extra emphasis on Giacomo and nudging me.

I made a little bit of a face at him and noticed that both Valentina and Jess had dropped their forks to stare at us. I looked at Matt and saw him smiling as he picked up another forkful of spaghetti. Why did he have to make this awkward?

"Yeah, I mean he's *kinda* cute." I wiped a bit of clam sauce at the corner of my mouth. "But I am not interested in dating anyone while I am here, and he probably isn't interested in me like that anyway."

The waiter came up to us and asked if we wanted any *dolci*, or dessert, allowing me to avoid the conversation. We ordered *galani*, a thin, flat dough fried and dusted with powdered sugar that was typical this time of year, and an order of *frittole*. We made sure to pair them with some macchiatos as well.

"I am exhausted from studying," Valentina said, slumping a little into her chair. "I was getting A's on everything back at Binghamton, but the professors here are relentless. They want to know the most minute details. This one question had the answer buried in the middle of one of the five books I had only a week to read. These poor Italians. There aren't even jobs for them when they graduate here."

It was true. Many Italians who graduate can't find jobs in their field and end up with something that has nothing to do with their degree. One of my cousins who worked hard at university got an economics degree and ended up working for her dad's restaurant as a bookkeeper.

The waiter brought our desserts and coffee to our table and placed the bill between all of us. My eyes grew wide. The *frittole* reminded me of the zeppoles you would find at Italian feasts. I bit into one and tasted the raisins and pine nuts and was surprised by the hint of orange. The *galani* were crunchy and delicately sweet, having the right touch of sweetness with powdered sugar sprinkled on top.

We looked over the bill together and I noticed that there was a service charge of two euros that was already added for each of us, something that kind of resembled what a tip would be.

"Grazie!" We called out after heading out after paying. It was still warm on the street, so we decided to continue walking to *Piazza San Marco*. We had finally reached the Grand Canal, or *Canal Grande*, and saw *Ponte Rialto*, the most famous bridge in Venice. A lot of people were stopped at the edge of the paved street leaning their back towards the stone railing and taking a picture. We waited our turn to do the same, trying to position ourselves to all fit in the picture at once and making sure the bridge was still showcased in the background. Matt took the phone from my hand and tried to see if he could do it, but luckily another tourist saw us struggling and offered to take the picture for us. We thanked him after and huddled around my phone to see how it came out.

"Oooh, yay! Send it to me!" Jess squealed.

I turned back towards the bridge and marvelled at how elegant it looked. There were shops lined at the top of the bridge that had delicately arched roofs. They were connected to an open arch in the center that peaked higher than the others. It had white stones that created a beautiful contrast to the waters underneath. Watching the gondolas pass under the bridge, and people eating at umbrella-topped tables by the base of the bridge made me want to paint the scene, even though I've never painted before. The bridge itself was lined with all different types of shops, some selling gold jewelry, and others souvenirs. Matt huffed out loud when Jess, Valentina, and I wanted to check out a leather goods shop and decided he would wait outside for us. We browsed through some of the colorful leather bags and wallets. I ultimately decided to get a new wallet, made of Italian light brown leather, one that would hold all of the coins that the euros had. We headed back across the bridge towards San Marco and stopped in front of a gelateria.

"Okay, I need to try *yogurt ai frutti di bosco*." I said, admiring the berry-flavored yogurt gelato in the window. "Please?" I begged, looking at them with pleading eyes.

"You don't need to convince me, Juliet. You know that." Matt said, giving me a smile.

Valentina and Jess ordered too and we leaned against a railing in front of one of the smaller canals that ran through Venice, enjoying our gelato.

"Guys, it's almost five, we should start looking for a hotel." Valentina announced while looking at her phone. "John's a lost cause since he's probably still gallivanting around with Kathryn. It should be somewhere around here. We are between the ferry to Murano and *Piazza San Marco*." She was vigorously typing something into her phone.

"There aren't that many hotels available." I checked my phone too and noticed the only ones that had rooms were way above our price range.

"How about this one?" Jess said, turning her phone to us to show pictures of a hotel.

"Wait, look at this one!" Matt interjected emphatically. "It has over 1,000 reviews on Tripadvisor and is listed as #3 for value in Venice."

"Let's go book it now so at least we don't have to worry for the rest of the night." I said, noticing Valentina had a worried look on her face.

"*Andiamo!*" Matt said and led the way to the hotel.

We walked up to it, and if it weren't for the pin on Google Maps telling us we arrived, we would've never known it was a hotel.

The facade was exactly the same as all of the other buildings next to it, with only a tiny sign above the door's archway that revealed the name of the hotel. We entered and were greeted in Italian by a friendly receptionist.

"*Salve.*" She said hello to us in a formal way.

Valentina started speaking first but became a little flustered and mixed in some Spanish and English words when asking for rooms. The receptionist smiled at her and asked if we spoke English as well.

"Yes." Valentina responded meekly, her mouth then set in a hard line and she had an almost defeated look in her eyes.

"Great." The receptionist stated, looking to see how many we were. "We have two rooms left, unfortunately. Many hotels in this price range are either full or closed so you're lucky. A lot of the owners closed this week for vacation since we were so busy the weeks before with Carnevale.

"That's fine," Jess interrupted. "We will take them. I will room with Valentina, and you two can room together." Jess said, looking at me.

I looked over at Matt who shrugged his shoulders.

"Okay, how much?" I replied to the receptionist. She went over the price and took our information down. She handed us two keys and showed us the elevator that we could take to go to our room. We looked at each other since the elevator was rather small and didn't look like it would fit all of us at once, so we opted for the stairs instead.

"Behave now." Jess quipped, smiling at both of us while we had reached our rooms. I looked at Jess with a raised eyebrow and half-smile, wondering where she got the courage to say that.

"Oh, we will." Matt shot right back, laughing as he put the key in the door to open it. "Do you mind if I take a quick shower before we head back out?" He asked all of us before he opened the door to the room.

"Great idea!" Jess said, noticing that Valentina was still quiet from before.

The room was immaculate inside. It had an old-world feel with dark red curtains and gold scroll decorations on the walls, but everything smelled clean and looked pristine. I took off my hat, as did Matt, and we dropped our bags in a little alcove at the entrance.

"I can see why it got good reviews," I said to Matt cheerfully, but then froze when I noticed only one Queen-sized bed.

Matt noticed it too and chuckled softly. "Don't worry Fiore, I'll sleep on the couch." He said, only using my last name a handful of times in all of the years we have known each other. I was about to respond when I saw him taking off his shirt.

His back was towards me and I could see the muscles in his shoulders clench as he pulled the shirt up over his head. I imagined he was toned since he would often talk about working out at the gym or playing soccer after classes back at Binghamton, but I never saw him without a shirt before and I couldn't stop looking. Matt turned around and caught me. I quickly looked down and away feeling guilty in my stomach. Why couldn't I control my feelings? I was acting like a teenage girl who'd never seen a boy shirtless before. I cleared my head of any other thoughts and decided to take out the outfit I packed to change into.

Matt showered quickly. I looked over to hear the bathroom door open and he tiptoed out with a towel wrapped around his bottom half. "I forgot to bring my clothes into the bathroom." He said apologetically as he picked them up and brought them in with him.

I tried not to look over as he said that but couldn't help notice how well-toned his chest was too out of the corner of my eye. I tried to keep myself busy by posting a picture of the four of us in front of Ponte Rialto on Instagram. I smiled at the picture since we all looked so happy.

Get a hold of yourself. Don't mix romance into this and ruin things. I kept thinking to myself. Matt came out changed, hair gelled perfectly back into place, and I noticed his familiar warm smell of citrus and woods was stronger. It did not help how I felt.

"All yours." He said, holding the door to the bathroom open for me. I made sure to remember to bring my clothes and makeup bag since I didn't want to go back out in only a towel to get them. I locked the door behind me and let out a deep breath, hoping the shower would calm down the reaction I had from Matt shirtless.

I let it run down my face and body. I quickly washed myself and left my hair in a messy bun while I refreshed my makeup. When I stepped out of the bathroom, Matt was looking down at his phone while sitting at the edge of the bed.

"I like this picture of all of us." He said, turning his phone towards me to show me the picture I just posted. I sat down next to him on the bed, looking at it. My stomach was somersaulting being so close to him and taking in his scent, but I forced my expression to stay neutral, not wanting to create any unnecessary complications between us.

He looked over at me, one side of his lips tugging into a smile, and said, "You looked cute in your hat, Juliet."

I felt a current of warmth rush through me and I looked down, not wanting to meet his eyes.

"Alright guys, hurry up! We still need to go to *Piazza San Marco!*" We heard Valentina yell from the other side of the door while knocking loudly at the same time. I was grateful for the interruption so I could compose myself.

"Ah, Valentina, always the same," Matt said, which made me laugh as I went over to open the door. Valentina had a huge smile on her face, definitely an improvement from when we left her.

The sun was almost setting as we stepped outside and there were fewer people in the streets than before. We headed straight to *Piazza San Marco* this time without stopping and got there in 10 minutes.

At the north end, there was a magnificent view of the *Basilica San Marco* to our left. It was a Gothic-style cathedral, with spires and statues scattered around the roof. Marble columns and arches with artwork meticulously drawn with a gold background added to the already impressive cathedral. We stopped and stared at it and took in the immense beauty of it. The piazza itself was a longer rectangle lined on the three sides with three-story buildings made of white stone. Shops lined the main floor under a series of arches that created a walkway that connected all of the sides. We walked towards the middle of the piazza and stared up at the tall bell tower that was at one end of the shops.

"You should see what they do at *Carnevale*." Valentina said to us while still staring at the bell tower. "They attach a wire that connects the tower to a platform in the middle of the piazza and a lady dressed up in a gown and mask actually *flies* down it." She used air quotes around the word *flies*.

"*Il Volo dell'Angelo*, right?" I asked, remembering the name.

"Yes, the flight of the angel." Jess nodded.

"Hey, look over there," Matt said, pointing to a kid with pigeons all around him. "We definitely need to do that!"

"Ew, gross, Matt. We try to avoid pigeons in New York City, why would I pay to have them on me?" Valentina said, her face scrunched up while she was shaking her head no.

"I'm doing it," I announced, stepping forward towards the vendor that was selling birdseed. "It'll make a great picture."

I went forward and handed the vendor the exact change for the bag of bird seeds. I gave some to Matt and to Jess while Valentina stood far from us, but not too far that she couldn't take pictures.

We held out our arms to the side, with seeds in our palms facing up, and watched a bunch of pigeons fly right to us. I closed my eyes and started laughing when I felt them pecking at the seeds in my hands and flapping their wings around my hair as they landed on my shoulders and arms. Once all of the seeds were gone, they flew off and I opened my eyes to see them flying towards another group of people with their arms outstretched and big smiles spread across their faces waiting to be attacked by them.

"Look at your faces in these pictures!" Valentina said, walking towards us with the phone facing us.

"Ha, look at you, Juliet! I can barely see your face with all of the pigeons surrounding you. And Jess, look at that one on your head, it looks like it's nesting!" Matt said, zooming into the picture and laughing.

"I am definitely washing my hair tonight before bed," Jess said, with a disgusted look on her face.

We walked towards the shops in the piazza and found a bar under the arches and sat around a table. We decided it would be a good idea to take in the views of the piazza and enjoy a drink. We each ordered a spritz, a drink made with prosecco and Campari, and the waiter gave it to us with a bowl of chips and a small plate with some bite-sized sandwiches made of prosciutto and soft cheese.

"Only in Italy do they make everything look classy," Jess said, taking a sip of her spritz.

"I can live like this," Matt said, popping the mini sandwich in his mouth. "I mean, the view isn't bad either." He continued, staring at two gorgeous girls walking by. One of the girls definitely looked back at him and gave him a smile. Valentina gave Matt a nudge and pretended to scold him while Jess shook her head and laughed.

Back at school, Matt had one serious girlfriend that I remembered. The first year we were there he was dating a girl that he had met the year before in high school. I remember seeing a picture of her on his phone, dark blond hair like his, great smile, and athletic since the picture was of her in a soccer uniform. They dated for another two years but broke up without Matt telling me why. He hasn't been with anyone since and proclaimed that he needed a break from relationships. Every once in a while I'd see him walking around campus with a girl, but nothing ever seemed serious. I never knew exactly what happened when he broke up with his ex and I always wondered if something hurt him quite a bit to make him want to stop dating.

"Pizza tonight?" Matt asked, breaking my thought.

"Yes!" We all said together.

We checked our phones and found a pizzeria close to us with a menu that had over 50 different pizza varieties. Matt had to try the one with hot dogs and french fries on it, while Jess and Valentina opted for roasted veggies and mushrooms. I saw one that had speck, gorgonzola and walnuts, and remembered that it was Giacomo's favorite.

"Per me una pizza bianca con speck, gorgonzola e noci." I said to the waiter after the others had already placed their orders.

They all looked at me with quizzical expressions, surprised that I had ordered that.

"What made you order that?" Valentina asked.

"I said I wanted to try everything while here and I never had this before!"

Our pizzas arrived quickly and we all dug in, hungry from walking all day. I took a bite of the pizza and could not believe how flavorful it was. The speck reminded me of a smokier prosciutto and the gorgonzola complemented it perfectly with the walnuts adding the right crunch.

"You need to try this." I said, cutting a slice for the others.

"Not for me." Jess said, taking a bite of her pizza.

"Sorry, I don't like anything that reminds me of blue cheese." Valentina added, shaking her head.

"I'm game," Matt said, pushing his plate away to slide the slice of pizza over. His fingers touched mine as he reached for the slice and those feelings from before rattled through me again. I had finally controlled my emotions enough to not look at Matt differently, and there I went again, my stomach laughing at my willpower to avoid any complications.

"Now that is good. Nice choice for a pizza. Makes me want to switch with you." He took a bite and moaned softly while chewing it.

On the way back to the hotel we stopped by a candy shop, figuring that since this was a mini-vacation we could have sweets, and filled up bags from wooden barrels full of candy.

When we reached our hotel and said goodnight to each other, that uneasy feeling crept back in my stomach as I realized I would be alone in the room with Matt again. I dropped my bag into the alcove, slipped off my shoes, and hung up my jacket, but moved back when Matt brushed past me to go to the bathroom.

"Sorry, I know how you girls are and how long you take to go to sleep, so I'm heading into the bathroom first." Matt proclaimed, closing the door behind him.

I was about to protest, but the door closed quickly and he already turned the water on. I decided to change into my pajamas as fast as I could and turned on the TV. This time I started understanding more Italian words as I watched the program. It was a show that reunited people and one man on it hadn't seen his childhood crush in years and was hoping to rekindle a romance. I got so entranced in watching it that I didn't realize Matt was standing next to me.

"Alright, let's take out the bag of candy and watch this." He said, reaching for the bag he bought. He sat on the bed, watching the show and popping fistfuls of candy into his mouth. I decided to get mine too and laid belly-down on the bed next to him.

"Did you try the sour peaches?" He asked, handing me one of his.

I took it and popped it into my mouth. "That's so good! Why

does all of the food taste better here?" I said, handing him one of the chocolates from my bag. "Try this one— it has caramel and hazelnut in it."

"I was actually thinking the same thing." He said, closing his eyes and chewing the chocolate a lot slower than he had with all of the candy before.

We continued watching the show until the end. When his child-hood sweetheart showed up she turned him down and told him he had his chance long ago, and too much time had passed.

"Well, that was a letdown," Matt said, as he turned to me and stole another chocolate from my bag.

"Hey!" I hid the bag behind my back away from him.

"Oh that's it, you are not hiding those chocolates from me after I let you eat mine. They're way too good. Get over here, Juliet!" He protested and tried to grab the bag from around my back.

I raised my arm holding the bag above my head, away from him, but he quickly reached for it, bumping into me and falling onto me against the bed. We both stopped laughing since his face was a few inches away from mine and he was looking straight into my eyes. His face leaned a little closer, and I looked down to his lips, which were slightly open, his breath shallow. He had all of his weight on his elbows, on my sides. My palms were placed against his chest, and I could feel his heart beating through his shirt. I didn't dare to breathe and just stayed there, not sure what to do next. A part of me wanted to kiss him, but the more sensible part was also saying how I shouldn't ruin something that was already perfect. I squeezed my eyes shut, praying that when I opened them, I wouldn't be faced with that decision. The sensible part won. My palms pushed him off me and he fell over on his back next to me on the bed.

"Wow. What kind of strength do you have? It's like you turned into the Incredible Hulk or something." Matt joked, obviously trying to change the mood from what was about to happen.

I wanted to kiss him at that moment. And, I still did. But I loved our friendship, and I didn't want to complicate anything while we were here. I smiled at him and made a muscle, pretending to be proud of my actual boney arms. He looked at me with a half-smile and went to get something out of his bag.

"I got this for you." He said, as he handed me a small, wrapped present.

I looked up at him surprised as I took the present and opened it. It was a beautiful bracelet, with small blue and turquoise crystals and Murano glass beads made with swirls of the same colors.

"Matt, this is beautiful. When did you get this?" I said putting it on. "You were with us the whole time."

"When you ladies were having fun buying bags and wallets in the leather shop on *Ponte Rialto*, I found this a few shops down. I know you love the color blue."

I was so touched by the gift, I was having trouble finding the right words to say. "Thanks, but you didn't have to do this."

"I wanted to. You have been my friend for a long time and I wanted to acknowledge that. Plus, you bought me that amazing hat, how could I not get something for you?"

I gave him a hug, taking in his smell as my head leaned against his chest. I never received anything this thoughtful from a boy before and couldn't believe how it was something I would've exactly picked out.

"Alright, I am brushing my teeth so we can get some rest." I grabbed my toothbrush and headed to the bathroom.

I took my time brushing my teeth and washing my face to take in all that happened. Those knots in my stomach that disappeared before came back even worse now that I realized I did, in fact, have feelings for him. It was how I felt the first time I met him and developed a crush.

He was already curled up on the couch, looking at his phone

when I stopped at the foot of the bed. "Matt, you don't actually have to sleep on the couch. The bed is big enough for both of us." I said to him as he looked over at me. "Some boundaries though," I added. "This is my side and that's yours." I proclaimed, drawing an imaginary line with my arm between the bed. "No pulling the covers off, no moving your long legs to my side, and definitely no snoring!"

He smiled and walked over to the opposite side from where I was. I could visibly see my hands shake as I rolled the bedspread off and threw the extra pillows. I literally invited Matt to sleep in the bed...what was I thinking? I couldn't let him sleep on the couch. His legs were too long to sleep comfortably on it and I definitely wasn't going on the couch either, so I was doing the right thing. He was about to sit on top of the bed when I heard his phone ring.

"Oh, I'm going to take this," Matt said as he looked down at the number on his phone screen. "It's my sister and I haven't spoken to her in a while. I'll go outside on the balcony."

A feeling of relief came over me. I looked at my phone and saw it was 11:30. I took a deep breath as I laid down against the soft pillow and closed my eyes and started to think of all of the events of the day, down to the bracelet Matt gave me.

12

Dodici

Cambiare (v)= to change

I must have slept completely through the night because when I opened my eyes, the sun was shining and I was in the middle of the bed by myself. I struggled to open my eyes since the room was so bright. Once they adjusted, I looked over at Matt to see him sleeping on the couch with a blanket covering him. The balcony shutter was left open and the light was pouring in. I got up quietly and snuck over to him trying not to wake him up.

"Hey," he said as I walked up to him, eyes still closed. His voice was groggy and he stretched his arms out and sat up on the couch. The blanket was still covering most of him. "You took up the whole bed when you went to sleep last night and I didn't want to wake you to move you over." He stared up at me with squinting eyes.

"You could've just pushed me over," I said feeling guilty.

"No, you were snoring so peacefully with your mouth open. I

didn't have the heart to do that to you." He said, smiling at me while I jokingly punched his arm.

"I do not snore, Matthew Connell!"

"Oh, you most certainly do, Juliet Fiore!" Matt yelled right back holding his arm as if I hurt him. "My sister kept me on the phone for an hour asking for advice about this boy she liked. She went through everything they've texted each other and she had me deciphering if he liked her or not. Was it that complicated when we were in high school?" He asked me while looking around for a shirt to put on.

"High school was always complicated, silly boy." I found it sweet that he had taken the time to listen to his sister and given her dating advice.

"Then she started talking about how she doesn't know what she should go to school for. I swear sometimes that girl overanalyzes everything."

"What's she into?" I remembered being in high school and thinking about all of the possibilities of what jobs I could get. I always leaned towards teaching though because my teachers were inspiring to me. They taught integral subjects that could possibly change a student's life one day. I still remembered my favorite teachers in high school, they were the ones that I truly wanted to be like.

"Honestly, I don't know." He said, bringing me back to the conversation. "She likes to draw a lot, but I'm not sure if she likes it enough to make a career out of it. I mean, most artists don't make a lot of money. I suggested that she work for my aunt at her real estate agency. You make good money and you don't even have to put in a lot of hours." Matt said while leaning back into the sofa with his arms behind his head.

"First of all, none of what you said is true," I said, shocked that he was acting so narrow-minded. "Artists can make great money and that's not the only job you can have if you are good at art. What about a graphic designer? Or an art teacher? Maybe a museum curator if she likes Art History. I mean there are plenty of jobs. She has to do something she *loves*!"

"Listen, I get that and all, but sometimes you have to take the easy route. For instance, my dad has an engineering firm, I would be an idiot not to work for him. Engineering wasn't my first choice, but at least I am guaranteed a job when I graduate." Matt said, reaching over to his bag and pulling out a shirt. I hadn't focused on the fact that he had been shirtless all of this time as he pulled the shirt over his head. The blanket was still covering his bottom half as he was sitting down.

"You still want to be a teacher, right? Did Verona change your mind at all? Summers off will be sweet if you do that."

"Yeah I do, but not just so I can have summers off." I hadn't thought too much about my future with all of the boy drama running through my head lately. "Plus, I'm not sure what type of teacher I want to be."

"Just be an Italian high school teacher! It's that easy. Your mom will plan your lessons, you won't have to worry about anything." Matt said, his arms moving around as if he were imitating an Italian while talking.

"*Matteo*, did you just yell at me like my mom does with your hands all over the place?" I quipped.

He shrugged his shoulders and I could tell that he had no interest in this conversation anymore.

"It's already nine," I said looking away. "You know Valentina is going to have a heart attack if we don't get ready soon. I'm sure she has already planned everything for us."

Sure enough, I saw Matt's phone light up on the armrest of the couch with a message from Valentina to our group chat.

"Yeah, you're definitely a psychic," Matt said as he checked his phone.

I read the message on my phone too. Valentina already got us the ferry times for us to visit Murano. I ran over and claimed the bath-room first as he was still on the couch not dressed. I took a shower and washed my hair quickly so Matt would have time to get ready too. I towel-dried my hair as much as I could and could almost hear the echoes of my nonna yelling at me not to go outside with wet hair. I put on some mascara and lip gloss, got dressed, and headed out into the room. Matt was patiently waiting by the bathroom door in his t-shirt and boxers and his toothbrush in his hand.

"Done *principessa*?" Matt said sarcastically to me, one eyebrow raised and a smirk on his face.

"Yes, and just so you know, my dad calls me that. So, *prego, papà*." I said moving out of the way so he could pass me through the door.

Ten minutes later, we grabbed all of our things from the room and were ready to check out.

"*Buongiorno!*" Jess greeted us enthusiastically as we met each other outside. "Valentina programmed the whole day already." She slightly rolled her eyes while saying this.

"What about me?" Valentina asked as she stepped outside after turning in all of our keys.

"Nothing, only that you will relax and we will figure out the plans along the way." Matt said, obviously mocking Valentina.

"Without me, you'd be lost, Matt," Valentina said in a haughty tone.

"Alright, Valentina, just don't stress. I liked the carefree Valentina from yesterday who didn't always have to have an answer to every-thing." Matt patted her on the back. Her shoulders relaxed and she looked down, biting her lip.

"No, you are right. It's just sometimes I can't help it," she said. "I know it's annoying, but I grew up in a house where my mom was always late to everything and my dad was always working and never home. Making schedules and showing up on time actually makes me feel like I'm in control. I know it's annoying, and I will try and learn to relax."

"Do you want me to lead the way?" Matt asked.

"Actually, yeah." She made a gesture like she was removing an imaginary captain's hat off of her head and placed it on Matt's.

"Okay if you say so. Let's do this, girls. *Andiamo!*" Matt said as he waved his finger in a circle above his head as if he was rounding us up.

I looked over at Valentina and wrapped an arm around her in a side hug. She looked over at me and gave me a small smile.

"*Andiamo!*" I repeated.

We decided to grab a quick bite to eat at the first espresso bar we saw. "You got lucky that this is a good bar." Valentina quipped to Matt.

"You see, not everything needs to be planned. Sometimes you get lucky." Matt said as he took a sip of his cappuccino. He decided we should walk straight towards the ferry next and see if there were any leaving for the island of Murano. He looked down at his phone to check the map and led us across the canals and through the narrow streets. We got there just in time to see a ferry approaching. Valentina ran up to the ticket window and ordered 4 tickets for the next trip to Murano.

"Seriously, Matt, you're too lucky. If we didn't make this ferry the next one wouldn't come for another 40 minutes." Valentina huffed, as she handed us our tickets.

"Sometimes it just happens." Matt replied back, shrugging his shoulders.

Valentina gave him a smile back and lifted her chin a little as she walked towards the ferry. I never took the time to think about why Valentina was the way she was. I always assumed that it was just her personality. I began to see her in a new light. We boarded the ferry and held onto the railings as it took off. It went faster than expected because it was smaller than the ones I usually ride on back home.

"By the way girls, if either of you were wondering if Juliet snores, stop wondering because the answer is yes. Yes, she does." Matt said, whispering loudly over to Valentina and Jess, purposely making sure I heard.

"I do not!" I proclaimed, pretending to be shocked as he said it.

"Oh right!" Jess said, remembering something. "I forgot to ask you guys, how did last night go?"

"Well, I slept on the couch, and *principessa* here took up the whole bed. Not as juicy as you guys might have been hoping." Matt said.

"*Boring!*" Jess replied back, pretending to be sad and pouting her lips. "We didn't stick you two in a room together for *that!*"

"*Sorry,*" I replied to Jess, playing along. I glanced towards Matt who was already looking at me smiling. I touched the glass beads on my bracelet and thought about it. I wonder what would've happened if I didn't think so much.

When we reached the island, Matt let Valentina take over. He announced out loud that he relinquished his power to her since he had no idea what to do.

Valentina laughed and then turned towards us. "Okay so, we could either take a tour or we could just stop by some of the shops and watch them make sculptures."

The three of us looked at each other and, as if we all read each other's minds, said "Stop by some shops" in unison.

We were in awe watching the glassmakers at work, seamlessly creating works of art from shapeless balls of glass. I made sure to take videos so my mom could have something to show her students.

At lunchtime, we walked around some of the streets and sat down at a restaurant for lunch at *Campo Stefano*, where a glass piece was on display in the middle of the piazza. It was probably 15 feet tall, with light and dark blue spikes sticking out of a cube.

"Yeah, that's not something you see back home," Jess said.

We continued to let Valentina lead the way and she suggested we go back to Venice to finish seeing *Palazzo Ducale*, behind the *Basilica San Marco*. We made sure to cross over the Bridge of Sighs. The history of it was fascinating. It was said to be the last view of the outside world a prisoner would see before crossing into the prison on the other side. The prisoner would then sigh their last breath of freedom. Our pace started slowing down when we made it back to the piazza and decided to head home.

"John texted me that they're already back, so we're on our own, again," Matt said, looking up from his phone.

We walked the way to the train station quickly, making it right on time to catch the train heading out to Verona. I sat down next to Matt while Jess and Valentina sat together a few seats away. I kept staring down at my bracelet, playing with beads and leaned my head against Matt's shoulder to relax. He looked over at me, gave me a gentle kiss on my head, and took out his phone to check out the pictures.

"This is a nice pic." He said, pointing out to one where I was standing on a small bridge over one of the canals, my back to the camera.

"When did you take that one?" I asked, cheeks still red from the kiss.

"Yesterday. You looked cute with your hat on watching the gondolas pass by." I liked how he always said what he genuinely thought. I smiled at him and we scrolled through the rest of the pictures. We shared our best ones with each other and posted a few on Instagram for our friends and family to see. I replied to some of the comments under my pictures and texted back with some friends as Matt was scrolling through his phone. Our knees were touching each other's and those feelings came back in my stomach. I was so frustrated with my feeble mind.

Matt looked over at me from his phone and then put it back in his bag. He wrapped one arm around me and squeezed me in closer to him. I settled into his chest and closed my eyes as the bumpy train ride calmed down any jitters I had. His thumb stroked my arm and I grabbed his fingers from across my chest. Our fingers interlocked and we both stayed still. I was sure Matt stopped breathing since his chest wasn't rising and I was afraid to look up. I still wasn't sure if I was willing to risk our friendship for what could be just a hookup. I realized I had stopped breathing too as I tried to gather the courage to turn my head and look up at him.

Just as I had built up some courage, by a pure coincidence of timing, the train's brakes squealed and we pulled up to the Verona station. Everyone around us started getting up and grabbing their bags and I got up to do the same, grateful for the excuse before I made any rash decisions. I waited for Matt to get up but noticed him staring down, pensive, with his lips pressed together. He stayed a few more seconds before standing up and grabbing his bag from the rack above the seat. We all filed out of the train and found the bus to take us back home.

"So, you like that bracelet?" Matt asked softly when we got on the bus, noticing that I had been playing with it. I looked over at him and he had a small smile on his face, but his eyes almost looked sad, not his usual expression.

"It's exactly what I would've picked," I said. His smile grew wider, but he was still calmer than before. He gently wrapped his fingers around my wrist to take a closer look at the bracelet. That jittery feeling came back again as he moved his hand down to hold mine. I looked at our fingers intertwined. The bus made a sharp turn that made me lose my balance and he grabbed my hand tighter to hold me steady. I looked up and thanked him and he opened his mouth and started to say something to me.

"We're home!" Valentina shouted, from the front of the bus,

interrupting the moment. Matt let go of me as we walked down the stairs of the bus.

"Juliet?!" I heard someone scream from down the street.

I squinted my eyes and saw Kristin and Ana waving their hands to me from down the road. Matt looked down at me and nodded his head.

"Go, Juliet. I'm probably going to go take a nap since that couch wasn't the best last night. I'll text you later." He nodded his head in their direction. I gave him a hug goodbye, longer than our usual ones, and quickly hugged Jess and Valentina before jogging over to meet Kristin and Ana.

"Oh my God, what was that about?" Ana whispered a little too loudly when I reached her. I looked back, hoping that Matt didn't hear, but he already reached his apartment building. "You hugged him goodbye?"

"I hugged Jess and Valentina bye too," I said, trying to act as if it were not a big deal.

"Oh no, we need to talk right now. I know you are tired, so this time we are coming to your apartment. Your miserable roommate isn't there, is she?" Kristin said, raising her eyebrow.

"No, she shouldn't be. Her name is *Elisa* by the way." I said, emphasizing her name instead, "and there isn't that much to talk about anyway."

"Uh-huh sure," Ana said, squinting her eyes at me.

Ana grabbed my hand and practically dragged me to my apartment. Before I could even put down my bag, Ana was getting the espresso pot ready.

"Okay, tell us everything!" Kristin said, pouring herself a cup.

I started with dinner in Venice, how Matt teased me about Giacomo, and how I mentioned I didn't want to get involved with anyone. Their faces lit up when I explained how we ended up sharing a hotel room and that we almost kissed, but I was too nervous.

They almost exploded with excitement at that tidbit. I went on to say how he bought me the bracelet. I showed it to them and got an audible "*ooo*" from Kristin. I ended with telling them about the train and bus back, how comfortable it felt to have my hand in his.

"So, what do you think is going to happen now?" Ana asked the same question I had been asking myself.

"I honestly don't know. A big part of me wants to try and see what will happen, but another part of me is afraid to ruin our friendship. What if we aren't good together in that way? Then it's nearly impossible to go back to being friends."

"Maybe it's worth a try." Ana offered, taking a sip of her espresso. "You may regret it if you don't."

I thought about what she said and I started to warm up to the idea that maybe I should give it a shot. We continued talking about some of the gossip that was happening in their apartment building, about how Ana saw the cute boy again but still didn't get his name.

"He smiled at me and I smiled back at him this time!" I could tell she was happy she had the courage.

"Now you need to get his number!" Kristin added, tapping her arm with her hand.

We talked about John and Kathryn, how they had ditched us and went off on their own. "He was never like that back at home," I explained, still shocked from how he was with her, but so happy for him.

"It was a fun trip, though," I said, covering my mouth as I stifled a yawn. Kristin and Ana decided it was time to go home too since we all had classes the next day and needed to wake up early.

Before I headed to bed, I plugged my phone into the charger not having realized the battery died. As soon as I turned on my phone, it pinged 3 times.

MATT: **I will never forget this pic.**

He had included a picture of me with pigeons all around.

MATT: **I had fun this weekend with you...even if you snore.**

MATT: **Good night, Fiore.**

I noticed the texts were from an hour ago, but I decided to text him back.

JULIET: **I do not snore! Buona notte Matteo.**

I put my earbuds in listening to Laura Pausini again since this time I needed her songs more than ever to clear my head of all of this confusion with Matt.

The next day I felt overwhelmed in my classes since I didn't do any reading over the weekend. I tried following along with the professors and taking notes, but none of it made sense. Matt noticed me quieter in our Italian class and asked if I was alright.

"I was supposed to read some chapters for my classes but completely forgot. I really need to catch up before I am too behind. I heard horror stories from Elisa about how hard these tests can be." I twirled my hair so much it wrapped around my index finger.

"Juliet, don't stress. You'll be fine. Breathe and *relax.*"

I took in a deep breath and let it out slowly as the teacher began to start her lesson. After class, I walked with Jess and Matt and waved bye to both of them as they headed off and I headed back home. Things seemed like they were back to normal with Matt. We were our old selves in class, with him even making me laugh when our Italian professor's back was turned to us. We did steal glances at each other during class, but we didn't hold hands or anything like we did on the bus the day before.

I was deep in thought sitting on the bus when I saw a familiar face get on a few stops later. Giacomo hopped on, dressed in a grey overcoat, with a black backpack slung over a shoulder. I haven't seen him in over a week and started feeling nervous. He made eye contact with me and nodded his head to say hi as he made his way over to me.

"*Ciao.*" He said, putting a hand on the side of my arm and squeezing it.

"*Ciao.* How are you?" My breath quickened after he touched my arm and I looked down to it. I remembered this weekend with Matt and feelings of guilt came over me. I shouldn't be feeling this way just with Giacomo touching my arm. I willed my breath to calm the rest of my body down. I looked back up at him, my expression now more serene, and asked him how his mom is doing.

"We went to a few new doctors and I feel better after spending some time with her." I saw a change in his expression as his shoulders relaxed and his lips pulled into a small smile, pressed together. I nodded my head sympathetically, listening as he described how the doctors were able to exclude some illnesses, but she still has to go to appointments weekly.

We reached our bus stop and got off together, now walking side by side to our building.

"Is that new?" Giacomo asked, pointing to my bracelet. I touched it and smiled.

"Yeah, we went to Venice this weekend and Matt bought it for me at a shop." I saw his expression change slightly as he looked down and kicked a little pebble in front of him.

"Oh, by the way," I said changing the subject. "Thank you for telling me about your favorite pizza. I tried it in Venice and it was *amazing!*"

His eyebrows raised and his smile grew wider.

I described the scene in *Piazza San Marco* where I was surrounded by pigeons and he started laughing and begged to see a picture of it. I swiped through my phone, and he smiled, commenting on some of the other pictures as we went through them.

"I am happy you had fun." He said when we reached our apartment building. "And I wanted to thank you for listening to me that day before I left. You really helped me. I wanted to text you, but I don't have your number. Can you give it to me?"

I thought back to the text he sent Marcello asking about me. We exchanged numbers and I complimented him on his English since he spoke better than the last time I was with him.

"*Grazie*. I found my old English textbooks from high school and studied them this week when I was home." He said, taking the key from his bag. "*Ciao*, Juliet."

"*Ciao*," I said, and continued up the stairs to my apartment.

It was good to see Giacomo in a better mood this week after he spent time with his mom. I tried to picture where he lived and what his house might look like. I thought about what it would be like to go there one day with him. I opened the door and saw Elisa sitting on her chair, with her back to the door scrolling through her phone.

"*Ciao*, Elisa!" I said, oddly happy to see her again too after the weekend.

"Hello!" She sounded like she was in a good mood and I was grateful.

"How was your weekend?" She patted the chair next to her so I could sit too.

I told her about Venice, skipping all of the details about what happened with Matt, but instead, I concentrated on just the food we ate and places we saw. I showed her the hat I bought and the new wallet I got myself along with other little souvenirs I picked up.

"That's a pretty bracelet too!" She lifted up my wrist to look at it.

"Thanks...Matt bought it for me." I hesitated saying the last part but didn't want to act like I was hiding anything.

She was silent as she just looked at me with raised eyebrows and then continued to turn my wrist and inspect the bracelet. She didn't say anything else when she put down my wrist, so instead of there being an awkward silence, I told her the story about the pigeons.

"I am sorry, but that is gross." She said, scrunching up her face in disgust. "But, I guess since you are a tourist, you must do what tourists do." She added, waving her hand in front of her.

I was getting used to adjusting to her mood swings and not responding to them. Ever since Valentina vented about her family situation and why she acts the way she does, I made a promise to not judge Elisa so quickly. I felt my phone vibrate with a text and took it out. I involuntarily smiled when I saw the text was from Giacomo.

GIACOMO: **I must know if this is true...do Americans actually put pineapple on pizza?**

JULIET: **Yes, but they also put pasta on it. At least we don't put horse meat on it like you do!**

GIACOMO: **Pasta?! No!!**

We continued texting back and forth until Elisa called me over asking if we were having dinner together. We got the ingredients together and decided on a simple pasta with some sauce and peas. I noticed that Elisa was great at eating small portions of her meals while I would feel guilty putting a second helping of pasta on my plate. We ate and chatted more before we finished up and cleared the table. Elisa went back to her room and I grabbed my phone and headed out to the balcony to text Matt.

JULIET: **Go out on your balcony and look left.**

I leaned against the balcony and waited a few minutes for him to appear. I could barely make out it was him but saw him waving as he spotted me when he stepped out.

MATT: **Well isn't that fitting, Juliet on a balcony.**

I laughed out loud and realized I was sort of too loud so I put my hand over my mouth to try to stifle it.

JULIET: **So, shouldn't you be on the street looking up at me, Romeo?**

I surprised myself by feeling bold enough to flirt a little.

MATT: **I will be right there!**

I saw him disappear back into the apartment and started panicking that he would actually come by. But then he came right back outside with Javier in his arms. I could see Javier was protesting for Matt to put him down and he screamed *"loco!"* while pointing to him.

JULIET: **You are absolutely crazy.**

I put my phone down and was still laughing at the scene with Javier. I loved how they formed a friendship right away. I wondered what it would be like to have a roommate who wasn't moody all the time and didn't try to sabotage your love life. I decided to say goodnight since I needed to spend the night catching up on all of the reading I was behind on and went back in to study.

13

Tredici

Cucinare (v) = to cook

The bar was quieter than it'd been since the weather was warmer and more people were just staying at the counter instead of sitting down. Jess and Valentina only stayed a few minutes too, but I decided to actually sit down, hoping my empty energy reservoir could be refueled with a strong espresso.

"*Ciao,* Gianni! *Oggi prendo un caffè doppio.*" I said, ordering a double espresso.

"*Sei stanca,* Juliet?" Gianni asked if I was tired while getting ready to prepare my espresso. I nodded my head. I was up really late last night studying. I was almost caught up but definitely needed the next two days to read the remaining chapters.

As soon as I got home after classes that day, I put on another pot of espresso and got straight to my books. I saw Giacomo had texted me again, this time asking if I would ever eat potatoes on my pizza and I responded that it doesn't scare me as much as horse meat. We texted a little more while I read until Elisa burst into my room.

"Come with me now, we are going to Giacomo's apartment to talk about Friday night!" She exclaimed, jumping up and down as she said it.

I wondered what she could be so excited about and followed her as she hurried to the door and held it open, waiting for me. I tried to catch up to her as she skipped down the stairs to Giacomo's apartment. We saw Luca holding the door open for us as soon as we reached his floor. We walked in to see Pietro with a big smile on his face.

"*Va bene, ragazzi.*" Pietro said as we filed into the apartment, taking seats around the table. Giacomo and Marcello came out of their rooms, smiling and chatting between themselves. We all found a seat. I sat between Marcello and Elisa and saw Giacomo sitting next to Luca on the other side. I peered over to him and met his glance. He was wearing dark wash jeans, a gray sweater, and dark gray sneakers. Every time I saw him, he was dressed nicely, even his hair had that perfect manicured messy look. I smiled, feeling my cheeks heat up, and then turned my attention back to Pietro, who was now standing on a chair.

"*Barbecue questo venerdì!*" He declared triumphantly, chest puffed as he tried to maintain a serious expression. We all let out a laugh since all he did was just say that there was a barbecue this Friday.

He got off the chair, now smiling, and sat down near us to go over the details of the barbecue for next weekend. I listened, curious why everyone was so excited about it. We made plans to go food shopping together on Thursday after classes and would all bring our own meal we made.

"*Allora, vieni?*" Pietro turned to me, asking if I was coming.

"*Certo!*" Sure, I said, happy that I had been included. I heard them talking more about what they would be making, what ingredients they needed, and noticed Marcello making a list of what everybody was saying.

I got excited watching everyone acting so animated about this barbecue. From what I understood, Marcello was making the drinks, while Luca was going to be the "grill-master". Elisa volunteered to make a dessert and I jumped in to help her too. Giacomo and Marcello were in charge of bringing sides.

I kept imagining what the party would be like since I had never been to one like this. The ones I was invited to back home just revolved around what alcohol was going to be there and how drunk everyone would get.

We went on to talk about our weekends and Marcello turned to me to ask how Venice was. I noticed Giacomo looking over at us every once in a while we were talking, and then turned his attention back to Pietro who was showing him a video on his phone.

I went to bed excited that night. Elisa was even happier than her normal self, going over all of the different desserts we could make. We settled on making a tiramisù, since it was a fan favorite. I texted Matt while I laid in bed for a few minutes since I missed a few of his texts from before.

The next day I felt more prepared for my classes. I met up with Matt and Jess in our Italian class and took our usual seats. Matt texted me throughout the class making me laugh and I shot him a pleading look to stop, but my phone kept vibrating with new texts coming in. I refused to turn it over and look at it, trying instead to pay attention to our teacher. Matt looked over at me, smiling, and kept nudging my leg to keep bothering me. After we left class, I smacked Matt across the arm and yelled at him for being so annoying.

"Ow!" He said, rubbing his arm. "When you stopped reading my texts I had to get your attention somehow. I'm having a big party Friday night so I wanted to make sure you will come."

"Friday?"

"Yeah, why?" His eyebrows furrowed.

"Giacomo, his roommates, and Elisa are all planning a barbecue that night and invited me. We are supposed to go food shopping Thursday together and bring our own dish." I hoped he could see how important this was to me.

"Well, can you come to my party instead? I think they would understand." He suggested, his voice full of hope when he asked. "Jess will be there, right, Jess?" He added, looking over to her.

"Yeah, but Juliet can't just cancel her plans. Her roommate already has it out for her. If she finds out that she ditched them to go to your party, it will make things worse between them." I was grateful that she understood.

"What if I came later on and tried to do both? You always say your friends in the building stay late."

"Okay, *finee*. That works." He said, smiling back at me.

"Awesome." I said, excited for the end of the week.

I said bye to Matt and Jess and took the bus back home. Once I reached my stop, I stepped off the bus and felt my phone buzz with an incoming message.

KRISTIN: **Hey Juliet, how are you doing in poetry? I am trying to follow, but I'm so confused!**

I had forgotten she was taking the same poetry class as me, but on a different day.

JULIET: **I'm studying for it now. Wanna meet in a few and study?**

KRISTIN: **I love you! Yes!!!**

I went to my room, grabbed my books, and headed over to Kristin's apartment.

"Seriously though, what is all of this?" She had a visibly disgusted look on her face. "How am I supposed to know what any of this actually means? I can't figure out any of the emotions from these lines!"

I understood what she meant and laughed at how frustrated she was getting. I was laying on my stomach on the couch while Ana was on the floor, lying on her back with a pillow and blanket under her. Kristin was sitting upright in a chair she pulled over.

"Okay, so the whole *Io* aspect of the poem is just the author trying to find himself through his adolescence. The *Io* refers to his soul and body together." I reached over to her, showing her the excerpts in my copy of the book.

"No, way too complicated for me." Kristin laughed, taking some chips from the bowl and munching on them. "I'm more of a what is x if a equals the sum of c and d. I can't do this." She grabbed her book again to keep reading.

My phone vibrated with a message from Matt and I sent him a quick picture of us studying. He promised he wouldn't bother us, but he did mention that I looked like a cute nerd reading my book.

"Juliet, why are you blushing?" Ana said, looking up at me.

"No, Matt just said I looked cute studying."

"Oooh, Matt. Come over Matt because I want to kiss you." Ana said in a joking way, mocking me. I threw a pillow at her.

"This is impossible. Juliet, what does he mean here?" I looked over to see Kristin's eyebrows knitted together and the corners of her mouth turned down. I moved down to the floor next to her, grabbed her book, and put an arm around her.

"We got this, Kristin. Let's break it down. The poet has lost his sense of self in a metaphysical way, but also in an artistic way. Here he is talking about trying to find out what his *Io* represents." I pointed out some passages to her, showed her the notes I took, and let her copy them.

"Okay, that makes more sense. You should be the one explaining it in front of the classroom. You literally did that better in 10 minutes than the professor ever has in class!"

I thanked her and then felt proud of myself. I was always so nervous to teach back home in front of students. But, maybe I actually *can* do this.

When I went back home that night, I found Elisa in the kitchen with a book opened in front of her. She looked up from her book and her expression seemed happier than normal.

"Are you excited for Friday?" She asked, not even giving me a chance to walk fully into the room.

"Definitely, it sounds like it's going to be so much fun. I can't wait to eat all of the food."

I didn't want to mention that I couldn't stay the whole night since she was in a good mood and I didn't know how she would react. I hoped that the barbecue would end before the party so there was no need for me to worry about letting anyone down.

"I'm also excited to make the tiramisù. My mom adds a bit of Baileys in her cream when she makes it." I said, letting her in on a big family secret we had on our version of it.

"Wow, that sounds like it would be really good!" She almost sounded surprised. "Let's make sure we get some when we go shopping on Thursday."

We went to bed early, chatting about what life was like when we were both in high school. Elisa was fascinated to find out how many sports and clubs my high school offered and wanted to hear what a typical day was like. She explained what school was like for her, a lot of studying and speaking exams in front of the class that made me shudder just imagining them. She talked about how much pressure she had from her family to make sure she went to college even though a lot of people don't graduate from it.

"Honestly, that sounds impossible, a lot of people go to college in the U.S. because it is almost a given." My classes at home were definitely challenging, but I wondered what it would be like to have grown up here in this type of education system.

"Many universities here have different classes just for foreigners because it is difficult to learn anything in a language that's not your native one. You should be proud that you can keep up with these classes." Elisa said, giving me what was maybe my first compliment ever from her.

I felt a little better after I thought about it and she was right. Many colleges had different programs for foreign exchange students, but Prof. Rossi warned us that we would take classes alongside other Italians. We didn't think much of it until we realized what it actually meant.

After an hour of talking, we both said goodnight and turned off the lights. I slipped into bed, pulled the covers over me, and a huge smile spread across my face as I imagined how much fun Friday would be. For some reason, I wasn't anxious at all about the party, like I had been at Binghamton or even at Matt's. I felt comfortable with all of them, almost as if I'd known them a lot longer than just the small time I've been here.

* * *

ELISA: **Don't take the bus home, we're all meeting here after classes.**

I was finishing up my last class and saw the text from Elisa with a link to where the grocery store was on Google Maps.

I was looking forward to seeing what a big supermarket looked like in Italy. Up to this point, I was getting all of my groceries at the little corner shop just past our bus stop and became friendly with Ivana and Bruno, the owners.

I waved to Elisa as I saw her, Marcello, and Luca, all together, walking towards our meeting point.

"*Ciao*, Juliet," Marcello said, with Luca echoing hello as well.

Elisa was on her phone texting. "Okay," she said, looking up at us. "Giacomo is coming in his car and Pietro is driving his too so we can all drive back with the groceries together. Pietro is finding a spot now so we can meet him at IperFamila." Elisa said this mostly to me and then translated it to the others.

We were pretty close to the supermarket, so we decided to walk the way there and we saw Pietro at the entrance waiting for us.

"*Aspettiamo Giacomo.*" He said, telling us to wait for him before we enter.

A few minutes later, Giacomo showed up smiling. I never would have thought going food shopping with friends in a supermarket would be the highlight of the day.

As we were loading the cart, I noticed the supermarket wasn't much different from the ones back home. The only real difference was the euro symbol next to all of the prices and a few products that I had not seen back home. The boys picked up various items to take pictures with, making me laugh uncontrollably. We must have looked insane to all of the other people there who were just trying to get their grocery shopping done but we didn't care. I took a picture of us all together and decided to post it on my Instagram.

"Oh, look, they have Baileys!" Elisa said, picking up a bottle and putting it in the cart.

Giacomo gave both of us a look and Elisa and I turned and decided to ignore him, keeping it our secret. We picked out four different varieties of potato chips, including a ketchup flavor which

I definitely had to try, and a few bottles of *aranciata*, orange soda, which was my personal favorite. At the checkout, Luca paid and we all split the bill into equal shares.

"Okay, *andiamo a casa!*" Elisa exclaimed as we followed Giacomo and Luca to his car. Pietro took Marcello home in his smaller car.

I climbed into the backseat of Giacomo's dark blue Alfa Romeo Stelvio. It was my dad's favorite Italian car brand. My dad was thrilled when Alfa Romeo finally came to the U.S. so he could buy one for himself. Luca and Giacomo loaded the bags in the trunk and Elisa joined me in the backseat.

"*Andiamo, ragazzi!*" Giacomo said, as he climbed into the driver's seat and started the car. Luca got into the passenger's seat, ducking a bit to get in, and we headed off back to the apartments.

"Why don't you drive your car to classes?" I asked Giacomo while we were at a traffic light, realizing that I always saw him take the bus to the city.

"It's actually very hard and expensive to find parking during the day near my classes, so the bus is much easier." He was looking at me through the rearview mirror.

"Giacomo, how did you get even better at English in only a week!" He didn't hesitate as much when he spoke this time.

"I told you, I studied the whole week when I was home." I could see his eyes crinkling while still looking at me through the mirror. I smiled back at him and then looked over at Elisa who had a confused expression on her face.

"*Hai studiato l'inglese, Giacomo?*" Elisa asked Giacomo in Italian if he studied English, her eyebrows raised.

He responded back in Italian while looking at the road, explaining how he studied from his old high school English books and practiced with some apps on his phone.

Elisa nodded her head, her lips pressed tightly together. She picked up her phone and started scrolling through her feeds.

I stared out of the window for the rest of the car ride, enjoying the distant view of the Prealps in the background. They were still covered with some snow.

My phone pinged and I noticed a text from Matt asking what I was doing in a supermarket posting pictures. I wrote him back explaining. I noticed that the three dots kept flashing as a response, but then would stop as I kept waiting for his reply. After a few minutes, he finally wrote me back.

MATT: **So, what time do you think you will come to my party?**

JULIET: **10? I'm not exactly sure. I haven't told them yet since I don't want them to think I'm ditching them at the first party they throw.**

...

More minutes passed, the dots flashing and then stopping, until I finally got a reply.

MATT: **Ok. I'll see you tomorrow then.**

The last message made me feel a little bit uneasy. It was so short for all of that time he spent waiting to reply back. Was he upset that I was still going to the barbecue? He seemed content with the plan I came up with, so why did his text seem so short? I decided to let it be and not thought much of it for the rest of the car ride until we got home.

Giacomo drove up to our apartment building and found a spot right near the door. Pietro pulled up right after us with Marcello jumping out and opening the trunk to grab the grocery bags.

Me and Elisa went to our apartment to put away the stuff we

bought for the tiramisù and then headed back to the guys' apartment. When we got back there, I looked over to see Giacomo and Pietro discussing how they should set up the party. He looked away from Pietro for a second and met my eyes.

"Juliet, can you come here? I want to show you the outside." Giacomo called for me, gesturing for me to follow him and Pietro.

We went out the balcony doors. I never realized how nice their set up was. They were on the first floor so their balcony wrapped around the whole side of the building to the back. They had a small volleyball net set up in the back and a little grill off to the side.

"Wow! It's so big back here!"

Pietro asked Giacomo in Italian how many chairs and tables they would need and if they had enough. Elisa had stepped outside after us, her face puzzled.

"What are you doing outside?"

"The boys are figuring out what we need and Giacomo wanted to show me back here. I never realized they had all of this space here."

Elisa nodded her head at me with her lips pursed, as if she wasn't trusting what I had just said.

I hoped she wasn't about to get moody again. I didn't know what set her off this time. It was starting to frustrate me that someone could go from being friendly one minute to cold the next. I gave her a quick smile, excused myself, and joined the rest of the guys inside who were talking about some soccer games that they recently watched.

"Alright, *buona notte!*" I shouted over the commotion of them arguing about which soccer team was stronger this season and why.

"Oh, *buona notte*, Juliet." Marcello turned to respond to me, the only one who apparently heard me. I texted Elisa that I was going upstairs to start making the coffee for the tiramisù and asked her to say goodnight to Giacomo and Pietro for me too. She responded right away, saying *okay*. I let out a sigh and went straight to the apartment.

I found all of the ingredients for the tiramisù, started the big espresso pot, and cracked the eggs to separate them. I figured I would get a head start before Elisa came up and we would finish the rest together.

A half-hour later she still hadn't come up, so I decided to finish making it myself. The longer the tiramisù was in the fridge, the more flavorful it became. I whipped up the egg whites, mixed the yolks with the mascarpone cheese and sugar, and added Bailey's cream, giving it the right kick.

My mom and I discovered this hack once by accident when we ran out of the traditional liquor we usually used and swapped it out for Baileys.

I started dipping the ladyfingers into the espresso when the door opened, and Elisa walked in.

"I thought we were doing it together." She huffed, looking upset.

"I texted you, but you didn't respond. It was getting late and I was afraid I would be too tired to help later. I'm sorry."

"No, it's fine. Here, at least I will finish this part up." She took the cookies from me and dipped them into the espresso. "Did you add sugar to the coffee?" She asked me, taking a sip of the espresso mixture as if she wouldn't trust my answer anyway.

"Yeah, and I put some milk in too. My mom says it tones the espresso flavor down a bit."

She nodded her head as she took a sip of the espresso and then continued to dip and place the cookies in the tray. I continued making the cream, folding the egg whites gently into the mascarpone mixture so we could pour half of it on the layer of cookies when Elisa was done. Elisa added another layer of cookies and we poured the rest of the mascarpone cream on top and grated some chocolate for a finishing touch.

"Look at us!" Elisa said, marveling at how good the tiramisù looked. She covered it with foil and put it in the fridge carefully. We both were exhausted by that point and decided to head to bed.

I laid down on my bed, the blanket still under me, and grabbed my phone to text Kristin and Ana.

KRISTIN: **Are you going to Matt's?**

JULIET: **Yeah, but around 10. The guys here are planning a bbq so I'll come after their party finishes.**

ANA: **Can't wait!**

I decided to text Matt too after with a simple *buona notte*. He texted back right away saying good night with a hug emoji. It was definitely a better response than before. I put in my earbuds to listen to Laura Pausini. My mixed emotions were making it difficult to sleep. I wanted to keep texting Matt, but I couldn't read his feelings through the text. I forced my eyes shut, and after a few songs, I finally closed my eyes and relaxed my body into sleep.

14

Quattordici

Scoprire (v)= to discover; to find out

I woke up smiling on Friday. I got my usual fix of espresso so that I would be more alert throughout the day and did some readings for my classes. In our Italian class, I sat in my usual seat with Jess and Matt and noticed he was definitely quieter than usual. He stole my pencil only once when his fell on the floor, and I glared at him grabbing another from my bag. His mouth turned up to a smile from the side, and he tapped the pencil on his desk as if to torment me further. I let out a chuckle, and I went back to taking notes.

"Wow, Matt, besides stealing my pencil, you were pretty focused today." I said, complimenting him as we walked out of class.

"I'm not that bad." He joked back.

We walked towards the bus stop and got on together when my phone vibrated with a text.

GIACOMO: **Ok, what is buffalo chicken and why do you put it on pizza?**

I smiled and chuckled softly to myself as I texted him back explaining what it was. Matt looked over with a quizzical expression and looked at my phone as I typed a message back.

"Let's see what Juliet finds so funny." He said, peering over my shoulder to look at my phone.

I startled, turning my head and seeing his face over my shoulder reading my text to Giacomo.

"So, you are texting Giacomo?" He asked, his lips closed into a small smile and his eyes narrowing slightly. I couldn't tell if he was teasing me or if he was a little mad.

"Yeah, we are comparing New York pizza toppings to Italian ones and seeing which are weirder."

"Okay. I see. Keep texting Giacomo about pizza flavors." I felt like he was judging me.

I put down my phone and asked Jess how classes were to change the subject. Matt just listened to her talk but didn't say anything, and a feeling of uneasiness crept up as I didn't know what was going through his mind.

"Where are my texts about pizza?" He asked after a little while, lightly touching my arm.

I opened my mouth to say something but wasn't really sure what. His expression softened as he stared back at me, and his thumb gently touched my arm now, creating a soft electrical current between us.

I looked down to the ground and smiled. I knew Jess was staring at us taking in this whole scene so I stepped back, blush creeping up my cheeks, not sure why I was feeling vulnerable.

"So tonight is going to be fun right?" I said, locking eyes with him again.

"I'll be waiting for you."

We reached our stop and got off. Halfway to our apartments, Matt gently grabbed my hand to stop me.

"Are you sure you are coming tonight?"

"Yes, I promise. I just can't ditch them right away. They've been planning all week for this." He let go of my hand and we continued walking.

"Okay, I'll see you tonight." He walked up to his building and turned around when he reached the door, giving me a quick wave before heading inside.

The mix of emotions I was feeling was quickly replaced when I entered the building. Both Giacomo and their neighbor's doors were opened and the guys were all trying to fit a table through them. I shook my head and let out a chuckle at the scene.

"*Mamma mia!*" Marcello exclaimed, pretending to wipe his forehead in an exaggerated way after they finally set it down in Giacomo's apartment.

"Need help?" I asked.

"*Prendi le sedie con* Pietro." Marcello said, asking me to go get chairs. He then started pulling the table across the kitchen towards the balcony.

"Come over around seven." Giacomo said in a strained voice, now lifting the table to move it over the lip of the balcony door. I said bye to all of them and skipped up the stairs.

Elisa was already in the apartment, scrolling through her phone. Her jet-black hair was shiny and pin-straight, and she was wearing a light pink sweater that hung off one shoulder and black high-waisted skinny jeans. She wore long skinny earrings with a little diamond on the end, and a light pink lip gloss that matched her shirt. She usually put on that much makeup, but today she lined her eyes and put on mascara.

"Hey, Elisa." I said, "You look so pretty today!" She batted her eyes back playfully and thanked me.

"What are you wearing?" She asked, with a face that read *I hope not that.*

"Honestly, I don't know yet. I'm not really sure how I should dress." I said.

"Let's see what you have." She got up from the chair and headed over to our room. Scanning through my closet, she took in everything I have and shook her head at most of them. She kept going through until she suddenly stopped and pulled something out.

"Oooh, I like this." It was my favorite blue sweater, just the right thickness and softness, not too elegant, but pretty enough to wear out at night. "Wear this with your white jeans." She handed me the sweater.

The weather was perfect these last few days, around mid 60's during the day and still in the 50's at night. We would probably need a light jacket if we stood out later, but for now, this sweater was perfect. I got dressed and took my time with my makeup, placing my phone against the backsplash of the bathroom sink and watching a tutorial.

I followed along, pausing in between the steps to make sure I lined my eyes correctly and used the right brushes to add some shine to the inner part of my lids and create a more dramatic effect on the rest. I dusted the bronzing powder on my face and highlighted the areas right above my cheekbones after I applied blush. I cleaned my eyebrows up, shaping them and filling them in. I played with my hair seeing what style I would put it in, and decided I would let it loose, curling a few pieces just to give it more volume. When I was done, I looked down at my phone to see it was a little after seven.

Elisa smiled at me when I came out and said I looked pretty too. She grabbed the tiramisù from the fridge and we walked down the stairs together, ready for the party.

I felt confident and had waited for this night the whole week, and couldn't wait to just relax with friends and have fun.

When we reached the apartment, Giacomo was next to the speakers adjusting the volume.

"I love this song!" I exclaimed, recognizing it from one that I had heard a few times while here. Giacomo turned around and stopped and stared at both of us.

"Che belle ragazze!" He declared, a smile forming as he complimented that we were both beautiful.

"Grazie." We said in unison, smiling at each other. Giacomo went back to adjusting the volume, and Luca was already outside grilling. Marcello was setting the tables while Pietro filled up some bowls with chips.

"Okay, what can we do to help?" I offered, after putting the tiramisù in the fridge. Pietro handed me a bowl of chips and I put it on the table and Elisa found the napkins and paper plates to set.

"Luca, everything smells amazing!" I said, patting him on his back. He shot up straight as I touched him.

"Thank you! Hope you came hungry." Elisa started talking to him in Italian and I left them to have their conversation.

The drinks were already out on the table. Pietro came up with the idea to toast the evening with our first drink. They decided on a spritz, with prosecco and Campari which reminded me of Venice and Matt. I checked my phone and saw no messages from him but didn't want to bother him since he was probably getting ready for the party. We brought our glasses together and I was about to drink when Giacomo interjected.

"Wait, Juliet. In Italy you first, um...how do you say *cin?*" Giacomo started to say but then Elisa helped him by adding the words *cheers.* "Yes, you say cheers, then look each other in the eyes, then touch the glass to the table before drinking."

I was still confused, but then he showed me what to do. I

followed along as we all yelled *cin* again, this time looking at each other in our eyes, clinking the glasses to the table, and then taking a sip. Since I didn't normally drink, my tolerance was very low. After a few sips, I already felt a little bit lighter. I finished it up and tried the ketchup potato chips. They reminded me of barbeque-flavored chips back home. Marcello started imitating all of us and we were dying since his impressions were spot on. Luca finished grilling up some of the food and we passed around plates before sitting down to eat. Giacomo and Pietro took out all of the sides and we filled our plates until there was no room left. I looked down at my plate and tried to make room between the chickpea salad, steak, and roasted potatoes, so I could add the zucchini on top of everything. I couldn't believe how everything tasted. I needed to suggest a party like this when I got home with my friends.

We continued to drink, laughing at Pietro who was telling us a story about how he went to say hi to a cute girl in his class but ended up tripping and knocking her to the floor. I noticed my cheeks were getting warmer and my body was starting to relax more. Everything was so funny. Even Elisa was laughing so hard at one point there were tears in her eyes which then made everyone else laugh harder. Luca started teasing Elisa by throwing some chickpeas at her when she wasn't looking. She pretended to be mad and acted like she didn't notice it, but then collected all of them and threw them right back at him.

"Karaoke time!" Marcello yelled, calling us to gather in front of the speaker as he put on some of their favorite Italian songs. They made sure I knew the lyrics so I could join in. I took my camera out and recorded us singing since I was sure it was something I would definitely want to remember.

Pietro got his guitar and started playing a song outside that had a beautiful melody to it that made everyone quiet down and sit beside him to listen. I sat down next to Marcello and Giacomo took a seat beside me.

"This is a good song." Giacomo whispered. "It's a song by Ultimo. I don't think many Americans know this singer, but he is really popular here in Italy."

I tried to imagine the words to the song as Pietro kept strumming the notes and felt them touch my core, making me feel warm from the inside out. I swayed along to each of the delicate notes and felt the syncopations of my heart align with the methodic rhythm.

I pulled out my phone to add it to my nighttime playlist and saw the screen light up. It was 10:15. We still didn't even have dessert yet. I debated whether or not I should text Matt and decided not to, since it would be easier to explain in person when I saw him. I was getting anxious and didn't want to leave before dessert.

"Drink this," Marcello said, noticing that I had been tapping my foot nervously. "My father always tells me to drink this before I take a test. Make sure you drink it all at once."

I didn't think twice and threw it into the back of my mouth. It felt like I swallowed fire.

"What was that!" I shouted, fanning my mouth.

"That was my father's *grappa*. Strong, right?" Marcello added, laughing at my reaction.

I nodded my head and went to pour aranciata in a glass and drank all of it when I heard my phone ping. I looked down to see a message from Kristin with a picture attached to it.

My heart stopped. I felt my head swirl and I grabbed onto a chair to hold myself steady. There was a picture of Matt, his back to the camera, making out with a girl with blond hair.

KRISTIN: **I am so sorry, but I thought you should know. I saw them go into his bedroom and close the door. Are you still at the bbq? Do you want us to come meet you?**

I sat down against the wall of the apartment building and slumped down. We weren't officially together so why was it bothering me so much? Was this what Kristin had warned me about? He obviously just wanted to hook up. Anger built up inside of me as I realized that all of this time he was just toying with me. I shook my head, angry that I fell for it. I actually believed he had real feelings for me, especially when we were on the train and holding hands. I thought tonight would have changed things in a different way when I went to his party. I was hesitant to kiss him back that night in Venice on the bed because I didn't want to change what we had, but now I felt like it had changed anyway.

I texted Kristin back that I would be fine, but I wasn't going to go to the party tonight. She agreed that it was for the best and that if I wanted company, she would get Ana and come and visit me. I turned off my phone and put it away. Giacomo saw me leaning against the wall and asked what was wrong.

"Nothing. Well, I'm confused. I thought someone wanted one thing, but instead, they wanted something completely different." I said, not wanting to reveal exactly what happened. He nodded his head as if he understood and brought me a piece of the tiramisù I made.

"Well, if it makes anything better," he put his hand on my shoulder and looked into my eyes, "you make the best tiramisù I have ever tasted."

"But Elisa and I both made it."

"No, Juliet. Elisa does not make tiramisù like this. This was you, I know it was."

I didn't want to argue, since he was kind of right. She just dipped the cookies in the espresso, but I put all of the ingredients together and added some special touches. I took a bite of the tiramisù and felt the sweet, creamy flavors melt on my tongue. At least that temporarily made me feel better. Giacomo still sat next to me as we both leaned against the wall, listening to Pietro strum another song on his guitar, while we ate our tiramisù.

"Now this is my absolute favorite song," Giacomo said, still holding the tiramisù plate in one hand and pointing with his fork towards Pietro.

I listened and closed my eyes. I never heard this song, but the sad melody was helping settle the uneasy feelings that were still left in me.

"You really like this song," Giacomo said, watching me sway along.

"I do, what is it?" I answered, still with my eyes closed and head against the wall.

"It's called *I Tuoi Particolari*, by that same singer, Ultimo. He has concerts all of the time all over Italy. We should go to one." Giacomo asked.

I opened my eyes and turned to look at him. "I would love that. Pietro is an amazing guitar player."

"Now try this." I looked up to see Marcello holding a small, yellow bottle in one hand while reaching out towards me with the other that had a small glass filled with the same yellow liquid. "*Limoncello*." He said, continuing to offer me the drink.

"Is this as strong as the *grappa*?" I asked him, a small smile forming on my face, I was still tipsy from the drinks before.

"No, this is only made with lemons, sugar, some alcohol, and *crema* inside, a bit of cream. It's very sweet. You will like it." He gestured that I should take the drink.

I reached for the drink and he poured another two glasses, one for himself and one for Giacomo, and we all raised them together and drank them in one shot.

"Wow, it's still strong, but good! There is definitely more than just *some* alcohol." I said.

"*Cosa bevete?*" Elisa came up to us, curious about what we were drinking. I hadn't spent too much time with her the whole barbecue since she was teasing Luca most of the night.

"Something strong." I answered, laughing and noticing that my head was definitely a little bit more than tipsy. "But I think I am done for tonight." I tried to stand up slowly, with my hands pressed against the wall for support.

Giacomo got up and held my arm so I wouldn't fall down. I noticed Elisa stared at Giacomo and then back at me with a somewhat icy glare, but I was too caught up in the night to even care about it. I looked over at Giacomo and thanked him and said I was heading to bed.

"Nooo, Juliet, stay a little more. Please?" His eyes pleaded.

"Okay."

I didn't want to be alone with all of the feelings I was weeding through. I went to the kitchen, got a glass of water, and turned on my phone to see if anyone texted.

My phone vibrated a few times and I saw a group text from Jess and Valentina.

JESS: **Call me.**

VALENTINA: **Juliet, are you coming here? The party is not that much fun. You should stay at the bbq.**

JULIET: **Kristin sent me a pic. I already know.**

JESS: **Do you want us to come by you?**

VALENTINA: **If you want to talk, we are here for you.**

I knew I had to stop feeling sad about this. We weren't dating and literally didn't even kiss. He didn't know if I liked him, so why am I getting all hung up on this?

JULIET: **Thank you but I am okay. He can kiss whoever he wants...**

I put my phone down and walked over to the others. They were now watching Marcello entertain them again with another imitation. I joined in, laughing with them, and Giacomo looked over at me and smiled, probably happy that I wasn't in such a sad mood like before.

Marcello continued by pretending to do a strip tease and then Luca came from behind and actually pulled down his pants. I could tell that the alcohol made him even bolder than he usually was and he didn't seem to care. We were all hysterical at that point with tears in our eyes, watching Marcello in his underwear and shirt on top of the table. He took off his shirt, swung it above his head a few times, and then proceeded to grab Pietro's guitar and pretended to rock with it.

"This is for you, Juliet! I am the naked cowboy from New York!" He yelled and continued to strum random notes in an exaggerated fashion.

At that point, we were all doubled down in laughter, trying to catch our breath. Marcello went on for a few minutes more, then cursed in Italian that it was too cold, and found his clothes to put back on. He took out his bottle of *limoncello* again, poured us all another glass, and we cheered and drank together. This was exactly what I needed. I looked around at all of my friends, grateful to have them at this moment. I caught Elisa, holding on to Luca's arm and whispering something in his ear. He smiled at her and whispered something back. I noticed her openly flirting with him a lot tonight.

They walked over to the side of the building together, out of every-one's eyesight.

Marcello started to calm down, probably since it was getting late and Pietro started cleaning up with Giacomo. I walked over to help them.

"Hai visto Elisa e Luca?" Pietro said, asking if we saw them both head into privacy on the side of the building.

"I told Luca to be careful, but he doesn't listen," Giacomo said.

We continued to put the chairs back inside, swept up all of the mess, and carried the table back. I decided it was time to head to my apartment and thanked them for the fun night.

"I'm sorry you were sad before Juliet, *ma sembri più felice adesso."* He finished saying in Italian that I seemed happier now.

"Tonight was a lot of fun, I'm glad I stayed," I told him. He smiled and gently squeezed my arm.

"I will see you on Monday. I am going back home early tomorrow morning."

I found Marcello passed out on a chair by the door and whis-pered good night to him so I wouldn't wake him up.

15

⧼❀⧽

Quindici

Riflettere (v)= to reflect

The next morning was definitely a different story. I was slightly hungover from the drinks and the hole in my stomach returned. The first image that popped in my head was the picture Kristin sent me last night. Then I started imagining what happened in his room. It felt like a fist wrapped around my stomach and grabbed hold of my insides. I couldn't stop myself from thinking of him hooking up with the other girl. I turned on my phone to face whatever texts there might be, only to find one from Ana.

ANA: **We are coming over to pick you up at 11am. Take a shower, get dressed, we are going shopping!**

I smiled. A shower was probably the best thing for my pounding headache anyway. Elisa was still snoring in her bed. I was asleep by the time she came upstairs last night so I wasn't sure what time she actually came home. I tip-toed in the room, gathered my stuff, and headed to the shower.

The heat woke me up and I kept turning the hot water nozzle more and more to make sure it stayed nice and warm. The picture of Matt and the girl kept flashing in my mind but I tried to drown them out instead with memories from last night. I scrubbed my whole body, made a mental note to buy more body wash since mine was almost done, and towel-dried my hair after stepping out.

I took a deep breath, let it out slowly, and wiped the fogged mirror. My eyes had dark circles under them. I put my hair back in a braid, got dressed, and headed out into the kitchen to see it was almost 11. I quickly grabbed a granola bar to eat and took some Advil, washing it down with water. I stood by the sink, drinking water until I heard Kristin and Ana knock on the door.

"Are you okay?" Kristin asked, stepping forward and giving me a hug. Ana joined us and we stood like that for a few seconds.

"I'm fine actually," I said, trying to convince myself. Maybe if I said it enough it would be true.

"I mean, it's not like we were together or anything. And like you said, maybe he was never looking for anything serious, so it's better this way." I said. They glanced at each other and nodded to me.

"Okay then, Juliet. We are too busy anyways to worry about boys because we are going to the biggest mall in this area! So get ready to shop!" Ana held both of my shoulders, shaking them, trying to pump me up too.

We got on a bus that led us into the city. Kristin said she already mapped out exactly where we needed to go. I started getting excited for a little retail therapy, it always soothed the soul.

"So, your choice, Juliet." Kristin started, "You can either talk to us about it and we can tell you everything, or we can forget about it and talk about shopping for today."

I thought about it for a second, but I just wanted to shop at a mall in Italy with my two good friends. "No, I don't want to know anything." Kristin nodded happily and Ana commended my choice as well.

We started to talk about what we were going to buy. Since the weather was getting warmer we should start looking for summery clothing. The bus let us off at the entrances of the mall, the exterior was very modern, which made sense since Kristin had mentioned it was built only a few years ago. The mall was two floors and had a rectangular shape, with stores lined around the outside and an opening in the center that looked down to the main level. I spotted a *profumeria* and decided to treat myself to a new scent.

"You know what, I need a fresh start, a new me!" I proclaimed out loud. I grabbed Kristin and Ana's hands and we pranced into the shop.

We sampled some of the perfumes before a shop assistant came up to us. *"Avete bisogno?"* She asked if we needed help, her face was void of any emotion while her arms were crossed in front of her. Her black hair was pulled back into a sleek bun and her outfit reminded me of something I might see a lawyer in New York City wearing— a black pencil skirt and wine-colored cardigan. I started to speak to her in Italian, explaining I was looking for a new scent, but she switched to English, probably detecting my accent when answering me.

"So, what do you want to do with this perfume?" She asked while leading me to a different section of perfumes on display. I was confused and trying to think of a response when she continued.

"Do you want to seem glamorous? Sophisticated? Professional? Do you want a certain boy to notice you?" She had one eyebrow slightly raised. She was a few inches taller than me thanks to her extremely high-heeled shoes.

"All of the above?" I answered when I couldn't think of a

response. She stared at me for a few seconds with her arms crossed in front and one hand under her chin.

"Okay, I know." She said, now pointing with her index finger in the air and directing me to the other side of the store. Kristin and Ana were still where they were before, trying more samples of perfumes.

"*Questo.*" She said, now switching to Italian to tell me this was the one. She sprayed some lightly on my wrist and I brought it to my nose.

"*È perfetto!*" I exclaimed, shocked how she could pick the right one for me on the first try.

"Would you like to try a lipstick too?" She asked, switching back to English. "I know the perfect one for your shade."

"Sure," I said. New lipstick always makes a girl feel better.

She looked through the different colors and chose a red shade and explained that the orange undertone would be perfect for me. She applied some with a q-tip on my lips and handed me a mirror to see.

"Wow, that *is* a nice shade!"

I moved my head from side to side while holding the mirror, admiring this bold new color for my lips.

"Do you have any body washes?" I asked, remembering that mine ran out.

She headed across the store and came back with a vanilla and patchouli-scented one. I thanked her again, gathered all of the new goodies in my arms, and went to the counter to pay.

"I love that lip color!" Ana said as we exited the store. "It's a nice fresh look."

It was only a little perfume and lipstick, but I felt good, definitely better than this morning. We stopped at another shop, this time trying on outfits and picking up some shirts and jeans.

"Okay, I have an idea," Ana said. "So one of my classmates told me that there is this bar in the city that is really nice and a lot of people our age hang out there on weekends. What if we go next Saturday?" Her eyes were pleading for us to say yes.

"Hmm, I guess so. I haven't really been out at night much since we got here." This new me was not going to say no to new, fun experiences. I had too much fun yesterday with the guys and Elisa to doubt myself again. Kristin looked over at me shocked but didn't say anything about it.

"We are going to have so much fun!" She looped her arm around mine and pulled me towards another shop.

We all bought a different pair of earrings. I opted for ones that were rose gold with a big sun-filled with tiny crystals on the post and a moon hanging from a chain that was connected to a heart. I was always afraid to buy anything bold, anything that would draw attention to me, but I put the earrings against my ear and smiled.

We passed by a little coffee stand and figured it was time for an espresso pause so we could sit. I had a few texts, one from Elisa that mentioned she was leaving for the weekend, and the others from Jess and Valentina.

VALENTINA: **Hey...just wondering what you were up to...**

JESS: **Let us know if you want company!**

I felt grateful that they were thinking of me, but I didn't want them to be sad for me. I was not going to let what happened last night ruin my time here.

JULIET: **Come to my apartment tomorrow and get ready to have lunch together, one that we are making!**

Jess wrote back right away, with five smiley face emojis, and

Valentina wrote back a few minutes later with a thumbs up. Still smiling, I started to put my phone in my bag when I noticed it vibrating. I picked up my phone, turned it over to the screen, and saw Matt's name lighting up.

I almost dropped it. My stomach sank and all of the dread from the night before came back. I was completely conflicted as I felt the vibrations from holding it in my hand. If I didn't answer, it would intensify the situation and I didn't want him to know he hurt me. I wanted to pretend I was fine.

If I answered and tried to talk normally, he would think everything was the same and we were still friends. I needed a few more minutes to think of what to do but didn't have them. Instead, I took a deep breath and pressed talk bringing my phone up to my ear.

"Hey." I said softly.

"Um, hi, Juliet. I uh, so, you didn't come to the party last night?"

"No, I wasn't feeling well so I decided to go back to my room," I said, a sort of halfway lie. I definitely hadn't felt well after what I saw, but I didn't want to bring it up.

"Oh, okay...are you home? I want to talk to you...and I ... I don't know, I guess I just wanted to see you." He stammered, not being able to express himself clearly.

I started getting angry at this point. What did he want to talk about? Tell me that he was sorry if I misunderstood something and that he kissed another girl? Sorry that he led me on all of this time? I decided to take a deep breath away from the phone as I covered the mouthpiece before I responded.

"No, actually I am at the mall with Kristin and Ana. I think we are staying late out here, so I don't know when I will be home." I said somewhat curtly, a little more difficult this time to hide my feelings.

"Okay. What about tomorrow? Listen, I just want to talk to you about something, but I need to do it in person." He added, with hope in his voice.

"I'm sorry, I have to go," I said, hanging up before he could say anything back and without also giving him a definite answer. I didn't want to talk to him. Not today and probably not even tomorrow. I know avoiding him was wrong, but I needed more time to think of how I should react.

"Was that Matt?" Kristin said, feeling the change in my mood.

I nodded silently, and she took me by my arms and lifted me out of my seat.

"Let's get some gelato." Ana said, smiling at me and dragging me along with them. I shuffled my feet to catch up. We walked to a little gelato stand that was a few shops down from the coffee place.

I ordered two ice cream flavors this time, chocolate and *stracciatella*, an Italian version of chocolate chip. I was acting exactly how people would after breakups, eating gallons of ice cream. Here I was too, trying to heal that pain that had opened up again, by scooping a huge spoonful of *stracciatella* in my mouth, but I was lucky enough to have Kristin and Ana by my side. We all sat there silently for a few minutes before Ana tapped my arm.

"Oh my God, don't look. But the guy with the dark blue pants and button-down shirt with brown hair is the guy I keep telling you guys about. The one with the smiles on the bus and the flirtatious looks." Ana said, in a loud whisper, glaring at us so we wouldn't look.

"But Ana, can I look?" I said, giggling when she even realized what she said didn't make sense.

"Yes, look, but don't make it obvious."

I was excited to see what he looked like so I casually turned, took a spoonful of my gelato and acted like I was just looking around. He seemed a few inches taller than me from where he was standing and his outfit seemed tailored, nothing baggy or hanging off of him.

His hair was cut short and neat and the way he was walking made it obvious that he must be an athlete. When he turned to the side, his expression seemed soft, and I could see why Ana had developed a crush on him.

"Oh, he's cute," Kristin said, nodding her head in a definite approval. "So what's the story with him?" She asked, now looking back at Ana.

"Well, we keep making eye contact whenever we are on the same bus or see each other out in the city. Our classes must be around the same time since we always see each other at the same time of day." She said, in between scoops. "But, every time I think he will say something, we just carry on and nothing happens. It's so frustrating! I need to just go up to him one day and talk but, I don't know. I get too sweaty." She threw her hands up in the air in an exaggerated way.

"Wait, who is that?" Kristin said, redirecting Ana's attention back to the boy. A tall, brown-haired girl walked up to him and gave him a big hug, and put her arm around him. They started laughing about something and then walked together down towards the opposite side of the mall.

"Of course...of *course* he has a pretty girlfriend." Ana muttered, "Okay, bad weekend for boys. Let's go girls, we need to get back."

We headed back home, a little quieter than we were on our way to the mall. I thanked them for taking me shopping since it helped me feel a little better.

"Text us if you are feeling lonely or just want some company." Kristin said as she hugged me goodbye before we entered our buildings. I gave Ana a hug too and walked up the stairs to my apartment.

16

Sedici

Fare la spesa = to go grocery shopping

The apartment was empty and I felt really alone for the first time in a while. I fought the urge to call Kristin again and ask her if they wanted to come over, but I was sure they wanted their space too. I put down my shopping bags in my room, took out my perfume and sprayed a little on, and then laid down on my bed, scrolling through the newsfeeds on my phone.

Matt didn't post anything from last night. I don't know why, but it made me angry. Angry at him, but more importantly myself. Things obviously happened last night and he must've had a good time. I knew that we were better off being friends, but I got attached anyway. He never even said he liked me or anything, it was just my mind getting ahead of itself and seeing things that were never actually there. In reality, he can kiss whoever he wants, it wasn't like we were dating. As I was holding my phone, my eyes went to my wrist to the bracelet he bought me. I still hadn't taken it off. Looking at it hurt even more so I took it off and placed it in my nightstand drawer.

I texted Jess and Valentina our plans for tomorrow and said we were going to cook a typical Italian dinner together. They responded and we settled on making homemade gnocchi with a meat sauce. Jess sent us a recipe for something called *torta rustica con spinaci* that would be a side dish. Valentina said she would be in charge of finding the dessert and sent us a recipe of a pie made with Nutella.

I was going to head out early the next day to buy everything before we met in my apartment to start cooking. I wanted to avoid going into their building and bumping into Matt. Since Elisa left, it also made a good excuse for them to come to me.

It started getting late and I wanted to lay down. I put my earbuds in and listened to Laura Pausini until I could fall asleep. As I searched through my playlist, the melody of the song that Pietro had played echoed in my ears and I wanted to find it. I tried to remember the name of it and typed in what I thought it was, but couldn't find anything. I looked at the time and figured it wasn't that late to text Giacomo.

JULIET: **Ciao, Giacomo...I'm sorry it's late, but what was the name of the song that Pietro was playing last night?**

Not even twenty seconds later, he replied.

GIACOMO: **Ciao, you can't sleep? :-) The singer is Ultimo, and that song you really loved is I Tuoi Particolari.**

I typed in the name, quickly found it, and added it to my playlist.

JULIET: **Grazie!**

GIACOMO: **Di niente...**

I wanted to talk more to Giacomo, but didn't know what else to say. I was about to put down my phone when it pinged again.

GIACOMO: **By the way, Elisa and Luca had a little fun last night.**

I immediately shot up and texted him back.

JULIET: **Wait, what happened?**

GIACOMO: **Ok, so don't say anything...but Luca said they kissed quite a bit.**

JULIET: **No way! They made out? This is big news! Are they dating? I had a feeling that something would happen...they are always flirting with each other...**

I was firing off messages at rapid speed back to him. I couldn't believe it finally happened.

GIACOMO: **Made out?**

I laughed to myself, realizing how American that expression must be.

JULIET: **It means passionate kissing, you know, more than just a peck.**

GIACOMO: **Oh! Luca said that Elisa did not respond to his texts today. I feel bad for him. He really likes Elisa, but she teases him a lot and I am not sure if she likes him.**

My heart fell for him. Why wouldn't she like him? He was so nice to her, they get along great, what would there not be to like?

JULIET: **I feel bad for Luca too. Maybe her phone is dead. Or maybe she's nervous about what happened and doesn't want to ruin their friendship?**

I felt like I knew about that a little too well lately.

GIACOMO: **You are too nice, Juliet. I don't know. I feel like she is leading him on.**

JULIET: **Leading him on? Giacomo, where did you learn that!!!**

I was proud of how he made no mistakes. I noticed my phone started ringing and saw Giacomo's name flash so I picked it up.

"Okay. *Stavo usando un traduttore per scrivere.*" Giacomo confessed as soon as I answered that he had been using a translating app to text me. He started laughing after that which made me start laughing too.

"And here I thought your English was perfect!" I said, smiling into the phone. We chatted more about how he thought that Elisa was just toying with Luca, but he couldn't understand why. He kept saying he didn't want to see his friend get hurt.

I remembered what Marcello told me. Elisa purposely flirted with Luca to get Giacomo jealous. But would she go that far? I didn't want to mention that to Giacomo and create more drama than there already was.

We switched subjects to what we were doing the next day, and I told him about my lunch date with Jess and Valentina and all of the food we were making.

"Homemade gnocchi?" Giacomo exclaimed after I told him. "Juliet, you need to make me dinner one day. Also, I want that tiramisù again. I told my mom about it, she wants to try it too." I was happy that Giacomo couldn't see me at this moment because my cheeks were heating up. He told my mom about my tiramisù?

"So how is she?" I asked, in a softer voice.

"Actually, we are waiting for an appointment with a new doctor. Hopefully, he will tell us what she has."

I heard his voice soften as well. I couldn't imagine how he felt not knowing what was going on. Even though my mom could annoy me from time to time, I would be lost without her. It made my heart break for Giacomo.

We talked a few minutes more before saying good night to each other. As I hung up, I was ready to sleep. I didn't need to listen to the song because talking to Giacomo relaxed me and put my mind at ease. I curled up in bed, hands under my pillow, and closed my eyes.

I woke up ready to take on the day. Jess and Valentina were meeting me early to go shopping for our lunch date. I felt bubbly walking next to them and talking about our plans for the day. The market has grown into a comforting place for me recently. I loved the colorful, fresh produce in baskets around the store, the smell of cheeses and meats hanging behind the counter and in the display case.

Bruno and Ivana, the owners, greeted us in Italian, remembering us from the past. Ivana was an older woman who looked like she always cooked fresh bread for her grandchildren and smiled with rosy cheeks. She wore a flowy, flowery dress and always had an apron hanging behind the counter. Her husband was a more serious man with a bushy dark mustache and a stout stature, he couldn't be more than five and a half feet tall, and wore the same white short-sleeve button-up shirt with airy tan slacks every time I saw him. Ivana helped us find what was on our list and insisted that we use a little butter in the sauce to bring out the flavors of the meat.

"*È un segreto!*" She said, winking while telling me it was a secret. I smiled and thanked her.

Back at the apartment, we put all of the ingredients out on the table. I put my phone down and we started reading the instructions for the Nutella pie. Jess crushed the cookies and mixed it with melted butter for the base. Valentina made the cream with vanilla and Nutella and poured it on top. I took out a piping bag that Elisa had, and with a very delicate hand, I circled the top, giving the cake a fancy edge.

"Jess, you peel the potatoes and I will cut them." Valentina directed, moving directly onto the next task and handing her the washed potatoes.

I started filling up a big pot with water and put it on the stove turning the gas up high. I was making my way over to Jess to help her with the potatoes when I heard a knock at the door. My heart immediately started racing and my palms were sweaty, I prayed that my nerves were for nothing and it wasn't who I thought it was. I grasped the door handle and slowly turned it.

There he was, hands in his pockets, shoulders shrugged up, and dressed in a white long-sleeved shirt and jeans. My heart stopped. I reminded myself to breathe and I looked back over at Jess and Valentina who stopped what they were doing to watch me open the door.

17

Diciassette

Parlare (v)= to talk

"Can I talk to you, Juliet?" He took one hand out of his pocket and ran it through his hair. He was nervously chewing on his lower lip, something he did before taking a test.

"Okay." I responded, trying not to watch his lips. They were the ones that drove this wedge between us. I stepped out into the hall and closed the door behind me.

"So," he started, looking down at the ground. "I know you know what happened at the party."

I tried to make my face as expressionless as possible, but it was hard. The picture of him lip locked with that girl polluted my memories. I tried my hardest to shove the image out of my mind and not think about what may have happened behind the confines of his room either.

"I just wanted to say this though," he continued when I didn't say anything, "I had way too many drinks waiting for you to show up, and..."

"You really don't have to explain anything." I interrupted. "Really. It's fine."

"Yeah, but, I want you to know nothing happened. I know it may not look that way, but I promise we didn't do more than kiss." He rubbed the back of his neck. "I don't want this to change what's between us."

"Nothing's changed, Matt. There was nothing to change. We're just *friends*. Always have been." It was hard to say that, but the more I did, the more I would believe it.

His eyes widened and I could tell I hit a soft spot. But I didn't care.

"Friends?"

"Yes, friends!" I didn't know why I was getting so angry. He comes here without an invitation, knocking on my door like a wounded puppy wanting to act like nothing's changed. But he was the one who messed it up. He couldn't have enough patience for me to show up to the party before he had to make out with some random girl.

"I'm glad you had fun." I continued. "Who you kiss is not my business. In fact, I am happy that you kissed someone!"

"Juliet, I..." He started to speak, but I interrupted him again.

"No, Matt. I am not looking for a relationship and you aren't either. We are here to have fun and that's it."

He looked down at my bare wrist. I rubbed it subconsciously feeling the absence of the bracelet.

"You're right Juliet, I don't know what I was thinking." His expression turned cold.

"I need to go back inside. 'Bye Matt." I didn't even give him a chance to respond before closing the door behind me.

I leaned my back against it, taking a breath. Frustration settled inside me in a way I'd never felt before. Matt was always the person who made me feel happy and light. I couldn't believe how much he hurt me from just a kiss.

I made eye contact with Jess and Valentina from across the room. They both looked sad for me but didn't say anything. After a few seconds, I opened the door a crack to see if he was still there, but he wasn't. He was gone.

"Juliet, he feels really bad," Jess said softly behind me. "He asked about you all day yesterday and begged us to talk to you. But we didn't want to interfere."

"I don't know why I let myself fall for him," I said.

"He really likes you, I don't think he ever wanted to just hook up." Valentina added.

"It's funny how he's open to you guys about how he feels but plays games with me! He only opens up about his feelings after he messes everything up." I couldn't believe how this happened. How could he be so immature? "If he really liked me he wouldn't have gotten drunk and made-out with the first girl he saw after I didn't show up right on time. He would have waited for me or texted me asking where I was." My anger was still bubbling beneath the surface but I knew I couldn't take it out on Jess and Valentina. I softened up a little bit, because it wasn't their fault. They just wanted to help.

"It just hurts," I said. "I was actually starting to fall for him and I thought it was mutual but I was afraid to kiss him because I didn't want to change the friendship we had. It didn't really matter though, because now it's ruined anyway."

This was the first time I was able to say how I felt to someone out loud. I felt a weight being lifted off my chest.

Jess came up to me and gave me a hug. She rested her head on my shoulder while squeezing me to her. Valentina came in too, wrapping her arms around both of us. We stood there for about 10 seconds before we heard the timer go off in the oven.

"Okay, the crostata is ready!" I said breaking away from them and walking to turn off the timer.

I needed to remember the new Juliet. The Juliet that's strong and won't let her feelings be played with. This Juliet would not let Matt ruin a day with my friends.

We all surrounded the oven, excited to see how it came out. As I opened it, we were instantly engulfed by the smell of Nutella that escaped from it. I grabbed the oven mitts, took it out, and we all high-fived each other at our first culinary success of the day.

"So, Jess, what are we going to do next?" Valentina asked, not as demanding as she usually was.

I was sure Valentina knew exactly what to do but wanted to give Jess a chance to take the wheel. I could see her waiting patiently for Jess to re-read the directions for the gnocchi so she could then tell us the next steps.

"We have to wait a few more minutes for the potatoes to boil, drain them, and then rice them," Jess said while grabbing a bowl and ricer.

Once the potatoes were done, we riced them into the bowl and measured out the flour and salt we needed. Jess mixed it all together and then we each broke off pieces, rolled them into a long snake-like tube, and cut it into small pieces.

"Now roll these pieces on the back of a fork. It says that this makes a ribbed surface so the sauce sticks better." Jess read.

Given some time between my conversation with Matt, I wondered if I was too abrupt with him. The hurt look on his face was one I never intended to give him, but at the moment it felt good that I did. I watched each gnocchi drop back on the table after I rolled them. I just wanted to feel the simplicity of making food with my hands and laughing with friends. I finished the last piece of gnocchi and we pushed it all to the side, getting ready to make the *torta rustica con spinaci*.

"Ok, let's get our pastry crust, mozzarella, spinach, potato, and onion ready. We need a pan to put the pastry crust on, and then we saute the spinach, potato, and onion together. We add an egg, chop up some mozzarella, put it all together, and pour it on the crust. Not bad at all!" Jess said.

We followed her lead as she reminded us what we needed to do and finished up our *torta rustica*. The sauce was next, I started by sauteing the onions and meat, and adding some spices in to make it tastier.

"Don't forget some butter!" Valentina said.

While that was cooking, we all sat down and I made them a spritz, which now became my cocktail of choice.

"How was yoga?" I asked Jess, remembering that she tried it out this week.

"I love it!" Her face was beaming. "I've gone three days this week so far with Jane. We get along so well."

"That's great! And how are classes, Valentina?" I said, turning towards her.

"You know, I dropped a class. It was too much. I couldn't keep up with everything and Matt was right in Venice. I am better as the more relaxed Valentina, the girl who doesn't need to plan every-thing. I can't promise I will change quickly, girls." She smiled and wagged her index finger to both of us. "But I promise that I'll try."

"We love you in every way, Valentina." Jess added, giving her a quick hug. "But, this relaxed Valentina is definitely more fun to hang out with!"

We laughed and I went to check on the sauce. The *torta rustica* was done, so I took it out and covered it to keep it warm. We grabbed a table cloth and silverware for the table and put on some Italian music to set the mood. We tried to play all of the songs that were popular now in Italy and sing along to them, but instead, we made total fools of ourselves, barely getting any words right. Once the sauce was done cooking, we boiled the gnocchi, drained them, and added the sauce.

"Ladies, we need to take a picture of this," I said, turning the camera towards us and smiling with all of the food in the background. I posted it to my page.

"This is amazing!" Valentina said in between fork fulls. The *torta rustica* turned out to be delicious and we made some espresso for our Nutella pie. I closed my eyes as the creamy and delicate taste of vanilla and Nutella landed on my tongue.

"That was perfect." I patted my stomach, content with everything we ate. "We should be proud."

"You know, I don't think I've ever done anything like that before. I was always afraid to cook and just bought everything already prepared. I'm glad we did this!" Jess said.

They stayed a little longer into the night and we watched a bunch of Italian TV. I thanked them again for being there for me.

"Of course, we will always be here for you," Jess said, giving me a hug. I walked them out, watching them go down the hall, and waved goodbye before they went down the stairs.

I went into my room and sat down on my bed against the headboard. That feeling of emptiness that took over my heart came back when the image of Matt standing at my door popped up as soon as they left. The internal push and pull that kept returning made it impossible to think clearly. On one hand, I wanted to hear Matt out. I wanted to see what he would say and maybe tell me it was a mistake. But then I thought about how easy it was for him to just kiss another girl after the weekend we spent together. I knew I needed advice so I took my phone out.

JULIET: **So...do you remember Matt? From my Italian class?**

...

DANIELLE: **Of course! The hottie that is obsessed with you.**

I let out a chuckle at her response. Exactly what I didn't need to hear.

JULIET: **Well, I thought we had something, but then he hooked up with another girl at a party. He came to me saying it was nothing, but I don't know. I mean, we were such good friends before, should I just let it be and stay friends?**

...

I waited a few minutes for her response.

DANIELLE: **Well, he's an ass to do that to you. You know what I always say, just do what feels right. If he really likes you, make him show it to you! You shouldn't have to question it.**

I let out my breath all in one huff after realizing I was holding it in.

JULIET: **You're right. Miss you!**

I put my phone down and headed to the bathroom. I took a shower with my new body wash, hoping that it would make me think clearly about what to do. The intensity of the patchouli mixed with vanilla enveloped my senses, without overpowering them. I finished showering, slipped into my pajamas, and went right into bed. I scrolled through my phone and noticed that Matt liked the picture that I posted before, and that I had a request from Giacomo to follow me. I accepted and requested to follow him as well. I was curious to see what his page looked like, so I clicked on his profile and started going through some of his pictures.

A part of me felt guilty prying into his personal life like this. But, it didn't stop me. I scrolled through to find pictures of him and his friends, some pictures of a cute, medium-sized brown dog, and some of his brothers and parents. His mom was a beautiful woman, with dark blonde hair and the same hazel eyes as Giacomo's. His dad was slightly taller, with mostly white hair and a face reminding me of an older version of Giacomo. I could see the resemblance between the brothers. They each had different characteristics from their parents.

One picture reminded me of the first picture I saw of him. He was facing sideways and smiling at something. I couldn't stop staring at the picture and his profile.

GIACOMO: **Are you finished looking at my pictures?**

I smiled and laughed to myself since he was probably doing the same with my profile.

JULIET: **Almost.**

GIACOMO: **Which is your favorite?**

JULIET: **This one.**

I attached a screenshot of his dog in a meadow, surrounded by wildflowers.

GIACOMO: **That one is my favorite, too.**

I was proud of my daring answers and I continued to stare again at the picture of him looking sideways. His hair was styled how it always was and he was wearing a t-shirt and jeans. I started thinking about the first time I saw his picture on Elisa's wall. An image flashed in my head when we went for a walk together and talked the whole time. It was silly of me to think something could happen with Giacomo, who lived 3,000 miles from me, when things didn't even work out with Matt who was only a 15-minute drive with light traffic. I put down my phone, not wanting to get caught up in any more of my feelings, and played Laura Pausini and Ultimo.

I woke up with instant dread. I had to go to Italian class and see Matt. My heart started to race thinking about it. I was walking towards my Italian class, the last class of the day, and tried calming myself down by breathing deeply through my nose and out of my mouth the whole way there. I finally reached the entrance of the building, went inside to the classroom, and found my usual seat, trying not to think about anything. Matt wasn't there and Jess walked through the door, just as class was starting.

I started getting worried and texted him to see where he was.

JULIET: **Are you coming to class today?**

He'd never missed class and I was honestly worried. I kept turning over my phone periodically to see if he responded, but he never did. Finally, more than 20 minutes later, I heard it vibrate on my desk.

MATT: **Busy. Lots of studying.**

My anxiety was instantly replaced with building anger after his short response. I kept thinking of all of the different things I wanted to write back to him. I honestly wanted to leave class now, go to his apartment and yell at him. Yell about how he played with my emotions, how he kissed someone else and then tried to apologize. I'd fallen for everything, I'd imagined being with him the night of his party, and thanked God Kristin had sent me that picture before anything serious happened.

Jess noticed I was not my usual self but, this time I didn't want to talk about it. I tried to smile and pretend that I was worried about all of the studying I had to do. We parted ways, saying goodbye as I took the bus back to the apartment.

Elisa was already there, getting dinner ready. She didn't look over at me when I walked in and kept turning her dinner on the stove and just said hi. Since I was still fuming from before, I definitely wasn't in the mood to be next to her, so I went straight to my room, took out all of the books I needed to catch up on, got my highlighter out, and started reading. Elisa walked in an hour later.

"Well, you don't look too happy." She stated, eyebrows raised and her arms crossed in front of her.

"I really don't want to talk about it," I said, not caring at this point if I replied too abruptly or if I wasn't polite. I was done trying to tiptoe around her. Why did I have to change myself so she wouldn't get mad at me?

"I am sorry, Juliet. I hope it's not about a boy, even though it usually always is. I think I made a mistake this time too, and I don't know what to do." She said.

I looked up and noticed she kept looking at her fingers and fidgeting in a nervous way.

"Do you want to talk?" I said, making room for her next to me.

"Honestly, yes." She grabbed her pillow from her bed to bring to mine. She sat on the edge and hugged her pillow to her chest. "You smell good." She said, leaning a little closer to me, noticing the new perfume I was wearing. "Well, anyway, I kissed Luca on Friday night, at the barbecue. I was drunk, he was making me laugh so much and it felt like it was the right thing to do." She was still fidgeting with her nails and looking down while hugging the pillow.

"So? What's wrong with that? Elisa, he is crazy about you! Do you see the way he looks at you?"

"I know he likes me. It's just that, I like someone else back home. Now I don't know what to say to Luca. I ignored his texts all weekend, and now it will be awkward when I see him." She looked up at me, and I could see worry in her face. She just got caught in the moment and kissed Luca.

"Elisa, I know you said you like someone else from back home, but I think you should give it a try with Luca. He's smart, funny, and good-looking. He makes you laugh, what more do you want?"

She didn't say anything for a minute but just looked at me with questioning eyes and her mouth pursed closed.

"Wow, Juliet." She finally said, in a sarcastic tone. "It sounds like you are very much team Luca." She continued to look at me, her mouth forming a half-smile while I tried to decipher what she meant by that.

I thought a bit before I responded. "Just follow your heart, and do what feels right. These answers don't always come from over-thinking and worrying. Sometimes you just have to wait and see."

She seemed more satisfied with that answer as she hopped off of my bed and went to the bathroom to get ready to sleep. I sat up in my bed, grabbed one of my books to keep studying when my phone vibrated with a message.

GIACOMO: **Look out your window, Juliet.**

I got up, walked across the room, opened the shutters, and looked down. There he was, on the patio, looking up at me, waving.

"So, is this a better way to chat?" I said, leaning over the window sill, smiling down at him. The sun had set, but there was still enough light outside where I could still see him.

"I never told you, but there was a picture I like of you." He said, still smiling up at me.

"Oh, what picture was that?" I asked, realizing I had done it in a little flirty tone. The wind was whipping my hair into my face so I tucked the strands behind my ears. He took out his phone and started typing something before looking up at me. My phone vibrated in my hand, and I saw the picture of me, holding the statue of Juliet's boob in Verona from almost a month ago.

I started laughing, my cheeks warm, and I was glad that he couldn't see that well from down below.

"Yeah, that was embarrassing." I said.

"Well, it's my favorite picture." He said, still smiling. I heard Elisa turn off the water.

"I have to go, *buona notte* Giacomo." I said.

"Good night, Juliet." He said before giving me one last smile and heading into his apartment.

I closed the shutters and window just as Elisa walked into the room, towel drying her hair, and her eyebrows pulled in together.

"Who were you talking to?" she asked, walking towards her bed.

"Oh, it was Giacomo. He was telling me something that Marcello did." I wasn't sure why I felt the need to lie but, I grabbed my stuff and headed off to the bathroom with a big smile still on my face.

18

Diciotto

Mi manchi= I miss you

The next few days were a bit of a blur. I met Jess and Valentina at the bar in between classes for espressos, chatting with Gianni about how the weather was warm for the middle of March. Elisa and I had been avoiding the guys' apartments because she was afraid of how she would act near Luca and I didn't feel comfortable going there alone. Matt showed up to our Italian class on Wednesday, right before class started, and was silent throughout. He said hi to me, but didn't act like himself at all. As soon as class was done, he told us he needed to meet his professor before his next class so he couldn't walk with us. I didn't know if he was telling the truth or making up an excuse, but I was glad he had at least shown up for class.

Elisa didn't mention Luca anymore and I never told her what happened with Matt. We had dinner together the next few nights and I finally felt as if I caught up with all of my studying.

I was taking the clothes out of the washer and hanging them up when I saw a text from Kristin.

KRISTIN: **Saturday, bar in the city. Dress hot! I want to see those new earrings and red lipstick on!**

I laughed at the text and sent back a thumbs up. I promised my-self I would go this time, convinced that it would be classier than the bars back home. I finished hanging the clothes and walked over to my closet, looking through it for an outfit to wear. I started to become excited, imagining what the bar would look like and how much fun I would have with Kristin and Ana.

***

"Wait, so if I'm not sure about something, I have to change how I conjugate the verb?" Jess whispered to me as the Italian teacher was going over the subjunctive mood.

I felt like my life was in the subjunctive mood where I was never sure of anything.

It was finally Friday and Matt was in Italian class, sitting in his usual seat right next to me. He looked over at me at the beginning of class and gave me a small smile, his eyes were definitely gentler than they'd been. I looked at him, giving him a small smile back, and hoped that this was the start of a new beginning for us.

After class, Jess excused herself, saying she needed to meet someone, even though I was sure she didn't. She just wanted us to talk alone.

We walked silently for a little while when he stopped. I turned around to him.

"I miss you, Juliet. I know it was me, and it was all my fault, but I really miss you." He said, looking at the ground, shaking his head.

I didn't know how to respond. I missed him too. I wanted things to go back to normal but I couldn't hide the fact that I was still hurt.

"Can you give me time?" I asked.

He nodded his head silently, sad and defeated. The look in his eyes was heartbreaking, but I couldn't bring myself to comfort him. We took the bus together in silence. We got off at our stop, still walking together when I saw Giacomo getting into his car in front of my building.

"*Ciao*, Juliet! *Ciao*, Matt!" He said as he threw his bag in his car. I forgot it was Friday and everyone was headed home for the weekend. Matt muttered a quick hello to him, and then bye. I walked over to Giacomo who noticed I was not my usual self and he asked what was wrong.

"Nothing. It's hard to be friends with someone who hurt you." I said to him, feeling like I needed to get that off my chest.

He looked at me for a few seconds, probably trying to think of what to say next.

"I know, I've been dealing with a similar situation with Luca lately." He said.

"Well, Luca definitely got his heart broken worse than me. I guess I was a lot luckier." I said.

"I'm sorry either way," Giacomo said, his face sympathetic as he looked at me.

"Have a good weekend." I offered, not wanting to take up any more of his time. He gave me a smile, got into his car, and started it. I headed inside the building, up the stairs, when my phone pinged.

GIACOMO: **And this is my other favorite picture.**

I looked out the building window to see he was still in his car and he hadn't left yet. The picture he attached was of me when I was five years old. I posted it about a year ago, right after I found it hidden in an old photo album. There I was, in oversized sunglasses, a bright yellow tank top, and red shorts, holding a chocolate ice cream, with the evidence I'd eaten it all over my face. I laughed at this picture, remembering that I loved it so much I had to post it. You could see the pure joy in my face from enjoying that ice cream cone and you could almost sense how carefree I must have been in that picture. I smiled again down at my phone, and looked out, noticing Giacomo was reversing his car, leaving to go home.

The next day, I texted Jess and Valentina and we decided to walk to the bar up the block together to get a cappuccino. Jess kept talking about Jane, and their plans for the next few days, and I noticed Valentina a little quieter than usual.

"Is everything okay?" I asked, trying to read her expression.

"Sorry, yes. Well....maybe not. It's just that Jess became close with Jane so quickly, and you have all of your Italian friends. I just feel like I am having trouble making friends here." She said, with a bit of sadness in her eyes.

"Well, when you keep telling people you don't want to hang out because you need to study, it doesn't make you the friendliest person," Jess said, smiling, but also making a point. I was actually surprised she had the guts to say something like that to her.

"I know, I know. I am getting better. Look, I went to Matt's party last night." She said and she looked at me, her eyes wider as she covered her mouth. She looked over at Jess, who shook her head slightly and then turned to me.

"I'm sorry, Juliet, we didn't want to tell you because we didn't think you would want to go. I didn't go because Jane wanted to hang out, but I told Valentina she should go. I'm sure you missed nothing." Jess explained to me.

I couldn't believe he didn't even invite me. Maybe things have changed for good between us. I wouldn't have gone anyway, I didn't feel ready, but I couldn't believe that I hadn't even been invited. I decided not to think about it and instead concentrate on getting ready for a fun night at the bar. We walked back home, said good-bye, and I headed to my apartment. Even though it was still really early, I figured it was the right moment to take my time and turn it into a self-care routine. I showered with my new body wash, let the conditioner sit in my hair longer than normal, and relaxed into the feeling of hot water running down my body, easing my muscles.

I painted my nails, noticing how much stronger they were thanks to the Italian water, and waited patiently as they dried while listening to some of the newer Italian songs. I started learning most of the words to the more popular songs and was able to sing along. Next, I started my makeup, using the foundation I saved for special occasions or nights out. My eye makeup turned out better than it ever had, and the red lipstick made me feel fierce.

I blew out my hair, section by section, flipped it over, and sprayed the roots with hairspray to give it more volume. Not only were my nails longer after staying here, but my hair wasn't as frizzy like it'd been back at home. I made sure to curl some pieces and then put on the new earrings that I had gotten, which were a little more daring than the studs I usually wore. I got dressed in a pair of black dressy shorts with sheer black tights underneath, a satin, light blue ruffled crop top, black heeled booties, and sprayed on my new perfume before I stepped in front of the mirror.

I hadn't felt this good since the barbecue, the last time I really got dressed up. I turned sideways, trying to see how my legs looked with my outfit and felt a burst of confidence fill me. I loved the daring, open, and adventurous Juliet staring back at me. I grabbed my clutch, put my red lipstick in it, and grabbed my short leather jacket just in case it got chilly later on. It was only six, but I texted Kristin and Ana that I would stop by their apartment since I didn't want to stay by myself anymore.

I hadn't been in the other apartment building since before Matt's party. I checked to see if I had my phone in my bag and quickly walked to the door, keeping my eyes down. I almost made it.

There he was, throwing the garbage out in the dumpster. I stopped, not sure if I should keep walking or go over to say hi, right as I decided to keep going, he looked up and made eye contact with me.

19

Diciannove

Cantare (v)= to sing

"Wow, Juliet. I almost didn't recognize you." Matt said, quickly glancing at my outfit and then looking back up at me. "You look beautiful." He took a deep breath and held it a few seconds before slowly blowing it out.

"Thanks," I whispered. The confidence I felt before was diminishing as nerves took over. I didn't know what else to say, and we stood together in a moment of silent awkwardness.

"Are you going out tonight?" He asked, positioning himself just like he had been outside the door of my apartment last Saturday—one arm in his pocket and the other arm behind the back of his neck, his elbow in the air.

"Yeah, with Kristin and Ana. There is this bar in the city that everyone goes to, so we wanted to check it out." I said.

"Oh, okay." He nodded, now taking the arm that was behind his neck and putting his hands in both of his pockets, his shoulders slightly shrugging. "Are you going inside? I'll walk with you."

I nodded and we walked together towards the apartment, still silent.

"The boys will be all over you tonight." He said, his eyes slightly closing and one side of his mouth tugging up. Why did he have to continue making things more awkward than they already were?

"Well, I'm not really going for that," I said. "I wanted to try out all of the new stuff I'd bought and figured it was the right night to do that."

He nodded as we walked up the stairs. He lived a floor below Kristin and Ana. "Can I walk with you to Kristin's apartment?"

"Yeah," I replied softly.

We reached their floor. I noticed Matt kept looking over at me as we walked together. We stopped a few feet before Kristin and Ana's door, not sure how to say bye.

"Be careful of those Italian boys." He finally said, giving me a wink.

I smiled and watched him take a few steps back and then turn around to walk away. When he reached the stairs, he looked at me and then nodded his head in my direction, giving me one last smile, before walking down.

I was much happier that we finally got to a good place, but all of my feelings still lingered, making our encounters so awkward. He looked cute with his messy hair, and the sleeves on his shirt rolled up to show his strong forearms, but I promised myself not to think about him in that way anymore. I knocked on their door and Kristin opened it, her eyes wide and her mouth slightly open when she saw me.

"You are freaking gorgeous!" She said, looking at me up and down. "Ana, get over here and look at our girl!" She turned her head to shout to Ana. Ana came to the door, her hair wrapped in a towel, and beamed at me.

"Yeah, Matt who?" She said, laughing.

I laughed but didn't want to tell them about the interaction I just had with him. I chatted with Kristin who was already ready. She was dressed in a simple, silver dress with thin straps and tall black boots that came above her knees. Her chestnut-colored hair was pulled into a high half-up half-down pony that gave it volume and made it look thicker than usual. She also had on lipstick but her shade was a little bit deeper of a red than mine, it went well with her emerald-colored eyes. Ana came out shortly after wearing faux leather pants, a white, tight cropped top, and an oversized but still tailored, black jacket. She wore simple, black strappy heels and had her hair pulled into a sleek, high bun. I was in awe at how amazing the two of them looked. We took the bus down to the city and Ana checked the map on her phone to find the bar.

"It's over here!" She said excitedly, pointing to where we needed to go.

We walked together, finally reaching the bar a few minutes later, and noticed it was already packed.

"Wow, this place is crazy!" I said, looking at Ana and thanking her for finding it for us. She pretended to bow, exaggerating her response, and both Kristin and I started laughing. The inside was modern, despite the outside resembling a historic building. It had eclectic furniture in bold colors and pendants of different geometric shapes hung from the ceiling. We found a seat and looked through the menu. We all ordered a prosecco and a few bites to eat so we wouldn't get drunk too quickly. More people began to enter the bar and the DJ started playing louder music while some people started dancing off to the side.

"Oh my God," Ana said, smacking Kristin's arm to get our attention, "He's here! My mystery guy is here!"

I looked over in the crowd to where she was pointing to and recognized the guy from the mall. He was talking to someone who had his back turned to me.

"But I thought you were over him. Didn't he have a girl all over him at the mall?" I asked, picturing the attractive brunette hugging him.

"Well, I got to thinking. Maybe it was his cousin? Or his friend? Why do I always have to think the worst? He doesn't walk with anyone in between classes. Wouldn't a girlfriend do that?" She said, trying to reason with us.

"You could be right, but I don't want you to get your hopes up though." I gave her a sympathetic look.

I spied on him a little more as he kept talking to the guy with his back turned. I kept staring at him until he turned around and locked eyes with me. My breath hitched when I realized it was Giacomo.

Ana's mystery guy was talking to Giacomo, and now he was smiling at me, and whispering something to Ana's guy. I saw him nod, whisper something back as Giacomo's eyes grew wide. Then they started walking in our direction.

"Are they walking towards us?" Ana whispered to me discreetly.

"I know the guy he's with, that's Giacomo!" I couldn't hold back my excitement.

"So what is Juliet doing in a bar in Verona?" Giacomo asked when he reached us, his arms crossed in front of himself, smiling.

"*Ciao*, Giacomo." I said, still trying to keep the calmest composure I could. I couldn't believe he was at the same bar as us and friends with Ana's mystery crush. "This is my friend Ana, and that's Kristin." I continued, now trying to grab Kristin's attention so she could put down her drink to say hi.

"Nice to meet you both," Giacomo said to them. "This is my friend, Roberto." He finally put a name to him.

I looked over at Ana, who still hadn't said hi, so I nudged her to say something. I barely heard anything come out of her mouth. I urged her with my eyes to say something else. Kristin said "Hi" right away, and continued drinking her prosecco, probably enjoying the drama unfolding in front of her.

"Do you ladies want to join us? We are here with a group of friends from my town. The only one that is missing is Luca." Giacomo said, pointing over to a group of three other guys.

"Sure!" I said, answering for everyone. I got up, followed them, and gestured to Kristin and Ana to do the same.

"I almost didn't recognize you," Giacomo said, a little closer to me. A shiver went through my spine. I'm sure the prosecco didn't help either.

He introduced me to his other friends, and they all said *ciao*, introducing themselves in Italian. I noticed Ana talking to Roberto, looking at the ground, unable to make eye contact. Kristin was at my side still sipping her prosecco.

"Cosa vogliono da bere?" One of Giacomo's friends asked what we wanted to drink, pointing to us.

I shrugged, afraid to suggest something that Italians normally wouldn't drink. After staying here for a while, I realized that Italians, like other cultures, had their own way of doing things and I wanted to make sure I fit in. Luckily, I heard Giacomo order something for us, relieving me of any decision I had to make. A few minutes later, one of his friends came back with three glasses of white wine. I was surprised that Italians drink wine on a night out.

"This is my friend's dad's wine. Tell me if you like it." Giacomo said, giving each of us a glass. I took a sip. It was smoother and different from the wines we were buying at the supermarket. I wasn't exactly sure what made a really good wine, but I was sure that this had to be pretty high quality.

"This is so good." I said, taking another sip. "Where is yours?" I asked, noticing Giacomo and another friend didn't have a glass.

"I'm driving tonight and so is my friend. But it's okay. I can still have fun without alcohol." He said. I looked over and noticed Kristin talking to another one of Giacomo's friends and then laughing at something he must have said.

"I have to tell you something," I said, a little closer to him, whispering in his ear so Ana wouldn't hear me. I looked over to make sure she was far enough away. "Ana has a crush on your friend Roberto."

"Crush?" Giacomo repeated, looking a little confused.

"*Una cotta.* Like when someone likes another person a lot, but the other person usually doesn't know."

Giacomo looked at me this time, with his head tilted slightly and a small smile on his face.

"Really?" He said, still smiling at me.

"But is he seeing someone? She doesn't want to get involved with him if he is."

"No, he actually isn't." He said. I started to relax and I took another sip of wine. I looked over at Ana, who had a smile on her face so wide, it made my heart burst. Roberto looked like he was into her too, with one hand on her arm as he kept leaning in to tell her something while she laughed. Kristin was now sitting down with Giacomo's friend and animatedly discussing something in Italian together. I never noticed that Kristin spoke Italian so well and loved listening in on her beautiful accent as she spoke.

"So two of my single friends found two of your single friends. They are single, right?" Giacomo asked, laughing a little but also questioning if they were.

"Yes, they actually are, and it looks like they're having fun."

"Do you want to sit over there?" Giacomo asked, pointing to an unoccupied table off in the corner.

"Sure," I said, before walking over to Kristin and Ana to tell them where I'd be. They nodded and went back to their conversations with their new friends.

We sat down and I noticed Giacomo was fidgeting a little. I was surprised he looked a little nervous, he always seemed confident 100% of the time. We started chatting and Giacomo told me all about his friends that were there. They all grew up near each other and usually played soccer in their town field on Saturday nights, but Roberto begged them to go to this club tonight. I told him about Kristin and Ana, how they've become my best friends in the short time we've known each other, and how they suggested we come here tonight, too. Kristin was still sitting and talking to her guy while Ana was on the dance floor with a drink and swaying to the music with Roberto.

"Giacomo, this is a good song!" I yelled when I recognized the song by Ultimo that was playing. I grabbed Giacomo by the arm and brought him to the dance floor.

We inched a little closer to each other since the music was loud and started moving along to the beat. When the chorus of the song came on, we both belted out the lyrics and I was proud that I finally got all of the words right. Giacomo looked over at me with his head pulled back.

"You can even sing in Italian now. Wow." He said, nodding his head. I was instantly glad that I studied the lyrics. The DJ then transitioned into another song by a band called Måneskin. We stepped closer to each other, smiling as we danced to the edgier rock song.

"*Questa è dedicata agli Azzurri, i vincitori degli Europei!*" The DJ announced the next song was dedicated to the Italian soccer team that had won the European Cup. The song was older and a little slower than the other songs the DJ played, but all of the Italians at the bar stopped what they were doing to sing along with it. I looked over at Giacomo, who was also singing along as if he couldn't help not to, and I joined in.

Notti magiche, inseguendo un goal
Sotto il cielo di un'estate italiana
E negli occhi tuoi voglia di vincere
Un'estate, un'avventura in più

He tilted his head and raised his eyebrows when I got all the words right. After it was over, another more upbeat song came on and everyone started mingling again.

"You are surprising me tonight, Juliet. First, you love my favorite singer, Ultimo, then you learn how to sing in Italian to the best songs, and then on top of it all, you look more beautiful every time I see you." He said the last part closer to my ear, sending shivers through my body, quickening my heartbeat.

He was looking right into my eyes. My heart was pounding so loud now, I could feel it in my eardrums. My instinct was to kiss him, but I knew I had to fight it. He kept staring at me, looking down to my lips, and then back at my eyes. I felt his fingers touch my hands, and I looked down at them as he interlaced them into mine. I stopped thinking and I closed my eyes, leaning into him.

When our lips touched, my body became a puddle on the floor. It was so gentle as he pressed his lips against mine, and it felt like they knew they were meant to be there as if this moment was destined to be. We continued kissing gently, this time my mouth opening slightly as his tongue gently touched my lower lip. I unlaced my fingers and touched his arm, feeling the definition underneath. Our kiss grew deeper, more passionate, his tongue sweeping into my mouth making my inner core burn. I pulled away, both of my hands holding on around his neck as I looked into his eyes again, now with a slightly glazed expression, as he looked into mine.

"*Mi piaci*, Juliet." He said, this time I knew exactly what he meant, *he liked me.* We began kissing again, and my head was still spinning.

I had kissed other guys before but I never felt electricity like this. It was all-consuming, it took the air out of my lungs, and above all, it kept me begging for more. My body pressed into his and I felt his hands on my lower back. We stopped for air and he wrapped his arms tighter around my waist, still looking into my eyes as if he were reading a book.

"I've wanted to kiss you since the first moment I saw you." He said as I became completely undone. "I really like you, Juliet." He let go of me and held my hands gently in his. "But I want to be sure that you are not with Matt. I saw how Luca is, and I don't want to get hurt either."

I couldn't think straight. I'd never been so sure of a kiss before. I didn't know where this would go but I needed to at least try. But I also wanted to be honest with him, so I told the truth. What happened with Matt, how my feelings changed for him after Venice, but then how he kissed another girl last week. Giacomo listened attentively as I told the story, but he didn't seem convinced.

"But do you have feelings for him, Juliet?" He asked, waiting for my response.

"I don't know how I feel about anything anymore," I responded, which was the absolute truth.

He looked at me with narrow eyes and a slight smile. He didn't seem completely satisfied with the answer, but nodded his head and pulled me closer to him. He was now leaning against the wall and still holding on to my hands as I stood close to him, trying to still steady my breath. I looked over and saw Ana coming towards me and gesturing that I should follow her.

"I'll be right back," I told Giacomo, letting go of his hands and following her. She led me to the bathroom and then started jumping up and down as soon as the door shut behind her.

"Oh my God! This is the best night ever!" She continued shrieking and I beamed too. She quickly told me that Roberto recognized her right away and said that he'd always wanted to talk to her but was too shy. She had told him the same thing and then they started dancing, talking, and then kissed. I told her about Giacomo's kiss too and we were all giddy when all of a sudden Kristin joined us.

"I see you two have found Italian boyfriends." She said, with a little smirk on her face.

"And what about your guy?" I said, asking her about the guy she had been talking to.

"Oh, Paolo?" She said, now a smile forming on her face. "It's nothing serious," she continued, her smile still growing wider, "but he *is* a good kisser." I was so happy for them it felt like my feet left the group and I was floating in a cloud of euphoria. I freshened up my lipstick and said bye to the girls.

I saw him, still standing where I left him, leaning against the wall, his head slightly moving to the beat of the song. He looked over at me, smiled, and I hurried towards him. I took his hands into mine, playing gently with his fingers before letting go of one hand and leaning into his side, resting my head on his shoulder. I wasn't questioning anything, and I didn't want to. I wanted to just be in this moment, with Giacomo, holding his hand and listening to these songs. I felt like my body had been screaming for this all of my life and I had never understood what it was saying until now. He turned his head towards me and softly kissed my forehead, making me melt even more. It was definitely too late— I was falling hard and didn't see the ground anywhere near. I turned my head slightly, met his lips to mine, and kissed him again, just for a few seconds this time, and let go as our foreheads kept touching and our lips stayed slightly apart. If there were a pause button, this would be the moment when I'd use it. I didn't have to worry about Kristin and Ana since they were fine, I wasn't worrying about school, I didn't worry about anything.

"What are you doing tomorrow?" He asked, pulling his head back to now look into my eyes.

"Nothing," I said.

"Can I take you somewhere?"

"Sure. Where?"

"One of my favorite towns. It's a long drive though, about two hours, but this is a beautiful time to see it before it starts getting too warm."

"I'm in," I said.

He kissed me again, this time pressing more firmly against my lips, and then pulled away, placing his hands on my face, shaking his head slightly.

"I don't want tonight to end." He said, and I nodded completely understanding what he meant. We swayed along to a few more songs, before noticing that the place wasn't as crowded as before. The time must've swept up from under us.

"I think I should go." It took everything I had in me to say that but I knew it was getting late and we needed to try to find a taxi since the buses weren't running anymore.

"Okay. Let me drive you and your friends back." He asked while holding my fingers and squeezing them lightly.

"It's okay, I don't want you to go out of your way for us, we can take a taxi back." I wanted him to say no though, so we could have a little more time together.

"Juliet, I told you I don't want this night to end, if I can spend 30 minutes more with you, I will."

I kissed him again and he wrapped his arms around my waist, pulling me into him. I pulled back and just looked at him, wanting to remember every second of this night. He let out a long breath, as if he'd forgotten to breathe, and grabbed my hand, leading me to where Roberto and Ana were.

Roberto was sitting on one of the benches against the wall and Ana was right next to him, her body sideways, facing him, one leg over his. They were holding hands and talking to each other but stopped to look at us as we reached up to them. Ana was glowing as she smiled at me. Roberto was still holding her hand as he started speaking in Italian to Giacomo.

"Okay, I will bring you girls home and Roberto will catch a ride with my other friend that is driving."

Ana got up, still holding Roberto's hand and I looked away as they kissed each other goodbye. Giacomo teased Roberto by patting his back and telling him to hurry up, with Roberto throwing Giacomo a curse back, which made him laugh. We found Kristin, who was still talking to Giacomo's other friend, and we all headed to his car. I sat in the front with Giacomo and Kristin and Ana slid in the back. I noticed they were whispering to each other and I was sure they were recounting everything that happened. Giacomo looked over at me and smiled after he snuck a glance in the rearview mirror of the girls giggling and whispering. I kept stealing glances at him while he was driving, and it took everything to stop me from going over and kissing him again. He was focused on driving, but every so often he would look over at me, making the heat rush to my cheeks. His lips were such a nice shape. I pulled in my lower lip, my tongue going slightly over it, trying to remember what it felt like to kiss him. When we finally reached the apartments, Kristin and Ana thanked Giacomo for the ride and then ran over to me to give me a hug.

"Text me later," Kristin whispered as she pulled back from the hug. I nodded and then saw them run off to their apartment.

Giacomo walked over to my side of the car. My stomach twisted as I realized there was nothing stopping him from staying the night since he probably still had clothes in his room.

"If I stay the night," he said as if reading my mind. "I won't be able to sleep knowing you are so close to me. I'll pick you up around 10 in the morning, is that okay?" He was holding both of my hands and rubbing his thumbs gently across my fingers.

"That's fine" I said, my breathing becoming more shallow and my cheeks turning pink from imagining what would happen if he did stay the night. I wouldn't sleep either since I felt like I couldn't stop touching or being close to him. He leaned in, gave me one last deep kiss, as if he couldn't resist anymore. His hands were around my waist, squeezing me as his kiss became stronger, needier. He pulled back, stared into my eyes, and shook his head.

"I can't stop, Juliet." He said, his eyes more playful now as he continued to look at me. I kissed him back, this time gently cupping his cheeks and bringing his face to mine.

"Okay, I need to go before I never leave." He finally let go of my waist, pulled away, and headed towards the driver's side of the car.

"I'll see you tomorrow." He said, giving me one last smile as he got into the car and slowly pulled away.

20

Venti

La Montagna (nf)= Mountain

KRISTIN: **Tell us everything!**

As soon as I stepped into my apartment, my phone pinged. I looked across the way at her building and noticed a few lights still on. I wondered if she was peeking through her window the whole time and she knew exactly when to text.

I decided to call her since it would be much easier to explain. She had me on speaker. Ana mentioned how she had made plans to see Roberto next weekend, and that she definitely liked him, but didn't want things to go so fast since she wasn't sure a long-distance relationship would work. Too late for me though, I wanted to see where it went. Kristin said Paolo was nice enough and definitely a good kisser, but she wasn't looking for anything serious with him. I told them I needed to sleep since Giacomo had made plans with me for the next day.

"Oh, Juliet. You are in *love!*" Ana teased.

"Please be careful and don't rush into anything," Kristin said, more in a serious tone.

I was throwing caution to the wind, but I couldn't help it. I went to bed, cuddled underneath the covers, imagining all of the kisses and praying it wasn't a dream.

I woke up to the sun shining through the opened slats in my shutters. I wasn't sure what to wear, so I figured jeans, a light grey long-sleeved peplum shirt, and my dark grey scarf would be fine. I tied my hair back in a loose braid and put on just a touch of mascara and eyeliner this time, adding my light pink lip gloss.

Giacomo arrived a little before ten and came straight up to my apartment. I opened the door and he wasted no time pulling me into him, picking me up slightly, and kissing me on my lips.

"I wanted to make sure it wasn't a dream." He said, putting me down but still holding on to me. He grabbed my hand and we headed out of the apartment, straight to his car.

As we were driving on the road, he explained how we were headed for a mountain town called Cortina, it was north of us, closer to the Austrian border. This whole time I never realized we were close to other European countries. Slovenia was to the east, Austria to the north, and Switzerland and France to the north-west. If you traveled three hours in any direction, you crossed the border into another country. Up north were the Dolomite mountains, a chain of mountains within the Alps. The soft, green mountains and hills in Verona were now being replaced by white and grey jagged rocks, jutting into the sky as if they'd claimed the landscape. I stared out the window at them, in awe at how they sprawled over the valleys and sprawled across the sky behind towns.

"Giacomo, this is so pretty. I can't believe I was missing out on this." I said, still craning my neck to see through the windows of his small car.

"I'm glad you like it, but we aren't even there yet!" He reached for my arm and I turned my head to look at him. "See, this is why you need me. I must show you all of the beautiful scenery throughout all of Italy."

"Okay, maybe I'll keep you around." I winked at him. He laughed and turned his attention back towards the road.

"Oh, by the way." He said. "Roberto has a *crush* on Ana."

"Wow, look at you using the word right!" I patted him on the shoulder, praising him like he was my student. "I know Ana likes him too, but she is afraid of what will happen when she leaves."

Giacomo was quiet for a few seconds, looking out in front of him. "Sometimes we can't control how we feel." He took my hand and I had a feeling we weren't talking about Ana and Roberto anymore. I looked down at our hands, caressing his fingers. The separation in the car between us was killing me. It took everything in me to resist pulling him over to me and kissing him. He pulled his hand back and shifted gears as we were climbing up higher in the mountains. Most cars here were manual, where you actually needed both of your feet to drive.

"I would love to learn how to drive a manual car." I said, looking at his hand shifting the gears seamlessly.

He glanced over at me, then turned his head back to the road. "I'll teach you."

I couldn't help but laugh as I watched over the rolling hills ahead of us and pictured what it would be like to drive over them.

He glanced over again, this time curious as to what I was thinking. "Are you imagining trying to drive up a hill?" He also started laughing.

"That was exactly the scene I was picturing, except the car is going backwards." I said, still laughing.

He squeezed my hand again, in between shifting the car back up because we were heading for a flatter road. "Don't worry, I won't let that happen." He was so confident, my body filled with a warmth that made me feel protected next to him.

We finally arrived at the small town, high up in the mountains. Giacomo had explained that it was one of the most famous ski towns in Italy and I could see why. The Dolomites looked like they were standing guard behind the town, protecting the shops and houses in the valley. It was a scene almost too perfect to exist in real life. The city had a town center with meadows and forests surrounding it.

"It's so beautiful," I said.

Giacomo parked the car in a lot that was close to the main street of Cortina. He turned off the ignition and looked at me before reaching over the console and pulling me closer to kiss him. It was soft at first, he had one hand on my cheek, right above my neck, but then he moved it behind my neck, to pull me even closer. I felt the blood rushing towards my stomach and below as I began to want more of him. He sensed that we were getting too heated and pulled away, struggling to not kiss me again.

"Juliet, I'm afraid if we don't get out of the car now, we never will."

He let go of my neck, we both opened our doors, meeting in the front of the car. We held hands and started making our way through the town.

The buildings reminded me of chalets that I would see at ski resorts. They were mostly cream-colored, with brown wooden balconies and gabled roofs that made you want to go inside and have a warm drink. The streets were cobblestone and people were walking around in thicker coats than they were down in Verona.

"I want to show you everything I love, and this is the first stop." Giacomo said, pulling me closer to him and rubbing my shoulders, keeping me warm.

"Well, it's truly... enchanting?" I said, looking for the right word.

"Does that sound right? I genuinely feel like I walked into a fairy-tale or a painting." I could smell the wood burning from the chimneys and people were walking side by side, arms hooked into each other. Cafes, shops, and hotels lined the cobbled street and Giacomo led me to a small bar in a little street off the main road.

"The sandwiches here are the best. I promise I will take you to a restaurant one day, but you have to try one."

I glanced inside and saw light wood paneling that matched the tables and chairs. There were red valances above the window that added to the already cozy feeling. It reminded me of a house I would see in a book like Hansel and Gretel. We sat down, the corner of Giacomo's eyes crinkling as he took my hands over the table. When the waiter came by, Giacomo let go to take the menus from him and thanked him after he read off the specials.

"I trust your taste in food ever since you told me about the pizza with speck, gorgonzola, and walnuts. Can you order what you think is the best?" I wanted to get what he really loved.

I saw his eyes light up and he sat up straighter. "I know exactly what you will like." He said, so confident and proud at the same time. When the waiter came back, he ordered for us, the only thing I could understand was *panino*, which didn't help since that meant *sandwich*.

"You know, Juliet. You were beautiful last night, but you are even more beautiful like this, sitting here, across from me, without a lot of makeup."

I couldn't stop my cheeks from turning red. I didn't know how to respond to that. I wasn't used to guys giving me such effortless compliments. Most guys I'd been with have been scared to be vulnerable and tell me how they really felt. I noticed my phone start vibrating and looked down to see it was my mom who was FaceTiming me.

"Sorry, it's my mom. I haven't talked to her in a week. Do you mind if I go outside to answer this real quick?"

"Not at all. Go."

I got up and hit the answer button.

"Hi, Mom! How's everything?" I said. She had a new haircut and my dad was in the background sitting at the kitchen table with a cup of coffee.

"Hi, honey! Everything is good. Dad wanted to know what you were up to too, so we figured we'd call you instead of texting you all of the time. Where are you? Are those the Dolomite Mountains I see?" I was impressed at how well she knew her Italian geography.

"Yeah, I'm actually in Cortina! It's so beautiful here, you would love it!" I said, switching my camera to show her the view. She started rattling off how it is a popular destination for the winter for Italians and I interrupted her before I got a history lesson for the next 10 minutes.

"I know, I know. Giacomo already told me that."

I squeezed my eyes shut after I said that since I didn't want to have to explain who he was. It slipped out and now I was prepared for the onslaught of questions.

"Giacomo?" I heard my dad repeat in the background. "Who is this Giacomo, Juliet?"

"No one, Dad. He is one of my roommate's friends. He brought all of us up to the mountains to see Cortina." I quickly recovered.

"Okay, sweetie." My mom said, not as convinced as my dad who had gone back to drinking his coffee.

"I have to go though, we are all having lunch and it's going to be ready soon." I made sure to stress *all*.

"I love you." She said, and I told them I loved them too and hung up. I took a deep breath and headed back to the cafe.

Giacomo was checking his phone and looked up, giving me his contagious smile. He put his phone in his pocket when I sat down.

"How're your parents?" He said. "Do you miss them?"

I hadn't really talked much about my family with him yet because they were so separated in my mind. Giacomo was associated with my life in Italy and my parents were part of the old Juliet who was nervous about every new experience she could have.

"They're good. It doesn't seem like much has changed since I left there." I said, picturing my Dad drinking his same cup of coffee out of the same mug, sitting at the same spot at the table every morning. "It's crazy though because I feel like I've changed so much."

"How so?" He asked, leaning back in his chair to listen.

"I'm not really sure honestly." I never really thought about what exactly was different now, just that I felt like I grew up a little bit more. I tried to put it into words. "Back at home, I was always nervous that nothing was going to work out. I was scared that I would never be able to become a teacher like I always wanted, or that everything was just going to go badly before it even happened." I thought about watching my mom teach her class back home and thinking I would never be a natural like her. "I guess what I am trying to say is I was scared to put myself out there and actually take risks. Coming to Italy was something I always knew I wanted to do, but I was terrified of it. I was nervous I wasn't going to meet anyone new who would mean a lot to me." I looked into his eyes, trying to read his face.

"So now, when you are in Verona, you feel more open to taking risks?"

"Yeah," I continued, thinking for a second. "Or something like that. I just feel like good things can happen once you start listening to your heart and saying yes, rather than overthinking and saying no."

"I think I know what you mean," he said. "I was never really like that. I always listen to my gut when making decisions. I believe that it is your body telling you deep down what is right and what is true."

The waiter came back to our table interrupting us with two

beautiful sandwiches on thick blocks of wood that looked like a mix between a cutting board and a trivet. We thanked him and he left.

"I do know what you mean." I continued looking down at my sandwich, stomach audibly growling. "Right now, my gut is screaming at me to put this sandwich inside of it."

He laughed and we each grabbed one-half of our sandwiches holding them up and admiring them before taking a huge bite. He was right again. The bread was a small loaf, still warm enough to make the melted cheese pull when I took a bite. The sandwich had slices of prosciutto, pickled mushrooms, and eggplant. It created a combination of flavors that I'd never tasted before.

"Oh my God," I said. "This is insane. I've never had a sandwich like this." I saw Giacomo's eyes twinkling and the corners of his mouth turned up as he watched me take another bite of the sandwich.

We both finished up quickly, devouring every crumb. Giacomo asked if I wanted another. I started laughing and shrugged saying that I'd have to just come back again. He asked the waiter for two coffees and a dessert.

"You need to try this. This is typical in this area. It's called *strudel di mele,* or apple strudel. It's actually Austrian, but you will find it around here, too." Giacomo said as the waiter handed us both a plate of the dessert.

The presentation of the dessert was lovely in itself. It looked like a puff pastry that was wrapped around chopped apples, raisins, and pignoli nuts. There was powdered sugar sprinkled on top and whipped cream to the side. I took a bite and closed my eyes. There was a slight crunch to the pignoli nuts that, combined with the taste of the warm cinnamon apples and raisins, melted into my mouth. When I opened them, I saw Giacomo taking a picture of me mid-bite.

"Hey!" I said, reaching for his phone.

"No, I'm keeping this." He said leaning back in his chair, away from me. "I need to remember your face eating this." He said as he put down his phone.

I chewed slowly, savoring the flavors, and smiled at him as I took another bite. "I'm afraid to see what else you really like," I said, my eyes playing with his. He shook his head slowly and still smiled at me as he finished drinking his espresso and I finished the strudel. I surprised myself with my bold response, but I did say I was going to start following my heart. When the bill came, I got my wallet out of my purse to help pay.

"Absolutely not, Juliet. I took you here, and I will pay for everything."

I thanked him, and we got up to walk outside. There were more people in the street than before, many holding onto a cold gelato despite the weather being so chilly. I looked at Giacomo, my eyes pleading to tell him what I wanted. He chuckled and just replied with *dopo*, later. I smiled, linking my arm through his and we walked towards a little shop, with trinkets in the window display.

Inside the shop, there were all different types of wooden dolls, ornaments, and toys. I spotted a checkered pattern in most of the different articles the store sold. I picked up a tablecloth and ran my fingers over the fabric, admiring the hearts and floral scroll that alternated in a red and white checkered pattern. I noticed underneath it was more colors of the same pattern that peaked through, one of an orange-gold color and another in a softer yellow. I placed it back and headed over to a wall full of magnets and glanced through them, taking in all of the various places around the town with *Cortina* labelled on the bottom. Right underneath the magnets, there were postcards of almost the same places, but with mostly the Dolomite Mountains in the background and an aerial view of the city. I looked around and saw little gnome statues in various poses.

"The gnomes are popular in mountain cities," Giacomo said, watching me look at one. "They say they bring luck." I picked up one, with a red, pointy felt hat covering its eyes, and white, long hair peeking out. Its white beard covered most of the face and it had a stumpy body, covered in grey felt, with mittens and shoes in the same red fabric. I'd never seen one like it before so I decided to buy it to remember Cortina. I walked it over to the register to pay, but Giacomo took it from me, saying it was part of the experience and that he had it.

"Now I have to show you something beautiful." He said as we exited the shop. "But we need to take my car and drive there."

21

Ventuno

Una bella vista= a beautiful view

We got in his car and drove out of the city down a narrow road up the mountain about 10 minutes away. He parked in a tiny parking lot and told me not to move or turn around yet. He got out of the car and reached my side and opened the door, telling me to close my eyes, and then turned me around, holding on to my shoulders. He moved his hands to the side of my shoulders, leaned into my ear, and whispered to open my eyes.

When I did, my mouth dropped. The whole city of Cortina was displayed in front of me. It looked so much smaller from this distance with the domineering mountains behind it. I looked around at where we were. We were on a meadow, much higher than the city, with the Dolomites still surrounding us. The sunlight reflected against the mountains, creating a magical pinkish-reddish hue on them.

"Wow." I said softly, still taking it all in. I turned to look at Giacomo, who was not staring at the view but staring at me, his eyes trying to read mine as he continued looking at me.

"And this is why I want to show you everything I love. You look at it with fresh eyes and appreciate it. You make me fall in love with everything all over again." He said, in a serious tone now, as he held both of my hands. We both leaned into each other and kissed, but not as passionately as before. It was a soft kiss that lasted a few seconds until he pushed back and said we should head back before it got too late. We stopped for a gelato on the way back since he had promised me one from before.

"Juliet, can you get my phone and choose one of my playlists?" He said when we got back in the car.

I felt excited that he was letting me go through them, something that he might have considered personal. I found Ultimo, clicked on it, and increased the volume. He smiled at me, squeezing my hand gently as we continued driving silently listening to the entire album.

We talked a bit here and there, but I mostly just looked out the window, watching the mountains turn to hills, and down into plains. When we reached our apartment building, the sun was starting to set behind them and the rays were peeking out from in between.

"Do you want to come to my apartment for coffee?" I asked, hoping he would say yes since I needed more time with him.

"Okay." He said, almost hesitantly. I could see him calculating something in his eyes as he looked to the side. His eyes met mine and he nodded his head again, almost as if he'd convinced himself to go.

My stomach was nervous because we hadn't been alone yet since everything had happened last night. Even though I was trying not to overthink, this was something important to me and I wanted to make sure I was 100% ready.

We walked up the stairs, holding hands from the car as I reached my apartment door. Elisa wasn't coming home until tomorrow so it was nice to know no one would be there. I got my key, opened the door slowly, and let Giacomo in before I closed it. He walked a few steps in, turned around, and watched me close the door. We both knew that I wasn't going to make coffee. He took a few steps towards me and took off my scarf and jacket and put it on the chair next to him. He took his off too and stepped closer to me. I put my hands around his neck and closed the space between us. I pulled him into me, and I could feel he was taken aback, but then he kissed me even deeper. His hands started moving down to the side of my stomach as I moved my hands up higher on his neck, now running my fingers through his hair. I couldn't get enough of him and needed to feel more of his skin, so I pulled myself back, looked at his eyes which were widened, as if he needed more too, and took his hand and led him towards my bedroom.

We kissed even more passionately as we made it to the bed and took off our shirts to feel more of each other. We laid on the bed near each other and he pushed me back gently so that I was laying on my back and he leaned against his elbow to look at me.

"*Sei bellissima.*" He told me in Italian that I was beautiful. Hearing it in Italian made me pull him in to kiss him and hold him tighter. I'd promised myself not to go too far, but I'd been willing to break my promise after that. As if he sensed me not being able to control myself, he moved his lips to my forehead, placed his hands to my side, and shifted away from me.

"Juliet, we can stop if you want, we can take it slow." He said. I realized he was right. I wanted him so badly at that point I wasn't even thinking clearly, pushing all of my judgments to the side and just wanting all of what he had. I took a few deep breaths, nodded my head as he pushed himself off the bed, and put on his shirt. I found mine, put it on too, but couldn't get myself to get off of the bed. He smiled, pulled my arms gently to get me up, and wrapped his arms around me in a big hug as I laid my head on his chest.

I felt as if I needed to pinch myself to make sure what was happening was real. From last night until now, it seemed like my brain couldn't comprehend all of the emotions my heart had been through. I took a deep breath, taking in the mix of fabric softener and sandalwood from his shirt.

"Are you hungry?" He asked, his hands rubbing my arms gently, still holding me tight to him.

"Actually, yes," I said, looking up at him before I planted another kiss on his lips.

We walked to the kitchen and I pulled out some bread and cheese, and we made sandwiches.

"I didn't realize I was so hungry!" I said as I took a bite. He laughed and then pushed his chair to face mine, and we ate with our legs interlocked with each other.

"So when are we going to try more of those pizza flavors we keep texting about?" He asked, his fingers gently touching mine.

"Hmm, well, anything but horse meat. Maybe one day this week."

"Okay. It's a date." He added, kissing me again gently, and getting up. "I'm going to start heading back. I'll see you tomorrow?" His hands now lifted my face to look at him.

I nodded my head, almost wanting to stop him and make him stay longer, but he grabbed his bag and headed for the door.

"So, no coffee?" I said, playfully teasing him and following him.

"I definitely don't need coffee now." He said, giving me one last kiss before I closed the door behind him. I covered my face with my hands as I tried to grasp what happened in the last 24 hours. I went from being depressed about Matt to not controlling myself with Giacomo.

I realized I hadn't checked my phone, so I went through it to see some messages. I had about seven unread messages, several from

Kristin and Ana wanting to know any updates, one from Jess and Valentina, and one from Matt.

Matt. 24 hours ago I asked him to give me time. I felt guilty that I was with Giacomo now, but I tried to remind myself that Matt was the one who kissed the other girl— I didn't do anything wrong. I felt confused because I wasn't sure if Matt still had hope for us and I didn't want to lead him on. What I felt with Giacomo today was all I could think about. It consumed me entirely and even if it was only going to last until I went home, I wanted to pursue it anyway. I opened his text which was from this morning before I left for Cortina.

22

Ventidue

Dire bugie- to tell lies

MATT: **How was last night?**

I debated what I should send back. I didn't feel right to tell him about Giacomo. I knew eventually I'd have to but figured the less I said, the better it would be.

JULIET: **It was fun :-)**

I put my phone down and replayed all of the scenes from yesterday to today with Giacomo and realized there was a feeling about him that I couldn't place. It was as if I had known him much longer than these few months and there was a sense of comfort when I was with him.

I texted Kristin and Ana back some details of today, leaving the juicier bits out since I wanted to keep those for myself. I laid in bed that night and scrolled through my feed when I saw a picture Giacomo posted of our table at the bar, both of our drinks on it and the menu in the middle. The caption just had a heart, with nothing else. I wasn't in the picture because I was talking to my parents, so the post was a little enigmatic. I double tapped the post, held my phone to my chest, and then scrolled through the rest of my feed still with a smile. That night I slept soundly.

The next day, I was getting ready for classes when Elisa popped into our room.

"Hey, I thought you usually came back to the apartment after classes," I said.

"Yeah, I know I just...I need to talk." She said, pacing around the room a little bit. "Remember when I said I liked someone else?"

"Yeah," I said. She told me that was the main reason why she didn't want to be with Luca.

"Well, I saw Giacomo's post last night on Instagram, and I think he likes someone." She said, with a little panic in her voice.

"Wait, you still like Giacomo? Elisa, didn't you say you like someone from your town, though?" My stomach dropped. How could she still be into him? I had a horrible feeling in my stomach. I completely forgot to think about what would happen if she found out about me and Giacomo. She has liked him for a while now and I feel bad that it was me he ended up falling for.

"I saw his post too and I thought it meant he liked the place," I said, trying to divert her suspicion so I had more time to think about what I should do.

"Yeah, you think so? I don't know. There were two glasses there and I could see a purse strap on the chair. Plus, he was in Cortina. You don't just go to Cortina with your mom." She added, still not convinced.

I panicked wondering how much of the purse strap you could

see. If she could see the whole purse then she would figure out it was mine. I needed to check the picture again quickly so I could hide that purse in case it was on the post.

"Sorry, my friend is texting me and it's important. Let me text her back quickly." I said, excusing myself out of the room so I could check my phone. I scrolled the feed as fast as I could and found the picture and breathed a sigh of relief when all you could see was a black strap wrapped across a chair. Lots of girls have black bags. The only thing I had to do now was talk to Giacomo and tell him to not say anything about us yet to anyone. I chewed on my bottom lip nervously, playing over different scenarios in my head. There goes me doing whatever feels right and not overthinking everything. That didn't last long. Now I was left in this mess, trying to spare Elisa's feelings but also needing to be with Giacomo. Elisa came to the kitchen, with a confused look on her face.

"I was waiting for you to come back to the bedroom and finish talking," she said. I started getting flustered and overwhelmed by all of what was going on.

"I'm sorry, I just, I'm late for class." I managed to say, going back into the bedroom as she followed behind me.

"I don't know, I really like him so much. Kissing Luca was a mistake, I just want to be friends with him. Hey, when did you get this?" She said, picking up the gnome I got from Cortina that I had on my bed.

My heart dropped. I looked at the gnome wondering how something so cute could betray me. My mind went 50 miles per minute trying to figure out an excuse to give her.

"My friends Ana and Kristin got it for me." I lied. "They visited some place in the mountains yesterday and brought it over to me last night."

"Oh, it's cute." She said and tossed the gnome back on the bed. I breathed a sigh of relief, but also started feeling horrible with all the lies that were piling on top of each other. I grabbed my coat and sneakers and started heading towards the door.

"I'll see you later!" I shouted. I didn't even have a chance to check my hair or makeup as I ran to the bus stop and waited for the bus.

I took out my phone and dialed Giacomo's number. He picked up on the second ring and just hearing his voice put me in a better mood. I explained everything that just happened with Elisa. I could tell he was getting angry at the situation and kept repeating that he didn't like her. I reminded him that she was still my roommate and maybe it was best if we acted like friends in front of her until we figured out what to do.

"I'm sorry, Juliet. I told Luca. I couldn't help it, you make me so happy I needed to tell my best friend." My heart melted and I wished he was here. I would take his face and kiss him all over.

"Do you think Luca will tell Elisa?"

"No, they haven't talked for over a week. He is still upset about what happened, but really happy for us."

"I miss you already." He added.

"I miss you too," I said softly back. We said goodbye and hung up the phone. I thought about what the rest of the week would look like. I wasn't sure if I'd be able to act normally in front of everyone when I was with Giacomo. I was half-listening through my classes literally daydreaming about a boy. I had to stop myself and try to focus on the lesson, but my mind kept bringing me back to him.

I met Jess and Valentina at the bar and they instantly noticed something was up. I gave an excuse that I'd been studying all night. I didn't want to tell them about Giacomo just yet. I had forgotten that I was going to see Matt later in Italian class, and my face dropped when I realized that I couldn't tell him either about Giacomo. My stomach twisted and turned as I had realized that being with Giacomo was creating even more problems than before. I wondered if it was just best that we stop being together since we would end up hurting more people in the end, but then I imagined not being able to kiss those lips or touch him, and I felt even worse.

"Juliet, *stai bene?*" Gianni asked me if I was alright, putting down the espresso cups he'd just cleaned, waiting for my answer.

"*Sì, sì...*" I answered quickly, giving him a reassuring smile even though I was betraying every feeling in my body.

As soon as I walked in the door of my Italian class with Jess, I noticed Matt was already there, waiting for us in his seat right next to mine. I mumbled a greeting to him and sat down, opening my book.

MATT: **Something is wrong—what happened?**

Halfway through class Matt had texted me. I looked over and saw him looking at me, with a worried expression on his face. My face was probably easier to read than I thought.

JULIET: **I don't feel so well.**

I surprised myself by coming up with a sort of lie quickly.

MATT: **I'm sorry. Where did you go yesterday? I stopped by your apartment but you weren't home. Jess and Valentina didn't even know where you went either.**

I honestly thought I might actually be sick.

JULIET: **I went to the city to go shopping with Kristin and Ana.**

The only person I'd been honest with this whole day was Giacomo, and all of these lies were making my stomach twist in knots. I took a deep breath, relaxed my shoulders, and tried again to just focus on the lesson. I saw Matt about to type a reply, but he put his phone away, probably also wanting to focus. After class was over, I was thankful to be departing from Matt. I said goodbye to him and grabbed my books, ready to go.

"My professor actually cancelled my next class, so I'm taking the bus back with you guys," Matt said, as he got up and followed me out the door.

I took another deep breath and prayed he wouldn't ask me any other questions that would have to make me lie more.

"So, Juliet, how many boys did you meet Saturday night?" He asked as we walked towards the bus.

"Um, none, why?" I answered.

"None really? Hard to believe especially with that red lipstick you had on." This time he was smiling sheepishly at me with an eyebrow slightly raised.

"No, honestly. I just had fun with Kristin and Ana and that's it. It was actually boring at the bar. I probably won't go again." I continued.

"Oh." He said, squinting at me trying to see past my words. He was right not to believe me. I wanted to tell him everything, but I wasn't sure how he would react.

"Did you guys get Giorgia's email?" Matt asked instead, looking at both Jess and I. "She wants to meet with all of us on Wednesday, after Italian class, to talk about how we're doing."

I was so grateful that Matt switched subjects to something I could finally be truthful about.

"Yeah I saw it. She wants to talk about how the exams will work here or something like that." Jess said, looking up from her phone. I noticed how quiet she'd been on the whole bus ride.

"I haven't checked my email in a while," I said as I scrolled through my phone looking for the message.

"We should all get pizza together after we meet with her," Matt said. Jess nodded her head, agreeing it was a good idea, and I did too. As long as we were all together, I could avoid having any awkward conversations with Matt.

"Jess, how was your weekend?" I said, finally asking after all of this time.

"I hung out with Jane and we checked out this art exhibit in Verona. It was my first exhibit, and I loved it. I feel like I should buy a beret now and a black and white striped shirt."

I laughed, the first time all day, happy for who she'd become in her short time here. We reached our stop and all got off. My smile began to fade as I realized Giacomo was home and everyone else was back and now the charade would begin.

I said bye to Matt and Jess and headed to my building. I entered the stairway slowly, almost as if asking time to slow down with me too. I didn't want to reach my apartment which held an inquisitive Elisa behind it.

23

Ventitré

Nascondere (v) - to hide

I entered the apartment to an empty kitchen. Elisa's bags and jacket were on the chair, and I could hear the shower running. I had a little bit of time. I started dinner, deciding on spaghetti with olives, capers, and a touch of oil, knowing she liked it too. I turned on some Italian music, recognizing the same songs that were playing at the bar with Giacomo, and hummed along, letting the beat pump through my body and put me in a better mood. I'd been softly singing at this point and focused on dinner, when I noticed Elisa standing next to me.

"Hey!" I said, somewhat startled to see her standing there, over my shoulder, watching me cook.

"What are you making?" She asked, walking over to where I was standing over the stove, while I added the spaghetti to the boiling water. "Olives and capers! Oh, my favorite!"

We ate together and I tried to subside the immense feeling of guilt that was boiling like the spaghetti water in my stomach. She carried the conversation and I just nodded or gave one answer replies. Every so often she would look over at me, her eyes narrowing a bit with my short answers, but then would continue talking ignoring whatever she was thinking.

"So, I've decided to stop avoiding Luca and I want to go down to their apartment tonight." She said, making me drop my fork onto my plate, creating a loud crash of metal against ceramic.

"Sorry," I said, picking up my fork and twirling some spaghetti around the prongs. "Umm, I don't know if I should go with you tonight. I have uhh...well, I should really do some studying." After lying effortlessly all day, I felt for some reason like I was at the stand getting interrogated for a crime I definitely committed.

"Juliet. Why are you acting so strange tonight? Of course you're going to come with me. Don't you miss the guys?"

"I mean, yeah I guess I do," I said putting down my fork and staring at my plate.

"So why wouldn't you want to come?" She kept looking straight into my eyes, trying to push her reasoning into me and also squeeze the answers out.

"Okay, okay. I'll come."

It won't be bad. I'll just act as I always do around them. I just need to be friendly and get through it.

I went to the bathroom to splash water on my face. I looked in the mirror and noticed that my face was pale from worrying all day. I put on some blush, a little eyeliner, mascara, and some lip gloss, hoping it would improve my complexion. My face brightened when I thought of seeing Giacomo. It was crazy how much I missed him even though I saw him about 24 hours ago. I grabbed my phone, met up with Elisa in the kitchen, and headed down the stairs to his apartment.

Luca answered the door with a surprised look when he saw the two of us together. He had a soccer ball in his hand and looked kind of sweaty. Giacomo was at the other end of the kitchen with two chairs set up to look like goals.

"I guess we interrupted a soccer game," Elisa said, as she moved past Luca and entered.

"*Ciao, ragazze.*" Luca replied, his voice less playful than normal.

"*Ciao.*" I said and followed Elisa inside. I looked over to the kitchen table and saw Marcello and Pietro sitting around it.

I locked eyes with Giacomo and all of those warm feelings from the night before rushed through my body. He smiled softly at me, staring at me with his intense eyes. I wanted to run over and kiss him, taking his face into my hands bringing him close to me, but I couldn't. I had to calm down.

Elisa walked over to the boys and started a conversation right away. I found a seat next to Marcello. He was hyper-focused on the sports' highlights playing on the TV and arguing with Pietro about which team deserved to win. Giacomo and Luca pulled over two chairs and sat down with the rest of us and started talking. Elisa was sitting across the table and was joining in on their conversation, while I was trying to stay as silent as I could, praying no one would ask me anything so the lying would stop.

Every once in a while Giacomo and I would steal glances at each other, and it was making it harder to stay in the room without touching him. I saw him take out his phone, type something quickly, put it back in his pocket, and continue talking to Luca about their classes.

I felt my own phone vibrate in my pocket and took it out.

GIACOMO: **I want to kiss you.**

I looked up to see Giacomo watching me read the message.

I fought back a small smile as I avoided looking at him. I saw him take out his phone again and I looked down at mine to see what he wrote.

GIACOMO: **I don't know if I can resist, especially how beautiful you look right now.**

I blushed and looked down at what I was wearing, realizing I wasn't dressed in anything special, just my favorite light-wash, ripped jeans and a plain white t-shirt. I put my phone under my chair so I wouldn't be tempted to look if he continued to text. He noticed me, let out a small laugh, and then continued talking to Luca, this time about something happening in their town.

A few minutes later, Pietro went to his room, deciding it was getting late, and I was about to use that as an excuse to leave too, but I noticed Elisa get up, and take the now empty seat next to Giacomo.

"*Allora*, Giacomo. *Cosa hai fatto questo weekend?*" She said, asking what he did this weekend. I held my breath, waiting to see how he was going to reply. He didn't look at her and instead kept his eyes downcast toward his phone.

"Cortina." He replied.

She did not seem satisfied with his answer, so she continued questioning him.

"*Ma, c'era una ragazza?*" She light-heartedly asked if there was a girl he went with.

"*Si, molto speciale.*" He said, his eyes still glued down, but a smile now forming on his lips.

Molto speciale, he'd said, someone very special! My heart skipped a beat. I turned to look at Elisa, whose expression had changed to hurt. I hated this situation we were in. Why did my happiness have to lead to someone else's pain? I couldn't help but feel sorry for her.

"Elisa, we should go back upstairs. It's getting late." I said so she had a way out of there. She nodded and began to grab her stuff. I gave Giacomo an apologetic look as we exited the apartment.

"I'm sorry, Elisa." I placed my hand on her shoulder as we walked up the stairs.

"Uggghhh." She sighed as a form of a response. She put the key into our apartment door, opened it, and huffed as she threw her bag on the chair.

"He is sweet, kind, smart, and of course handsome on top of everything. He is everything I want in a guy," she said. She didn't know just yet how much I completely agreed with her. "My last boyfriend was horrible to me, and I didn't realize until after."

I'd never heard anything about Elisa's past relationships before. "How was he horrible?" I said. She piqued my interest.

"In so many ways!" She said, taking a seat. "For example, every time I'd eat ice cream or something not traditionally healthy, he'd judge me and say it was going to make me fat."

"Oh my God Elisa, that's terrible," I said. I've heard about abusive relationships before and knew that they, unfortunately, happened all the time, but none of my friends had ever been in one.

"Yes, I know. I didn't even realize that he was mentally abusive until after I broke up with him and had a talk with someone I trust, who'd been in a similar situation as mine. Also," she continued, thinking about something else, "every time I'd put on makeup or get dressed up really pretty, he'd always find something wrong with it. He never made me feel good enough. I honestly don't know why I put up with him all of that time. I was so blind in what I thought was love, and couldn't see the truth. When I became friends with Giacomo, I realized that not all guys are like that. He was sweet and kind from the first day. The only problem was that he's just not interested in me in that way. I thought flirting with Luca would make him see that I was desirable, but look at what happened with that. That just created a giant mess."

It all made sense now, the jealousy and the desire to get him when she couldn't. The only problem was I felt the same way about him and I didn't know how to stop. I tried to think of what to say to her but couldn't come up with anything. I took a chair and sat down next to her and just listened. Even though I was the one making her life harder, I wanted her to know that I was there for her.

"I need to stop. He told us he went to Cortina with a girl who is *"molto speciale"* anyway, so I can't keep thinking I have a chance. I have to move on."

I was relieved that she realized her determination and persistence to be with Giacomo was not healthy for her but knew she would still feel hurt if she realized that I was the one he mentioned tonight.

"I'm really sorry Elisa for what you went through in the past. You are a beautiful girl and you deserve someone who will love every part of you. I promise you will find someone like that, even if it's not Giacomo."

She gave me a slight smile. "Thank you for listening. I really appreciate it."

We went into our individual beds, ready to turn in for the night. I went to grab my earbuds from my bedside table and searched for my phone, but couldn't find it. It did not take me long to realize where it was.

"Oh no, I think I left my phone in their apartment," I said, looking all around my dresser and then in the kitchen. "I'll be right back!" I shouted, as I opened the door and headed downstairs.

I ran down the stairs and I rapidly knocked on Giacomo's door. A few moments later, he opened it, my phone already in his hand.

"I was hoping you would remember and come down here to get it." He said, his eyes playful and his mouth forming a smile as he held the phone a little higher, out of my reach.

I tried to reach over and grab my phone back, but he pulled his arm away even further and grabbed my waist. I didn't even protest because all I wanted since this morning was to be alone with him. He lowered his other arm, wrapped it around my waist, and kissed my forehead, nose, and then my lips gently.

I hadn't even looked to see if anyone was in the room. I nuzzled into his chest, forgetting all of what Elisa confessed to me before.

"This is not going to be easy." Giacomo said, and I nodded my head against his chest in agreement. I held him for a few seconds more, then pulled away, looking up at him.

I got lost in his hazel eyes, noticing how the green and brown specks fused together to create a color that was unique to him, as he said, "Do not make any plans for Saturday, I want to show you where I live."

I didn't have any plans and told him I was free.

"I'm leaving early on Friday to go home. I want to bring my mom to a new doctor, but I will come back Saturday morning to pick you up." He added.

"Okay." I said.

I didn't want Elisa to get suspicious, so I had to start heading back upstairs. I brought his lips closer to mine and this time gave him a greedy, fervent kiss goodnight. As I pulled my head back, I noticed his eyes were still closed.

"*Mi fai impazzire*— you make me crazy, Juliet." He opened his eyes and they were burning hot.

I smiled, kissed him one last time, and ran upstairs before anything else would happen. I took a minute to compose myself before I entered my apartment. When I walked into our bedroom, Elisa was already asleep. I got my earbuds, turned on my nighttime playlist, and tucked myself in, hoping that the morning would make things clearer.

24

Ventiquattro

Complicato (adj)= complicated

"Buon giorno!"

I opened my eyes and looked around, groggy from sleep. Elisa was standing over my bed with a smile spread across her face.

"Wow, you're in a good mood," I said to her as I got up and headed towards the kitchen to make coffee.

"It's a new day!" She said, making her bed.

I got dressed quickly, put my hair back in a braid, and started walking to the bus stop. Kristin and Ana were already there and waved.

"Hey girls! I missed you!" I said. I hugged both of them and started chatting. Since I had already filled them in about Giacomo Sunday night, I was more curious about what was going on with them and the guys they'd met at the bar.

"So, I met up with Roberto at a bar for a cup of coffee the other day, and we have plans to get together again this weekend," Ana said, her face lighting up. "The only thing is, I have no clue what to wear and I need help with my makeup."

"That's amazing! Don't worry, we can go through your closet this week and pick something out. What about you Kristin?" I turned towards her.

"I have been texting Paolo, but nothing serious. He just came out of a long-term relationship and to be honest, I don't want to get too involved while I'm here, so it's been nice to have no strings attached." Kristin added.

"That's great! I'm happy for both of you." I said.

"What about *Giacomo*?" Kristin added, smiling.

"Well, it's kind of complicated..." I started, but then I noticed a few more people showed up at the bus stop and I didn't want to talk about it anymore.

"Our apartment, after classes tonight," Ana said, making a date. I agreed and saw the bus pulling up to our stop.

Classes went quickly, I met Jess and Valentina midday at our usual bar and Gianni commented that I looked much better than yesterday. That night, before going to Ana and Kristin's apartment, I texted Giacomo for a few minutes since he still wasn't home from his classes. He kept telling me how excited he was for Saturday. I tried to get excited too but every time I did, Elisa's face would pop up in my head and I'd replay in my mind everything she told me. I hated feeling guilty about falling so hard for someone.

I walked over to Kristin and Ana's apartment and instantly unloaded everything onto them. They listened quietly while I ranted and exposed all of the feelings and thoughts that have been swirling around my head.

"So..." Kristin said afterward, processing the entire situation. "She said she doesn't like him anymore right?"

"Yeah, she said she needed to start moving on and that she

needs to stop having feelings for him. Which I am extremely happy about for her, but I think it's way too early to say that I am seeing Giacomo." I paused, thinking about what I should do. "Is it even right that I stay with Giacomo? I tried picturing myself telling him I wouldn't be able to be with him and my whole body shouts no. Am I a bad person?"

"Well, at least Elisa said she doesn't like him anymore, so that's good news, but she can't just turn off a switch and stop having feelings for him. Seeing you with him will be hard for her but no, I don't think you are a bad person for liking him. Giacomo said from the beginning he wasn't interested in her. He didn't play games with her, he was just nice to her. It's not your fault and you cannot stop your life for her." Kristin said.

I got up and hugged her. "Thank you." She laughed and Ana joined in, all three of us huddled together.

I felt my phone vibrate a few times in my pocket and pulled it out to see messages from Giacomo. He was home and wanted to see me. It was physically painful to tell him I couldn't tonight since I was with Kristin and Ana and then needed to do some reading for school. He replied with a sad face but said he understood.

We continued chatting about random things that happened during our classes, some high school memories, and laughed at some old pictures of ourselves when we were younger. I noticed it was getting late, and needed to get back to my apartment.

As I walked past Giacomo's door on the way to my apartment, a part of me was pulling towards it, just wanting to say hi, especially since Kristin made me feel better about being with him. I still wanted to give Elisa time, and I really did need to read for my classes since I was planning on spending all of Saturday with Giacomo.

****

Jess, Valentina, and I met up the next day at the bar and sat in our usual seats. We were about to order something when Gianni put three cappuccino mugs in front of us.

"*Marocchino.*" He said, telling us the name of the coffee as he served it to us in a cappuccino mug. I checked my phone and it was definitely after 2pm.

"But Gianni, you said no cappuccinos after 11am. What's this?" I said.

"*No, va bene.*" He continued, telling me it was okay. "*C'è caffè, latte, e nutella. Questo lo offre la casa.*" He said, telling us that it was on the house. I looked at the drink and noticed there was frothy milk with a dusting of cocoa powder on top. We all took a sip, not knowing what to expect. The Nutella hit my mouth with the perfect touch of sweetness, without overpowering the coffee.

"*Wow! Delizioso.*" Valentina said. Gianni was a very serious guy and usually didn't smile too much, but if you looked at him then you never would have known. We thanked him and then he went on to serve other customers.

"So, what time is the meeting again?" Jess asked both of us.

"What meeting?" I asked, looking at both of them.

"Juliet, remember? We are meeting Giorgia tonight in her office, then we are going out for pizza after. Even John is coming tonight." Valentina explained.

No, I did not remember. Another night that I wouldn't be able to see Giacomo. "I completely forgot. Do you want to meet us after our Italian class to walk over to her office?" I asked Valentina since she was the only one not in our class.

"I'm actually skipping my last class and meeting up with a girl from my art history class to walk with," Valentina added with excitement in her voice.

"No way, that's great!" I said.

"Yeah, it's funny because it's the same girl that helped me copy her notes. She's so brilliant that I didn't think she would want to hang out with me. I was intimidated to even ask her to. But, a few days ago," she said, grabbing my arm showcasing her excitement, "I just asked her if she wanted to meet up for coffee and chat, and she invited me to hang out with her and her other friends at a bar! She told me they meet up all the time and have crazy discussions about politics, art, and writers. They all seem so cool."

"They *do* sound cool. I feel like you would get along really well with a group like that." I said. I hoped that this would change things for her here and that she would finally enjoy her time more.

We parted after that, all going to our next classes, and I met up with Jess again in our Italian class later on. Matt was already there, smiling and happier than he'd been in the last few weeks.

"So what are you so happy about?" I asked.

"Nothing, just happy." He said, smiling even wider to show his teeth

"I don't know, Matt," Jess said, jumping in on our conversation, "seems kind of suspicious."

"Alright, alright I'll give." he said, throwing his hands up, and still grinning, "I'm having another party this Friday night and I'm really excited about it. You both need to come this time. I don't want to hear any excuses at all. I'm even making paella."

"Okay, you convinced me," I said, hoping it would help revert our relationship back to how it was, "I'll go and I'll bake some cookies."

"Oh my God, yes. Cookies!" said Jess. "I'll be there too, with a bottle of wine that I may or may not feel like sharing."

I laughed and forgot for a moment that class was about to start and the classroom was pretty much quiet except for our conversation.

"Can you text Valentina the info too?" Matt asked more quietly.

"Of course," Jess said.

When class was over, the three of us made our way over to

Giorgia's office. Personally, I was daydreaming about paella and hoping that Friday would bring only good memories. I turned towards Matt.

"Are you sure you know how to cook paella?" I joked.

"Wow, you really don't trust me, do you?" He quipped back as he looked over at me.

"I don't know, Javier's paella is pretty top-notch, might be kind of hard to compete with it," I responded.

"I promise it'll blow your mind." He said, making a gesture with his hands of something exploding.

When we reached Giorgia's office I realized that I was excited to see her again. Memories of my first day here with my bags came back to me as I remembered the mixed feelings I had. The fear and excitement hit me as I stood in front of the building. So much had changed in the few months that I'd been here.

25

Venticinque

Un rapporto (nm)= a relationship

Giorgia was sitting behind her desk with her black stiletto heels propped up onto the dark wood. She had her cat-eye, red reading glasses perched halfway down her nose as she looked up from the papers she was reading. She was still dressed fashionably, in dark grey slacks and a white short-sleeved dress shirt that had a V-neck and a belt. With her free hand, she gestured for the five of us to take a seat.

"I've heard great things from your professors about all five of you." She started, her eyeglasses falling slightly on her nose as she looked above them with her eyes at us. "Matthew, you did well on a writing exam I see. And Valentina, your professors have raved about you saying you are just like the Italian students. Jess and Juliet, your professors have praised your work as well. John, I see that you have done well on your marketing project. Just remember, there are bigger exams coming up in the next few months so make sure you don't fall behind. You should still travel, and take in all of what Italy has to offer, but try to find a balance."

I was so happy to hear her praise. It made me feel like the hard work I did paid off. She told us some more information on upcoming events pertaining to the end of the semester, and we took down notes of important dates and things we needed to remember. We all got up to leave and she stopped me before I was about to go.

"Juliet, can you stay just a little bit longer?" She took out my papers and separated them from the bunch.

"Of course," I said, sitting back down and suddenly nervous, feeling the sweat begin to moisten my hands. The rest of them left, saying they would wait outside for me.

"Don't be nervous Juliet," Giorgia said, noticing me sitting rigidly in the chair, "I just want to talk. I remember reading in your application that you wanted to be a teacher. How would you like to teach here for a year after you graduate? You are graduating this year, right?"

My mind took a second to catch up to her words. "Yes, I am," I said, still processing. "What would that mean exactly, though?" I asked, wondering where I would live and what I'd be teaching.

"Well, my husband is from England and runs a local language school here that offers English to all age groups. We always could use more teachers since our program is growing. You would be teaching English. Think about it, and if you are interested, you would just have to take an intensive course this summer and then you can start teaching this September. I'll send you an email with all of the information and you can let me know if you are interested."

I absorbed what she said and thanked her before I left. As exciting as that sounded, there was no way I could put off a year from getting my Master's. I did keep thinking about it though as I caught up with the others who were waiting for me outside of the building.

We decided on a pizzeria that was nearby so we wouldn't have to wait too long to get some food in our stomachs. I took out my phone while we were seated and texted Giacomo that I had a meeting with my director and now I was at a pizzeria with my friends. He texted back a sad face and asked if he could meet me quickly when I came back.

GIACOMO: **Come to my apartment. You are allowed to visit me, right?**

JULIET: **Ok, but only for a few minutes!**

"Here's to us and all of the hard work we did!" Jess said, raising her glass of beer as we all did the same and clinked them together.

"So what did Georgia stop you about? Is everything okay?" Matt asked me as Valentina was talking to Jess about the new friends she had made. John was seated next to Valentina, already halfway finished with his beer.

"She wanted to know if I was interested in teaching English here for a year, starting September. I guess she saw my file and knows that I want to be a teacher, but I'm not so sure I do anymore."

Matt's eyebrows raised as I was telling him this, probably surprised too from what Giorgia said.

"Anyway, I'm not thinking that far ahead. I want to pass these classes so I can graduate on time."

"Are you bummed that we can't attend our graduation in person?" He asked, now his face in a neutral expression.

"Not really. Look at where we are and this view! This trip was definitely worth it no matter what."

Matt smiled and nodded his head. We continued chatting until the pizzas came and then everybody became silent, mesmerized by each of the individual pies in front of them.

"Wow, I was so hungry." Matt said, with a mouthful of pizza in his mouth.

"That's gross, Matt. You can't talk with your mouth full!" Valentina said, wearing her disgust on her face.

Matt, in order to properly annoy Valentina thoroughly, continued talking with his mouth full which made Jess and I laugh and Valentina shaded her eyes away.

"Alright, alright, I'm done," Matt said clearly now, but still smiling at Valentina. "Anyway, are we ready for Friday night guys? Ready to see my paella skills in the flesh?"

"You bet I am," I said, "That lunch you made me that time was very good, but I don't know if it was up to par with a professional paella chef. There's a lot of ingredients that go into that dish." I looked at him and noticed he'd stopped eating when I mentioned the lunch. It was right when I thought I could possibly be something more with Matt. Before the barbecue, before Giacomo, before all of the mess that happened. I noticed that he must've come to the same realization as me because his facial expression changed and then he turned his body toward John.

"Make sure you bring your girl, John," Matt said, getting his attention.

"Oooh, you need to tell us more about Kathryn," Jess added, visibly interested.

"Well," John started, shifting in his seat, looking uncomfortable. "She's sweet, fun, and we can talk for hours."

All four of us leaned towards John, as our mouths stood slightly agape. This was definitely not the same John we knew from before.

"Wait, *talk for hours?* Who are you?" Jess said, voicing what we probably had all been thinking.

John let out a laugh and relaxed slightly back in his seat. "I know, I know. I don't have the best reputation with girls. But I just feel different with her. I really like her. It just feels right."

The corner of my mouth pulled up after hearing that. *It just feels right.* Those same feelings that I couldn't express about Giacomo were exactly that—it just felt right.

After we finished up and paid, we walked to the bus stop to go back home. Matt walked next to me, his hands in his pockets as usual. I could tell he was thinking about something.

"So, this time you will make it?" He asked, his face now changing more to hope as he asked me.

I nodded yes, and he seemed content as we boarded the bus and headed back home. My mood instantly lifted as I remembered that I was going to visit Giacomo. I figured I would knock on his door, and if anyone else answered, I could pretend I was looking for Elisa before heading back to our apartment thinking she would be there. I started playing out different scenarios in my head of different excuses in case anyone else opened the door. Then I remembered Luca already knew and Marcello and Pietro probably wouldn't care. I lifted my hand to knock on the door.

"I was waiting for you." He said as soon as he opened the door, not even giving me a chance to knock a second time. I quickly looked over his shoulder and saw no one else there and then looked behind me and saw the hall empty. He took me in and kissed me so deeply that it made me want to drop my bags.

"So, you had a beer and pizza tonight." He said, his mouth forming a playful grin as he said that. "How was it?"

"Delicious. Also, my director said she was proud of us." I said, pretending to brush off an imaginary crumb on my shoulder which made Giacomo laugh. "Matt invited me to a party Friday night at his apartment," I added, not wanting to hide anything from him.

"Oh, did he?" He said, still holding on to me and kissing my forehead.

"Yes, and I promised to make lemon cookies. He is making the paella and wants us to try it." I added while kissing him back on his forehead. I panicked and looked over our shoulders again. I'd never felt paranoid like this before. Once I realized we were still alone, I kissed him again on his nose and then on his lips.

"Okay, but Saturday you are mine." He said, pulling me again closely to him and giving me a deeper kiss than the playful ones I'd been giving him. I didn't want to risk it anymore, so I pushed away from him, held his face in my hands, and gave him one more kiss goodnight before going upstairs.

***

The next day passed so quickly between lessons and reading that I didn't even realize it was time for dinner when I checked the time. I stepped in the kitchen and saw Elisa putting some salad and grilled chicken on two dishes on the table.

"You were so captivated by your reading, I figured I'd make you dinner." She said and then placed the bowl on the table. "I wanted to surprise you."

"Wow, thanks so much! It smells delicious." I said. I instantly felt the guilt creep up, but I reminded myself of what Kristin told me and that it wasn't mine or Giacomo's fault what happened between us. We ate and chatted about our day, and then both of our phones vibrated at the same time. Elisa went to get hers first and turned it around to check the message.

"So Marcello texted me that they are all downstairs watching a show and he wants to know if we want to join them." She said as I checked to see the same message sent to me too.

"It's okay, you can go, I kind of want to stay in," I said.

"Juliet, enough of this. You keep saying no, but then come down anyway. You've read enough for one day. Finish up eating and let's go!" She added, her tone serious but her face showing a more playful expression.

"Alright fine," I said. I didn't know why I couldn't ever tell Elisa no. We put the dishes in the sink, leaving them for later and I followed her out the door down to the boys' apartment.

We walked in the door and Giacomo's eyes lit up as soon as he saw me. I gave him a smile back. I'd recognized the show that they were watching from another time we were together, but they spoke so fast that I couldn't keep up. I hoped I could understand more than last time, especially since I had been listening to more music and shows in Italian.

Elisa sat down next to Pietro and Marcello and I took the only other free seat available, next to Giacomo.

I felt myself blushing as I tried to keep my head straight and not gaze at him. I heard Giacomo let out a small laugh, probably because I still couldn't face him, and my face was getting redder as the minutes passed. He pressed his palm against my knee under the table, out of everyone's sight, and squeezed my knee gently which made me calm down. I sat a little further back in my chair, waiting for my cheeks to return to a normal color before I could say or do anything next. Everyone else was focused on watching the TV as a segment played about the inequalities of Southern and Northern Italians. The reporter was interviewing a Southern Italian man who was lamenting about how he was getting passed over jobs because of his accent. While I was proud that I was now finally able to understand almost everything, the man's words were stuck in my head.

"Wait," I said, causing everyone to turn their head towards me, "So is there really this difference between Northern and Southern Italians?" I asked everyone.

"Yes, there is, but of course, not everyone feels like this, there are some people that believe in the stereotypes of Southern Italians. Obviously, we don't," Elisa said, gesturing to everyone in the room, "But you should hear some of the comments people say." The others nodded their heads in agreement.

I thought back to how so many people here had commented that my accent was southern. I only now realized that they may have been judging me poorly because of it. Back in New York, I would just say I was Italian, never realizing that there was a difference in what *part* of Italy I came from.

"What do they say about Southern Italians?" I asked, now curious to know more.

"Well," Marcello said, looking a little uneasy since they all knew I was Southern Italian, "they say that they are lazy, in the mafia, and don't want to work." He blurted out.

"Wow, I never realized this. I assumed everyone loved pizza and pasta and that was it." I said, laughing a little to lighten the humor.

"Now who's the one saying stereotypes?" Giacomo said, his eyes teasing me. I looked over to him and smiled.

We continued watching the show, the reporter now interviewing others about their experiences with profiling. I felt that I was treated differently in stores at times when I would try to speak Italian, but I couldn't imagine an Italian feeling that way in their own country.

"But even if they all speak Italian, not their dialects, you can still hear that they are from the South?" I asked, still trying to wrap my brain around all of it.

They all nodded their heads with expressions of sympathy in their eyes. I felt bad for my relatives. I'd never known that they'd gone through something like this and it made me want to see them and hug them.

In a few weeks, I'll see my grandparents for the Easter break. I felt like I needed more time here and prayed that the next few weeks would go slowly. Elisa was chatting with Luca, which made me feel happy for both of them. Luca said something that made her laugh, and I finally saw her relaxed near him. Marcello looked at both Giacomo and me and gestured towards Luca and Elisa as if to say *finally, things are back to normal.*

Pietro opened the balcony door and we followed him outside, while Elisa and Luca stayed in, still talking. The weather was warm that night, so we all leaned against the railing enjoying the night sky and the silence. Pietro and Marcello started talking to each other and Giacomo looked over at me, his face hard to read.

"Juliet, did you ever see the volleyball court we set up in the back?" He asked, his face still neutral.

I was about to respond yes, but I saw him shake his head no quickly as if I was supposed to say *no* out loud.

"No?" I said, laughing as it came out as a question. He dropped his head, then turned around and told the guys where we were going.

As soon as we turned the corner and were out of sight, he leaned against the wall and pulled me against him. My legs were slightly weak since I was not expecting this moment at all. His intoxicating smell overpowered me as I knew I needed more of him at that moment and didn't even care if we got caught. Our lips finally touched, at first a delicate song playing until passion had taken over and my heart began thumping, creating a beat that I felt coming out of my chest. I pulled back, caught my breath, and waited for my brain to connect back to the rest of my body, before I looked back into his eyes.

"I can't wait until Saturday." Was all he said, and all I could do was nod my head. He let out a breath, and we both walked back around the corner, our hands not touching, but wanting to, to where Pietro and Marcello were.

I peered into the apartment and saw Elisa still talking to Luca. She made eye contact when she saw me and we both gestured to each other at the same time we should go up.

"Have a great weekend if I don't see you," I told the boys. I stared at Giacomo a second longer. I wanted to make him show me the volleyball court again.

Elisa followed me upstairs, not saying much, but in a good mood as we both then said our goodnights, going straight in our beds.

****

The next day, Matt sat down next to me in class and bumped my shoulder, displaying a huge "up-to-no-good" grin.

"Hey." he said.

"Hey," I said, shoving him back.

"It's Friday."

"I know! I'm very ready for the weekend."

When I got back to my apartment after, I texted Giacomo to see how the doctor appointments had gone with his mom. I was nervous to see where he lived and maybe meet some of his friends. He hadn't mentioned I would meet his parents, but would I? It was definitely a possibility. I contemplated asking him but figured I wouldn't, to see where the day took me.

I put on jeans and one of my comfy shirts and tied my hair back in a ponytail. I refreshed my mascara that I had put on in the morning and got the cookies out from the oven that I'd baked. The smell from them took over the whole kitchen and instantly put me in a better mood. I met up with Kristin and Ana before heading over to Matt's. Jess and Valentina were already there and I gave them both big hugs when I saw them. John was at the other side of the room with his arm around Kathryn. I made sure to wave hello to them. I turned around and spied Matt by the stove, concentrating on the paella, and decided I would say hi to him later. I put the cookies on a table where the other food was and Jess poured us all a glass from the bottle of wine she brought.

"Well, there goes a bottle already!" She said, laughing as she poured the last drop into Ana's glass. "It's finally nice to meet you both since Juliet has talked about you two so much."

"I thought you all knew each other," I yelled over the music that Javier had just turned on. They all chatted with each other, asking questions about their lives at home when all of a sudden, I felt an arm on my shoulder and turned around to see Matt standing behind me, beaming. He was wearing a blue and black checkered, flannel shirt, and tan pants.

"So, are you ready ladies to try the best paella you've ever tasted in your life?" He said.

"You bet I am. My expectations are very high." I said.

We walked over to the table, where he'd already placed a few servings into paper bowls. He handed us each one filled with yellow rice, roasted chicken, sausage, peppers, and peas.

"Wait, before you try, we need to all bring our forks together and cheers," Matt said, taking a bite forkful of rice and holding it up. We all obeyed, bringing them together and laughing as we said "cheers" in unison.

I brought the fork to my mouth and widened my eyes as the rich flavors marinated my tongue.

"Wow, Matt! That's awesome. Don't tell Javier," I continued bringing my voice down so that only he could hear me, "but I think it might be even better than Javier's."

"Probably beginner's luck," He said, even though I could tell he was waiting for someone to say something along those lines. "I added some more spices than he does and I think it brought out the chicken flavor even more. Plus, I found this new butcher in the city and I got the meat from there. It's definitely higher quality."

"Well, I'm very impressed. You've really outdone yourself with this. It was definitely worth the hype." I could tell that I made his night.

"Thank you." He put his hand on my shoulder and looked into

my eyes. I quickly looked away not wanting to expand the tension. "Who needs a drink? I know I do." He started pouring some liquor and coke into plastic cups to pass around.

"I'm okay," I said, pushing away the one he was offering me. "I need to get up early tomorrow and I already drank a glass of wine," I said. Jess took a glass from him and so did Kristin, while Ana and Valentina also refused.

"Where are you going?" Jess asked, turning to me and sipping from her cup. It took me a second to realize my mistake. I was backed into a corner and couldn't find my way out.

"Actually, Giacomo, you know Elisa's friend? He is going to pick me up tomorrow morning and we are going to visit his town." I didn't want to hide in front of them anymore.

"Oh, awesome!" Jess said, her eyes widening. "You'll have so much fun!" She looked at Matt and then down at the ground before excusing herself saying she needed to use the restroom, and grabbed Valentina along with her. Kristin and Ana understood as well and moved over to the other side of the room, excusing themselves too.

"So, you are seeing Giacomo." Matt said, his expression hard to read.

"Yeah, he invited me to see where he is from," I answered meekly. He looked to the side, his expression hardened. When he turned back there was a flicker of anger in his eyes.

"I thought you didn't want a relationship here? I thought you were going to focus on school." The volume of his voice had increased enough for some of the people around us to turn around. I pulled his arm to follow me outside on the balcony so we wouldn't cause a scene.

"I know I said that, and I'm not sure what's happening with Giacomo or if it will even last." I saw his anger soften into sadness.

"I just thought if anyone would've been able to change your mind about dating in Verona, it would've been me. We have fun together and I've always been there for you."

"Matt," I said, taking his hand and looking into his eyes. "You *have* always been there for me and I love the relationship we have." I looked out towards my apartment building, knowing that Giacomo wasn't there but feeling pulled and torn in that direction. "I just think that it needs to stay like this, and that maybe we weren't meant to be anything more than just friends."

He clenched his jaw and turned his eyes to the side before looking back at me. I swore I saw a few tears in his eyes before he blinked back his emotions rapidly. "I don't even know what to say to that." He pulled his hand back and put both in his pockets and shrugged his shoulders up. "You know what? I don't want to talk about this anymore. Tonight was supposed to be fun. And this? This will ruin it for me."

"Okay, I understand," I said, starting to feel my own emotions well up inside of me. "Take your time." He opened the door of the balcony, joined the colored lights and music of the inside, and left me outside.

I wanted to follow him but knew it would only make things worse. I stood outside looking into the night sky, unable to see the stars or the hills behind the city. If I went after him I would only say something that would hurt him more. I put down my drink, my stomach churning anything that I had already eaten, and I went back inside.

I saw him in the far corner of the apartment, leaning against the wall talking to Javier and another girl. I looked up at him, trying to get his attention, but as soon as his eyes met mine, he quickly looked away and put his hands in his pocket. I bit down on my lip, telling myself I would not get upset and walked over to Kristin and Ana. My lips were quivering slightly, my fingers clenched to my sides, and they both put an arm around me and took me outside of the party.

"Let's just go back to my apartment." Kristin offered and I nodded my head. "Just text Jess and Valentina that you left early in case they were wondering where you went."

I took out my phone and sent the message. They responded back quickly, saying they were excited for my date with Giacomo but hoped everything was okay with Matt. I didn't know what to write back, so I didn't respond.

26

Ventisei

Conoscere (v)= to know, be familiar with

I slept on Kristin and Ana's couch that night because I didn't want to be alone. They brought me pillows and blankets and I felt grateful to have them as my friends. We stayed up pretty late talking about anything other than boys. I even showed Ana how to apply her makeup differently.

The next morning, I hugged Ana and Kristin, thanking them over and over for being there. I ran over to my apartment to get ready before Giacomo came. The ominous feeling of guilt kept returning and I tried to push away all of the faces of the people I hurt by being with Giacomo.

I heard a soft knock on the door and opened it to find Giacomo, one arm against the frame and his other hand holding his car keys by his side.

"I'm not coming in, because we will never leave." He said, giving me a sweet kiss hello.

I grabbed my bag, locked the door behind us, and headed outside. As we were walking towards his car, I saw Matt jogging towards the apartment, probably coming back from a run.

I hesitated before stepping into the car. I didn't want to hide from him, but I also didn't want to hurt him. As I stood there, he kept jogging towards his building, refusing to look in my direction. Giacomo watched me in silence while I stood with one foot in his car.

"Is everything okay?" He asked, craning his neck to look at me through the passenger's side.

I took a breath and lowered myself into the seat.

"I told Matt last night about us and it didn't go too well," I said. I continued to explain to him what happened and how I didn't want to hurt him, but I felt that I already did.

"You should never hide something that makes you happy." He reached over to squeeze my hand, looking me in the eyes.

We drove silently for a little while, listening to another one of his favorite singers, Ligabue, whose warm lyrics reminded me of Ultimo. I added a few of the songs I heard to my playlist as we drove along. About a half-hour in, he begged me to put on my music.

"No, I can't," I said, putting my phone away. "It's not the same as your music. It doesn't sound as effortlessly classy and beautiful."

"I want to know what type of music you like." He said as he disconnected his phone from the car. "Just because it's different doesn't automatically mean that it's bad. Please?" He stopped looking at the road for a second to glance my way.

"Okay, okay. I will put on the playlist I used to listen to when I walked between classes." I plugged in my phone and played "Honeybee" by The Head and the Heart. "I like to listen to all types of music, but I need to be able to feel the emotion behind the lyrics.

I think that's why I like listening to Italian music so much. It's so powerful."

"This song is good. It's very sweet sounding." He said. "Like you." He squeezed my knee and I let my guard down, allowing the playlist to play through.

We started approaching his town and he pointed out little things from his past along the way. It reminded me of a nativity scene perched on a hilltop. I couldn't believe the view of the valleys below us. There was a church with a bell tower in the main square, and two small bars next to it with older men playing cards, drinking glasses of wine. We drove up a narrow street that only one car could pass at a time, and he had to honk his horn on the curve to make sure no one was coming the opposite way. We turned into a small courtyard and he parked his car in front of an ivy-covered building with cream stucco peeking out between some of the vines. I looked over at him and realized we were probably in front of his house.

"My parents are dying to meet you. Is it okay if we see them first?" He turned and asked, his hands holding the key, waiting to turn the car off.

"Of course, it's okay." My heartbeat began to quicken. "I'm not going to lie though, I'm nervous Giacomo, what if they don't like me?" I looked down to see my fingers trembling slightly. I didn't think I was going to meet his parents right away.

"Don't worry Juliet." He said reaching over to grab my trembling hands. "They'll love you. I didn't tell you because I didn't want you to get nervous. If you don't want to meet them, you don't have to, no pressure. She did make an amazing risotto that you might want to try though." He said and then gave me a sweet kiss.

"Okay, the risotto convinced me. Let's go." I said, opening the door.

He laughed and got out of the car. His mother answered the door, greeting him with a smile and a huge hug. His dog ran out right after her, running over to me and I bent down to pet him. I looked back over at his mom and noticed she looked the same in the pictures he had posted, except a little more tired, probably from how she had been feeling lately. Her hair was styled away from her face, with her wavy blond locks just brushing the tops of her shoulders. She was slightly shorter than me and was dressed in a loose-fitting floral blouse with matching dark blue slacks. She looked over at me, continuing to smile, and then she held out her arms to wrap me in a hug.

"Adeso ho capio el parche el sta imparando l'inglese." She said, as she pulled back and smiled at me with a genuinely warm smile that made me feel like I already knew her. I knew Italian, could understand almost every TV show and song, but I looked to Giacomo for help because I didn't understand a word she'd said.

"She's speaking the dialect to you, sorry. She just said now she knows why I am learning English." He was bent down, hugging his dog, and looked up to his mom shaking his head. *"L'italiano, mamma!"* He said, now reminding her to speak Italian, not dialect to me.

"Va bene, va bene." She said, her hands still on my shoulders as she escorted us inside. *"Sono Carla."* She added, telling me her name. We walked into a foyer where there were stairs leading up to the second floor and a doorway leading into the rest of the house. His mother led me through the doorway into a dining room and den. The decor reminded me of Cortina, with wooden trinkets lining the fireplace mantel and soft yellows and oranges brightening the room.

The room had a cozy feel to it that made me want to take a seat on the couch and face the fireplace with a cup of warm coffee in my hands and a book next to me. The table in the den was already set with four places. His house gave me a good feeling.

His dad walked into the dining room and greeted me with a handshake.

"Piacere, sono Luciano." He said, introducing himself to me. He

was more serious than his mom, but his eyes had a gentle look to them. I looked over at Giacomo and I could see his expression was relaxed but proud. He pulled a chair out for me next to him, and we sat down while his mom brought us dishes of risotto.

"Pretend you like it, even if you don't," Giacomo whispered as she placed the dish down in front of me. His mom playfully yelled at Giacomo to not speak English, and he nodded his head that he wouldn't anymore. "It's a risotto with porcini mushrooms. It's my favorite thing she makes." He added as we waited for his mom to take a seat before we began eating.

I took a forkful of the risotto, making sure to get a piece of mushroom on it too, and moaned slightly. I'd never expected something as simple as rice could be turned into a work of art that had my taste buds melt. Giacomo hit the side of my leg and I quickly apologized in Italian after realizing I sort of moaned out loud. I complimented his mom that I had never had a dish that tasted this good before. His mom looked over at Giacomo with a slight smile, then back at me and thanked me for the compliment.

She brought out another dish called *peperonata*, which was a sort of stew made with tomatoes, peppers, eggplants, and onions. I didn't hesitate to take a second helping since it was so good. Afterward, we had a cup of espresso and some fresh baked cookies. Giacomo carried a few dirty dishes back to the kitchen and I helped him, carrying some of the food back too. He gave me a quick kiss before his mom came in to bring in the rest of the stuff.

I offered to help his mom wash the dishes. She protested, but I told her that I would feel better if I could do anything to help after the delicious meal she made. Giacomo excused himself after his dad called him over to check something in their yard while I stayed to help his mom dry the dishes.

"*Giacomo mi ha detto che fai un buon tiramisù.*" She told me in Italian this time, not in dialect, how Giacomo said I make a good tiramisù. She added that I would have to make it next time together with her. I responded that I definitely would as I continued helping her dry the rest of the dishes. She stopped washing for a second, walked over to a framed picture of a little boy in a meadow, and pointed to it.

"*Questo è Giacomo*," she said. "*Era molto timido da bambino, e balbettava quando parlava.*" She explained how he was very shy when he was young and stuttered. It was difficult for me to imagine him as shy or stuttering as a little boy.

"*Ho cantato sempre con lui.*" She then said how she would always sing with him and explained how it helped his stuttering go away. I stopped drying the dishes as she told me that the doctors didn't think that it would work back then, saying she was wasting her time, but she kept trying and had him singing songs every night before bed. Tears formed in her eyes as she said how some of his classmates would tease him, but she told him to be strong and not let it bother him, that he was smart anyway. I could hear the pride in her voice as she told me how he eventually stopped stuttering, and how she has been proud of how hard he'd worked for everything.

I smiled picturing his mom helping him when he was young and making sure he would never doubt himself and feel down. I could see why Giacomo wanted to do everything he could to help her. She had an effortless way of making you feel comfortable next to her, like you just wanted to sit down next to her and listen to what she had to say.

Giacomo came in smiling to see us together chatting. "She used Italian, I hope." He said, and his mother gave him a look as if she understood what he was saying. "Follow me, I'll show you the rest of the house." I looked back at his mom, silently thanking her with a smile. She nodded back gently to me, her mouth turning up slightly before going back to washing the dishes.

He took my hand and led me across the dining room and up the stairs to the second floor.

"Your mom is amazing, Giacomo. I never knew you stuttered." I said, squeezing his hand.

His cheeks slightly flushed. I grabbed his face gently between my hands and kissed his forehead.

The hallway upstairs was the same color as the rest of the house, with yellow bubbly paint covering the wall. There were some black and white pictures hanging up, with who I assumed were his grandparents. He led me to the end of the hallway and stopped in front of a bedroom.

"This is my room. I cleaned it last night, so hopefully it's okay." He said, opening the door.

The walls were the same color as the hallway and there was a big armoire against one wall. It took up the entirety of the space along it. Italians didn't have closets like we did back home but instead used floor-to-ceiling armoires to store their clothes. There were multiple, colorful murals painted all over his room, one of a bulldog in yellow and blue, another of the ocean with palm trees, and one of a shark.

"So that's the mascot of the Hellas Verona soccer team." He said, pointing to the bulldog. "I got inspired to paint the beach one time after being stuck in the house one summer with a broken foot, and that shark, over there, is something I copied off a book I saw."

"You painted these?" I asked, taking in the detail he added to the bulldog's fur and collar.

"Do you like them?"

"Are you kidding? They're amazing! You're so talented!" I got closer to the murals to admire each one of them. I remembered my art teacher having some sort of pity for me back in high school because even though I tried my best, I still lacked basic art skills.

"What?" I said as I saw him staring at me while I was looking at the murals.

"You are so passionate about everything. When you love something, you literally moan and make noises. You make everyone around you feel like a better person and you don't even realize you are doing it."

I stopped and took in the words he said. I'd never received a compliment like that before. It made me feel good about myself, something I was at war with feeling these past few weeks.

"I feel safe with you. Like I am at home." I said, stepping a little closer to him. He came a little closer too and we both stopped a few feet away from each other.

"Did you feel something that day when we first met?" His eyes jumped between mine and his expression turned serious.

"I did. I actually felt something when I saw your picture hanging by Elisa's bed." I admitted, slightly embarrassed.

"You did? So, you thought I was cute. And here I thought you liked me for my personality." He said, his expression changing to a playful one.

"I also felt something that first night on the balcony, and definitely during that walk, but I didn't think you liked me in a serious way." It felt good to reveal myself to him and become vulnerable.

"I liked you a lot right from the beginning but thought I'd lost you when I saw you become closer with Matt."

We stepped a little closer to each other, our vulnerability creating a magnetic-like attraction dragging us closer with each admission.

"It would've always been you, Giacomo," I said, stepping towards him until the tips of our shoes were touching and he was looking down at me. I felt his breath on my mouth, making me want him.

"Juliet, I..." He started to say, but I took his mouth into mine, I needed to feel him to let him know how much of me he had, how my heart was his. He responded back with a kiss that was even deeper, his tongue sweeping inside my mouth as his hands went to the top of my neck, bringing me even closer to him. His hands then moved down, towards my waist, still with his mouth on mine, sucking all of the air out of my body. We now moved against the mural, one of his arms was leaning against the wall for support as our kiss became more passionate, and his other arm grabbed tighter to my waist. I suddenly came to my senses, realized that his parents were just downstairs, and pulled back, enough for him to stop.

"We can't Giacomo, your parents..." I stammered as I was trying to get my breath back. He was flushed too, but looked down and nodded his head.

"Let's go meet up with my friends. I want to introduce you to them." He said, stepping back and bringing me into his arms, and giving me gentle kisses on my face.

I thanked his parents again on the way out the door, and they both hugged me goodbye telling me how happy they were to meet me. Giacomo put his arm around my shoulder and we walked to his car and drove to the town square. We were meeting his friends at one of the bars out front. I recognized a few of them including Luca. Roberto made plans with Ana in the city so he wouldn't be here, but there were some other friends with their girlfriends as well that he introduced me to.

We sat down at the bar and they asked me questions about my life in New York. I heard embarrassing stories about Giacomo when he was younger from some of his friends. We decided to go out to a pizzeria after to keep the night going. His friends made me feel like I fit in and I felt comfortable around them, too. Giacomo kept his hand on mine the whole night, squeezing it every once in a while, and looking over at me with a smile. I could see how happy he was that we were hanging out in his hometown.

After I enjoyed *panna cotta* for dessert, a custard with caramelized sugar on top, we decided it was time to go back to the apartment.

We said our goodbyes, the girlfriends surprising me with hugs, and headed to his car and started the trip back.

"My friends loved you, my parents loved you. Juliet, you are winning over everyone." Giacomo said, taking my hand and kissing the back of it before he had to shift gears again.

I wanted to do everything with him— see new places, try new things. I'd never had this feeling about anyone before and I was afraid to lose it. Unwelcome thoughts popped into my brain that I fought hard to suppress. I needed to focus on the present. I needed to focus on being with him.

He stopped in front of the apartments about an hour later, and we both froze, unsure of what should happen next. I could feel the tension build, unable to escape, pushing me closer to him.

27

※

Ventisette

Innamorarsi (v)= to fall in love

"I can come upstairs for a while." He said, his voice barely perceptible as if he was afraid to quell that desire that continued to build and create tangible energy between us.

"Okay." Was all I could respond back. We walked silently, all the way to my apartment, through my door, still not daring to utter a word or break the intensity that was there. I took off my jacket and placed my bag on the chair as I walked in and he placed his jacket on top. Still silent, I took his hand and led him straight to my bedroom, feeling the need to close the door behind him, as if I had to contain this built-up energy between us. He stood in front of me, taking both of my arms in his hands, and he looked down, staring into my eyes with a gaze so intense that held me in.

"I love you, Juliet." The words echoed throughout my body, releasing that energy that had been built up inside. Those were words that I would remember forever, this moment, as I would look back on. I reached up to him, pulling his head towards mine as an answer. My body asked me to do it, and wanted him closer to me. He cradled his hands under my legs and back, swept me up, his mouth still locked on mine, and then placed me on the bed, placing gentle kisses all over me.

****

When we woke up the next morning, our legs were intertwined and my head was resting on his chest while his fingers were playing with my hair.

"*Buongiorno, bella.*" He said as I looked up to him. Last night was so magical, every cell of my body was still glowing.

"So now that my friends and mom embarrassed me about what I was like when I was younger, I want to hear all about what young Juliet was like."

I told him how I was pretty fearless when I was younger, climbing trees in my backyard and throwing footballs around with the neighborhood boys.

"I could throw a perfect spiral!"

Giacomo started laughing and then made me promise to show him one time. I explained how my mom would bring me to her school and have me help her teach. I'd then go home, line up my dolls, and pretend to be a teacher too.

"So, you always knew that you wanted to be a teacher?"

"I did, but a few years ago I tried teaching one of her classes, and it was not at all what I expected. My mom made it seem so effortless, but when I got in front of the class, my mind went blank. It was as if I had forgotten to speak even English!"

He laughed and then turned to me, pushing a strand of hair behind my ear, and looking into my eyes. I loved his touch, at times both gentle and strong, and I felt relaxed talking to him, wanting to tell him everything there was to know about me.

"For some reason, I started doubting myself as I got older. Like I'm not so sure of myself or anything that I do. My mom is this amazing teacher and I know she is pushing me to be like her, but what if I'm not?"

"Not sure of yourself? Juliet, you are beautiful and full of life. What are you unsure of?"

"Maybe I'm like that with you, but I'm not that way all of the time." I took his hand again and gently touched his fingers. "Well, anyway, I still have to do my Master's when I go back so I can start teaching. I started applying to several schools and will probably hear back from them in June. I can become a substitute teacher while going to school and then hopefully start teaching right after."

"Sounds to me like you have everything planned already. By the way, I think you will be amazing in anything you want to do. You make people happier when they are around you. You even make me want to be better."

"Well, maybe everyone except Elisa," I said, laughing and squeezing his fingers that were still locked with mine.

"I don't think anything can make Elisa happy." He added, chuckling too.

I kissed him again, and placed my hand delicately on his face, moving closer to him, not wanting this time we had together to end.

"I can't hide this anymore Juliet. I know you don't want to hurt Elisa's feelings, but I need to kiss and hold you every time I see you."

I felt like that too. I was visiting my grandparents next week for the Easter break and wanted to wait until I came back the following week. I explained that to him, and he grunted, but agreed that we could wait until then.

"When are you leaving?"

"Next Sunday."

"I was hoping to spend Easter with you, but I understand. I can share you with your grandparents." He said, a playful grin forming on his face. "But when you come back, you are all mine, I will not share you with anyone." And with that, he grabbed me close to him and tickled me.

My face turned red from laughing, my body squirming and becoming rigid as he continued tickling me. He eventually stopped by planting kisses all over my face until I stopped laughing and relaxed in his arms.

"Do you want to get something to eat?" He asked and I nodded yes, emphatically, pulling him up off the bed. We walked together, hand in hand, to the little bar that was just past the bus stop, sat down, and talked while sipping our cappuccinos.

"It is safe here, Juliet. Otherwise, if we were back at the apartment, I would not be able to keep my hands off of you." The corners of his mouth turned up as his eyes playfully danced with mine.

"Do you want to stay at our cabin in the mountains with me next weekend? My parents might join us in the morning, but after that, some of my friends are coming up in the afternoon to go hiking. I was thinking you could stay over and I'll drive you to the airport the next day to visit your grandparents."

"That sounds perfect," I said. We walked back to the apartments, holding hands and enjoying the warm air that was around us.

"Let's go to Verona today. I want to show you the city the way I know it. Plus, we need to do something there." He turned to me, holding both of my hands as he asked.

"I would love that," I said, curious about what he needed to do while there.

We took his car into the city and parked in a lot close to the Arena. We walked under the city's arches, dividing the area where cars were not able to cross and walked towards *Via Mazzini*, the same street I'd visited the first time I came here.

"So, I imagine you have already seen *Via Mazzini*, right?" Giacomo asked as we walked past the Louis Vuitton store on the left and Intimissimi on the right.

"It was actually one of the first places I visited when I got here," I said, remembering the five of us exploring the city.

"We need to just visit one place down here. It's a few more minutes this way."

His vagueness made me excited. I didn't ask where we were headed and just followed. A few minutes later, we stopped in front of Juliet's house. Confused, I looked over to Giacomo.

"I know you touched her statue, but now we need to do something else." He gave me a wink and his dimple popped in his cheek as he held my hand and led me behind the tourists that were waiting to go in. He stopped in the covered archway, borrowed a marker from another tourist, took out a post-it note from his pocket, and wrote both of our names surrounded by a heart on it before sticking it on the wall.

"Giacomo, what is that for and how did you have a post-it note in your pocket?"

He let out a laugh before he answered. "This is what you do when you are in love with someone and want to spend forever with them."

My heart melted again, these past few weeks had made me feel emotions I had never known existed. He took my hand again, this time leading me away from Juliet's house and across to another road I hadn't been on.

"Now we are going to eat at one of my favorite restaurants. I promised you I would take you to a restaurant, Juliet."

I looked down and noticed I was wearing jeans and a t-shirt, nothing fancy enough to go to a restaurant in Italy since they were usually very formal.

"Don't worry about your outfit," he said. "I know the owner. My dad did some woodwork for him and they became friendly. Let's go." He pulled my hand along and his pace quickened.

There was a lighted sign on top of the doorway with an old-fashioned lantern hanging underneath. The facade was made of a light and dark brown brick, alternating in color, and it had a historical feel to it. A waiter greeted us as we walked in and quickly sat us down at a table off in a corner.

Giacomo looked over at me and saw I was playing with my fingers and quickly put his hand on mine. "I'm sorry, I didn't tell you before. Sometimes I listen to what my heart tells me and I usually don't plan anything. I saw you before, under the archway in Juliet's house, and wanted to bring you here. You look beautiful in every way though, whether you are dressed up or in jeans."

I closed my eyes, took a deep breath in through my nose, and instantly felt better. I loved what he said. He just listened to his heart and it took him here. From how I was, always overthinking, I wanted to sometimes do just that. I took the menu, looked through it, and decided on pumpkin gnocchi in a light cream sauce. I made Giacomo order the rest since I wasn't sure what to get, especially since restaurants in Italy expect you to order all of the courses.

Our appetizer came, a meat and cheese platter filled with local delicacies and adorned with ribbons of vegetables. We tried the local *salame* which was softer than the one I was used to back home. I tried the different cheeses, Giacomo naming each one, and I found a new favorite called Monte Veronese coming from the mountains near Giacomo's home. After all of this time in Italy, I still couldn't believe that I was finding new favorite foods that I loved.

Our first course arrived, the orange gnocchi vibrant in look, but delicate in flavor had my taste buds thanking me for each bite. Giacomo offered me his risotto made with red radish and wine that was equally delicious. He ordered a steak sliced thin with rucola and parmesan for the second course, and another order of a local fish on a bed of grilled fennel drizzled with a balsamic glaze. We shared both dishes, trying to figure out which we liked more, and finished both of the plates before we could decide.

We both ordered dessert, this time opting for a souffle and cream-filled pastry, that resembled a cream puff. We shared our desserts too, enjoying each bite of it as we talked about his house in the mountains and the next weekend.

"It is the house that my mother grew up in." He said. "It has been in our family for over 100 years, with her grandparents living there before. I can tell she misses it because every chance she gets, she goes back and stays there. My dad loves it too but also loves the town we live in now, so they made a compromise to stay there some weekends until they both retire."

"I can't wait to see it." We finished up, Giacomo graciously paying, as we continued wandering the city, walking along the Adige River, and stopping in front of historic buildings that Giacomo knew. We passed by a donut stand that opened up only from 10pm to 3am and sold donuts through a make-shift hole in a door.

"We need to come back one night and have them!" I said, my eyes begging him.

"Okay, my Juliet." He said, his arm now around my shoulder while I held on to his fingers.

We walked back to the car, figuring it was time to go back. Giacomo still needed to go back home to get clothes for the week since he hadn't planned on staying over last night and hadn't brought anything.

He drove me to the apartment and kissed me in front of the building.

"I'll call you later." He said, squeezing my hand and then letting go as he walked back to his car.

I watched him go and headed up to my apartment, texting Kristin and Ana to see how they were.

KRISTIN: **Let's meet— come over now!**

I headed straight there instead of going upstairs and saw Ana was at the door waiting for me to come in.

2 8

Ventotto

Uscire (v)= to go out

"So, I heard someone hung out with Roberto!" I said in a teasing way to Ana as she held the door open.

"And I heard someone met all of Giacomo's friends!" She said, teasing me right back. Kristin was looking at both of us, clearly enjoying the scene as we sat around the table and started talking about our weekend.

Ana went on to say how she met up with Roberto in the city, and they had dinner together and then watched a movie.

"I mean, I like him, but we don't have much in common. I don't see this lasting more than these months here. With my ex, back home, there was a connection. It was like sparks when we were together," she said.

Kristin said the same about Paolo, Giacomo's other friend that she talked to at the bar. "He's cute, and we text here and there, but we aren't serious, it's more just to have fun together."

"So, tell us about Giacomo!" Ana said, fishing for information from me.

"I feel that connection, and the sparks. Probably way too many sparks." I added, chuckling. "But I am letting my heart take me along on this and not really thinking of what happens June 3rd, when I have to go back home."

"Don't think about it, you have two months. Just enjoy each second you have now, together." Kristin said, Ana nodding her head and agreeing too.

"Wait, so did you guys, you know..." Kristin said, her words trailing off before she was able to finish asking me.

I held the espresso cup in front of my eyes and nodded yes, not able to hold back the huge, blushing grin I was giving.

"What!" They both shrieked, jumping up and grabbing my arm. "So, how was it? You need to talk, Juliet."

"It was. *perfect*. I mean, I've truly never felt this way."

They were both holding their espresso cups and staring at me, not saying a word.

"She's not telling us any more." Ana said, turning to face Kristin now who was smiling back at her. "Okay, we get it, you don't kiss and tell, but at least we know why you are really smiling right now."

We all laughed and continued to talk more about what our plans were for the week. I noticed it was getting late so I hugged them goodnight and started walking down the steps to the main floor. My heart jumped when I saw Matt, walking up the other side, and I almost wanted to reach out to him but stopped myself.

"Hey." I said, stopping on the stairs to look at him.

"Hi." He said, avoiding eye contact with me as he kept going up the stairs, getting closer to me and not stopping. I was hoping he would say something more, anything more, but I knew he needed time, just as I needed before. I hesitated a second and then continued down the stairs past him. I stopped at the bottom to look up at him swinging the door behind him, snapping it shut at the top of the stairs.

I texted Jess and Valentina, and they both told me about their weekend. Jess hung out with Jane and went to a yoga retreat in a neighboring city, while Valentina hung out with her new friends on both days. They asked about Giacomo and I told them I spent the weekend with him. We were all happy for each other and then I laid on my bed, waiting for his call.

We talked for a few hours, chatting about how he was helping his dad design a new wall unit for a customer. He explained that his Dad's woodworking gig started out as a hobby- something to make extra money while he wasn't in the hospital working as a nurse. Giacomo explained helping him when he was younger, first by handing him the right tools until he was old enough to use them correctly. He said he felt at peace working in the woodshop with his dad, sometimes creating new designs with him for their own house.

"I hadn't seen anything you made though."

"I'll show you at our cabin on Saturday."

"I can't wait." We hung up and I went to sleep dreaming about next weekend even though it was only Sunday night.

* * *

To my relief, I woke up on Monday with an email from my Italian teacher saying that class was cancelled. I saw Elisa later in the day and she seemed happier than normal lately. We had dinner together, and I texted Giacomo that I wouldn't be able to see him.

The next few days dragged along since I wasn't able to see Giacomo. We decided that it was better to focus on our school work so we could spend the weekend together and not have to worry about our classes. I walked with Jess to Italian class on Wednesday and instantly noticed Matt's empty seat. I refrained from texting him to give him space.

Elisa begged me to come with her downstairs to see the boys that night. I didn't give in and said I needed to catch up with reading. Right as she closed the door behind her I saw the screen of my phone light up with a text on the table next to me.

GIACOMO: **I need to see you. Three days is too long. Meet me outside.**

I felt a rush of excitement run through me as I ran downstairs and met him outside. We ran quickly to the side of the other building and kissed each other passionately trying to make up for the few days we hadn't seen each other.

"I can't do this anymore." He said, between breaths as he pulled away. "I want to see you every day."

"After I come back from my grandparents' house, I promise you will." I said, taking his face into mine and kissing him again.

We walked back separately to our apartments, and we then continued to text each other all night.

I was excited when the next two days passed quickly. The kiss I had with Giacomo was the adrenaline rush I needed to push me through to the end of the week. Matt finally showed up to our Italian class on Friday, still quiet and not saying much to us. Jess was wondering what changed.

"He isn't happy I am with Giacomo," I told her.

"I know, but you two were never actually together. He obviously regrets messing up what you had and I feel bad for him but he can't stay angry and hurt forever. He's still really hung up on you and it probably hurts to know you've moved on."

"I feel bad for him too. Before all of this, he was a really good friend. If I could go back, I would take back Venice."

"I know you like Giacomo, Juliet, but he lives in Italy. You and Matt have always seemed like the perfect match to me, laughing at each other's jokes and always teasing. You both live near each other and you were practically best friends. Maybe think about that before you go ahead with Giacomo?"

Her words echoed through me as I thought about them. I didn't even want to think about it. I'd thought that there could have been more with Matt, but now I was with Giacomo and couldn't think of anyone else but him.

"It's all a lot to think about," I said, but I felt that my heart already knew the answer.

We didn't say much else after that on the way home. I had stopped by Kristin and Ana's for the night, eating together and drinking a glass of wine as we relaxed and talked about our week. I slept on the couch in their apartment, not wanting to go back to an empty apartment, alone with my thoughts.

***

Giacomo picked me up early the next day and we headed straight to his parent's cabin in the mountains.

"My parents are actually meeting us there. I hope you don't mind." He said, while playing with my fingers and rubbing his thumb against them.

"I don't mind at all. I really like your parents. Has your mom been okay though to drive up there?"

"She has. The new doctor she saw last time gave her a list of things to take and avoid, and she's had more energy lately because of it. But he did say he wants to do more tests." He also explained in Italian that she would need a CT scan, but it might take a few weeks before she can get an appointment. I'd forgotten that their health care system is different and sometimes you need to wait for routine visits or scans.

We reached the cabin by taking a long, graveled road that was surrounded by a meadow on each side. It was a small bright yellow-stucco house with brown shutters and was surrounded by views of soft, rolling hills and nearby towns. I could understand why his mother missed it. The view was absolutely breathtaking.

His parents waved to us as we arrived, giving us both hugs as we got out of the car. His mom definitely had more pep in her step as she took me by my hand and showed me around the cabin. She named some of the towns that we could see on the other hilltops and pointed to the other houses close by where some of her relatives still lived.

She brought up some sauce that she made at home and boiled some pasta for us to eat together. They asked me some questions about New York and what life was like there. Afterward, we cleared the table and I looked down to see elegant etchings in the wood, my hand running over it to feel all of the different textures.

"*L'ha fatto Giacomo e il suo papà.*" Giacomo's mom said, telling me Giacomo and his dad made it.

"*È bellissimo.*" I said, still feeling the table and admiring it. I'd never seen anything like it before.

"It's actually made with olive trees. You don't see much furniture made of olive because no one wants to chop them down. The older the olive tree is, the better the olives it produces." Giacomo explained. I looked over and could see how happy he was in his eyes and saw his father look over too. I complimented him in Italian as well.

His parents stayed for an hour longer before leaving and telling me they hoped we would get together again. Giacomo and I decided to lay a blanket outside and enjoy the view until his friends came.

"Do you sell the stuff you make?" I asked Giacomo, while we were both laying on our backs, my hand in his against his chest.

"Sometimes. I use the money to buy books for my classes or I save it to spend in a restaurant with the girl I love." He said, squeezing my hand.

I let out a small laugh and then kissed him on his cheek. "Do you love doing it?"

"I do. But I'm not sure if I can make money on just that, so I figured I can be an engineer and do that as a hobby, like what my dad does."

I nodded my head, still taking in the view of the cloudless sky and hearing some birds chirping in the distance. The meadow around us was starting to bloom, some flowers poking through, and I got up on my elbows to capture the moment in my memories. A pit in my stomach grew as reality hit me.

"Giacomo, as much as I love you and love spending time with you, what will happen in June when I leave?" I turned to him and saw worry now taking over his face.

Giacomo took his hand to mine and kissed it. "I wanted to talk to you about that. I was thinking I could stay with you for the summer. And then we will do long distance for a year until I graduate. I am not worried. I will miss you, but it will go fast."

"You text me saying how you miss me after just a day not seeing me. Are you sure you can last more than that?" I said, teasing him.

"For you, I will do that and more." He said, kissing my hand again. He took my face and brought his lips to mine, kissing me deeply until we were interrupted.

"Giacomo, *basta!*" I looked up, noticing it was Luca, telling us to stop and pretending to act grossed out. We both quickly got up, laughing as we saw the rest of his friends behind him. They bought bags of groceries with them for a barbecue outside.

We spent the night laughing all together, drinking wine, and having fun. It reminded me of the barbecue we had back at his apartment, but this time I was with Giacomo, and my heart felt full. His friends stayed until almost past midnight, drinking, singing some songs they all knew. After they had all left, we went back up to his room, finally able to spend time alone, taking in as much as we could of each other, my heart heavy that I wouldn't see him for a week.

29

Ventinove

La Fattoria (nf)- the farm

Giacomo drove me to the airport the next day, but my heart continued to ache for all of the time we would be apart. If I felt this sad for a week, what would happen when I couldn't see him for months? I didn't want to even think about that a second more as I boarded the plane, took my seat, and put my earbuds in, ready for the next few hours of traveling.

My grandparents were at the arrival area waiting to pick me up. Their hair was a little whiter than the last time I saw them. My grandmother was wearing a plain pale yellow, flowy blouse and tan pants and my grandfather was in his usual short-sleeved white button-up shirt with the top two buttons undone. They always tended to dress the same every day no matter what they were planning on doing for the day. I waved to them and ran over to hug them and took in their smell of clean cotton and sun.

"Come si?" My nonno asked how I was in the dialect I'd grown up with which made my ears perk up. It hit me that there was a big difference between the way Giacomo and his friends spoke to the way they spoke here. I promised myself I would always be proud to be from Southern Italy. I responded back in dialect and gave them both an extra hug before heading to the car.

On the way back to their house I asked them if they were ever treated negatively because of their accent. My grandparents thought about it, but both responded that they may have, but they never noticed it. My grandfather went on to explain how he lived for a while in Switzerland because he couldn't find any jobs down here, but everyone he met treated him nicely, but not overly friendly.

My grandparents spoiled me back at their house, making all of my favorite foods— seafood salad, homemade pasta with the fresh tomato sauce and hot pepper sprinkled on top, and pickled vegetables. They wanted to hear about my adventures, but I made sure to avoid mentioning Giacomo since I hadn't even told my parents about him. Thinking about Giacomo made me curious to hear their story and how they fell in love.

"Nonna, come hai conosciuto il nonno?" I asked her how she met my nonno while grabbing a piece of bread and putting 'nduja, a spicy sausage spread, on top.

"Allora, molti anni fa..." She started, emphasizing it was many years ago. *"...il tuo nonno era fidanzato con una mia amica..."* My nonno laughed as he saw the expression of shock on my face after she had just revealed that he had been engaged to another girl, one of her friends.

"Aspetta," She continued, telling me to wait so I could hear the rest of the story. She went on to say how it had been arranged, something common back then, and how both her friend and my nonno weren't happy. My nonno was listening quietly, nodding his

head and agreeing with her as she talked. I listened too, not daring to say anything or even eat as she continued the rest of the story.

"*Poi, durante una festa, ho ballato e parlato con il nonno...*" They danced at a party, and couldn't stop talking about all of their shared interests. She was afraid that her friend would get mad at her that night, but she had noticed she was talking to another guy, her childhood crush, someone her parents had refused her to marry.

I still held onto the bread, my mouth opening slightly as I listened to the story, not having imagined that any drama could have existed back then.

"*Dopo...*" she continued, and then explained how my nonno and the girl decided to tell their parents that they were breaking up their engagement since they were both in love with other people. Their parents were angry with them, refused to speak to them, so they each ran away and got married to the real person they loved, without their family.

"*Cosa?*" I said in shock, not ready to hear that. I'd wondered why I never saw a picture of my nonna and nonno on their wedding day but thought it was because they either lost their pictures or they didn't have access to a camera. Instead, here she was telling me they practically eloped.

"*Non fare quello che abbiamo fatto noi!*" She sternly told me not to do what she did, but then smiled after. "*Erano tempi diversi.*"

The times were different, but the complications of love were always the same.

We finished up our dinner, changing topics to what we were going to do the rest of the week and how we would go to my cousin's house for Easter Sunday.

I helped my grandparents on their small farm and took pictures of the baby bunnies to post on my feed. Giacomo liked it right away and texted me to FaceTime him so I could show him what the farm looked like. I checked to see that my grandparents were on the other side of the fence before I called him.

"I didn't believe you that you worked on a farm." He said as I showed him around. "Okay, I want to see you collect the eggs from the chickens."

I walked over to the usual spots that I'd remembered from the last time and, sure enough, there were eggs. Giacomo was laughing as I showed him the three I found and then asked to see the pigs.

"Oh no. I am afraid of them." I said, "One time they escaped their pen and chased me around the farm. I'm sorry but there are no pigs on this tour." I laughed as I remembered younger me running around yelling for my grandparents. I showed him around a little more before hanging up and promising to text later.

The next few days were relaxing with my grandparents, but I started missing Giacomo. I realized it was going to be hard when I went back home. Thoughts kept swirling around in my head and as much as I tried not to overthink, they still popped up like unwanted ads on the internet. *How often would we visit each other when I get home? How long would it be for? Would I have to move here? What if I end up teaching on Long Island? Would I give that up for him and move to Italy? Would he come live with me?*

I frequently caught myself turning off my brain so I could concentrate on spending quality time with my grandparents. I walked towards the garden and my nonno showed me all of the fruit trees that were flowering, quizzing me as he would point to each one to see if I knew what they were. I'd just guessed *arancio,* or *orange tree,* correctly by chance, but he laughed as I incorrectly identified the rest. It was nice to see Calabria in the springtime. The land had a different look to it. The fields were green instead of dry yellow like they are in the summer months, and the gardens seemed bare with just a few sprouts coming up.

Easter finally came and my nonna and I prepared a traditional dessert called *cuzzupa* that was popular around this time. I helped her grate lemon zest into the flour and egg mixture, and then rolled it out into smaller ropes once done. I watched her effortlessly make a braid, press a whole egg on top, and cover it with strips of leftover dough. We brought it with us to my cousin's house and admired all of the *cuzzupe* they made, with the dough shaped into the initials of their names and even one into a fish.

It was nice to hear them all speak in the dialect I grew up with. All of this time up North I never realized how much I'd missed it. I asked my oldest cousin, Giuseppe, if he'd ever been treated differently being from the South. He responded by saying he'd felt it a little when he went skiing up near Milano in the North. He was at a local shop wanting to buy ski pants and noticed the shop assistant was talking to him more abruptly than the person in front of him with a Northern accent. It didn't bother him that much, he said, but he definitely was aware of it. He did go on to say that many others treated him normally.

"Ma, è vero che la pizza è più buona al sud?" I asked him if it was true the pizzas were better down south.

He had turned to me at that point and said very seriously, *"È vero,* it's true." But then a smile slowly spread on his face. He explained how the South was known for its pizza, with Naples being the best place for it. "Maybe that is not right for me to say, but it's true." He said, switching to English and making me laugh.

One of my cousins chimed in saying that the media is sometimes unfair to people in the South, always showing Naples as the center of crime and never talking about the positive stories that come out of it. The conversation reminded me a lot of some cities back in the United States. Some were always put in a negative light that made people assume the worst of them without having even stepped foot there. I guess that each country had its own skeletons, and I was wrong to put Italy on a pedestal these years, thinking it couldn't have them too.

As sad as I was about my time down south with my grandparents was done, I was itching to see Giacomo. Monday morning arrived and I gave my grandparents big hugs as I boarded my flight back up north. Giacomo had promised to pick me up at the airport and FaceTimed me up until I boarded my plane- already bombarding me with questions about my family and the holiday. When the doors to the arrival waiting area opened, I spotted Giacomo right away. He had his phone in one hand and he was on his toes trying to look for me over the crowd. I ran straight to him and he lifted me in the air as he kissed me.

30

Trenta

La Verità (nf) = the truth

"I missed you, my Juliet." He continued giving me soft kisses all over my face.

"I missed you so much," I said, kissing him back.

We drove back to the apartment since no one would be back until the next day. I took him straight to my apartment, and we barely made it through the door before our shoes and jackets were off and we ran to my bedroom.

Afterward, we laid there, holding each other tightly, absorbing each other, and making up for all the time we spent apart.

"Okay, you promised that we'd tell Elisa that we are together, right?" Giacomo said, now turning to me.

I'd forgotten that arrangement we made and it instantly started making me nervous. But he was right, we needed to let Elisa know and stop hiding around.

"How about we pretend that we got together recently?" I offered, trying to think of ways that wouldn't hurt her as much.

"We can tell her whatever you want as long as I can hold your hand and kiss you when I want."

"Okay, we can let her know."

We decided to go down to Giacomo's apartment for the night since he knew for sure that Luca wouldn't be back and surprise him in the morning. I never knew how Elisa would react to anything and I definitely didn't want her walking in on us in bed. I woke up next to him and planted kisses all over his face while he was still sleeping. He pretended to be asleep until he pulled me in, tickling me all over which made me laugh uncontrollably.

"I need to go get changed for classes!" I said, coming back to reality and going into the bathroom to look at myself in the mirror. My hair was a mess and my makeup was smudged under my eyes, but I was happy, truly happy. I headed back out into the kitchen, smiling, and headed towards the door.

"I'll see you later," I shouted back at Giacomo as I opened the door to go outside. Elisa was standing there, holding her hand up in a fist about to knock.

"Juliet? What are you doing here?" She asked, a shocked expression on her face as she stared at me, still in my pajamas, and Giacomo walking out of his room in nothing but his boxers. I saw Elisa look at him, back at me, then back at him. Giacomo froze, not knowing if he should go back and get dressed or stay there to see how she would react.

"What's going on?" She said, through closed teeth. Her nose twitched and her eyes narrowed, and I realized the worst possible thing I could have imagined just happened.

"Elisa, I wanted to tell you. I'm so sorry, you definitely shouldn't have found out about this in this way. We started seeing each other recently, and ..."

"This is what happens when it's recent?" She said, pointing towards the both of us. "This is not recent, this has been a while." Her face turned redder and her hands now formed fists to her side. Giacomo had quickly put on a shirt and pants and was by my side and started telling Elisa to calm down in Italian.

"Don't tell me to calm down! You lied to me, both of you. Why? To spare my feelings? Because you felt bad for me? Did you think I wouldn't be able to handle it?" Her eyes were burning with fury and her hands were both tightened into fists at her sides. She looked back and forth between us for a while, visually disgusted with our actions. "I can't even look at either of you. I don't want to see you both for a while. I'm asking to switch roommates."

"Elisa, don't!" I said, calling after her as she stormed back up to our apartment. I didn't know whether to follow her or give her time to cool off. Giacomo hugged me from behind, apologizing that he caused all of this.

"It's not your fault, we did nothing wrong." I kept repeating this, but it felt like a lie. Matt hated me and now Elisa hated me, all because I was in love with Giacomo.

I needed to get dressed for classes but figured I would skip the first one and wait until Elisa left the apartment. When I saw her take the bus from Giacomo's window, I went back up to my apartment to get ready as fast as I could, not even caring what my hair looked like. I texted Elisa that we should talk before she did anything, but as I figured, she didn't text me back.

I could barely concentrate in class and forgot to take notes. Giacomo kept texting me to see if I was okay, but Elisa still hadn't texted back. Back at the apartment, I sent a message to Kristin and Ana explaining what happened and they told me I could stay with them until she cooled down. I thought about it and decided that it might be a good idea to sleep somewhere else so I could give her the space she needed. I left a note for Elisa, apologizing for hurting her and having her find out in this way, on her pillow. I grabbed a few outfits from the armoire, my toothbrush, and body wash, and headed over to Kristin and Ana's.

I felt that I should wait until Elisa calmed down to see Giacomo again and he agreed, but it was as if I was punishing myself too. Kristin and Ana listened as I described how Elisa reacted and they both assured me that she will probably calm down in a few days and I should wait to talk to her. I slept on the couch that night, my earbuds in, listening to music.

The next day I met up with Jess before we reached our Italian class. The last conversation we had echoed in my head. She told me about her weekend, how she hung out with Jane. I almost felt jealous of the drama-free relationship they had. As we entered our class, I saw Matt sitting in his usual seat, his lips pressed, looking down and scrolling through his phone. I took my seat next to him and he muttered "Hi" still without looking up.

"Hey. Did you spend Easter with Javier?" I tried to make conversation with him, grasping at the first neutral topic I could think of.

"Yeah." He said bluntly, purposely trying to halt the conversation.

"Did you make anything else new to eat?" I asked, nudging him.

"No, just the usual." He said while continuing to scroll through his phone.

Jess's comment still echoed through me. *He really likes you...I always thought you should be together...is it really going to last with Giacomo?* I did have feelings for him in Venice, and that week after I really thought about making something happen between us. I tried not to entertain that thought since I was genuinely happy with Giacomo. A part of me kept those questions coming back as if I wasn't sure if I was making the right choice.

My phone vibrated in my hand with a message from Giacomo on the bus home from class.

GIACOMO: **Elisa went home for the week. Marcello ran into her leaving with bags and she said she was coming back on Monday.**

It made it easier that I could go back to my apartment and sleep in my own bed for the next few days without having to worry about confronting Elisa.

I got off the bus and stopped by Giacomo's apartment to see how he was.

"I'm sorry, *amore.*" He said, kissing me softly on my forehead and wrapping his arms tightly around me. I stayed against his chest, needing to feel him until I saw Marcello walk into the kitchen with a smile on his face.

"*Basta!*" He shouted *enough*, pretending to be serious but he had a smirk on his face when he said it. Giacomo said something back in Italian that made Marcello laugh more. I realized that we didn't need to hide anymore. Almost everyone knew at this point, and it felt liberating to be able to hug him when I wanted to. Of course, my brain had to then flash an image of Elisa and Matt, both hurt, which then made that happiness short-lived.

We both walked over to the table and sat next to Marcello who was already seated with his feet up on another chair.

"Elisa is one cranky girl. You'd wonder what you guys did that was so bad." He put his hands behind his head as he leaned back into the chair more. "All I know is that I don't want her angry at me." He continued, laughing. "But don't worry. Let her cool down, and wait for her to come back. I guess this is Karma, right, Juliet?"

"Karma?" I repeated, not sure why he would mention that.

"Well, look at how she treated Luca. It wasn't fair what she did to him, now she knows how it feels." He added, leaning back in his chair again like he was sharing his wisdom with us.

"I still feel bad though. She is my roommate and I didn't want to hurt her."

"But she can hurt Luca? I don't know Juliet, you're not wrong. If you two are in *love*, then don't let her bother you." He added, his arms gesturing passionately as he was explaining this.

I let out a breath and saw Giacomo do the same. We both looked at each other and I could see in his eyes that he agreed with Marcello. He took his arm, wrapped it around me. Marcello made a disgusted face at both of us, dramatically getting up from his chair, and pushing it in before letting out a laugh and going to his room.

"Let's do something this weekend. I want to show you *il Lago di Garda*, the lake that is 30 minutes from here. It's still not warm enough to go swimming, but I promise you will love it." Giacomo said, holding my hand in his.

That was exactly what I needed. I needed to focus on exploring Italy and taking advantage of it while I was here. Giorgia had told us about the lake and it definitely piqued my interest.

"That sounds wonderful," I said. He pulled me back in close to him, giving me kisses all over that made me laugh.

"*Basta*, Giacomo!" I said, now imitating Marcello yelling at him like before. He kept me close as we looked through his phone, searching for different things to do while there.

31

❦

Trentuno

Un dipinto (nm) = a painting; a portrait

The next few days of classes went quickly, Matt was still not talk-ative in class, but at least he started answering in fuller sentences, even sometimes adding on to our conversations.

Kristin and Ana had plans for the weekend too, so we made sure to get together at night and hang out during the week. Jess and Valentina were both spending most of the time with their new friends, but we still met up with me at the bar for Gianni to serve us some coffees.

Giacomo went home Friday night to help his dad on a piece he was working on but promised to meet me at the apartment Satur-day morning. I got up early, not sure what time he would come, and made sure I was ready for the day at the lake. I heard a knock and ran to the door to greet him.

"Ciao, bella." He said, his hazel eyes twinkling and his mouth

curved into a smile that made me want to kiss it before I said hello back.

I noticed he was holding something behind him and I tried to peer over his shoulder to see.

"*Aspetta*, wait. You have to be careful with this because it took me a long time." He took the object out from behind his back and walked deeper into my apartment, resting it on the table. It was in the shape of a flat rectangle. It was a little bigger than a tablet, wrapped in light brown paper with a note on it. I took the note off and read it.

Sei la mia vita, Juliet. I loved you before, love you now, and will love you forever.

Tears formed in my eyes as I read it and I felt goosebumps prickle all over my skin. I looked up at him trying to blink away my tears. His eyes softly met mine, and his hand brushed against me to push the package closer to me to open.

"I hope you like it, Juliet."

I went to open it carefully, not sure what to expect. As I finished tearing off the last bit of paper, I noticed it was the back of a canvas. I turned it around and my mouth dropped. It was a painting of a girl with brown hair, facing away, surrounded by a landscape of mountains around her.

"You...you painted this?"

"Yes. I took a picture of you that day we were up in the mountains because I wanted to remember how you looked. I needed to draw you and wanted you to have it."

I stared at the painting, noticing the brush strokes that defined each strand of my brown hair and the slight breeze blowing through it. The grey and green strokes on the mountains were mixed with black to show shadows that I would've never known to create. I was speechless. I looked at him, not even sure what to say next.

"So, what do you think?" His eyes scanned mine, looking for an answer.

I shook my head and just looked into his eyes. "*Ti amo*, Giacomo." My heart answered for me. No one had ever painted anything for me or created something special like this. I took his face in my hands, stared into his eyes, and kissed him gently, wanting to thank him for all of these memories and moments he's made and shared with me. I wanted to thank him for making me feel more alive than I'd ever felt and for making me feel exactly like that girl in the painting— full of wonder and happiness, excited to take in all of the beauty there was in the world.

"On to our next adventure?" He said, now pulling his head back and moving his hands around my waist.

"I can't wait," I responded, pulling him into me and laying my head against his chest. He kissed the top of my head, squeezed me tight to him, and then took my hand in his.

"*Andiamo, amore.*" He said, taking his keys and still holding my hand.

Amore. Love. This was love. The feeling that made me want to share everything I have with someone else. I wanted to spend all of our moments together and to capture every emotion and memory to always remember. I squeezed his hand and headed out the door, ready for another day to spend together.

"And that's a Lamborghini," Giacomo said, pointing to the blue car that whizzed past us.

"But it said *Polizia* on the side. Don't tell me that the police here drive Lamborghinis!"

He started laughing and shook his head.

"Well, not all of them. It's usually only for the highways to catch people who are speeding. I haven't seen many, only here where the Germans and Austrians come down to Italy on vacation and don't remember we have speed limits."

I laughed and noticed that the cars were definitely driving faster than the highway back at home. The speed limit at home was always around 55 - 65mph and people definitely went faster than that but here the cars felt like they were going around 80mph or more on average.

We finally arrived in a small town, Lazise, and enjoyed a gelato by the lake. We admired the Garda Mountains, a part of the Alps, bordering it. The town had a medieval feel to it, with turrets framing the stone castle that was at the entrance of the town. A stone archway connected us to the main square where shops and restaurants were filled with people just taking in the view.

The next town we visited was Bardolino, a 10-minute drive north of Lazise. It was a more bustling and elegant town. Giacomo explained how it is known for the wine and elegant eateries and of course beautiful views as well.

We sat at a restaurant outside, watching boaters go by and little kids throwing pieces of crackers to the ducks in the lake. We stayed outside most of the day, enjoying the sunset behind the mountains, the rays still peering over for a few moments more. They created a gorgeous wispy display of orange and pinks in the sky. On the drive back home, Giacomo drove along the lake instead of taking the main roads so I was able to enjoy the view one more time. He stayed over that night in my apartment, his arms wrapped around me, as we slept close to each other.

We decided to stay at the apartment the next day, both of us studying for our classes together. Every once in a while, he would crumple a paper and throw it over to me and laugh when I got mad. I could never get seriously mad at him since his smile could instantly make me forgive him.

He slept in his apartment that night and I decided to stay up in mine, hoping that Elisa would come back. I ran through the different scenarios in my head of what she would say, but in all of them, I hoped she would forgive me.

The next morning, she hadn't shown up before classes. She normally didn't, which is why I still had hope for later in the day. I felt prepared for the day, finally getting the courage to answer questions in Italian, and Matt seemed in a better spirit when I saw him in our Italian class. I prayed that with how good this day was going, Elisa would be in our apartment, ready to talk and forgive me.

I ran up to the apartment and opened the door to find her still not there. I slumped down in the chair, now slightly depressed. We were supposed to hug and I would say I am sorry I hurt her. She would forgive me, and we would make dinner together, laughing about something silly that happened during our classes. I still kept hoping that maybe she would come back later, but when eight o'clock came and went, I texted Giacomo, and he said he hadn't seen her either. I was just about to give up hope and head into bed when the door opened. I ran out into the kitchen and saw it was her.

She didn't say anything as she took off her jacket, hung it up, and put her shoes on the rack neatly. I noticed she had a bag of groceries in her hand along with some books in the other.

"Hi, Elisa," I said, softly.

"Hi. I'm sorry, but I don't want to talk right now. I forgive you, don't worry, but I just don't want to talk about it." From her tone, it didn't sound like she forgave me, but I was content that she had at least acknowledged I was there.

She was quiet for the rest of the night, making dinner by herself, and eating while reading a book. I texted Giacomo what had happened and he thought it was a good sign that she talked to me at all.

I fell asleep earlier that night, not waiting for Elisa to come into the bedroom because I wouldn't know how to act or what to say.

The next morning, she was already gone by the time I woke up. We continued the next few days, still politely saying hello, a few words here and there, but nothing more than that. One night she did have dinner with me, and we talked a little more. She hardly went down to visit the boys, saying she had to study and I went down to visit Giacomo alone. Giacomo made plans with me each weekend to do something new and this time we were going to see Milano with Roberto, Ana, Kristin, and Paolo.

Valentina started not showing up at the bar anymore because her friends had the same plans at a different bar. Jess was still close with Jane, spending almost every minute they had free together, which made me so happy for her too. I felt that everything was finally fixing itself in the last month of the trip.

3 2

❦

Trentadue

Una gita (nf)= a trip; an outing; an excursion

"So, where are we exactly?" Kristin said, tilting her head while looking at the map on her phone.

"I think we are close to *Piazza Duomo.*" I said, looking around and shading my eyes from the sun. "Wait, isn't that it?" I took Kristin's phone from her. "It's right there!" I said, pointing to it.

The city of Milano took on a life that reminded me of New York with people in the streets and energy in the air that made you feel like you could take on anything. We all took the train in from Verona and decided to walk as much of Milano as we could.

Kristin put her phone away and we followed the streets that would lead us to the piazza. We rounded the corner of a busy street when all of a sudden there was an open piazza in front of us. In front of that piazza, in the middle of this bustling city with buildings like any other you had seen before, stood a cathedral.

It was one of the most beautiful sights I had ever seen. The delicate and ornate details of the gothic-style architecture stood out so blaringly against the buildings that surrounded it. It made it even more beautiful the fact that it didn't look like it belonged there at all. There were statues and spires all on the facade, with details that I imagined took years to create. I stood there, mouth slightly agape as I took in all of its beauty. I finally looked over at Ana and Kristin who were equally mesmerized, their expressions similar to mine.

"Wow." All three of us said at the same time. We heard chuckling from behind us, as the boys were enjoying our reactions.

"It's beautiful, isn't it?" Giacomo said, coming up from behind me and wrapping his arms around my stomach.

"Like nothing I have ever seen."

"Come on, there's so much more to show you." His eyes were playful as he pulled my hand to follow the rest of them.

"Really, Giacomo?" I said as we stood in front of the McDonald's across from the cathedral. He started laughing and then shook his head.

"Well, it's lunchtime, and I don't know if you've ever seen a McDonald's like this."

He was right. I was surprised at how modern and elegant it was. There was a full espresso bar to the right when you walked in and electronic ordering stations straight ahead. Everything was immaculate and I almost felt like I was in an upscale restaurant back home.

"I swear these hamburgers taste better too," I said, biting into one. We all sat down at adjoining tables and started eating. I realized it was crazy to have fast food in a country where they prided themselves on taking their time when cooking. For example, a simple dish of rice for them turns into the elegance of risotto, rice that has been cooked so long that the starches released make it a creamy masterpiece.

We stayed in Milano for a while, taking the train back together and laughing at the boys teasing each other in Italian. We had all made plans to visit Florence the next week and Bologna the weekend after, trying to take in as much of Italy as we could before we left.

Elisa was opening up to me more. She still wouldn't come down to the boys' apartment, but we were now having full-on conversations about our classes and professors, still never mentioning Giacomo or what happened on the weekends. Matt seemed friendlier too, going back to teasing me more in Italian class and almost feeling like we were back to normal.

The Italians seemed excited to welcome the warmer weather that May brought in, with more cyclists on the roads ringing their bells as they swerved around you, and at least every other person with gelato in their hands walking down the streets. Exams were coming up in all my classes now that we were in our last few weeks, and as excited I was to see my family again at home, I became more anxious realizing it would mean I wouldn't see Giacomo.

We'd talked about it a few times but mostly tried to avoid discussing it. We made a plan that he'd come to visit me right away this summer, spending the month with me on Long Island, and then I would start my Master's program back home, but come back to Italy in December. Then we would figure out who would go where for the next summer, but at least for now, we had plans to see each other as much as we could.

***

"Matt, your Italian is fine. The teacher still adores you even if you scroll through your phone most of the class. I'm sure you'll do well on the exam."

Matt was nervously chewing his bottom lip, looking over the notes to study for our Italian final.

"Juliet, this subjunctive mood, tense, whatever it is, is not normal. What is this? If I say *I think*, I have to change the verb endings? Who does stuff like that?"

"Apparently the Italians do," I said, taking his notes away from him. We were walking towards our Italian class together, definitely in a better place than we'd been the month before.

"No, no, no. I can barely remember the conditional mood, tense, ughhh, I give up." He said, dramatically throwing his hands in the air which made me laugh.

"Sure, laugh at my expense. We have another week of Italian before our test. I'm going to ace all of my engineering classes with ease, but fail Italian."

We both laughed as he looked over, now smiling at me with closed lips. "Are you ready to go home, Juliet?"

That knotty feeling in my stomach came back as he said that. He knew I was seeing Giacomo, but I never talked about it to him. We hadn't bumped into each other together again and he never asked me about him after that party, so I didn't feel the need to bring it up either.

"Not really. I finally feel like I am just getting used to the way of life here now. It stinks that we have to go back home so soon." He nodded his head silently too, and we both entered the building, ready to start class.

33

Trentatré

I met up with Giacomo after classes one day in the city. We got ice cream and sat by the *Arena*, watching a magician entertaining a crowd for the hope of some euros in exchange.

"The new doctor my mom saw is confident that he will properly diagnose her after the results from the CT scan come in. I pray it's good news."

I squeezed his hand and saw his expression change to worry. I knew how much he'd been worried for her and prayed it was something that could easily be cured. We got up after our ice cream was done and wandered through the streets of Verona. We came up to a little shop that was selling framed artwork and decided to check it out. Giacomo's phone rang, his mom's name flashing on the screen, so he waited outside talking to her while I walked in the shop, greeting the owner.

The shop had some paintings hanging on the walls of various still lifes and landscapes, something you would see in any art shop. The display in the center of the shop had unframed works, a mix between those that'd been reprinted from the walls and originals as well. I browsed through them, flipping through paintings of the arena and statues of Juliet until I spotted a familiar landscape. I pulled it out, looked at the inscription under it, and noticed I had, in fact, recognized the area. It was the town where Giacomo's family had their cabin, the town where his mother was born. I was so excited by my find that I went to the register and bought it, before Giacomo saw what I was doing. I thanked the owner, took my change, and headed outside, just as Giacomo was hanging up.

"So, what did you buy?" His face was curious, trying to peek at the painting.

"I saw this and I know how much your mom loves the cabin. So I bought it for her." I handed it to Giacomo and could see from his expression that he didn't know what to say.

"She will love this, Juliet." He took my cheeks in his hands and kissed me gently on my lips, then on my eyes, and finally on my nose.

"Let's give this to her on Friday together. Are we still okay to go to the cabin this weekend?" We made plans to spend the whole weekend together at the cabins, trying to squeeze every minute of the time we had left.

That weekend I held the painting up for his mom to completely take it in. Tears formed in her eyes as she took it from me, holding it in front of her. She gave me a big hug, one that reminded me of the ones my mom would give me, and quickly found a spot on the wall to hang it up. His father joked that we wouldn't need to visit the cabin that much more since we could just look at the painting now, and his mother jokingly batted him on his arm.

We spent the whole weekend hiking in the nearby mountains,

cooking meals together, and relaxing in front of the fire outside, watching the clear night sky. My brain was trying to record every moment, so I could dream of this time when I was back home.

I still hadn't told my parents about him and figured it was best if I told them once I got home. He would come to visit a month later and they would fall in love with him, understanding exactly why I did too.

****

We had only three more weeks of classes and my nerves were catching up to me. I tried not to think about it every time I was with Giacomo, but it hung over us, heavy in the air as if we could feel it, but chose to ignore it.

I had my final exam in Italian class on Friday, the first class to finish early. Giacomo had given me a kiss that morning and told me I would ace it, but I was worried that the black clouds and drizzling weather were an ominous warning that I wouldn't do that well.

"Well that bright pink raincoat you are wearing will at least make everyone around you happy. That is really bright though, Juliet." Giacomo said, watching me out the door.

I pushed him a little as I looked down and had to agree it was a blaring color, the fuchsia pink made me easy to spot in a crowd. I remembered finding it in a little shop near Binghamton and thought it would make me happier on gloomy, rainy days.

"I'll pick you up tomorrow. We should be finished right after lunch." He was helping his dad finish up a project that night and would deliver it to the client the next day, so I figured it was best if I stood back and studied for my other exams that were coming up.

The rain was relentless all day, kicking my nerves into a higher gear before the Italian test. I met up with Jess and Matt and we were all silent as we walked together towards class.

"This is it, guys, the moment it's all led up to." Jess said, laughing and taking both of our hands and pulling us into the classroom. We were walking so slowly before that, nervously checking our phones as if something magically would appear on them that would calm us down. Giacomo had texted me *in bocca al lupo*, for good luck—which I never understood how it could mean that since they are literally telling you to go in the wolf's mouth.

Crepi. I would make sure to respond, or *death* to the wolf. Definitely odd, but I guess us saying *break a leg* didn't make any sense either.

The exam was a lot easier than I'd imagined because I'd actually studied hard and practiced the new expressions and verbs. Giacomo helped me study too, perfecting my pronunciation of *e* and *è*.

"We did it!" Matt said, fist pumping in the air as we walked out of the exam.

"It wasn't as bad as I thought, but I completely forgot the subjunctive and how to conjugate it," Jess said a little nervously, probably remembering what answers she put down. "Oh well, at least that's over with."

"I feel good about it," I said, my nerves finally relaxing from all of the tension that clung on all day.

"Let's celebrate with a drink at the bar. My treat ladies."

I was about to protest, but Jess grabbed my hand dragging me and I realized I hadn't spent much time with them this past month.

"Okay, one drink, but then I need to go back. I am exhausted from all of the worrying."

"One drink, Juliet, come on," Matt said, his smile wide and his face lighting up, instantly making me happy too.

We walked over to the bar up the road from our apartments after we got off the bus. Matt ordered us all an *aperitivo*, and the waiter brought us cocktail drinks made with prosecco, and some small sandwiches to snack on. We raised our glasses and toasted to doing well on our first exam.

"Here's to the rest of them, too!" He said, as we brought our glasses together again and cheered. We were happy, chatting about some of the memories we had together these past months and sad that it was all going to be over soon. Matt ordered us another round even though I had waved my hands and protested, but Jess convinced me that I needed it and should just drink it with them.

"I need to get home while I can still walk. By all means, stay more if you want, but *buona notte*." I said, after finishing up the second drink.

"I'm actually meeting Jane here in ten minutes, so I'm going to stay if you don't mind, Juliet. Matt, can you walk back with her so she's not alone?"

I looked over at Matt, who looked at Jess quizzically, then back at me before he shrugged his shoulders and said "Sure."

It was still raining outside so I put the hood of my raincoat on. We were mostly silent on the walk back. I looked over to see Matt's hands in his pockets, his shoulders tense, probably trying to brave the rain that was drizzling on him.

We reached my building and I turned to say goodbye to Matt when he grabbed my hand to stop me.

"What's the matter?" I asked, looking down at his hand on mine.

"Juliet, I need to tell you something, something I should have told you a long time ago."

My heart started racing. Please don't say what I think you are going to say. I was hoping that the two drinks in his body weren't giving him the courage to say something he would regret.

"I have to go inside, it's raining a lot now Matt."

"I made a mistake that night." His eyes were intense and glued to mine.

"We don't need to talk about it. It's in the past." I held his stare trying to convince him to not say what I knew he was going to.

"No, we do. We do because that mistake has eaten me alive these past months. It caused me to lose my best friend. Juliet, I waited for you that night. I thought about that night after Venice and had imagined something different. But, I got jealous that you liked Giacomo after I saw you texting him. When you didn't show up at our party like you promised, I got mad. I thought you'd chosen him over me and I did something stupid. I know it hurt you, but I did it more to hurt me too."

I stared at him, taking in everything he was saying, and still not responding. My jeans were soaked, my shoes were in a puddle, but my body was numb so I didn't feel any of it.

"I always liked you, Juliet. From the first day in Prof. Rossi's class. I thought you were this sweet, funny girl who made me feel better, who laughed at my jokes. And after my girlfriend cheated on me and broke my heart, being next to you in class made me feel better. That's why I took Italian, I just wanted to be near you. I realized that I liked you, really liked you, Juliet when we got here, but I was afraid to ruin our friendship so I never asked you out. I was afraid you would say no and then I would lose you. But what happened in Venice was perfect. I knew you felt something too, but you were nervous like me. I was willing to wait, Juliet, but I messed up that night."

In all of these years that I'd known him, I'd never heard him talk this much at once, or be this vulnerable with me.

He took two steps closer to me, his hair was all wet as the rain was still pouring down but he seemed oblivious to everything. "Juliet, I love you. I think of only you." He took another two steps closer. "We were meant to be together." He took the last two steps, looked down at me and hesitated before he kissed me.

My body froze. His mouth was gentle, his lips parting mine and his tongue caressing my tongue. My head was swirling and I was unable to react out of full shock. His hands made their way to my hip and I finally regained my senses to push him away.

Giacomo. I thought, but I must have said it aloud because Matt repeated his name.

"Giacomo. Matt, I am with Giacomo."

"We are leaving in three weeks, Juliet. How can you stay with him?" He said, his voice now getting louder.

"He will visit and then I'll visit him," I said, my voice soft since I wasn't still sure of what was going on.

"Juliet, do you think that will work? That's impossible. We live near each other. When we go home, we can see each other every day if we want to. You really don't think he will cheat on you when you go back home?"

Now my blood was boiling. Why was he saying this? He didn't know how Giacomo felt about me. I was so angry that he always thought he knew everything. I couldn't help but say the one thing that I knew would get him as mad as I was.

"You shouldn't be an engineer!" I shouted, this time louder than he was, over the pouring rain.

"What?" He answered, still an inflection of anger and now uncertainty in his voice wondering.

"You shouldn't be an engineer, Matt. That's the easy way for you and you even said it yourself. It's not your passion. It's what your dad does and it will be easy for you."

"What does this have to do with what we were talking about?" His voice was now growing even angrier.

"Because you don't do things that are easy in life if you don't truly love them. I chose to be a teacher Matt, not because it's easy or what my mom does, but because I wanted to. I'm in love with Giacomo, Matt. I know it might not be easy to live so far away from him but my heart is telling me it's the right thing to do."

I saw the hurt in his eyes, even through the rain. He was my best friend, someone I thought I could've been with before all of it changed. I knew we could've worked as a couple, but I wasn't sure if it would've ever been true love. It never would've felt like I felt with Giacomo.

He shook his head, took a hand, and brushed it over his hair making the water drip down.

"So, that's it." He said as he put his hands in his pocket, looking down.

"I'm sorry, Matt. I never meant to hurt you."

"No, no. This is not it, Juliet. I'm sorry, as much as you think it will last with Giacomo, it won't." He hesitated as if he was going to say something else, but shook his head and walked back up to his apartment. I was still frozen, not knowing what to do. I stood there in the rain, now completely soaked and I looked up at my balcony to notice my kitchen light on. I didn't care if it stayed on the whole night because I couldn't stay alone after this. I needed Giacomo. I needed my friends. I called Kristin, who picked up on the first ring and asked if I could stay over. She waited for me outside of her door and wrapped her arms around me and then helped take off my raincoat. I told her and Ana the whole story, what had happened, and they both listened, nodding their heads and not saying one word until I was done.

"Change into this and go to bed," Ana said, lending me her pajamas and bringing me an extra pillow and blanket.

I couldn't fall asleep because all I could think about was what I was going to tell Giacomo. I was still shocked that Matt kissed me. I imagined all of the different ways he would react and each scenario made my stomach hurt more. I tossed and turned the whole night on the couch, not actually sleeping, only replaying the whole night in my head until tears formed in my eyes. I felt them fall down my cheeks, as I started feeling my chest rise and fall, not being able to catch my breath. I cried silently, in the dark, feeling bad for all of the people I'd hurt. I would've never imagined back in February I would be crying on a friend's couch about Matt. So much had happened these past few months here that my body couldn't handle it. I put in my earbuds, put on Laura Pausini, and finally fell asleep, tears still falling down.

34

Trentaquattro

Avere paura (v) = to be afraid

The next day I decided to head back to my apartment to get ready to see Giacomo in the afternoon. I still didn't know how I would tell him what happened, but when I would, it would have to be in person. I opened my door, remembering I forgot to turn off the kitchen light, but I was shocked to see it turned off already. Did I imagine it? I decided to just take a shower and get dressed. I texted Giacomo, seeing how it was going with his dad, but realized he was probably still busy since he didn't text back.

A few hours passed and I was starting to get worried at the lack of response. I texted him again, asking if he was alright, but still no text back. My stomach had an unsettling feeling as my mind created more what-ifs. What if he saw Matt kissing me? I tried to keep myself busy by cleaning the apartment and listening to some new songs, but when a few more hours passed and there was still no word from him, I knew something was wrong.

JULIET: **Giacomo? Please text me back— I am worried.**

The whole day passed, I hadn't heard from him and my mind was creating more what-if scenarios. My heart ached not hearing from him, even if it was just a simple text exchange of pizza toppings. I sunk into my bed, grabbed my pillow tight, and squeezed my eyes shut so the tears wouldn't escape. This sudden detachment from him was pulling my heart and emotions into a dark pit, one that felt like there would be no bottom and my emotions would be swallowed by it even more. I would have given anything to feel his arms wrapped around me, or his kiss, or hearing him say he was there for me. I had to find a way to reach him.

I texted Ana to get in touch with Roberto to see if he knew where Giacomo was.

ANA: **Juliet, what happened? Is everything ok? Roberto said Giacomo hasn't answered his text.**

JULIET: **No, it's fine. I thought we were hanging out today but forgot he was busy.**

For some reason I didn't want Ana to feel sorry for me, so I tried to pretend everything was okay even though I wanted to run to her and Kristin.

I didn't even know how I slept that night, blasting the music louder into my ears as if I was punishing myself for why Giacomo had been ignoring me. The whole night I tossed in bed, my emotions ranging from panic that I was sure something bad had happened, to anger that he hadn't reached out to me, to worry that he somehow saw Matt kiss me. I clutched my phone tight to me and prayed that somehow, the next day, everything would go back to normal.

****

"Juliet?"

I woke up abruptly after I heard a muffled voice calling my name through the door. I grabbed my phone off the nightstand and ran to the door to open it.

I saw Jess standing there, her smiling face quickly changing to a mix between surprise and shock when she saw me.

I opened the door wider to let her in. I noticed she was almost afraid to come closer to me and her eyebrows knitted together.

"Juliet, are you okay? Your face is puffy and your eyes are red."

I touched my face, not knowing what to expect by just feeling it, and squeezed my eyes shut so I wouldn't cry anymore.

"I'm fine. It was a long night and I had a fight with my mom, nothing really." I couldn't tell her the truth either, that I had been worried sick about Giacomo and he wasn't returning my texts or calls.

"Oh, I'm sorry. Well, I wanted to know if you wanted to come to breakfast with me and Jane, but we can bring something back for you here."

"It's okay, I'm actually not hungry. I'm going to just put on a pot of tea and go back to bed." I was afraid my quivering voice would give away the fact that I was about to cry again.

Jess's eyes narrowed as if she were trying to read me, and she reached out a hand to squeeze my arm. "I am here if you want to talk." She let go of my arm, pressed her lips into a small smile, and looked back at me before she left.

I slumped to the ground and the tears started flowing out, and I didn't stop them. I didn't want to.

My heart jumped when my phone pinged, and I turned it over fast to see who it was.

KRISTIN: **Thinking of you...do you want company?**

ANA: ♡

I couldn't just stay here and drown in my tears. I needed to go, face him, and see why he wasn't returning my calls.

JULIET: **I'm ok. I'm actually meeting Giacomo.**

I lied replying back to them. Well, it wasn't really a lie since that was exactly what I had planned to do, he just didn't know yet.

35

Trentacinque

Una decisione (nf) = a decision

I took the bus down to Verona and switched to another bus to go to his town. It dropped me off in his town's piazza and I trekked up to his house.

"*Ciao*, Juliet." His mom greeted me at the door, somewhat surprised to see me. Her expression was sadder this time and my stomach twisted in more knots, praying this was just all a misunderstanding and Giacomo just lost his phone.

"*C'è* Giacomo?" I asked if he was there. She nodded, telling me he was in the back, working on a project.

I went around and saw him, his body leaning over, sanding what looked like an antique door. He looked up, his eyes met mine, and he didn't say anything as his face also remained expressionless. He knew. Somehow, he knew.

"Giacomo, I wanted to tell you..."

"Juliet, we need to talk."

"I know, I have to tell you..."

"I don't think we should date anymore. It won't work out."

Ripping the air out of my lungs would have been less painful than what he'd just told me. I stood there, not moving, not knowing how to respond.

"You are leaving in a few weeks, Juliet. It will never work. We keep saying it will, but it won't."

"Don't say that Giacomo, you don't mean it. I love you."

"It's not love. It can't be. We haven't known each other that long."

A knife, twisted into my sides, would have hurt me less. My body was numb and my mind couldn't understand the reality that was in front of me, the words he was saying.

"Giacomo..." I pleaded, tears streaming down my cheeks.

"I am sorry, Juliet. I need to finish this." He looked down, continued sanding the door, his eyes cold, not daring to look back at me. I didn't know what to do. I stood there, a few seconds more before my brain commanded my legs to walk away. I needed to run. Run away from all of this. I ran down to the bus stop, took the first bus out of his town, and called Kristin and Ana.

They met me down in the city, wherever the bus had stopped last, and they hugged me, saying it would be okay.

"We are here for you, Juliet. Let's go back to our place and we will take care of you." Ana said, her arm around me, gently guiding me to the bus stop to go back to the apartments.

I decided to stay at their place that night. They grabbed a bunch of clothes and toiletries from my apartment to help me last a few days there, without having to go back. I didn't want to leave this apartment and bump into Matt or Giacomo. How could I have managed to lose my boyfriend and best friend all in one day?

All of the choices I had made were wrong. I chose to be with

Matt and then he kissed another girl. I chose Giacomo, which made Elisa hate me and I lost Matt again. And, in the end of all of this, I still lost Giacomo. I started questioning every choice I'd made. A memory flashed back to when I couldn't even get through a lesson of teaching. I started panicking and felt my chest rise and fall rapidly. I needed to breathe. I needed to go home. My stomach twisted so much that I started feeling homesick. I wanted my bedroom, my parents, and the warmth of the house, comfortable and safe, away from all of the mess that I'd created. I covered my face with my hands, trying to stop the tears from coming again.

"It's okay, Juliet," Ana said softly next to me, an arm wrapped around my shoulders. "Here, let me do your hair." She went to grab a brush and sat down next to me, taking strands of my hair and brushing it gently. I realized I hadn't brushed it since the day before and didn't even want to know what it looked like.

"Juliet, I brought you one of the croissants you love from the bar. You need to eat." Kristin said, placing the croissant on a small plate next to me.

"I am so lucky that I have you two, but I'm sorry. I don't deserve you as friends. All you do is help clean up my messes." More tears streamed down my eyes. I never did anything for them.

"Juliet, we will always be there for you. That's what being a friend is. It isn't a give-and-take relationship. Sometimes you need us more, but then there will be times when I will need you. Besides, who helped me finally understand the poetry we were going over in class?" Kristin said, her eyebrows shooting up and her head tilting to the side.

I still felt guilty, but let out a laugh at her expression. Ana handed me a tissue and I blotted my eyes and took a deep breath in to slow the tears from falling.

We ended up all sitting on the couch, watching movies that made us laugh and eating popcorn together. I kept looking at my phone, praying that he would text me, but knew deep down that he wouldn't. I tried to stay strong, not wanting to show Kristin and Ana that I was still devastated inside, and forced myself to laugh at the silly scenes in the movie we were watching. I think they knew deep down I would break again.

I spent two more days in their apartment, inside and skipping classes. Ana and Kristin stayed with me on Monday, they both went back to classes on Tuesday after I pushed them to go, promising them I was okay.

I wasn't though. My fingers hovered over the phone, wanting to press Giacomo's name and hear his voice. I missed him, I wanted to lay my head against his chest, hear his heartbeat and hold him tight. I wanted his fingers playing with mine, touching my face, and pulling me to him, kissing me delicately.

Most of all, I wanted to hear his voice. His smile when I was silly, his confidence when I didn't have any, and that feeling of warmth and safety that I felt when I was near him. It was as if I was home next to him. My body now felt like it was deprived of something without him, something it had become used to having, and now that it wasn't there, it screamed and begged for him. I had never felt like this before and I finally understood all of those songs of heartbreak.

36

Trentasei

Il Voto (nm) = grade

It was Wednesday before I made the trek back to my apartment, choosing a time when I was sure Giacomo was still in class. I opened the door to see Elisa at the kitchen table.

"Oh hi, Juliet. Where were you? We were all worried about you!"

"I was staying at Kristin and Ana's."

"Is everything okay? Your hair is a mess!"

"Yes, I'm fine." I snipped back, definitely not in the mood to hear criticism from her.

"Well, I'm going down to the boys' apartment if you want to come."

"No, I'll stay here," I replied, not even attempting to come up with an excuse. I wasn't sure if she knew about us breaking up yet. My head was still hurting from all of the crying that I just wanted to forget about everything and try to move on.

I went to my room, a pit forming in my stomach as I looked over to my bed, memories of Giacomo lying next to me flashing in my head. I shoved all of the memories aside and convinced myself I needed to study and concentrate on passing the exams that were coming up. I pulled my books out, put my earbuds in, and forced myself to read.

I went to classes on Thursday, and I met Jess at the bar for an espresso. I tried to smile as much as I could and pretend everything was okay, but Jess kept looking at me skeptically as if she saw right through me. I was happy that she didn't press for any details, instead, I just kept asking what she'd been doing with Jane.

That night Elisa made dinner for me, seeming somewhat happier than her usual self. She hadn't asked about Giacomo, so I assumed she knew we broke up.

"One more week for me and then it's summer vacation! So the apartment will be all yours the week after." She said, her voice in probably a higher pitch than I had ever heard.

I was somewhat happy when I thought about having the apartment to myself until I realized I would be completely alone. I wasn't ready to be alone with all of these feelings inside of me, even if it was with Elisa, who hadn't been that much of a friend.

I stepped out to walk over and meet Kristin and Ana when I saw Jess and Valentina outside, laughing with Jane about something. Although I was happy for them, a pang of jealousy hit me as I realized they didn't suffer this heartache that had consumed me entirely, not even letting me enjoy my last weeks here.

I was about to start walking again when I now looked over and saw him, the first time in almost a week.

There he was, talking to Marcello and laughing about something, on his way to board the bus.

He was happy without me. Some selfish part of me was hoping

that he was as miserable as I was, but instead, he seemed like nothing was bothering him.

I shook my head, not letting myself go back to that dark place, and walked over to Kristin and Ana's to study.

***

"Explain it one more time to me, Juliet."

"Okay, in this poem, Pascoli is talking about and referencing Greek mythology. But this one, over here, it's more about the current events that were going on in his time."

We'd been studying together for hours, while Ana sat next to us with her engineering books opened and a pencil in her mouth.

"I never thought I'd be grateful to study formulas. I don't know how you two do it." She said, taking the pencil out of her mouth and shaking her head.

"That's funny because I feel the exact opposite as you," I said back after peering at a part of her textbook. There were so many different letters and equations that it gave me a headache just looking at it.

We all laughed and went back to studying. I needed this distraction from Giacomo. My heart was still jumping, hoping anytime my phone would go off, and it would be him saying how he made a mistake and missed me. Deep down I knew it was over, but my heart held on to the little shred of hope that I left there, praying that things would go back to the way they were. Praying my phone would light up and display his name.

I looked back up to Kristin and Ana and made a promise that I would try to be my best for them since they'd been so good to me, and not mope around for the remainder of the time I had in Italy. I also promised myself that I was going to do well on those exams and not let a heartache get in the way of getting the highest scores I could.

***

On the day of my first exam, I wasn't sure of what to expect, but Kristin and Ana had prepared me enough since many of the European university exams are similar. When it was my turn to take it, I sat in front of the professor, answering his questions about the different books we read, and then gave my opinion on certain topics. My fingers were shaking, so I held on to the books in my lap so I wouldn't reveal exactly how nervous I was.

"Mom! I got a 27 out of 30! Can you believe that?! And the professor complimented my Italian!" I shrieked into the phone as soon as she picked up.

"Well, I'm not surprised, I knew you would do well. I'm so proud of you. You know I can't wait to see you, right?"

I felt a little tug in my chest. I missed her too and a part of me was ready to go home. Another part still felt that I needed to be here, despite all that I went through. Something felt unfinished.

"I know. I love you, Mom. The next one will be harder though, so I'm not sure I will do that well."

The next exam had been tougher, and this time I scored 23, still better than what I'd thought I'd get. I walked around the city after I was done and took off my jacket, letting the strong sun hit my arms. I looked down at them, and noticed a slight tan forming, reminding me that summer was approaching. I noticed a lot of people were walking around, eating their gelato, another reminder that summer was just around the corner. I sat down on a bench, relaxed my shoulders, took a deep breath, absorbing the view around me.

I decided after a while to take the bus back, even though I didn't want to leave the city. I needed the stillness. The time alone to feel connected with myself again after the flurry of emotions I'd gone through this past week. I stepped off the bus when it reached my stop, in a better place than I had been, and walked into the apartment building.

I climbed the steps slowly, still relaxed from before when I looked up to see him, coming out of his apartment.

We both froze, neither one of us knowing what to say for the next few seconds.

37

❧

Trentasette

Affrontare (v) = to confront someone

"Hi." Was all that my heart and brain would allow me to say. My heart was beating too loudly for my brain to focus on anything else.

"Hi, Juliet."

"Can I talk to you?" I stammered.

"I'm going to meet Marcello at the bar."

"It will only be a second."

"Okay." He turned, opened his apartment door, and we walked in together.

I looked around the apartment and saw no one was there. My hands were fidgeting nervously as I was trying to think of what I was going to say.

"What really happened, Giacomo?"

He hesitated, let out a sigh as if he were thinking of what he should say.

"Elisa sent me a picture that night of you kissing Matt."

I couldn't believe it. She was home that night. She must've taken a picture from the balcony.

"Giacomo, he kissed me. He came towards me uninvited. I pushed him away but it was too late. I was so confused because he was telling me he loved me and that we should be together. He took that opportunity because he was finally being vulnerable with me."

"But that's the thing, Juliet, you *should* be together." His eyes looked hurt as he was saying it. "Juliet, my mom has cancer. I can't visit you this summer, I need to be here to help her with her treatments. Matt loves you too and lives so close to you. It would make sense for you to be with him."

"She has cancer?"

"Yes. We found out that Friday."

Tears came to my eyes as I imagined what he must be feeling. He found out on that Friday, the same day that Elisa had sent him the picture of Matt kissing me. I saw his mom two days after and she already knew what she had. He was having the worst day of his life and I was caught up in myself again. I wanted to hug him, to take him in my arms and tell him I would be there for him. My heart kept pushing my body to hug him, but I couldn't move. I stood there, still frozen from his words.

"I'm sorry. I'm really sorry. It is not fair." I saw tears forming in the corner of his eyes, his expression hardening as if he didn't want those tears to come down.

"I know. I need to go though. Marcello is waiting for me." He walked out of the apartment, waiting for me to leave too so he could lock the door. I was hoping he would say something else, but he just stood there, still quiet as he just turned to look at me.

"You should go, Juliet." He said as he held the door open. I stepped out and he closed the door, then headed out to the street, not looking back at me. My heart followed him. I couldn't feel anything else as I watched him go from the front door of his apartment. I knew for certain I would never be walking in there again. I prayed he would come back, pick me up, kiss me all over, and then I could soothe him, telling him his mom would be okay and I would be there for him no matter what. He didn't though, and I walked up the stairs not feeling a single thing.

All of that time that we were together after Giacomo had broken up with me, Elisa had known. She knew what she'd done and just smiled like everything was okay. Anger built up inside of me, imagining her smirk after realizing she'd broken us up. That relaxed feeling I had before was far gone, replaced by this fire that was building up slowly inside. What would I say to her if she came back? My brain started hurting and I didn't want to think about her anymore, so I put my earbuds in, blasted my music, and laid on my bed, praying I would never see her again.

She never showed up that night at the apartment, and when I came back from the city the next day, all of her stuff was already moved out, her bed and dresser were left empty. I was glad that I didn't have to say goodbye to her, but a part of me felt pity for her. I couldn't believe that she was that bad of a person that she would do something like that to someone she shared a room with, someone at one point she may have considered a friend.

Maybe it was because I deserved it. After all, she was in love with Giacomo too, and I didn't spare her feelings. I picked up my phone, scrolled through my feed, and tried to distract myself when I saw a message pop up.

MATT: **Juliet, we need to talk. I'm sorry, I really am.**

I hadn't seen him or wanted to talk to him since that night. I went to put the phone down again but decided instead that we needed to talk.

JULIET: **Are you home? I'll meet you there.**

MATT: **Yes. Thanks.**

I knocked on the door when I reached his apartment, louder than I probably should have. I realized I had my fists clenched to my sides and loosened them as soon as I heard the door open.

His hair was messy, like I was used to seeing in our Italian class, and his expression was drawn, something I hadn't really seen on him.

"You had no right to kiss me, Matt," I said before he opened the door fully. He shook his head, looked down, and opened the door wider, motioning for me to come in.

I stormed through, dropped my bag, and turned to him, ready to yell.

"I'm sorry, Juliet." His hands were raised up by his shoulders as he took a step back from me. "It was wrong and I wasn't thinking."

"He broke up with me, Matt! Elisa somehow took a picture of that kiss and sent it to him! You ruined the best relationship I've ever had." I said.

His mouth dropped and he ran both of his hands through his hair.

"Oh my God Juliet. I never meant... I mean, I didn't mean for that..."

"Didn't you, Matt? Didn't you? Because it looked like you knew exactly what you were trying to do when you kissed me."

A pained expression now crossed his face and it looked like he wanted to say something. I shook my head, grabbed my bag, and started heading to the door.

"It doesn't matter anymore, none of it does. He made it clear that we weren't getting back together."

"Juliet, I am sorry. I really am. I shouldn't have kissed you, if I could take it all back, I would."

I hesitated with my hand on the doorknob, looked back at Matt, took a deep breath, opened the door and left.

***

KRISTIN: **Study session now.**

My phone pinged as soon as I reached my apartment, breaking my thoughts from what had just happened.

JULIET: **Come by my apartment, no one is here!**

I felt relief when they came by a few minutes later, a pile of books in each of their hands, and smiles on their faces. I wanted a distraction and I didn't want to tell them what had just happened, especially since my life had been full of so much drama up to that point. Instead, I grabbed a bag of chips, poured them into a bowl, and placed it next to us as we studied.

I felt better that I had confronted Matt. A selfish part of me wanted to make him feel terrible for what happened. The shock on his face kept replaying in my head, but a small part of me also missed our friendship. Italy was supposed to be an adventure for us, something we could look back on and talk about when we were older, but now all it did was put a huge dent in our friendship, possibly ruining it forever. I kept thinking of his face, how his eyes showed sincerity in his apology, but my feelings were still too raw to even think about accepting it. I took a deep breath, letting my shoulders drop as I exhaled, and forced myself to focus on studying instead.

We studied all night, getting ready for our last test which turned out to be our poetry class. Ana was studying for a physics test she had the next day and we kept the espresso pot going most of the night to make sure we were awake.

***

"I got a 28!" Kristin shouted, hugging me as we jumped up and down. "Considering you're jumping with me I'm assuming you did well too." She laughed and released me.

I couldn't contain my happiness. "So, I *may* have gotten a perfect score," I said smiling so hard it hurt my cheeks.

"Oh my God, Juliet! Congrats! I knew you had it in you" She gave me another hug.

***

"Brave, ragazze!" Gianni said, after Jess, Valentina, and I told him we all aced our exams. He went to grab something underneath the counter and put a box in front of each of us.

"Che bella!" I exclaimed after opening it to reveal an espresso cup with the logo of the bar and a matching saucer. *"Grazie, Gianni."* We thanked him, admiring our new cups. He explained how he wanted us to remember him and the bar and how he wanted to make sure we came back in the future.

I felt the usual tug in my heart, the one that pulled in both directions, at times telling me to stay more, and at other times wanting the comfort of home. This was just another memory of my time spent here, something I would look back on and have stories to share with others.

We got off the bus, chatted about our plans for the last weeks, and headed back to our apartments after saying bye. I walked into my apartment building and saw Giacomo's door. Something drew me to it. I knew inside me that we weren't done talking. I didn't say everything I wanted to say last time. Before I even had a chance to protest my body's reaction, I found myself knocking on his door.

Luca answered, surprised to see me and I asked if Giacomo was home. He went to go get him, and Giacomo showed up at the door, his face hard to read.

We walked outside together, on the balcony, to the same spot where we kissed before.

"Giacomo, you need to know this." I started. "I love you. I still do. I know you said it wasn't love, but I don't think you believe that. It was love. And I know it will be hard, but we can try and make it work. Maybe I can come back in August for a month before I start my Master's program. I know you wanted to visit me, but I don't mind coming to you, especially since you need to be there for your mom. We can..."

"Juliet, we can't. You can't." He cut me off so abruptly that it surprised me. "You need to focus on yourself and not worry about me over here. You have everything in New York. You will be with your family and friends. We can't do it."

I stood there, my eyes locked on his, hoping he would say something else, tell me he would try even though it would be hard, but he said nothing. I shivered as a small breeze touched my arms, almost as if it were pushing me to leave and not say anything more. But I couldn't. This could not be it for us.

"I can't give up on us, Giacomo. I won't. It was love. I know it's hard, but so is everything else."

He didn't respond, but he took my hand in his, touching my fingers gently. He brought them to his lips, closing his eyes, and kissing them before pulling his fingers away.

"I'm sorry, Juliet. This is just how it has to be." He turned and left. He left me there, my heart open, vulnerable, and waiting. Waiting for something that wasn't there, that I couldn't have. Tears streamed down my cheeks as I walked out of the apartment. An empty feeling consumed my whole body. There was nothing more I could do, nothing I could say to change it. I went upstairs and sat, my earbuds in, staring at the painting of the girl in front of the mountains that Giacomo made. I didn't feel like that girl anymore. She was free. She sat on that meadow with the view of the mountains all around her and a heart full of love. More tears streamed down my face as I put it down, closed my eyes, and slept.

38

Trentotto

Finire (v)= to finish

"Yes, Ma. I have everything. I checked under my bed twice, inside all of the cabinets and even outside on the balcony. I got your lists, and everything is finally packed." I said, on the phone.

I was leaving. I said goodbye to Kristin and Ana the night before, crying and hugging them, but promising that we would FaceTime as soon as we could. I saw Marcello and Pietro talking in front of their apartments and hugged them goodbye. I noticed over Marcello's shoulder that the door to Giacomo's room was open and his mattress was bare.

I had finally made peace with it, and promised myself I would try to move on as best as I could. I gave a slight nod to Matt when I saw him at the bus stop, and I noticed he was looking at me, his eyes almost pleading for me to talk to him. I didn't have the energy to be mad anymore.

"Hey." I said, one side of my mouth turning up as I relaxed my shoulders and looked at him.

"Hey." He said, his hand gripping his bag and his lips now forming a small smile. "Are you ready?"

There were too many answers to that question, and I wasn't sure of how to answer any of them. I didn't know if I was truly ready to go home and leave everything behind, but at the same time, I wanted to hug my parents, sleep in my own bed, and not have all of these emotions that I had felt this past month.

"I'm not sure."

He nodded his head, lips pressed together, and he shifted his gaze past my head. I turned around and saw Jess and Valentina, dragging their bags behind them, walking to the bus stop.

"Can you believe John is staying for four more weeks?" Valentina said after she dropped her luggage in front of her.

"Yeah, then he is staying with Kathryn's family for a year! Talk about a shock, right?" Jess added.

Matt and I shook our heads, laughing. This was definitely not something we had expected from John. This whole trip turned out to be a lot of unexpected events in the end.

We all looked at each other silently and I could feel the energy between us mixed with both sadness and excitement.

"This view. We will never get this view back." Jess said as she stared at the rolling hills and distant Prealps that were visible on the clear day.

"I know. I will miss my friends too. I finally found a group of friends that understood me, that I could be myself around." Valentina added in a soft voice, her gaze directed to the ground.

"I promised Javier I have to visit him in Valencia. He wants me to go during the winter break and I might take him up on that."

I didn't want to say what I missed, there was too much. The walk to the bus stop, the espressos at the bar with friends, the views, and Giacomo. Especially Giacomo.

We took the bus to the city, boarded the train, and headed to the airport. We got our seats, this time we all sat next to each other in a row of 4, Matt and Valentina sitting at the ends, with Jess and I in the middle. I chose the seat next to Matt.

As we landed, we decided to stick together through security and wait until we all got our luggage. We all gave each other one last hug before we went through the doors where our families were waiting for us.

"I'll call you tomorrow." Matt said as he hugged me, warmer and tighter than I had expected.

The doors dividing the baggage claim and the waiting area slid open and I spotted my parents right away. Warm tears splashed against my cheeks as I ran up to them, hugging them after all of the time we spent apart.

We talked on the whole drive home, I told them all about the views and different cities I visited. I mentioned I met Giacomo, my mom's eyebrows raised as I briefly said he was a nice boy that lived in the same building as me.

I talked about Kristin and Ana, how we had planned to meet up every year and that we promised to keep in touch in between. I also talked about Jess and Valentina, and how they'd made new friends too.

We ordered Japanese that night, something I didn't feel was the same back in Italy. As we were clearing the table, my mom came over to me and put her hand on mine.

"Juliet. You aren't sad like this just from missing two friends. I know that look. Do you want to talk?"

I let out a sigh and hoped it wasn't obvious that my heart still ached to be back in Italy, at least then I would be closer to Giacomo even if he wasn't mine anymore.

"It was pretty serious with Giacomo." I went on to tell her everything, from how I had thought there might be something with Matt, to how I had kissed Giacomo at the bar and how all of my feelings had changed.

She listened, her face sympathetic as a few tears had escaped from my eyes as I was recounting the stories. It felt nice to dispatch my load onto her. I had been afraid all this time to tell her anything since she had warned me before I left to not get involved with any boys. She was usually the hardest on me, which always made me run to my dad for advice. But this time, I just spilled my heart out.

"I know how you feel, Juliet." Her expression changed to concern as she walked me over to the kitchen table and gestured to sit next to her.

"It wasn't easy when I met your dad. I knew he was the one from that moment he walked over to me and introduced himself, but I know how hard it can be, leaving your country and family behind. It's not easy for your dad. But, sometimes, we can't help what happens. I know it's silly to believe in destiny, fate, soulmates, whatever you want to call it, but sometimes you just know. And with all of the ugly in this world, is it so bad to think that it might be real?"

My face pulled back quickly in surprise to hear my mom say that. She was not telling me I was being silly and overreacting about a boy I had only known for a few months, instead, she was empathetic. I started to realize for the first time the way she truly felt. My dad gave up everything and moved to stay with her. But Giacomo couldn't. I wasn't even sure if he still wanted to be with me.

I hugged my mom. A hug that thanked her for everything and expressed how much I missed her and needed her, one that helped me fill a little of that empty feeling in my heart.

I went upstairs to my room to start unpacking, trying to get myself settled back home. I looked over to the middle of my room. It'd been sitting there for about two days now, unpacked and holding all of my time abroad. It was time to admit that whatever we had was over and that I was back home, back to my regular life. I reached over to grab the heavy luggage. It was frayed all around the sides and the zipper looked as if it were going to burst from the amount of clothes and souvenirs I packed into it. I debated whether I could actually do it; unzip the bag and reveal everything from my trip. Tears were already forming around my eyes as I began to pull on the zipper. The contents spilled out as if they were finally taking a deep breath after being hidden for so long. I was afraid to see it, afraid of what emotions were going to well up inside of me. As I turned back around to face the suitcase, there it was.

I saw the corner of the painting he made of me. I looked away, tears sliding down my cheeks, but then decided to just face it and open it. I unzipped it all the way, took out the painting and held it out in front of me. My heart still ached, though getting better each day, and I knew I just needed time.

I found a place in my room to hang it up, knowing it would hurt me every time I looked at it, but would also remind me of the beauty of that moment.

A few weeks passed and I started getting into a routine, waking up at 6, going for a run around my neighborhood, and then heading over to our usual spot at the beach with my mom. We were spending so much time together, trying to make up for all of those months I was away, that my dad was starting to tease us that he was jealous.

I started hearing back from several of the Master's programs at some local colleges I'd applied to, getting accepted to all of them. I should have been excited, but there was a part of me that still doubted if I was doing the right thing by wanting to be a teacher. I found out that Matt had applied to some of the same colleges when we met up one afternoon at a Starbucks. We wanted to have the closest feel to Italy we could and figured that the Starbucks between both of our houses would have to do for now.

"So, how's working for your dad?" I asked.

"Well, it's not what I expected it to be. Maybe I just have to get used to it." I noticed the corners of his lips were turned down and there was an almost sad look in his eyes.

"I did buy a ticket to visit Javier in December though." A pang of jealousy hit me as I realized that I didn't have plans anymore, I would be staying close to home.

We never mentioned anything that had happened in Italy, almost as if it were a silent agreement between us that we would move on and try to get back to where we were. I could still feel a change between us, not the same as before we left, but the rift was healing, even if it was slowly.

DANIELLE: **Missed you at graduation. Are you back? You were supposed to bring me back a hottie!**

I hadn't kept in touch with her throughout most of the trip, but the best thing about our friendship was that there were no expectations. We would always pick right up where we last left off.

JULIET: **Yes..but there is way too much to text. We need to meet up...are you coming to the city soon?**

As I was waiting for her to reply, I opened my email and noticed a familiar name in the sender's box. *Giorgia.* I opened the email quickly, curious to see what she wrote.

Ciao Juliet,

I imagine you are settling back home, trying to get used to what your life before Verona was like. I was wondering if you were still interested in the teaching opportunity I told you about. My husband's school is looking for English teachers and from what I heard about you from your professors, you would be perfect! A course is starting in the middle of July here, in Verona, and then you will have your certification a month later to teach!

Write back and let me know if you are interested. I've attached the website and information for the course you would need to attend.

Respectfully yours,

Giorgia

My heart pulled to the screen. My fingers hovered over the keyboard, ready to type a response before I had even had a chance to think about it. This felt right. I could try teaching and see if I liked it before going through two years of school here. I only needed to do that one-month course and then I could teach. If I didn't like teaching, then I could come back home and start a different Master's program. Plus, I could do this in a city with beautiful views and history all around it.

My fingers couldn't type a fast enough reply. All I wanted to do was just write YES, in all caps, as a quick response before she changed her mind, but I realized it was the middle of the night in Italy and she wouldn't see the email anyway until the next morning.

Danielle had texted back in the meantime, and I called her, telling her I might not be able to meet up after all.

I sat down with my parents after I sent that email and explained exactly what I wanted to do. I was prepared for them to say no, that they didn't think it was a good idea, so I was surprised when they both agreed it might be exactly what I needed. I ran to my room, clicked on the link to the course's website that was attached to the email and filled out all of their online forms to take the course in July. My heart was racing and my fingers were determined to type as fast as they could. I felt like things were starting to make sense again.

The next day, Giorgia wrote back that she was happy I had accepted and said she would call down to the person leading the intensive teaching course to make sure I got a spot. The day after that, my spot in the course was confirmed and I bought my tickets, ready to leave two weeks after that.

I met up with Matt again, at the same Starbucks, and told him all about my teaching plans in Verona.

"Wow, Juliet. You're ready to go back already?"

"I am. But it's more so I can see if I want to actually teach. I will never get a chance like this once I start teaching here, so I might as well take advantage of this opportunity while I can."

"There goes our streak of being in the same Italian class." He said, chuckling.

"Are you happy, Matt?" I said, seriously.

"I don't know." He stopped laughing and looked me in the eye. "Maybe you were right. Maybe I'm not an engineer. The only time I felt proud of something I did was that time I made paella for everyone. Maybe I never thought about what I actually liked before." He paused for a moment. "What about you? Are you happy?"

I thought about it. I was definitely happier than when I came back from Italy, slowly putting back together all of the pieces that had fallen those last few weeks. I had been unsure of applying to the teaching programs here, but now I felt confident about going back to Verona.

"I will be," I said.

39

Trentanove

Ritornare (v) = to return

"Okay, Juliet. Do you have everything? Do you have my lists?" This time my mom was teasing me as I packed to leave for the year.

The year. I was going to spend every season in Italy, from picking olives in the late fall to cherries at the beginning of June. I was excited this time, no nerves, no worrying what it would be like, instead just excited to start this adventure.

The ride to the airport seemed so familiar. I hugged my parents goodbye, this time not as sad since I knew I would see them for Christmas and FaceTime them as much as I could.

I landed in Milano, a half-hour earlier thanks to a favorable jet stream and no turbulence. My bags were one of the first to come out and I headed to the train station. I stared out of the train window to the Alps in the background. A warmth filled my stomach as if I were back home. I sat back, not even wanting to put my earbuds in, since all I wanted to do was listen to the people around me speak in Italian. That month home made me realize how much I missed it.

I met Giorgia at her office on time. She set me up with an apartment near the school for a great price and I would start paying rent only when I started working in September. I thanked her and couldn't wait to settle into my new place.

The apartment was small, with a living area and kitchenette as soon as you entered and a little bedroom off to the side. I didn't care how small it was, it was mine and I didn't have a roommate to share it with. I unpacked my luggage and started filling in the wardrobe.

I enjoyed decorating my apartment, searching for finds at the outdoor market, and making sure to give the apartment a cozy feel that would make me feel at home for the next year. I took care placing trinkets on the different shelves and picking curtains that reminded me of the pattern I had seen in the mountains nearby. I stood in the middle of my apartment and became excited for this new chapter in my life, one where I felt more sure and stronger about myself. I couldn't wait to see what the next few months would be like.

***

I stirred my espresso with a spoon, staring at the computer screen, nervous for the start of the intensive course.

Giorgia emailed me the night before, going over all of the details, reminding me that it went from 8:30 until 5pm through the week and until 12pm on Saturday. I mulled over the email again, taking a sip of the espresso and checking the time on my phone.

MOM: **In bocca al lupo!**

It was almost two in the morning there, and I smiled imagining her staying up to make sure she could text me before it started.

JULIET: **Love you and thanks, Mom.**

The little time we had together this summer had brought us closer, especially when she comforted me after I came home.

I decided to walk to the course, giving myself extra time to find the building and situate myself before it started. I walked for about fifteen minutes before I found the building that Giorgia had described. I took the elevator to the third floor, where a sign pointing to the direction of the Cambridge CELTA course greeted me as I got off. I took a seat, nodding hello to a few of the classmates that had arrived there before me, and checked my phone nervously, not knowing what else to do. A few more people arrived, and then two instructors came in and greeted us, explaining what the course would entail.

"Good morning everyone! We have a nice mix of students from all over. Megan, Keymoni, Simone, and Michael are all from England, Penelope and Robert are from Ireland, and Juliet and Jasmine are from the States. It will be an intensive course, you will need to rely on each other at times, you will have homework at night, and then you will have to prepare lessons for the next day. There are no absences in this class. If you want to pass the course, you will need to be here every day for the next month."

We all collectively let out a nervous chuckle and followed along as they explained the syllabus and our schedule.

When the end of the day finally had arrived, we all said good-bye, our exhaustion evident, and headed out, back to our homes. Although it was intensive, an energy of excitement filled me as I walked through Verona and I couldn't wait to wake up the next day to go back.

I woke up early, at 6:30, and decided to save time and make espresso at home so I had a few minutes extra to review our first assignment. I dipped some *cantucci* I had bought on my way home from the course last night and bit into them as I kept thinking of different ways I could teach the classroom vocabulary the instructor had given us.

I could have students walk around the classroom and point out the different objects that I called out in English. Or, I could have them draw their ideal classroom and label the different items. I became excited as I thought of all of the different ways and jotted them down so I could remember to share them with the others during our class discussion.

I grew closer to my classmates over the next few weeks, meeting up with them after class at bars and pizzerias, and going over assignments together. The instructor separated us into two smaller groups and we each had 20 minutes to teach a group of actual students something we'd prepared.

I was excited and nervous to actually start testing out my teaching skills in front of real students. The instructor said we would get our final grade based on how well we prepared and taught our lessons, and interacted with our students.

The day before I was to teach a lesson, I ran it over with my mom, making sure it was okay.

"You're a natural, Juliet. The lesson is perfect, better than anything I would have come up with. Text me as soon as you finish it!" A sense of pride filled my chest.

After we all had our turn teaching, the instructor critiqued and complemented our lessons, taking apart what didn't work and highlighting what did. I was excited that the only critique I got was that I needed to give more time to let the students respond, instead of jumping to the next person right away. Something I could easily work on.

Keymoni met me at a bar for a spritz after classes one day and promised to reveal all of her favorite local shops in Verona since she had been living there already for a year. It was nice to make a new friend, but I still missed Kristin and Ana, remembering all of the times we had together. Keymoni showed me which shop sold the best fruit, which butcher had the best cuts, and she even introduced me to what turned out to be my favorite bookshop, quietly hidden away in an unassuming street.

After two more weeks, we'd finished the course and received our final grades, celebrating all together as a class. The instructors came out with us to a pizzeria to toast the fact that we'd all passed, with Keymoni and I scoring the highest marks out of everyone.

JULIET: **So, it turns out I may actually like teaching...**

I texted my mom, wanting to share my feelings with her after all the doubts I had this past year. She responded back with 10 different emojis, ranging from a thumbs up to an ecstatic smiling face. I laughed and then checked the text from Giorgia that reminded me I would need to meet with her husband, James, to go over my job that was starting in a week.

***

"So, I heard you are quite a natural teacher from the Cambridge instructors. Giorgia always has an eye for these things. I mean, she has an eye for everything, she picked me, didn't she?" James said, moving out a chair so I could sit in front of his desk. He was tall and lanky, hair disheveled, and his outfit looked like something I would picture an English detective wearing in a movie from the '80s.

"Here is your schedule. You have one beginners' course on a Monday, Wednesday, and Friday; two advanced courses on Tuesday and Thursday; and then you are travelling to several public schools as a guest lecturer Monday through Friday."

"Guest lecturer?" I asked, not quite sure what it entailed.

"Oh, that's right, back in the States you don't use this. Here they have a native speaker join the language teacher to review pronunciation and do some activities with them. It's as if you help teach the course for one hour a week. Not all schools provide this, but many do."

I became excited as he showed me the courses and the names of the students I would have. It all suddenly felt real to me now that I had names of my own actual students. I shook his hand, thanked him, and left.

"I'm so excited Mom. You have to see the classes I am teaching! James said that he might have a little kid's class ready for me at the end of September. Imagine?" My mom had already started classes and called me in between periods to see how I was doing. I could tell she was genuinely happy for me and thought that this was the best decision I made for myself.

* * *

I kept turning the tiny spoon in my espresso cup and checking my phone as if the time would miraculously jump ten minutes as each minute passed. It was the first day of classes and my stomach was in complete knots, even though I had reviewed my lessons ten times. I spent the whole night choosing five different outfits before I finally settled on one. I wanted to make sure that I didn't seem like a young 22-year-old, but instead a mature one that was ready to teach. I chose a black pencil skirt, light blue button-down shirt, and Mary-Jane style shoes with a small heel. I kept checking to make sure my hair was in place, testing the clips that held the few pieces of my hair back to see if they were secure enough. I grabbed my new dark blue leather bag, something I had bought to celebrate the start of my new job, filled it with a bottle of water and some snacks and started walking to work.

I loved the fact that I could walk there. I felt like I belonged this time. I didn't have the feeling that I needed to take in everything I saw like before. Now, I was a part of this city, a productive member going about on a normal day of work.

The air was still warm for the beginning of September. I looked around, smiled at some passersby that had gelatos in their hands, and made a mental note that I deserved one at the end of class. I almost reached the school but turned around when I thought I heard my name.

I searched through the people and shook my head, thinking I must have just been hearing things, and continued walking towards the building. I reached for the door, grabbed the handle when I felt a tap on my shoulder.

40

Quaranta

Una sorpresa (nf)= A surprise

"Juliet?"

"Giacomo?" I hadn't seen him in almost three months. His skin was tanned from the summer, the sleeves rolled up on his shirt showing it off, and, as if it wasn't fair, he was even more handsome than before. My body started betraying me, becoming nervous from just seeing him.

"What are you doing here?"

"I actually started work today. I'm teaching at this school."

He stood there, silent for a few seconds more before he started again.

"I thought you were finishing school there. I thought you couldn't come back."

"Giorgia offered me a job here at her husband's school. I wasn't sure what I was going to do, so I decided to try this."

I could see his eyes jumping back and forth to mine, probably thinking of what to say.

"I missed you. I missed you so much that I thought I was dreaming when I saw you just now." He said, and my heart fell, again, those days I had spent with him came flooding back. That feeling that I had rushed back in, ready to take the spot he left behind.

"Can I see you for coffee some time?" He asked, softly, his eyes begging for me to say yes.

"Sure."

We both stood there, not knowing what to say or do before I said goodbye and turned into my school. Out of all of the days and times I had been in Verona, I had to see him now, right before my first class. My heart was still racing from the meeting and I tried to breathe deeply to calm myself down before walking into the prep area. I'd missed him. But, he'd broken my heart so badly that I couldn't go back. I didn't want to go through that same pain all over again, especially now that I finally felt I was in a good place.

Despite what had happened, I felt exhilarated after I was done teaching. The students smiled back at my jokes, the ones they understood anyway, and I even got a compliment from a woman a little older than me telling me that I was a natural teacher. I wanted to text my mom right away, but I saw I had an unread message.

GIACOMO: **You are even more beautiful than I remembered, Juliet.**

I kept reading the message as I walked back to my apartment, afraid to let my heart open to him again and what I would feel. I decided not to text him back, hoping that those feelings I had every time I thought of him would go away. It was good to see him, and I would have lied to myself that I had not hoped for a chance to see him again, but my heart had slowly stitched itself together and I couldn't let him back in and undo it.

The next few days went by fast. I spent the day preparing my lessons and then teaching at night. I usually would leave the school at 9:30, after the last class, and walk home to my apartment, past people sitting outside, enjoying the crisp September nights until they lasted.

I grabbed my bag after my last class on Friday night and headed out to enjoy the well-deserved weekend. Some of my colleagues wanted to meet up for a pizza after, but I decided I would just head back to my apartment and start the new book I'd picked up earlier that day from the bookshop.

I opened the door and stepped out, my eyes adjusting to the dark sky. My heart leapt into my throat and I stood still. I saw Giacomo standing in front of the building, hands in his pockets as if he had been waiting there for a while. My heart slumped and lurched toward him, mad that the rest of my body wasn't responding.

"Hi," I said, my eyes closing slightly as I wondered what he was doing there.

"I didn't want to ruin your plans. You had plans, Juliet. You were going to school in New York and I was afraid if we were still together, it would be too hard to stay all of that time apart."

"What do you mean?"

"Juliet, I am the hard choice. You had to give up a lot to stay with me. When I saw that picture of you and Matt, I knew he loved you too and you would have an easier life with him. I thought if I told you I didn't love you, you would go back home, be with him, and have an easier life."

"How do you get to choose what is right for me?" I said, my face turning red from the anger built up inside me. "I wasn't allowed to choose? I chose you, Giacomo. I would have always chosen you!"

I didn't know what was happening, but all of a sudden, he walked over and kissed me, took my head in his hands, and pushed his lips hard into mine. My lips remembered his, my body felt relief after all of those months without his embrace, without his hands touching my skin. We finally pulled apart, our foreheads still touching, our breath still connected, his hands now wrapped around my waist.

"I love you, Juliet. I wasn't living these months without you. I went through each day waiting for it to finish, to only start it again. I thought about you every single day and hoped you were happy back at home. When I saw you the other day, when I saw you...."

I kissed him now, this time not wanting to let go. I didn't care if we were in the middle of the street, with everyone watching us, I realized that I had also never stopped loving him all of these months, instead trying to convince myself that I was fine without him. I could feel the stitches in my heart healing with his words and touch, something I had secretly wished for all along, and finally, my heart was full.

EPILOGUE: 8 MONTHS LATER...

La scelta giusta= the right choice

"Giacomo, we are going to be late. Hurry up and get your jacket! Your parents are already on their way to the cabin!"

Giacomo was rushing out of the bedroom, still putting on his socks with his shoes tucked under his arm.

"Juliet, your clothes are everywhere in the closet, there is no room for mine!"

He had decided to officially move in two weeks before, after spending every night at my apartment the past month.

"Okay, I'll make room. Make sure you get the rice salad in the fridge, your mom said she loved the way I made it."

Giacomo glared at me teasingly and went over to get it out of the fridge. It was already May, the weather hinting at summer's close arrival, and we had decided to spend the day at the cabin with his parents, celebrating the good news on his mom's latest scan.

I had also decided to stay an extra year here teaching, James practically begging since my students raved to him about me. I found out I loved teaching. My favorite age group was the little kids where I would make puppets with them and act out different scenes from the fairy tales we read together.

"Okay, do we have everything Giacomo? *Andiamo!*" We walked down the two flights of stairs, out the front door, and onto the cobbled street. People were riding their bikes and walking in groups, just enjoying a relaxed Sunday morning with a gelato in their hands. Giacomo took my hand in his, our fingers interlaced in each other's, and kissed me on my forehead as we walked toward his car.

"Did your parents buy the tickets yet?" He asked as I was about to open the car door.

"They did. They're coming June 29th, and staying up here for two weeks before going down south for another two more." My parents had decided they would come down to see me this time since Giacomo and I had visited them for Christmas. I was excited to finally show them Verona, a city that might not be everyone's first destination when they visited Italy, but would always be mine.

We drove up to his cabin, the base of the Alps getting closer, as Ultimo's velvety voice entered our ears. He held my hand and I knew that all of the choices we had made, led us to this perfect moment.

Acknowledgements

I had the words in this book in me for so long, I felt like they just burst out and demanded to be written on paper. This story and all of the experiences in here wouldn't have happened without my parents. I owe this to them. They are the ones that encouraged me to study abroad and to experience all of the amazing things Italy has to offer. I tried to capture as much as I could in this book, but make sure to visit www.alessiasaint.com to read more about the places, music, and food mentioned!

Arianna and Matteo- I know, somewhere deep down, it was you two who brought me and papà together. You both somehow, from up above, coordinated everything so we could meet and have you two. You are my life and I will always do everything for you!

Rocco, Rosa- thank you for listening to me talk incessantly about the book and for all of your help- I love you and thank you for encouraging me to pursue it!

To my first beta reader- Denise. Thank you for reading this and for pushing me to take this story to the next level! **My other beta readers- Sheryl, Kris-** thank you for making me pursue this story as well!

My girls- Kelly, Nicole, and Noreen- Thank you for reading this and for listening to me during our walks. I am grateful to have friends like you!

Maria D.- My editor and savior- you envisioned exactly how this book should be and I would not have trusted this with anyone else! Thank you for being patient with me!

Antonella, Maria - Thank you for being my connection to Italy here and for sharing my excitement with this book! Love you both!

To all of my relatives near and far- Love you all and so proud that we are keeping our Italian traditions alive!

To my Italian professors at Binghamton- Prof. Stewart and Prof. Lavalva-

Thank you for inspiring me to learn more about the Italian language and culture and for all of your help studying abroad!

Ivana e Bruno- Vi ringrazio per tutto quello che avete fatto per me- sono fortunata di avervi conosciuti e mi avete sempre trattato come una figlia! Vi voglio bene!

Moreno, Giovanna, Luca, e Lara- Grazie di avermi accolto nella vostra famiglia! Vi voglio bene!

Monica- Sono fortunata di averti avuta come compagna di stanza! Grazie di aver fatto la mia esperienza in Italia davvero unica e divertente!

Ai miei nonni- Vi voglio bene! Grazie per tutto quello che mi avete insegnato nella vita!

Jacopo- Without you, this book wouldn't exist as well. *Sei la mia vita*, you are my life. Forgetting that key to my luggage brought me to you...and maybe with a little magic of touching Juliet's statue too. I love you more than I will ever be able to express and the fact that you believed in me to write this book gave me all the strength I needed to finish it. *Ti amerò per sempre.*

Mom and Dad- From our trips to Nonna and Nonno's house, to actually letting me go and live in Italy after, you have helped me become the person I am now. I now know how difficult it must have been to let me go and I hope to have the same courage as you when it comes to that time. You have sacrificed so much for me and still want to give me more. I love you more than I will ever be able to express!

My hope is for you, the reader, to fall in love with Italy and the language and whatever small flicker of desire you had to travel there will burst into a flame!

Le Ricette: Recipes

Lots of delicious food was mentioned in this book- try your hand at some of these recipes below to really feel like you are in Italy!

Juliet's Lemon Cookies

makes about 48 cookies

2 eggs

1 cup of sugar

½ cup of milk

½ cup of corn oil

3 ¾ cup of all-purpose flour

3 teaspoons of baking powder

2 teaspoons of lemon extract

<u>For the glaze:</u>

1 cup of confectioners' sugar, sifted

2 tablespoons of milk

1 ½ teaspoons of lemon extract

1. Preheat the oven to 350 degrees. Have greased cookie sheets ready.
2. In a large bowl, combine eggs and sugar and beat until mixture is thick and turns pale yellow. Add the milk and corn oil and mix well. Add the flour, baking powder, and lemon extract, and mix until well blended.
3. Drop dough by teaspoonful onto prepared cookie sheets and bake for 12 to 14 minutes. Cool cookies on a rack set over wax paper.
4. For the glaze- combine all ingredients and mix well and brush on top of cookies (or let drizzle!)

Ivana's Tiramisù
400g pack of Savoiardi cookies (ladyfingers)
2 cups of espresso
8 tbsp sugar
2 tbsp milk
1/2 shot plus 1 shot of Baileys
4 eggs, separated
400 g. mascarpone
1/4 cup crushed Amaretti cookies (optional)
cocoa powder

1. Prepare 2 cups of espresso and pour into a bowl. Add 2 tbsp of sugar, a 1/2 shot glass of Baileys, and 2 tbsp of milk. Stir and set aside to let cool. (There will be left over)

2. Separate eggs and place egg whites in a medium-sized bowl. Place yolks in a large mixing bowl with 6 tbsp of sugar and beat for two minutes. Stop mixer and add mascarpone, 1 shot of Baileys and mix gently until combined.

3. Whip egg whites to stiff peaks, fold gently with a spatula into mascarpone mixture. Set aside.

4. Set out a tray (lasagne pans work- 9"x13") and check how to lay out ladyfingers before proceeding with the next step. When ready, dip ladyfingers quickly into the espresso mixture and then place it down in the tray.

5. After the first layer is complete, pour 2 cups of mascarpone mixture on the ladyfingers and spread so that it covers the whole layer.

6. Sprinkle 1/4 cup of crushed amaretti cookies on top of the bottom layer. (This is optional but gives it a great flavor!)

7. Then repeat the steps to add the next layer on top, omitting the crushed amaretti cookies. Cover and set in the fridge for at least 6 hours. (You will have extra cookies, mascarpone mixture, and coffee to make a smaller, personal-sized tiramisù!)

8. Right before serving, sprinkle cocoa powder on top to completely cover the top layer of cream and serve!

Potato croquettes
makes about 19
3/4 cup seasoned bread crumbs + 1 cup
3 lb Russet potatoes
20 pieces of mozzarella cut in small ¼"x 2" lengths
3 eggs
1.5 cups grated cheese (locatelli or parmesan)

1. Boil potatoes for about 40 minutes. When done, drain and let sit to cool down.
2. Peel (can run under cold water if too hot) and rice potatoes in a large bowl.
3. Add 3/4 cup of flavored breadcrumbs, one egg, and 1.5 cups of grated cheese and mix well until combined.
4. Grab about a 1/4 cup of potato mixture and flatten it against your palm. Take a piece of mozzarella, and wrap potato mixture around it. Make sure mixture is closed around the mozzarella and is rolled nicely in a cylinder shape.
5. When finished, lightly beat two eggs and place them in one bowl and then place 1 cup of seasoned breadcrumbs in another bowl. Dip each croquette in egg and then in breadcrumbs. Set on another plate ready to fry.
6. Put completed potato croquettes in the fridge for 1 hour to set before frying.
7. When ready to fry, use a deep fryer or a pot with 4" of oil to fry (can be olive oil, peanut oil, or any frying oil you prefer).
8. Fry each croquette for about a minute on each side, waiting for a nice golden-brown color. Set on paper towels to absorb oil after you take them out.
9. Enjoy!

Mamma Maria's Seafood Salad
1lb of Raw Shrimp
1lb of calamari cut in rings
1lb of Imitation crab meat
Lemon juice (can be bottled)
2-3 stalks of celery
1 jar of sliced manzanilla olives
1-2 Tbsp of capers
Fresh parsley
1 lemon
Garlic powder
Black pepper
Salt
Extra Virgin Olive oil
1 clove of garlic minced

1. First, wash the shrimp and calamari with lemon juice separately.
2. Place the shrimp in boiling water for five minutes. After they are done, put them in a bowl of ice water for another five minutes.
3. Repeat the same steps for the calamari.
4. Cut the shrimp and calamari into smaller pieces. Place them in a bowl.
5. Prepare the imitation crab meat by washing it in lemon juice and then drain it. Cut it into pieces and add them to the bowl.
6. Chop celery and add to the bowl along with capers (can be 1 to 2 tbsp, depending on your preference- make sure they are drained of juice).
7. Drain olives and rinse them under cold water. Add them to the bowl along with chopped parsley (your preference on amount), black pepper, extra virgin olive oil, a little salt (again, your preference), garlic powder and the minced clove of garlic.
8. Mix all together and let sit for a few hours. Before serving, add the juice of a fresh squeezed lemon and mix again.

Visit www.alessiasaint.com for more recipes from this book!